ONCE A JAILBIRD

Hans Fallada was born Rudolf Wilhelm Adolf Ditzen in 1893 in Greifswald, north-east Germany, and took his pen-name from a Brothers Grimm fairy tale. He spent much of his life in prison or in psychiatric care, yet produced some of the most significant German novels of the twentieth century, including *Little Man, What Now?*, *Iron Gustav*, *A Small Circus*, *The Drinker* and *Alone in Berlin*, the last of which was only published in English for the first time in 2009, to near-universal acclaim. He died in Berlin in 1947.

Jenny Williams is Professor Emeritus at Dublin City University. She has worked on Fallada's life and writings for many years and is the author of *More Lives than One: A Biography of Hans Fallada*, which is also published by Penguin.

HANS FALLADA

Once a Jailbird

Translated by ERIC SUTTON

Revised by NICHOLAS JACOBS, GARDIS CRAMER VON LAUE
and LINDEN LAWSON

Afterword by
Jenny Williams

PENGUIN BOOKS

PENGUIN CLASSICS

Published by the Penguin Group
Penguin Books Ltd, 80 Strand, London WC2R 0RL, England
Penguin Group (USA) Inc., 375 Hudson Street, New York, New York 10014, USA
Penguin Group (Canada), 90 Eglinton Avenue East, Suite 700, Toronto, Ontario, Canada M4P 2Y3
(a division of Pearson Penguin Canada Inc.)
Penguin Ireland, 25 St Stephen's Green, Dublin 2, Ireland (a division of Penguin Books Ltd)
Penguin Group (Australia), 250 Camberwell Road, Camberwell, Victoria 3124, Australia
(a division of Pearson Australia Group Pty Ltd)
Penguin Books India Pvt Ltd, 11 Community Centre, Panchsheel Park, New Delhi – 110 017, India
Penguin Group (NZ), 67 Apollo Drive, Rosedale, Auckland 0632, New Zealand
(a division of Pearson New Zealand Ltd)
Penguin Books (South Africa) (Pty) Ltd, Block D, Rosebank Office Park,
181 Jan Smuts Avenue, Parktown North, Gauteng 2193, South Africa

Penguin Books Ltd, Registered Offices: 80 Strand, London WC2R 0RL, England

www.penguin.com

First published as *Wer Einmal Aus Dem Blechnapf Frißt* in Germany by Rowohlt 1934
First published in English as *Who Once Eats Out of the Tin Bowl* in Great Britain by Putnam 1934
First published as *Once a Jailbird*, in this revised edition, in Penguin Classics 2012
001

Set in 10.5/13 pt Monotype Dante
Typeset by Jouve (UK), Milton Keynes
Printed in England by Clays Ltd, St Ives plc

ISBN: 978–0–141–19654–1

www.greenpenguin.co.uk

Penguin Books is committed to a sustainable
future for our business, our readers and our planet.
This book is made from Forest Stewardship
Council™ certified paper.

ALWAYS LEARNING PEARSON

Contents

I
Time-expired

I

Prisoner Willi Kufalt was pacing up and down his cell. Five paces forward, five paces back. Five paces forward again.

He stopped for a moment under the window. It was opened slantwise, as far as the iron shutters allowed, and through it he could hear the shuffle of many feet and the intermittent shout of a warder: 'Keep your distance! Five paces apart!'

Section C4 were having their recreation period, walking round and round in a circle for half an hour in the open air.

'No talking! Get it?' shouted the warder outside, and the feet shuffled on and on.

The prisoner walked to the door, stood beside it and listened; not a sound in the whole vast building.

'If Werner doesn't write today,' he thought, 'I must go to the chaplain and beg to be taken into the Home. Where else can I go? My earnings won't come to more than three hundred marks. And they'll soon be gone.'

He stood and listened. In twenty minutes recreation would be over. Then his section would go down. He must try to grab a bit of tobacco before that. He couldn't be without tobacco for his last two days.

He opened his little cupboard and looked inside; of course there was no tobacco there. He must rub up his plate too, or Rusch would be on to him. Polish? Ernst would get some for him.

He put his coat, cap and scarf on the table. Even if it was a warm bright May day outside, scarf and cap were compulsory.

'Well, only two more days of it. Then I can dress as I please.'

He tried to imagine what his life would then be like, but could not . . . 'I'll be walking along the street, and there'll be a pub, and I'll open the door and say: Waiter, a glass of beer . . .'

Outside, in the Central Hall, Rusch, the chief warder, was knocking his keys against the iron grille. The noise echoed through the entire building and could be heard in all 640 cells.

'He's always making a row, the old bastard,' growled Kufalt. 'Something upset you, Ruschy? . . . If I only knew what to do when I come out. They'll ask me where I want to be sent . . . and if I haven't got a job, my earnings here will be handed over to the Welfare Office, for me to draw a bit every week. Nothing doing! I'd sooner pull off a job with Batzke . . .'

He looked abstractedly at his jacket, the blue sleeve of which was adorned with three stripes of white tape. This meant that he was a 'category three' man, in other words a prisoner whose conduct promised 'permanent improvement and continued good behaviour on release'.

'And how I had to crawl to get them! And were they worth it? A bit of tobacco, half an hour more recreation, wireless one evening a week, and my cell not locked in the daytime . . .'

True: the cell doors of category three men were not locked, merely left ajar. But it was a strange sort of favour; he was not to push the door wide when he chose, go out into the corridor, or walk even a couple of steps along it. That was forbidden. If he did that, he would be degraded. The point was that he knew the door was open; it was a preparation for the world outside where doors are not locked . . . a gradual acclimatization, devised by an official brain.

The prisoner stood under the window again and wondered for a moment whether he could climb up and look out. Perhaps he would see a woman across the walls . . .

No, better not – save it up for Wednesday.

Restlessly he picked up his net and made six, eight, ten meshes. As he did so it occurred to him that he might wangle some polish as well as tobacco from the nets orderly – he dropped the wooden needle and walked to the door.

For a moment he stopped and wondered whether he should try. Then an idea came into his mind: he quickly unbuttoned his trousers, went to the bucket and laid his morning egg. He tipped some water over it, closed the lid, did up his trousers, and grasped the bucket in both hands.

'If he catches me, I'll say they've forgotten to empty my bucket today,' he said to himself; and pushed the door open with his elbow.

II

He glanced over his shoulder at the glass cubicle in the Central Hall, where, like a spider in its web, the chief warder usually sat and watched all the corridors and all the cell doors. But Kufalt was in luck; Rusch was not there. In his place sat a senior warder who was reading a newspaper, bored by the whole business.

Kufalt tiptoed along the passage to the toilets. On his way he passed the nets orderly's cell and paused for a moment; there was a quarrel going on inside. One, an oily voice, he knew; it was the nets instructor. But the other . . .

He stood and listened. Then he went on.

The toilets were a hive of activity. The orderlies of C2 and C4 had slipped in to have a smoke.

And somebody else was there.

'That you, Emil Bruhn? You must be finishing your stretch too, pretty soon?'

Kufalt tipped his bucket into the sink as he spoke.

'You filthy scumbag! Can't you see we're smoking?' said an orderly angrily.

'Shut up, you scab,' retorted Kufalt. 'How long have you been in, eh? Six months? And talking about filthy scumbags! You ought to have stayed outside if you couldn't do without a flush and plug. Shut your face! I'm category three, I am – any of you got a smoke?'

'Here, Willi,' said little Emil Bruhn, giving him a whole packet and some cigarette papers. 'You can keep it all. I've got plenty till Wednesday.'

'Wednesday? Are you getting out on Wednesday? Me too.'

'Are you sticking around this town?'

'No way. With all the prison officers about! I'm going to Hamburg.'

'Got a job there?'

'No, not yet. But I'll sort something out, through my relations . . . or maybe the chaplain . . . I'll manage.' And Kufalt smiled a rather thin smile.

'I've got a job already. I'm starting here in the timber works. Nest boxes for hens – piecework. I'll earn at least fifty marks a week, the manager says.'

'Too right,' assented Kufalt. 'You've been at it for nine years.'

'Ten and a half,' said little fair-haired Bruhn, and blinked his watery blue eyes. He had a round, good-humoured head, rather like a seal. 'It was eleven years really; only they gave me an extra six months' probation.'

'Jesus, Emil, I would not have taken it! Six months as a gift – and how long will you be out on probation?'

'Three years.'

'You're a bloody fool. If you so much as smash a window when you're pissed, or get rowdy on the street, you'll have to serve your six months. I'd have served the whole time out.'

'Yes, but, Willi, when you've done a ten-and-a-half-year stretch . . .'

'They were all on at me, the governor, and the schoolmaster and the chaplain, to apply for probation. But I'm not such a fool. When I come out on Wednesday, I'm in the clear . . .'

'But your application was refused,' butted in one of the orderlies.

'Refused? I didn't make one; you'd better get your ears cleaned out.'

'Well, that's what the storeman's orderly told me.'

'Oh, did he? And what kind of bastard do you think he is? He kicks the kids' behinds and pinches the pennies their mums have given them to go and buy the supper. To hell with him! Got any polish?'

'And the orderly also said . . .'

'Oh, bollocks. Got any polish? Show me – good, I'll have it. You won't get it back again. I've got a lot of cleaning to do. Now don't you start talking. Besides I've got a bar of soap among my things, I'll give you that in exchange. Come to the discharge cell on Wednesday. Shall I slip a letter out for you too? Right. Discharge cell, Wednesday morning.'

The C2 orderly remarked: 'Getting above himself, he is. All uppity because he's out the day after tomorrow.'

Kufalt suddenly turned on him: 'Uppity, am I? You're crazy! It's all shit to me whether I stick in here a couple more weeks or not. I've done 260 weeks – 1,825 days – mind that – and you think I'm uppity because I'm getting out?'

Then he turned more calmly to little Bruhn: 'Now listen, Emil – ah, you want to bunk. Recreation will soon be over. Get up to category three at twelve o'clock today . . .'

'I can manage. Petrow's on duty with our lot on F landing. He'll fix it.'

'Good. I've got something to say to you. And now get lost.'

'Bye, Willi.'

'Bye, Emil.'

'And now . . .' said Kufalt, picking up his emptied bucket. 'By the way, does anyone know what's up with the nets orderly?'

'Someone's split on him; and now he's for it.'

'How do you mean?'

'He smuggled letters with the dirty washing to someone in the women's prison.'

'To which of 'em?'

'I don't know. A small dark one, I think.'

'I know her,' said Kufalt. 'She's from Altona. The burglar's girl. She's done in half a dozen lads, and pinched the swag . . . Who's orderly now?'

'I don't know him. He's new – put in by the nets instructor. A fat Jew – fraudulent bankruptcy, they say . . .'

'Ah?' said Kufalt, recalling a word or two he had heard as he passed the cell door with his bucket. 'So that's how it is. Well, I've had my eye on that slimy old Nets for quite a while; now I'm going to set him up. Shove your head out, mate, and see if the coast's clear. Ker-rist,' he cried in despair, 'what kind of suckers are they sending us now?

They bash the door open fit to bring the bloody house down. Just look out and see whether Rusch is in the glass cubicle. Not? Then I'll go and pay a visit to old Nets. Morning.'

He picked up his bucket and went back to his cell.

III

On the way back Kufalt glanced down at the glass cubicle; there the position was unchanged, Senior Warder Suhr still had his nose in the paper.

When Kufalt reached the nets orderly's cell he stepped aside, flattened himself against the wall by the door, and listened.

There he stood, in blue dungarees and a striped prison shirt, his feet in list slippers, with a pointed yellowish nose, pale and thin, but noticeably pot-bellied. About twenty-eight years old. His brown eyes should have been frank and friendly, but they looked haunted, and furtive, and unsteady. His hair was brown. He stood and listened, and tried to catch what was being said. He still held the bucket in front of him with both hands.

One of the voices said excitedly: 'You give me back that ten marks. Why does my wife keep on sending you money?'

And the smooth, oily voice of the nets instructor answered: 'I do what I can for you. You ought to be very grateful to me for getting the work inspector to make you nets orderly.'

'Grateful!' said the other angrily. 'I'd sooner have done paper bags. This yarn tears your hands to shreds.'

'That's only for the first few weeks,' said the instructor comfortingly. 'You'll get used to it. Paper bags is much worse. All those who stick bags come to me.'

'You'll have to get me a pair of nail scissors – all my nails are torn . . .'

'You must report that to the storeman on Wednesday. He's got a pair of nail scissors. Then you'll be sent for to cut your nails.'

'When?'

'When the storeman has time. Saturday or Monday – maybe even Friday.'

'You're crazy!' shouted the other. 'What do you think my hands'll be like by Monday? The whole net's covered with blood – you can see for yourself!'

His voice rose to a roar.

Kufalt, outside the door, grinned. He knew what it was like when your hands began to bleed from the sharp sisal yarn and the harsh threads were drawn through the cuts next day. True, no one had told him that the storeman had a pair of scissors. He had trimmed his torn nails with bits of broken crockery.

'That's right, get mad, my friend,' he thought to himself. 'I hope you'll be doing a long stretch and find out all about it for yourself. But my bucket's started stinking like hell again. I'll have to clean it out with hydrochloric. If I go before the doctor today, I'll get the infirmary orderly to cough up a bit . . .'

'Hand over that ten marks. I won't have you fool me. I want my money.'

'Now we don't need to quarrel, do we, Herr Rosenthal?' said the instructor imploringly. 'What do you want with money in this place? I get you everything you need. I'll even buy you a pair of nail scissors – but cash in prison, that might get us into a real mess.'

'Don't play the fool with me,' said prisoner Rosenthal. 'You're not a real official. You haven't taken any oaths. You're just an agent of the net manufacturers, to give out the work. You don't run any risks.'

'But what do you want with cash? Tell me that, anyhow.'

'I want it to buy tobacco.'

'That can't be true, Herr Rosenthal. You can get tobacco from me. What do you want the money for?'

The other man was silent.

'If you tell me, you can have it. But I want to know who gets it and what for. There's some that are straight, and they're all right.'

'Straight?'

'They don't do the dirty on us, Herr Rosenthal, they don't shaft us, they don't do us down, they don't squeal. That's what the word means here.'

'I'll tell you,' whispered the other – and Kufalt had to lay his ear against the crack of the door to hear what he said; 'but you mustn't breathe a word. There's a big dark brute who'd kill me if I gave him away, he told me. He's in the boiler room – he made up to me in the recreation period . . .'

'Ah, Batzke,' said the other. 'There's a right crook.'

'He promised me that if I gave him ten marks – look, you won't give me away, will you? Right opposite my window, on the other side of the street, beyond the wall, there's a house.' Rosenthal swallowed, drew a deep breath, and went on: 'I can see right into the windows; and twice I've seen a woman there. And the man swore that if I'd give him ten marks she'd stand stark naked at the window tomorrow morning at five o'clock, and I could see her. Now hand over those ten marks. This place is killing me, I'm half mad already. Come on now.'

'Well, that's a neat bit of work, that is,' said the other, in a tone of admiration and pride. 'But if Batzke says he will, he'll do it. And he won't split. Here you are . . .'

Kufalt thrust his foot into the crack of the door, pushed it open, and with one step was inside; he said in a low voice, 'Halves, or I'll split!' and waited.

The pair looked at him dumbfounded. The instructor, fishy-eyed, round-faced and bearded like a walrus, stood with his wallet in his hand, and stared; under the window, pallid, bloated, dark and rather fat, stood the new nets orderly, Rosenthal, shivering with fear.

Kufalt put down his bucket with a flourish.

'Now then, we don't want any argument, Uncle Nets, or I'll talk, and get you a stretch for yourself. You got the last orderly jugged so as to give his job to this old grafter. Don't look so scared, you dumb bastard, it'll only cost you your money. I'll be at the window tomorrow at five myself. So out with it. How much? Well, we can't exactly split it, I don't know how much you've had. I'm cheap; a hundred marks.'

'It's no good, Rosenthal,' said the instructor resignedly. 'We'll have to cough up if you don't want to get at least eight weeks' solitary. I know Kufalt.'

'It's cold in the solitary cells, young man,' grinned Kufalt. 'When you've dossed on stone for three days, the marrow in your bones will turn to ice. Well, how about it?'

'It's up to you, Herr Rosenthal,' urged the instructor.

Two strokes of a bell boomed through the building. The whole landing leapt to life, bolts began to rattle . . .

'Quick, or I'll go straight to the chief.'

'Please, Herr Rosenthal!'

'I'll put Batzke on to you, you fat swine, he's my mate. He'll knock your head off.'

'Herr Rosenthal, please . . .'

'All right, give it him . . . but you've got to stand in with me, Instructor.'

'On account,' said Kufalt, and spat on the hundred-mark note. 'I'll be outside the day after tomorrow, fatty, and I'll think of you when I'm with the girls. Now, Uncle Nets, you put my bucket in my cell while I'm at recreation. And some hydrochloric too, or there'll be trouble. Morning!'

And Kufalt darted down the corridor to his cell.

IV

Eighty noisy, chattering prisoners clopped down the four iron staircases leading to the ground floor. There, at the door into the yard, stood two warders, repeating mechanically: 'Keep your distance. No talking. Keep your distance. Anyone talking will be reported.'

But the prisoners did talk. Only when near the warders were they silent; once they had passed, they dropped into that loud whisper that carries just further than five paces, though the speaker's lips must never move or he would be reported at once.

Kufalt was in high form. He conversed simultaneously with the man in front of him and the one behind, who were anxious to get anything they could out of the category three man.

'It's all balls that category two are to hear the wireless. Don't you believe a word of it, mate.'

'Yes, I'll be out the day after tomorrow . . . Don't yet know. Perhaps I'll pull off a job again, perhaps I'll go into my brother-in-law's office.'

'How are they going to get 125 category two men into the schoolroom? There's only room for fifty at the most. You're a twerp. You'll believe anything.'

'My brother-in-law? I don't mind telling you. He's got a felt slipper factory, if you must know. I might get you taken on there.'

'Hold your tongue, Kufalt,' said the warder. 'It's always you category three men that give trouble.'

'I didn't speak, sir, I was only breathing hard.'

'You'd better hold your tongue or I'll report you.'

'All my things are with the storeman. All immaculate, silk-lined tails and patent shoes. Hey, I wonder what it'll feel like after five years!'

'Oh, let that ape of a warder gibber if he wants to. I know something that'll keep him quiet. He had me make a shopping bag and a hammock for him.'

'There's only one thing I'm anxious about . . . How long have you been in? Three months? Tell me, do the women still wear such short skirts? I heard they were wearing long ones again . . .'

'Can't prove it, eh? I'll just say to the governor: you'll find a double mesh in the fourth row of the net bag, and he'll be for it.'

'Well, thank God. So you can see their thighs when they sit down? And bare flesh when they're bicycling?'

'Step out, Kufalt, I don't know what's up with you today. Do you want to spend your last days in solitary? Get over to the wall – that's our reserved box for category three gents.'

Kufalt went, and stood alone. Those in the circle jeered at him as they passed: 'What about category three now! Grafters! Wireless and all, eh? Proud of your three stripes, aren't you? Bum-suckers!'

'You can all . . .' he began, and then he thought: 'Hundred marks. Fine. Now I'll have at least four hundred marks, and if Werner Pause writes today and sends me some money . . .' 'Hey, Warder Steinitz, how much is a third-class ticket to Hamburg?'

'Are you talking to me? Hold your tongue, or I'll have you put in solitary.'

'Oh, please not, sir! Well, I should have plenty of time today to make you another shopping bag.'

'Insolent, eh? I'll clip you with these keys if you aren't careful.'

'I really should have time for it today, sir. And the pound of margarine you promised me for the hammock hasn't turned up.'

'You young scab! Trying a little blackmail on your last day, are you? Sneaky little rat – oh well, get back into line, why should I bother about you any more. Five paces' distance – and keep your mouth shut, Kufalt.'

'Very well, sir, I won't say a word.'

It is May; the sky is blue beyond the wall, and above it the chestnuts are in flower. The circular yard round which the prisoners are marching has been planted with swedes, which are just coming up – a patch of meagre yellowish green against the melancholy bleak background of cinders, dusty earth and cement.

They walk in a circle and whisper. They walk in a circle and whisper. They walk in a circle and whisper.

V

Back in his cell, Willi Kufalt collapsed. That was what always happened. When he was with other people he prattled on and threw his weight about, and posed as the old experienced lag who could never be fooled; but alone with himself, he was very much alone, and grew timid and despondent.

'I shouldn't have acted like that to Warder Steinitz,' he thought. 'It was mean. Just to show the new blokes I had him in my pocket. It's not worth it, I do everything wrong – how will I get on outside?'

If only his brother-in-law would write . . . Outside was the world, full of towns, and the towns full of rooms, one of which he would have to rent: and looking for jobs, and the money that would too soon be spent – and what then?

He stared into vacancy. Scarcely eighty-four hours until the moment of his release, for which he had so yearned during five long years. And now he was afraid. He had liked being here, he had soon adapted himself to the atmosphere and ways of the place; he had quickly learnt when a man should be humble and when he could speak up. His cell was always spotless, his bucket lid had always shone like a mirror, and he had washed the cement floor of his cell twice a week with graphite and turpentine until it gleamed like an ape's arse.

He had always made his allotted amount of net, sometimes twice and even three times as much, so that he had been able to buy little luxuries for himself and tobacco. He had reached category two, then three: a model prisoner, whose cell was visited by committees and who always gave a sensible and modest answer to their questions.

'Yes, sir, I feel very well here.'

'No, sir, I'm sure it is doing me good.'

'No, sir, I have no complaints.'

But sometimes – and he grinned as he recalled how the girl students training to become welfare workers had asked him so inquisitively what his crime had been; and instead of answering, 'Embezzlement and forgery,' he had said humbly: 'Incest. I slept with my sister, I'm sorry to say.'

He recalled the face of the police inspector, grinning delightedly at the joke, and the eager-eyed girl student who came up closer to him. A nice girl, who had often brought him pleasing thoughts as he fell asleep.

It had been a good time, too, when he had to arrange the altar for the Catholic priest, even though he had strongly objected to Kufalt as a Protestant. But there were no 'reliable Catholics' in the place – it was really a dig by the Protestant officials at the Catholic priest.

He had stood behind the organ and pumped air into the bellows and the choirmaster always gave him a cigar; and on one occasion the choir of the Catholic church had come, and the girls sent him chocolate and some good toilet soap. Rusch, the chief warder, had taken it away from him afterwards. 'Brothel, brothel!' he had said when he came into Kufalt's cell and sniffed. 'It smells like a brothel here.' And he had rummaged around until he found it, and the old soda soap had to be brought out again.

No, he had had a good time, all in all, and the prospect of release rather bewildered him. He felt quite unprepared, and he would gladly have stayed inside another six or eight weeks to get ready to leave. Or was it that he was beginning to get a little crazed? He had often noticed that the quietest and most sensible prisoners cracked up just before their release and acted crazily. Had he reached that stage?

Perhaps he had; never before would he have risked that business with the nets instructor and the fat Jew, entering the cell like that, nor spoken up to Warder Steinitz as he had done.

If only his brother-in-law would write. Had the chief warder given out the post that day? He was a pig you couldn't trust; if he didn't feel like it, he wouldn't give out any post for three days.

Kufalt walked a step or two and stopped. He had always set the wash-basin on the top of the cupboard so that the edges met within a millimetre; and now it stood at least a centimetre back.

He opened the cupboard door.

'So old Nets, the dirty dog, has been going through my cell. Hasn't given up hope of his hundred marks. All right, my lad, just you wait.'

Kufalt threw a suspicious look at the peephole in the door, and grabbed his scarf. Something crackled encouragingly in its folds. But it then occurred to him that in half an hour at most he would have to appear before the doctor and undress, and must not have a hundred mark note on him. The nets instructor would know that, and search his cell again . . .

Kufalt frowned and pondered. He knew of course that there was no hiding place in the cell of which the officials were not well aware. Indeed they had a list, a warder had once told him; there were 211 ways of concealing an object in a cell; and he cursed the thought.

But what he had to find now was a hiding place that would serve for an hour and a half. The inspection by the doctor would not last longer, and that's all the time Nets would have to search his cell.

In the back of the hymn book? No, that was a bad place. In the mattress? That would do, but he did not have enough time to slit it and sew it up again in the half-hour before his examination. Besides, he would first have to get the proper thread from the saddler's room.

What a pity he had emptied his bucket; it wouldn't have damaged the note to slip it into the muck at the bottom for an hour and a half, but unfortunately the bucket was empty.

Should he stick it to the underside of the table with bits of bread?

He began to roll the pellets of bread, and then he stopped; the trick was too well known, and one glance under the table was enough.

Kufalt was growing nervous. A bell was ringing for the end of the last recreation period; in a quarter of an hour he would have to go before the doctor. Should he take the note with him? He could roll it up very tight and push it up his behind. But perhaps the nets instructor might tip off the head screw in the infirmary, and they would search him properly – they might very well examine him for cancer of the rectum!

He was at a loss. This was what would happen when he got outside. There were so many possibilities, and a 'but' to all of them. A man must make up his mind, but that was just what he could not do. How should he? In these five years he had been deprived of all power of decision. They had said, 'Eat,' and he had eaten. They had said, 'Go out,' and he had gone; and 'Write,' and he had written his letter.

The ventilator was not a bad place. But too well known, much too well known. There was a crack in the planking of his bed – but a single look would catch the glint of paper. He could stand the stool on the table and put the note on the electric light shade, but that was a common trick; besides, anyone might see him through the peephole in the door when he got onto the table.

He turned quickly round and looked at the peephole. Ah! There was a goggle eye, a fishy eye that he knew well.

In a fury of feigned rage he leapt at the door and hammered on it, shouting: 'Get away from the peephole, damn you!'

A sudden crash, the door flew open, and there stood the chief warder, Rusch.

Now for a bit of acting, for Rusch liked none but his own jokes. You had to be humble to the chief warder, and Kufalt played his part to perfection as he stammered: 'I *beg* your pardon, sir, I do beg your pardon, I thought it was that rat of an orderly who's always sneaking after my tobacco.'

'Eh? What's that? Don't make a racket. You'll have all the paint off the door.'

'There's never a speck of what there shouldn't be in my cell, you know that, sir,' said Kufalt in an ingratiating tone; 'not a scratch in the varnish.'

The chief warder – a rather stubbly Napoleon, the real ruler of the prison, curt, always springing something unexpected, embittered enemy of every reform, of the grading of prisoners, of the governor, of the officials, and of every prisoner – made no reply but marched up to the little cupboard on which hung a list of personal effects and special privileges.

'How about the birds?' he asked.

'Birds?' said Kufalt, with a bewildered grin.

'Birds! Birds!' snarled the despot, and tapped the list. 'There are two canaries down here. Where are they? Swapped already, eh?'

'But, sir,' said Kufalt reproachfully, thinking anxiously of the hundred-mark note still hidden in his scarf. 'They died when the central heating went wrong this winter. I told you about it.'

'That's a lie, a damn lie. Maass the shoemaker has two too many. They're yours. You swapped 'em.'

'But, sir, I told you they were dead. I went to the glass cubicle and reported it.'

The chief warder stood beneath the window. His back was turned to the prisoner, who could see only his fat white hands fumbling with the keys.

'If he would only go!' prayed Kufalt inwardly. 'At any moment I'll have to go to the doctor, and with the note in my scarf. I shall get rumbled, and hauled up.'

'Category three,' growled the chief. 'Always category three. All the trouble in the place . . . About your money . . .'

'Yes?' said Kufalt, as the other paused.

'Welfare Office. You can draw five marks a week.'

'Oh, please,' implored Kufalt, 'you won't do that, sir, I've always kept my cell so tidy.'

'What's that? Oh, won't I? Tidy, eh? What about those birds? Hahaha!'

'Haha!' laughed Kufalt obsequiously.

'What's up with the nets instructor and the new nets orderly?' asked the chief, with a sudden change of tone.

'New orderly?' asked Kufalt. 'Is there a new one? I've never seen him.'

'Liar! You can't fool me. You were with them in the cell for ten minutes.'

'I was not, sir, I was only out of my cell for recreation today.'

The chief warder passed a finger meditatively over the top of the cupboard. He examined his finger with an air of satisfaction, and then sniffed it. No; not a speck of dust. He walked briskly to the door. 'So you'll draw your money through the Welfare Office.'

Kufalt reflected feverishly: 'If I say nothing now, he'll go, and I can hide the hundred, but I'll be tied to the welfare people. If I squeal, I'll lose the hundred, but I'll get my pay in cash. Though not for certain.'

'Sir . . .'

'Hey?'

'I *was* in the cell with them . . .'

The other waited. Then – 'Well?'

'He gets letters for the fat Jew. You have him searched and see.'

'Only letters?'

'Well, he wouldn't do it for love.'

'Do you know anything?'

'Have him searched, sir. This very day – you'll find something.'

The door opened: 'Kufalt for the doctor.'

Kufalt looked at the chief warder.

'Get along,' said the other indulgently. 'All birds die in this place.'

'Well, I've stitched up that bastard of an instructor,' thought Kufalt as he shuffled downstairs. 'He won't have time to go through my cell now, though it wouldn't matter, God knows! The note's still on me, damn!'

VI

The warder stood by the balustrade and watched Kufalt depart. 'Get a move on, Kufalt. Acts as if he doesn't know all about it. You've been to the doctor often enough.'

'That isn't true,' thought Kufalt. 'Since he reported me for shamming, when I sprained my thumb and couldn't weave, I haven't been near him more than three times. And I wasn't kidding, my thumb really was sprained.'

No, it looked bad for shifting the note. All the corridors were crowded with men reporting to the governor, the police inspector, the work inspector, the doctor, the chaplain and the schoolmaster – on all the landings bolts were rattling, keys clicking, officials running about with lists and prisoners slouching along in their blue dungarees.

'I'm always messing up. And when I do get a bit feisty and try to pull off anything, I muck it up. I'll never make a real crook . . .'

Below he was greeted by Senior Warder Petrow, an East Prussian, who had been a warder before the war and was very popular with all the prisoners.

'Well, Kufalt, old man, time's up, eh? You see it's gone like lightning. Did the chief give you solitary? You could have done the last bit on your head! How long? Five years? Time passes like an express train, mate; and won't the girls be pleased with what you've saved up for them!'

Fat Petrow snorted amiably, and the prisoners grinned agreement.

'Well, fall in, Kufalt. No, not beside Batzke, he talks, and the old man's always peering out of his glass cubicle. Here – and three paces apart. Now then, you with the specs, you're a new hand, aren't you? Think you're walking to Hamburg, eh? Stop here, my boy, put in a little time with us . . . Don't go any further.'

The thirty prisoners already waiting for the doctor's inspection were joined by more and more from all landings. Kufalt noticed the little carpenter, Emil Bruhn, and waved to him from where he stood.

'It'll go on for ever again today,' he groaned to the man in front; 'the grub's sure to be ice-cold when we get back. And there's peas today.'

The man in front turned round. He was a tall lanky fellow in an incredible get-up – trousers consisting almost entirely of light and dark blue patches, a waistcoat so short that a hand's width of shirt could be seen between the lower edge of it and his trousers, and a jacket with arms that reached only to the elbows. And above it, a small, pallid, evil head.

'Well, you're a fine sight, I must say,' said Kufalt. 'You must have got across the storeman. They've made a proper guy of you. How long are you in for?'

'Are you speaking to me?' said the beanpole. 'Can we talk here?'

'No. But you don't need to throw your weight about; all our buckets will be emptied at the same time. How long have you got?'

'I was sentenced to two years' imprisonment. But I'm innocent. Two witnesses committed perjury. I've written to the Public Prosecutor's office.'

'Oh, we all talk about perjury when we come in,' said Kufalt soothingly. 'That's natural. What was written up outside your cell before your case came on?'

'Written? What do you mean? Oh, yes – "prisoner on remand".'

'Well, that means Innocent. And what is written there now?'

'Convict.'

'And that means Guilty. It's all quite simple. When you're in jug, you're guilty, it's no use making any fuss about it. A sentence is a sentence. And don't start any talk about perjury here, it won't get you anywhere. There's some of us here that'll put you through it if you do.'

'Pardon me, I am innocent, my wife and my secretary will find themselves in jail for perjury. Listen, let me tell you about it . . .'

But he got no further. A violent jingle of keys came from the glass cubicle. 'Herr Petrow! Will you please attend to what's going on. That tall fellow there, Menzel, keeps on talking to Kufalt.'

Petrow dashed savagely up to the innocent convict. 'Do you want me to pull out your rotten teeth, you big bastard? Do you think you're in a Jews' school, eh? Quick march, left, right, left, right, to the cell, and you can talk to the iron door till the doctor comes.'

The door clicked, the bewildered prisoner disappeared, and as he passed Petrow whispered, with a twinkle in his eye: 'Put the wind up him, didn't I? Don't you get pally with that lad, he's always going to the governor and the inspector and he tells everything he hears.'

Petrow was already ten paces away. There stood two men in brown uniforms by themselves, smart-looking lifers, no doubt on their way elsewhere. And the pair had moved three steps forward, from the linoleum onto the waxed cement floor, to make contact with the other prisoners, probably for tobacco . . .

'Keep on the brown lino, please – don't move off the lino, you there!'

The men did not look up, they stared straight in front of them and did not move. Kufalt once more observed that lifers treated the prison officials in quite a different way. Ordinary prisoners jollied them, and tried to get on terms with them; but for these men, an official simply did not exist.

This time Petrow burst into a real fury: 'Get back onto that lino!'

The pair heard nothing, saw nothing. As though by accident, they each took one step, two steps, three steps – and again stood on the linoleum. They did not so much as look at the warder.

The infirmary door opened, and the infirmary chief warder appeared in a white jacket. 'Prisoners to see the doctor!'

'Double file – into the infirmary,' shouted Petrow.

But at that moment all the carefully maintained discipline and decorum collapsed. With a hubbub of talk and hurrying feet the fifty prisoners jostled along a narrow passage and down some steps into the infirmary. Petrow tried to keep the two lifers at least in view, but they were at once lost among the others; they whispered, hands grabbing.

'Just you wait, you miserable swine, I'll have that tobacco off you . . . Now then, move aside you two!'

'All prisoners in double file, eyes to the wall and back to back. Take off shoes and slippers and place them in front of you,' ordered the infirmary chief warder.

A name was called, and the prisoner vanished into the doctor's room, followed by the chief warder.

'This is going to last for hours,' sighed Kufalt to little Bruhn, who was standing beside him.

'I'm not so sure, Willi,' whispered Bruhn. 'He often gets through sixty in half an hour. Hello, there's a row going on.'

From the doctor's room came curses and shouts, and a prisoner emerged, red with fury. 'But I'm really ill, I'll complain to the Prison Board, I won't stand it . . .'

'Move on, move on,' said the chief warder, pushing the man out.

'Malingering scum,' the doctor was heard to shout. 'I'll teach 'em! Next!'

'Doesn't look too good today,' said Batzke, from the other side of Kufalt. 'If he starts on the first one like that . . .'

'Anyhow, we'll be through quicker. I want to get in some football. Are you coming?'

'Don't know yet. My dripping's all gone, I'll have to wangle some more.'

'Will we have to take all our clothes off?' asked Kufalt.

And Batzke: 'We had to at Fuhlsbüttel. I don't know what they do here in Prussia.'

'Course not,' whispered Bruhn from the other side. 'He won't even look at us.'

'Don't be so sure,' said Kufalt. 'It says in the Prison Regulations that prisoners are to be thoroughly examined before release as to their health and their capacity for work.'

'It says a lot in those regulations.'

'Then you think we won't have to undress?'

'What have you got tucked away in your pants, eh? Halves, or . . . ?'

'Silence over there,' shouted Petrow; 'if you don't want a crack on the head with my keys.'

'Oh, please, sir, can I be excused? I've got such a pain in my guts, I'm afraid to go in to the doctor,' grinned Kufalt.

'All right, go and shit then, old codger. Over to the toilets. Now mind – no smoking, or there'll be trouble with the doctor.'

'Of course not, sir.'

And Kufalt disappeared into the toilet, and left the door ajar. For safety's sake he pulled down his trousers; then he stood with his back against the peephole, hurriedly took the note out of his scarf, pushed it down into his sock ('no halves, Batzke'), stood up, flushed the toilet, and took his place in the ranks again.

Petrow stuck his head round the toilet door to check, and withdrew it with a look of satisfaction. 'You haven't smoked – good boy, Kufalt.'

Kufalt felt really touched by this approbation.

But Batzke whispered: 'Well, Kufalt, how about it? Will you cough it up or . . . ?'

Kufalt parried: 'What about the fat Jew and the naked tart? Cut it out, nothing doing here!'

'Aha!' grinned Batzke. 'So you too stung the little swine, did you? Good for you, lad!'

From the corner growled a menacing voice: 'How long am I to be kept on this cold floor in my socks? It's a scandal. I'll complain.'

Petrow grinned: 'Ah, the gentlemen lifers. Medical officer's orders; I can do nothing. You must complain to the medical officer.'

'I'd like to know why it's allowed too,' said Kufalt softly to Bruhn. 'I've caught a dozen colds standing around on this cold floor.'

'So we won't scratch the orderlies' lino,' said Batzke.

'Wrong,' said Bruhn, who knew everything. 'Six or eight years ago a prisoner hit the doctor over the head with his slippers. Since then all prisoners have had to wait in their socks.'

'It's a bloody shame,' growled Kufalt. 'We have to catch cold here just because . . .'

'We're just cattle,' said Batzke. 'But outside I'll show folks what sort of animal I am!'

The prisoners had melted away like snow in the sun; there had been more outbursts, more shouts, indignant protests and whining, but in the end the infirmary chief warder's heavy shoulder had edged them through the door, where Petrow received them, listened sympathetically to their complaints, and bustled them away, delighted to have got them back from the infirmary.

The only ones left were the two lifers and the discharges.

'Now for a row,' said Kufalt warningly.

'I don't think so,' said Bruhn sceptically. 'I'd be surprised if there was.'

And in five minutes the two reappeared from the doctor's room, with the same expressionless faces, followed this time by the medical officer himself. 'The chief warder will bring you the medicine. And the cotton wool. Right.'

'Those lads know how to fix him,' said Kufalt enviously.

'Oh, he's just a coward,' said Bruhn. 'They're lifers, probably – and they don't risk anything if they give him one on the jaw. A lifer's always a lifer. The doctor knows that well enough.'

'Eyes ahead! These are the men due for discharge this week, sir.'

'Right.' The medical officer did not look up. 'They can be taken away. All in good health, all fit for work, chief warder.'

'And that's what we've waited an hour for,' said Bruhn.

'Well, I'll put in a stiff complaint when I get out,' said Kufalt.

'Cattle must be treated like cattle,' grinned Batzke. 'The old pill-pusher's right.'

VII

When Kufalt got back to his cell, he found something else to make him indignant. Dinner had been given out in the meantime and his bowl stood on the table, but there was only one ladleful in it. Lousy bastards! Was he to go on an empty belly these last few days? Peas too – which he liked so much!

But as Kufalt sat there and crammed the food into his mouth – he had to bolt it, as the bell for the category three men's recreation might ring at any moment – a sudden nausea came over him. That had happened several times during his five years; for weeks and even months he could not get the sloppy mixture down.

Listlessly he stirred the bowl, to see whether a bit of pork might have strayed into it – in vain.

He tipped the stuff into his bucket, cleaned the plate and smeared a slice of bread with dripping. His dripping tasted fine; the tailors stewed it up for him on the ironing stove, with apples and onions. They were very decent to him, and never took more than a quarter off the pound for their 'work'; others had to give up a half or even three-quarters, and the new boys got nothing back at all. The tailors always told them that the chief warder had confiscated it and that it was very decent of them to take all the blame. And they had to put up with it.

Kufalt squatted on his stool and yawned. He would like to have had a bit of a snooze on his bed, but the chief warder might ring the bell at any moment; it was already time.

How the time dragged, these last few days and weeks! It would not pass, it stayed, it stuck, it would not pass. Every free minute he had he had always sat down to knot, but now he could not, he would never knot another mesh. He cared for nothing now. The thought of freedom left him cold. Werner would be sure not to write, and then he would have to go and beg the chaplain for help.

The best thing for him would be a decent safe wage – small it might be, but it must be sure. No more dealings with crooks; he would get some quiet little room, where insignificant Willi Kufalt could sit and keep warm through the winter. A cinema now and again. And a nice office job, and so on and so on. He wanted nothing better. Amen.

The bell rang.

He sat up, picked up his cap and scarf, felt for the note to make sure it was still safe in his sock – and there was Steinitz at the open door: 'Recreation – category three!'

They gathered round the glass cubicle, eleven manikins out of six hundred.

'All here?' asked Petrow.

'No, Batzke's not here yet.'

'Having a snooze, is he? Someone go and wake him up.'

'No, he won't come.'

'Oh? Well, I know what'll happen. They'll soon knock off the extra recreation period when they see we don't use it.'

'Who's got the football?'

'We need a new one. This one's past mending.'

'Rubbish, shoemaker! Of course it can be mended, you lazy sod.'

'The gentlemen who are going out tomorrow might cough up ten marks out of their pay, eh?'

'I need my money for myself, thank you.'

'Well hello, why are we going through the cellar today, sir?'

'It's nearer.'

'And it's forbidden.'

'It isn't. Who said so?'

'Rusch.'

'Oh, I fart at what he forbids.'

'There's somebody!'

'Hi, Bruhn, are you coming with us?'

'Fine, Emil, we can have a bit of a chat.'

'Petrow slipped me out, Rusch isn't in the building. Good work, eh, Willi?'

'Well, that's rich! He's not even category two, Senior Warder, sir!'

'I don't see anything. I don't know how Bruhn came out.'

'Shut your mouth, you jealous pig. Can't you let Bruhn come out with us once in a while?'

'You idiot, when *I* want anything you get all worked up about it.'

'It's different with Bruhn, no warder minds about Bruhn.'

'Different – because he's your boyfriend, eh? Listen, I won't stand for it, I'll squeal.'

'All right, squeal if you dare. I know a thing or two about you . . .'

They were outside. It was the Junior Prison's recreation ground, where they played football and were allowed to walk about without supervision – Petrow had gone off straight away – as a preparation for freedom, surrounded, of course, by a wall five metres high.

'Come along, Willi, don't mind him. I'm here anyhow.'

'Yes, come on. Let's walk by the wall, then we won't disturb the game.'

'I've a good mind to give you one in the jaw – think a lot of yourself, don't you?'

'All right, do, if you've got any guts.'

'Guts, eh? I'll soon show you, you dirty scab . . .'

'Now then, shoemaker, are we playing football or not?'

'I wouldn't dirty my hands on you – clear off with your boyfriend. But I'll tell Rusch . . . '

'Oh, come on, Willi.'

'The shoemaker's a pig, Emil. But I'll tell you what he's making all this fuss about. I sold him my two canaries for four packets of tobacco. And Rusch found out. So he's lost the birds *and* the tobacco. That's what's bugging him, it's nothing to do with you.'

'When's the shoemaker due to come out? He's going crazy already.'

'Too right! He's got three years to go yet. But he sucks up to everyone, and secretly mends the warders' shoes, and now he wants to join the Catholic Church; he'll get out on probation all right.'

'Yes, he'll fix it, he knows what's what.'

They were walking up and down under the wall in the warm May sunshine. Not a blade of green grass, not a leaf to be seen, but the sky was deeply blue, and after the bleak cells the sun seemed doubly bright and warm. It warmed them to the bones, their limbs loosened; their tense, watchful and defensive mood was relaxed, and they both became easy and quiet.

'Hey, Willi,' said Bruhn.

He was a plump, friendly young man, only just twenty-eight, who had been in prison since he was seventeen. With his light blue eyes, his ruddy round face and his flaxen hair he looked like a large child. But on the card in his cell was written 'Robbery and murder', and he had received the maximum sentence for those underage, at that time – fifteen years. And yet he did not appear as anything of the kind; he was a pleasant young man and popular with everyone. He had never tried to ingratiate himself, and yet he was liked by all.

In fact, when he mentioned the subject, which he did very seldom and with an air of hopeless resignation, he maintained that he had been unjustly convicted. It had not been murder for robbery, but manslaughter in a fit of fury and despair; he had killed the captain of the barge, who tortured him, his cabin-boy, beyond all human endurance. The fact that he could not bring himself to leave the gold watch on the corpse when he threw it into the water was in his view quite a separate matter. He had not killed the man to get his watch.

So the two young men walked up and down in the sunshine, with five, and eleven, years of jail behind them; in two days all would be over, and life would smile on them again.

'Hey, Willi,' said little Bruhn.

'Yes, Emil?'

'I asked you this before, in the toilets: why don't you stay here? In this town, I mean. No, don't answer yet; we might take a room together, it would be cheaper. And if you don't get a job at once, you could cook and wash and do the housework. I'll be earning good money. And in the evenings we could smarten ourselves up and go out.'

'But I must get a job, Emil. I couldn't do your housework for ever.'

'You'll get a job all right. Just at the beginning, I meant. If you were stronger I would fix you up at the timber yard, but you'll have to get some sort of clerk's job for a start . . . The old man likes you, he's sure to help.'

'Oh, the governor? But he can't do just what he likes. And, Emil, this is such a hole, warders around everywhere, and the lads on outside work, and there's the prison always under your nose, and in three days the cops would all know where you'd come from. And there'd be talk, and the landlady would hear about it, and she'd give you notice . . .'

'But we'll find a landlady that doesn't mind.'

'Yes, but even if we could she'd pile on the rent.'

'I don't think so, Willi, really I don't think so. There are some. But I'll try to get hold of a decent girl, not a tart, and marry, and have a shop of my own, and children . . .'

'Would you tell her?'

'I don't know. I'd have to see. But better not.'

'But you'd have to tell her, Emil. Otherwise you'd always be afraid it would come out, and she'd bolt.'

They stood in the bright sunlight, not looking at each other, but staring at the grey sand before them in which Kufalt was burrowing with his slipper.

Bruhn tried again: 'Come with me, Willi.'

And Kufalt: 'No. No. It would be like being in the clink again. We would always be talking about our life here. No, no.'

'No!' said Bruhn too.

'We've both been in it up to our necks together; we've wangled what we could, done the dirty on the other lads and sucked up to the warders – but now it's over.'

'Yes,' said Bruhn.

'And there's another thing . . . Do you know, when I was a boy at school, I fell in love – from afar, we didn't speak to each other more than twice, and once I saw her fixing her stocking in the gardens. That was when girls still wore long skirts, you know . . .'

'Yes,' said Bruhn.

'But that was nothing compared to the first year here, when you had the cell opposite me, on the other side of the passage, and I saw you in the morning. You only had a shirt and trousers on, and you put your bucket and water jug outside the door. And your shirt was open at the neck. Then you smiled, and I used to wait till the door opened, hoping to see you . . . And then you slipped me the first note . . .'

'Yes, through that big orderly, Tietjen, who was in for burglary. He was safe, he was up to it himself.'

'And then the first time, in the shower room, when the warder turned round and you crept under my shower and hid behind the screen when he looked . . . God, we've had some good times in this old place . . .'

'Yes,' said Bruhn; 'but a girl's better.'

Kufalt pondered: 'Well, you see, I've been thinking that if we were together it would just go on as before . . .'

'No,' said Bruhn; 'not when there are girls around.'

'Yes,' said Kufalt. 'And it must all come to an end. It was great, but it must come to an end now. We're making a fresh start, and I want to be like everybody else.'

'So you've made up your mind to go to Hamburg?'

'Yes, to Hamburg; no one will ask questions there.'

'All right, only mind you keep straight there, Willi. Shall we walk a bit further?'

'Yes, the sun's quite warm today.'

'I shall fix up with Krüger, then,' said little Bruhn. 'He comes out on 16 May.'

Kufalt was taken aback. 'You can't mean that, Emil. He's no good.'

'No, I know. And he always pinches our tobacco. And he's been dropped on three times for robbing the men on his shift.'

'There you go.'

'But what am I to do? I must have someone, I can't stick it alone. And there's not many people want to take up with a murderer, you know.'

'Yes, but not Krüger.'

'But who else is there? You've said you won't.'

'Not for that reason, Emil.'

'And I must have someone to help me, Willi. I've been eleven years in jug, and I don't know my way around. I'm often terrified, I think I'll get into a mess again and spend the rest of my life doing time.'

'That's just why you shouldn't take up with Krüger.'

'Then you come with me.'

'No, I can't. I want to go to Hamburg.'

'Then I'll go with Krüger.'

For a while they walked in silence, side by side. Then Bruhn said:

'I want to ask you something else, Willi. You know about such things . . .'

'What things?'

'Money. Savings bank books.'

'A little, perhaps.'

'When a bloke . . . has a savings bank book in my name, and he has the receipt for it, can he draw any of the money? He can't, can he?'

'Usually he could, if the savings book isn't actually closed, or notice has been given. Usually he can. Have you got a savings book?'

'Yes. No. One has been taken out for me.'

'Before you came in?'

'No, here . . .'

'Look, you had better tell me all about it, Emil, I shan't split. Perhaps I can help.'

'I've always worked in Shed 3, first with the cabinetmakers, and afterwards I was on nest boxes for Steguweit's . . .'

'Yes?'

'And then at the big poultry exhibition Steguweit got the gold medal for his nest boxes, and a lot of orders. So, to get us on with the job, his foremen used to slip us tobacco on the quiet. That was when there was no smoking allowed in the prison at all.'

'Before my time . . .'

'Yes, and then it came out, and there was a row, and no more tobacco. But they fixed up something else. We didn't see why we should work the skin off our hands just to make money for Steguweit, and we knocked the nest boxes together to pass the time. Then one day the foremen came along and promised us twenty pfennigs for every nest box over fifteen per day per man. And the money would be paid into a savings account under each man's name. And when we came out, we were to go along and draw the cash.'

'Sounds all right! And did you deliver the goods?'

'Didn't we just! There were days when we turned out thirty-two or even thirty-five extra. By God, it was a sweat, you should have seen my hands sometimes.'

'And was the money paid in all right?'

'Absolutely. In the first year there was already more than two hundred marks; and in the next it was more. It must be well over a thousand by now.'

'Well, then, ask for the savings book; and just take it when he shows it you.'

'Yes, but he doesn't show it any more. Too risky, he says, he's afraid of a stink, he says. A lot of men have come out and made a stink and gone to the governor because they said the money wasn't right. And Steguweit said to the governor it was all bollocks, there had never been any savings books, because it wasn't legal for prisoners to earn any extra money.'

'Some of them must have come back here in the meantime, what did they say?'

'Steguweit asked some of them what the hell they were talking about, he knew nothing of any savings books. And when they turned nasty, he threatened them with the police. He gave twenty marks or even fifty to some who pressed him, but what's that against the hundreds that they ought to have had. And I've got the most anyhow, I was there from the beginning.'

'And what do the foremen say?'

'That the guys are telling lies. That they got the money, but won't admit it because they threw it all away at once on drink and women.'

'Well, that's possible. The ones that get back into the clink again are shits. But why don't they show you the book? That's a bad sign. You ought to report Steguweit. No, that won't work, I wouldn't do that. You'd get yourself another stretch for blackmail, like Sethe there over by the wall.'

'That was some business with the chef, wasn't it?'

'Yes, don't talk about it, I see red whenever I think of it. He'd be coming out the day after tomorrow, and now he's got to do another three months because I couldn't hold my tongue. He'd like to do me in. Let's drop it . . .'

'I thought,' said little Bruhn, 'that at the worst I could go to the old man. He's a decent bloke, and helps us when he can.'

'Sure, when he can. But he can't do all he wants.'

'Why not? He's only got to ask the prisoners in Shed 3, and he'll find I'm speaking the truth.'

'But even if he believes you, he can't do anything. These savings accounts were against the regulations, and he can't help you over a thing like that. After all, old Sethe's business wasn't so very bad, but he got another three months for it.'

They were standing in a corner. The football players were tired, and were lying against the wall in the sun, sleeping and smoking. 'Smoking again, the bloody fools,' grumbled Kufalt. 'They know it's forbidden to smoke here in front of the Junior Prison. Well, never mind, the day after tomorrow I'll be a category above category three, I don't care what happens to 'em. Well, old Sethe was potato-peeler in the kitchen, and spent his six or eight years in the potato cellar, peeling potatoes. And once every month he reported to the work inspector and asked for another job, he said he'd been in the potato cellar long enough, he wanted to get out into the air. And he was always refused. Eventually he found out that the chef had got at the inspector so that Sethe shouldn't be let out of the cellar, because he did as much as two other potato-peelers. That's what happens if you work hard in this place.'

'I know.'

'So he begged the smarmy old brute to let him out, he said the damp dark cellar was getting on his nerves; and he was told to stick it out for another three months and then he could join the gardeners in the spring. But the chef said this again and again, and Sethe got mad in the end.

'He knew a lot about the kitchen and he also knew that every Wednesday and Saturday the chef shoved five or six pounds of meat under his jacket and carried it home. The prison officers are allowed to take shavings out of the carpenter's shop as kindling, they put it into a sack and carry it home in a wheelbarrow. But in the chef's sack there were shavings on top, and peas and lentils and barley and semolina underneath. And the joke was that Sethe usually had to push the old swine's wheelbarrow to his house.

'Well, Sethe kept on thinking how he could shaft the chef, so that another man would get the job and he could get out of the cellar.

Eventually he told me the whole yarn, and said: "Kufalt, what shall I do?" And I said: "Sethe, the whole thing's as plain as the nose on your face; let's go to the governor." And he said: "To the old man? Not on your life. I'd be shit scared." And I said: "I don't see why, it's a perfectly simple story, and we'll fix it so you don't get into trouble." And he said: "I wish to God I'd never told you, I know I'll be for it, you're too green." And I said: "I'm not green, and you'll be on garden work inside of a week." And I reported to the governor.

'I tell you I felt pretty pissed off with that chef, the fat pig; to think of the old grafter pinching what little meat we get, from us poor half-starved prisoners.'

'And what did the old man say?'

'Well, the governor listened, shook his bald head and said: "So that's what's going on. I had heard something, but I didn't know how it was carried out." And I said to him: "Yes, but Sethe mustn't get into trouble. How about if you stand by the gate next Wednesday or Saturday at six o'clock? The chef will be along with his barrow of shavings, and Sethe in front. And if there's only shavings in the sack Sethe will blink as he passes, but if he keeps his eyes open you can stop him and nab the old swine." "Yes," said the governor; "that's a very good scheme, we'll do so. Thank you, Kufalt."

' "Now," I said to Sethe; "it will be all right." And he was delighted. But the next Wednesday he said: "The governor wasn't there, and there were three tins of corned beef in the sack." And on the Saturday he said: "They've squealed to the chef, I know it by the way he treats me."

'And when the whole thing burst open, Sethe was hauled in for libelling prison officers. And the cooks stood and swore to a man that they had never seen the chef pinching meat or peas, and that it wasn't possible anyhow, and old Daddy Sethe got three months. And he would have come out the day after tomorrow.'

'But perhaps he was trying it on. Why should the governor do such a thing?'

'The governor didn't, it was the Prison Board that did it. They couldn't have a prisoner putting it across an old officer. Now be sensible, do what I tell you and don't go to the governor.'

'I don't know, Willi. It's different in my case.'

'Of course it's different in your case. But what's the same is that Sethe's a convict and so are you, and they won't believe us from the very start. Do what I say. Shut your trap and be glad when you're outside and have got a job.'

'Do you really mean it, Willi?'

'Of course. I would do the same myself, Emil.'

VIII

In the afternoon Kufalt was suddenly seized by an urgent impulse to work. He had really meant only to clean his cell, but then he noticed that his net was about two thousand knots short, and if he stuck to it he could finish the job and draw another eighteen pfennigs on discharge.

So he started knotting as if the Devil were after him. But it turned out a bit crooked, and a herring net always looks awful if the knots are not even. But the main thing was the eighteen pfennigs, and if the orderly stretched the net as he should do, it was plenty good enough for any old trawler.

Then, when he had finished the net, he sat on the floor and scoured it. That is a job that you need to get the hang of – just a touch of turpentine and graphite, or the floor won't take a polish, however much it is brushed. And then he made patterns, as was the fad at the moment in the Central Prison: you cut a stencil out of a bit of cardboard and then brushed the floor through the stencil against the grain, and so you made bright patterns on the floor, some light and some dark, of flowers and stars and little galloping beasts. There was no compulsion to do it, but it was amusing and pleased the eye of Chief Warder Rusch, who warmed to such artists.

When he had finished this, he went on to polish the metal. The most difficult bit was the underside of the bucket lid, which comes into direct contact with the urine and excrement and is always covered with a whitish slimy film. Well, he knew how to do it. The best thing was to attack it first with the hardest burnt brick you could get hold of, then . . .

At first he had been upset by the stench that rose from the open bucket, but now he never noticed it. The bucket stank, nothing could be done, and it would stink for some time, for the cells were small and badly aired.

Then you took a little polish . . .

But that moment the door of his cell opened, and the nets instructor came in with the orderly. It was no longer Rosenthal, but a new face.

'Well, Instructor,' grinned Kufalt, and went on busily with his polishing. 'So we've got another orderly, eh? Quick as baking biscuits.'

The man did not reply, but said to his assistant: 'There you are, take the net and the yarn and the iron rod and – where have you put your knife, Kufalt?'

'It's in the cupboard by the Bible. No, on the window ledge. I've finished the unit, Instructor.'

'Eh? Please put the lid on the bucket. It stinks like the plague in here.'

'Your shop smells like violets, I suppose. The last unit, of course. And mind you see I get the doings.'

'You've done sixteen since the first of the month. Put the lid on that bucket at once.'

'Can't, I'm polishing it. Hey, you lout behind there, pick up the net, please, and don't scratch my floor. Can't you see I've just polished it?'

The prisoner, a 'colleger', as Kufalt had seen at once, said: 'Don't you speak to me like that, I won't have it. And put the lid on your bucket, didn't you hear? There's a filthy stink in here.'

'I won't talk to you, boy, I'm sure you're in for pinching your old aunt's savings. What do you mean, sixteen, Instructor? There's seventeen now, and I'll be paid for them tomorrow, or there'll be a row.'

'Now, Kufalt, don't get cheeky,' he almost begged; 'or I shall have to call the chief warder.'

But Kufalt had lost his temper and said: 'Then call him, I've got something I'd like to tell him. Don't stare like that, take the net, you dope, and get out of my cell! So you want to do me out of a unit, do you?'

The nets instructor was in despair: 'Look, Kufalt, you're crazy. The work inspector asked early this morning for the work lists of the prisoners due for discharge. I can't alter anything now, Kufalt. Do be sensible.'

'Then you should have told me,' roared Kufalt.

'You were with the doctor.'

'That doesn't matter. Do you think I'm going to give you four thousand five hundred knots? Bring that net back, I'll unpick it again!'

'Kufalt!' begged the instructor. 'Do be sensible. It'll take you six or eight hours to undo all those knots.'

'I don't care,' shouted Kufalt. 'It's victimization. You're trying to get back at me by not paying for the job. I know you well. Give me that net, or I'll chuck the bucket and all the muck inside it . . .'

'What's all this!' said a voice from the door, and the master of the Central Prison, Chief Warder Rusch, thrust his large person into the cell. 'Chuck the bucket, would you? And all the muck, hey? Well, you'll clear up the mess yourself, mind!'

'And the man was due for discharge the day after tomorrow,' said the instructor, with a sudden return of confidence.

'That's not your business,' broke in Kufalt once more. 'You've no right to say that! You're not an official here. I'll report you to the governor. You've always tried to do me down since the very start. I haven't forgotten how you always gave me the worst yarn and always said my knots weren't tight enough. And I pulled until I sprained my thumb, and you just laughed and said: "Not tight enough!"'

'Why are you shouting like this, Kufalt?' asked the chief warder. 'Are you ill?'

'I'm not ill at all, but I've done seventeen units, and the instructor says he'll only allow sixteen. Is that just? I thought we were treated justly here!'

'If the man has done seventeen, then he must be paid for seventeen,' observed Rusch.

'But the work inspector . . .'

'What! But, but—? Has he done seventeen?'

'Yes, but . . .'

'What! But, but—? Then he's to be paid for seventeen. Got that?'

'But I've already sent in the lists.'

'Then just say you've made a mistake.'

Kufalt grinned and broke in: 'It's just because he thinks I shopped him over Rosenthal. That's why I'm to be done out of a unit, and that's why I'm so mad.'

The chief warder looked, and waited. This was his hour. It was then he reaped his harvest; when the denizens of his kingdom said what they thought about each other, he collected his evidence against prisoners and the graded punishment system, and found the material for his reports. There was nothing that he did not know or hear; and in his office, the governor wrung his hands despairingly and cried: 'Is there not one just man . . . ?'

The instructor flushed purple, and swallowed: 'Herr Rusch, if anyone deserves to be shopped . . .'

'Hey, what's this?' asked Rusch with a large and genial air. 'You don't mean our model lad, Willi Kufalt. Why, just look round his cell, do you know another like it in the place? It's as bright and shining as an ape's arse.'

And Kufalt felt so confident that he too had a go at the instructor. 'So I ought to be shopped, eh? You've got something on me, eh? Are you sworn in as an assistant official?'

At this the nets instructor burst out in a fury: 'You blackmailer! I tell you, Chief Warder . . .' And then, though his face was purple, he thought better of it and said: 'You'll be paid for your seventeen units, Kufalt; even if I myself have to give you the eighteen pfennigs at the gate the day after tomorrow. You'll get them all right.'

And he departed. The chief warder stood with an air of baffled wrath.

'No letters for me, sir?' asked Kufalt.

'Letters? Letters? You'll get your letters at the proper time. And you'd better not be so cheeky. The instructor is your superior. I shall write on your discharge sheet that your conduct was bad, Kufalt.

Then you won't even get into category two when you come in again.'

So saying, he slammed the door before Kufalt could fly into a rage again.

IX

At eight o'clock category three had their wireless evening. It was pleasantly hushed in the building; two or three warders on night duty padded round in list slippers, quietly and cautiously opening the doors of the category three men's cells, which had already been locked for the night. And the prisoners went softly down to the schoolroom. For nothing is worse in a prison than any noise at night. If the prisoners' precious night's rest is disturbed, the place becomes a pandemonium of shouts and yells and howls.

The twelve men gathered in the schoolroom, where it was still fairly light, and the shoemaker was already busy over the receiver.

'What's on?' asked Kufalt, but the shoemaker was still smarting from their encounter in the middle of the day, and did not reply.

Batzke answered in his stead; tall Batzke, who trafficked in naked female charms and looked after the boiler room: 'A Verdi opera. Want to listen?'

'No, thanks. I can't understand why they don't put on something funny in the evening. They might remember the prisoners.'

Batzke droned his usual refrain: 'Why should they? They're glad they don't have to. They're bloody glad to be rid of us – cattle, that's what we are.'

The wireless had started, and the pair strolled up and down the long gangway near the desks.

'Got any tobacco? Hey Batzke, how do you get such good tobacco here? I've learnt a thing or two since I've been in, but you . . .'

'When you've done a fourteen-year stretch like I have,' said Batzke, from the vantage of his thirty-six years, 'you'll know this shop even better than you do now.'

'Not for me,' cried Kufalt. 'Sooner be dead.'

'Don't say that,' said Batzke encouragingly. 'You enjoy your time outside all the more.'

'No, thanks, I'm running straight now.'

'Don't you try it,' warned Batzke; 'you'll never keep it up. You'll knock around for a few months looking for a job. And perhaps you'll find a job, and sweat yourself to death to keep it. But then it'll come out somehow that you've been in the clink, and the boss'll put you on the street, or the other blokes – they're always the worst – won't work with a criminal. I've tried it all. And when you're beat, and haven't eaten for three days, and pinch something, and get caught, they say: "Just what we thought; good thing we threw that bloke out." That's what they're like, and if you've got any sense you'll listen to me, and won't even start to run straight. You come along with me.'

'But you get nabbed and back in the clink again.'

'Not so easily, when you've had a rest and got a bit of money. It's only when you're starving and get the wind up, and have to have money, that you get caught. Of course they nab you sometime, but you'll last out a bit if you're with me.'

'But aren't there some that don't ever come back?'

'How many, eh? Look, how long have you been inside? How many have you seen come back in that time? Well, then! And those that don't come back here are doing time somewhere else. But I shan't do my next job in Prussia; I shall do a bit of housebreaking in Hamburg, and I'll buy a plan of the place so as to make sure I don't get over the border into Altona. Fuhlsbüttel is much better than Prussia, category two are allowed to play football.'

'But I don't want to start burgling – I've no guts for that sort of thing.'

'No need to, my lad; I can see that myself. You couldn't do much with arms like yours. But I've been looking for someone like you for a long time. You're a scholar, you know grand words and a bit of English parley-voo, and that's where I fall down. You don't suppose I like smashing things up.'

Kufalt felt flattered.

'I've tried and tried,' went on Batzke, 'but I can't get away with it.

I had a go at the bogus marriage game, the risk isn't much and you don't need to pay out any money for the tarts, but do you think I could pick up one decent girl? I watched how it was done, on the racecourse and in bars, and I had my nails manicured – no good. The smart alecs got off with all the girls worth having, and I was left with a slavey or at best a housemaid with two hundred marks in the savings bank – no use to me.'

'I could show you how to behave.'

'That's just it. I'm up to anything, I can split a safe with an acetylene burner as well as any man. But I only get the small jobs, it's the others who get away with the big ones. That's what riles a man when he understands his profession.'

'But a man doesn't need any education for burgling, Walter.'

'You've no notion. I ought to be able to get into a club as Dr Batzke, or travel in a luxury train without the cops smelling what's up at once, or run up the steps of a posh house so that the porter doesn't dare to ask what I want – that's where you've got to fill me in.'

'I'm sure you know all that already. You've soaked up more champagne in your life than I have.'

'Sure . . . but just soaked it up . . . and along with tarts. To drink champagne, and carry on a conversation with a real lady, and not start feeling under her blouse after the third glass – that's what I want to learn.'

They paced up and down. The others were talking, smoking, quarrelling, and two were playing chess in a corner. Verdi's melodies were drowned by the din.

Walter Batzke warmed to his theme: 'We'll have a fine time, my lad. When we come out now we'll both have money and see a bit of life, I tell you. Do you know what you'll do the first night?'

'No. What should I do?'

'Well, you don't know much, do you! You'll pick up a nice little tart in the Reeperbahn or the Freiheit and go along home with her. And when she asks about the cash, you slap your discharge sheet on the table and say: "It's on you tonight, love. Send for some fizz!"'

'She'd spit in my face!'

'You're clueless! The first night out of clink is free with all the whores in Hamburg. That's a fact. You can believe me. They'll all let you.'

'Really?'

'Word of honour. Well, and on the Sunday I'll be out.'

'Shall I come and meet you at the station?' asked Kufalt.

'No, better not. I'll have to go home first and see my old woman.'

'I never knew you were married?'

'I'm not – do I look it? No, I've got an old widow, about fifty, who can't find another man, so I give her what she wants, and I get two fine rooms for it, and a bath, and good grub – all the very best, my lad. Perhaps you can come and live there, we'll see – Harvestehuder Weg, Widow Antonie Hermann. She belongs to the big shipping firm, you'll have heard of it?'

'Do you think she'll have waited for you all these years?'

'Well, what do you think? Of course she'll have got another bloke, and of course she's no idea I'm coming out. But you know me, I don't stand for any nonsense. I'll just say to the bloke: "The Raven is back. Get out!" And when he packs his stuff, I'll see he doesn't get away with much of what he's got out of her.'

This amused Kufalt, and he grinned: 'Won't she mind?'

'She? I know where the whip's kept, and after I've given her a hiding she won't look at anyone else.'

Kufalt suddenly turned giddy; the smoke was thick, the evening muggy, the music of the opera came from very far away. The widow on the Harvestehuder Weg, the shipping business she owned, the whip, the Raven – it was a bit too much. But when a man's done a five-year stretch, nothing seems impossible. A man goes through strange experiences in jail.

So he made no comment, and said: 'Where shall we meet? And when?'

'I'll tell you,' said Batzke – 'we'll meet at the Central Station – no, there are always so many cops around there, they all know me. We'll meet at eight on the Town Hall Square under the horse's tail.'

'Where's that?'

'Under the horse's tail? Ever been in Hamburg?'

'Only a few days.'

'There's a statue of Kaiser Wilhelm on the Town Hall Square, on horseback. Everyone in Hamburg knows "under the horse's tail".'

'Good. I'll find it. At eight, then.'

'Right. And put your best suit on. We'll make a night of it.'

'Sure. It won't be my fault if we don't.'

'Nor mine.'

X

Through the sleeping prison, now almost dark, Kufalt crept behind the night warder in his socks, his slippers in his hand.

The warder opened the cell door and stood for a moment hesitating with his fingers on the switch. 'You can go to bed without a light for once, Kufalt; otherwise in ten minutes I'll have to go up four flights of stairs again. I've been sawing wood at home all day, and I'm dog-tired.'

'Of course,' said Kufalt. 'I don't mind. Goodnight, Herr Thiessen.'

'Goodnight, Kufalt. Is this your last night?'

'Last but one.'

'How long have you been in?'

'Five years.'

'That's a long time. Yes,' continued the old man, shaking his head. 'It's a pretty long time. You'll be surprised when you get outside. Five million unemployed. It's hard, Kufalt, it's hard. Both my sons are out of work.'

'I've learnt to wait.'

'Have you? Not in here. No one has ever learnt that here. Well, if I don't see you again, Kufalt, all the best. You won't find life easy, you'll find it very hard. I wonder if you'll stick it. Once a jailbird . . .'

The old man stood waiting, for Kufalt had almost finished undressing by the landing light.

'You haven't been a bad bloke, Kufalt, but a bit too easy-going. Hard-working, yes. And civil when you were treated civil. But you were always off in a temper when anything went wrong. And you took up all the shithouse gossip. Five million unemployed, Kufalt . . .'

'You aren't exactly cheering me up, Herr Thiessen.'

'You'll be cheerful enough when you get out, the girls and the booze'll do that for you – cheerfulness isn't much. Just keep on remembering, Kufalt, that there's about seven hundred cells in this building – they don't care who gets inside. And we don't care whom we turn the key on either.'

'But everyone is different, Herr Thiessen.'

'Outside, yes. But in here you're all alike, you know that yourself, Kufalt. You find it out pretty quick. Well, get along to bed. I see you've pulled your bed down already; that's what I like, only the decent blokes do that. There are others. The worst is Batzke, who takes down his bed from the hook at twelve o'clock at night and then slams it onto the stone floor so as to wake the whole building. Sleep well – your last night but one.'

'Goodnight, Herr Thiessen. And thank you very much. For everything.'

XI

It was not dark in the cell. Moonlight shone through the window. Kufalt stood up on his bed, and pulled himself up to the metal sill. He could just get one knee onto the narrow sill, and he hung there, looking out into the night.

It was very still. The bark of a dog and the tramp of the nightwatchman in the yard only made the stillness deeper.

No; no stars. He could not see the moon either, only its radiance in the air. The dark, long, heavy shadows yonder were the walls, and the globed shapes above them were the chestnut trees. They were in blossom, but they did not smell. Chestnuts only smell from quite near at hand, and the smell is unpleasant, like the smell of sperm.

But they would still be in blossom when he came out. He could walk under them when they were in bloom, he could visit them when their foliage turned a deeper green, when the first yellow leaves came, when the fruit burst, when they were bare of leaves, and when they bloomed again – he could always go and see them, he could go anywhere he liked, how he liked, and when he liked.

He found it hard to realize. During five long years he had clung to that sill hundreds of times, always in danger of dragging the sill down or of discovery by the warder; and now all that was over.

'Thiessen was talking rubbish,' he thought. 'He doesn't understand anything any more; after all, a warder is a lifer too. As for his sons – I know for a fact that the youngest robbed someone's till and would be in here if his father wasn't paying it off. And his wages don't amount to much.'

He felt a craving for a cigarette and clambered down. As he groped in the darkness for his trousers, where he kept his tobacco, an unusual feeling suddenly came over him . . . he stopped . . .

'I won't,' he said; 'I won't do it any more. The old bloke's always been very decent to all of us. It's like the night outside, it gets dark, the moon comes out, and then it's light again, it's all quite simple . . .'

He tried to clear his thoughts. 'All these scams only make things harder; everything was much simpler when I just sat in my cell, before I was up to any of the old lags' games. I must make things easier again. Otherwise I shan't get through, I'm too weak, he's right. Everything beats me. A bloke must make a clean start, it doesn't matter how. Perhaps I'll go to the chaplain tomorrow.'

He rolled the cigarette and lit it. 'I must stick it out, I'll start the first thing tomorrow, I won't look out of the window at five o'clock to see Batzke's tart.'

He sat in his shirt on the edge of the bed and stared into vacancy, desolate. The cigarette ash fell unnoticed on his spotless floor, patterned with the stars, and sun, and moon.

2

Release

I

Whether Kufalt, had he woken at five in the morning, would have rejected the charms of a naked girl's body, remains doubtful. He did not wake up until a quarter to six, when two sharp strokes of the bell indicated that it was time to get up and wash.

He leapt off his bed and made it with special care, for that day the final cell inspection would take place. Then, a wash in the enamel food bowl instead of in the gleaming nickel basin, which there would be no more time to polish.

When the orderlies came past for the buckets and the water at about six o'clock, when bolts rattled and keys clashed, Kufalt had long since started polishing the cement floor. The pattern had to be picked out again, it had got smudged during the night. Then he drew up the inventory, as laid down by age-long prescription, so that the chief warder could see at a glance that all was there.

And all this time he kept thinking of his dream of the night before. The dream of the first few weeks of his imprisonment had returned once more.

He was running towards a dark wood deep in snow. He had to run very fast, the police were on his track. It was night, and bitter winter weather, the forest was vast, he had seen on a map that the road through it was eighteen kilometres long. But he must get to the further side of it, where there was another railway line, where they would not look for him, and he might escape.

Before he plunged into that vast forest that was to envelop him for four dark hours, he had to pass through a village; and in the inn the windows were still lit. He went in and asked for a schnapps. And another. And another. He felt as though he would never be warm again. He bought a bottle of brandy, stowed it away in his briefcase and paid.

Then he noticed that two men were watching him, one of them young and pale and foxy-faced; the other old and bloated, with only a few remaining hairs on his bald, scabby scalp. Two tramps.

'Much snow on the roads?' croaked the older man.

'Yes,' replied Kufalt, waiting for the change from his hundred-mark note. He had the wallet in his hand, and the young fox's eyes were fixed on it with a look of insatiable greed.

'There's more snow to come, mate,' growled the older man. 'It's no night for walking.'

'No,' he said shortly, and put the wallet back in his pocket. He said 'Good evening' to the landlord and went towards the door. As he passed the table where the two men were sitting, the young one got up and said in an imploring tone: 'Buy us a schnapps – we're frozen. We are on the way to Quanz too.'

But he walked quickly past, as though he had not heard.

Outside, the wind flung a whirl of snow into his face. He had to fight against it step by step; beyond the fields stood the dark mass of the forest, a few hundred metres away.

'I ought to have bought them a grog,' he said reproachfully to himself. 'Then they'd have stayed where they were for a quarter of an hour, and I'd have got a start. They're after my money. Why did he say they were going to Quanz *too*? How does he know where I'm going?'

He tried to walk back the way he had come. But he could not find it; the snow had drifted across the road.

'It will be quieter in the forest. But the snow will be lying deep. Eighteen kilometres to go! I'm crazy, wasn't I all right in Berlin? As soon as I get into the forest I'll take the thousand-mark notes out of my wallet and hide them about me somewhere. Then they'll only find the change out of the hundred, and they're welcome to that.'

He moved on against wind and snow. The alcohol flamed up in him, he steamed with warmth. The snow was pleasantly cool against his face.

Then a sudden stillness fell, he had reached the shelter of the trees. Only a few steps further. There stood a clump of firs by the side of the road, he would hide behind it; he plunged into a snowdrift in the ditch and struggled through it onto firm ground. When he reached it, he did not begin by shaking the snow off his clothes. He put a foot on a heap of stones by the roadside, and hastily untied his bootlaces. His boots were good ones, with long waterproof uppers, and the foot inside was dry and warm. Carefully he eased the flattened thousand-mark notes – there were unfortunately only three left – between sock and skin, made sure that they were lying neatly and securely, and pulled the boot on again.

Then he stood up. He took a long swig from his bottle. He was now quite calm and confident. They would never catch him, none of them. He would be one too many for them. He had only to step out briskly and they would never catch him up.

And so began his journey. It was more difficult, but also easier than he had thought. He saw and heard no more of the two men; but the snow lay terribly deep, in great drifts beside the paths, into which he sank up to the armpits. He slipped so often off the road that finally, when he felt the ground giving way beneath his feet, and himself sliding into the ditch, he flung himself in the opposite direction and usually recovered his footing.

From time to time he cleared the snow off a milestone and flashed his lamp onto the figures. He made only slow progress. He did not do more than about three kilometres an hour. It was a good thing he had the brandy with him, but even so he would not catch the early train at Quanz; besides he must first go to a hotel there and sleep and sleep.

When he threw the emptied bottle into the snow, he still had four kilometres to go. He could not reach Quanz before eight. For the last bit of the way he was merely staggering forward, though the road was now outside the forest and swept by the wind almost clear of snow.

Then he found himself sitting on his bed at the Eagle at Quanz; the room was icy, and the stove, just lit, smoked. He kept on stumbling and falling asleep; but he knew he must undress, he could not sleep in his wet clothes. His limbs were stiff, and his bones congealed.

He peeled off his sock . . .

He stiffened and stared dumbfounded. Then his fingers came to the aid of his eyes. They found a soft mass of paper-pulp, almost colourless – paper that had been rubbed for eight hours between a moist foot and a sock.

Three thousand – his last money, the last proceeds of his crime. He flung himself onto the bed and lay as he had fallen, his mind a blank. A little later, he ordered some cognac to be brought up to his room, and hot red wine with cloves and sugar.

For three days he stayed in bed, drinking all the time, until the money in his wallet was spent. Then he made his way to the police station in Quanz, a small town of three thousand inhabitants, and gave himself up. All was at an end.

All this had really happened to him, more than five years ago. And it had passed over Kufalt's dreaming vision on many many nights during the first months after his arrest; that night march through the forest, and the moment when he had picked the pulped notes out of his sock. That had been the worst shock of his life. It had broken his pride for ever, and destroyed all his self-esteem. He was no use, even as a criminal. He would never tell that story, he always said he had squandered all the money, including the three thousand.

Later on the dream had come less often, but it still returned from time to time. And it had come last night. The new life was beginning, the old chains were clinking.

But it was noticeable that the dream had changed; one trifling detail had altered.

He remembered exactly: last night too he had put his foot on the stone by the roadside, unlaced his boot and taken it off. Only . . . it was not the three thousand-mark notes that he had slipped into his sock, it was a hundred-mark one . . .

It was *the* hundred-mark note!

II

Willi Kufalt sat there lost in thought. He fingered his sock doubtfully. 'I really ought to give it back to the instructor. But I can't do that. I'd sooner tear it up.'

He had a clear sense of the new life that was now to begin. Something like the moonlight of the night before. 'A clean break,' he said to himself, 'and a fresh start.'

He felt in his sock . . .

Then he let his hand fall. He stood up with a jerk and posted himself in watchful attitude under the window, as Chief Warder Rusch stepped into the cell.

The section warder stood at the door.

The chief warder did not look at the prisoner. First he inspected the bucket, then the inventory on the table, and then the arrangement of plates, brushes, boxes and tins of polish on the floor. Something must have annoyed him: he first jingled his keys, and then kicked the brushes apart with the toe of his boot.

'Polishing brushes first, then clothes brushes,' he commanded.

Kufalt walked across the floor, bent down, and laid the brushes in the required order.

'Learnt a bit, hey?' said Rusch more graciously. 'Pigsty days over, hey?'

'Yes,' said Kufalt, reflecting that he had here, for instance, learnt to wash his plate, and eat with his netting knife, a blackened stump of blade, merely to preserve the prescribed spotless sheen of the other objects.

The chief warder walked towards the door. But there was still something: he stopped and looked meditatively at the cupboard. He passed a finger lightly along the edge of it.

'Herr Suhm,' he said, 'give out notepaper. I'll carry on.'

The section warder disappeared.

'This man Sethe,' said Rusch, contemplating the ceiling; 'will he appeal?'

Kufalt reflected for a moment. He really did not know whether the old potato-peeler would accept his three months for insulting the chef, or whether he would appeal, for they were no longer on speaking terms. But he would rather not let Rusch know that.

'I think he will, sir,' he said.

'Better not. Better not be a fool. Tell him to accept his punishment.

Then with probation he'll be out tomorrow. Otherwise – he'll stay inside. Detention – and maybe other charges.'

'Ha,' thought Kufalt, 'they think they've got him taped. Old Sethe's done an eight-year stretch, and they know every day's one too many for him now. That's how they mean to get him.'

And aloud: 'I could speak to him at twelve this morning. But I don't think it'll be any good, sir. He's sore with rage.'

'Better not be a fool Accept it. Then probation. Otherwise – he's in for another stretch.' The chief warder paused. Then he said ominously: 'And then . . .'

He broke off, *very* ominously.

'Yes, and then,' thought Kufalt. 'I know what you mean. It isn't at all certain Sethe would come out in three months. Those lice in the kitchen would set about him in the cellar, and a prisoner isn't a witness. They'd knock him around so he could hear himself shout. Warders would turn the screws on him now and again – he's pretty near boiling over as it is – until he said something silly. Insulting an official again. And if he gets violent – doesn't matter whether he does or not; they'll keep him inside till he's fit for the madhouse . . .'

'Yes, it would be stupid to appeal,' agreed Kufalt.

'Of course,' said the chief warder benignly. 'Tell him so. Better report to registrar – he'll be here today. Released tomorrow at seven.'

'Yes, sir,' said Kufalt, knowing he would not say a word to Sethe.

The chief warder nodded: 'That's right. Always were a sensible chap – except when you weren't. Hurry up. Take you to the governor straight away. Keep your mouth shut.'

The chief warder went to inspect some other cells and see if they were neat and clean.

Kufalt didn't move.

See the governor before eight o'clock! His brother-in-law Werner had written. Perhaps his sister had herself come to fetch him. But it was one day too early for that. It was about something else, of course; about Sethe. Why had the chief warder said at the end, 'Keep your mouth shut'?

He would say what he liked to the governor. Governor Greve was the only man in the building to whom one could tell everything. He could not do much, his officers always overruled him, but he was a decent man, he did what he could. And he only wanted to do what was decent.

Kufalt again thought of his hundred-mark note. But he didn't finger his sock any more. He put away the inventory. 'Pah! Fancy starting to be decent here! Nothing doing.'

And he went on: 'I'd have been a right fool to tear up that note. They're all alike, outside as well as in. Sethe – they mean to do in the old man after his eight years in the clink. And I'm to start being decent? I don't think.'

The chief warder put his head through the door and said: 'Come along.'

III

Kufalt was always specially glad to get out of the prison buildings and go 'up in front'.

He walked half a pace in advance of the chief warder, past the glass cubicle in the Central Hall. Here the scene was quite different; here were the large cells of the artisans, the shoemakers and the tailors, the lithographers and the librarian. Here the cell doors stood wide open, and the workers went in and out, to the lavatory or the instructor, carrying irons or strips of leather.

But then came the great iron door.

The chief warder turned the key twice; Kufalt stepped through the door, and stood in the office corridor. A bleak corridor, with whitewashed walls, the linoleum on the floor gleaming and spotless, and an endless line of doors. Kufalt knew them all: visitors' room, schoolmaster, chaplain, another visitors' room, the work inspector's two clerks, governor's anteroom and office, and senior warder of the postal service; and in the opposite direction on the other side – telephone exchange, police inspector, work inspector, steward, cashier, accounts inspector, doctor, Young Prisoners' Welfare, conference room, investigating magistrate and Admission.

Almost all these rooms he had entered, with requests or petitions, to receive reprimands, or to sign documents. Here had his fate been settled, his hopes raised or dashed.

The police inspector had once kept on promising to visit him for three months, and never came; since when he had hated him. The schoolmaster had once given him twenty almost new magazines to take to his cell; indeed he had always been decent. With the work inspector he had had many conflicts, because their estimates of work done did not agree. On one occasion the steward had been a little too generous with supplies for two months, and at the end of that quarter the grub had been such that one could only think of hunger, hunger, hunger. The chaplain – there wasn't much to be said about him. He was already over sixty, and had been in the jail for forty years; the chilliest Pharisee on this chilly earth.

The governor, on the other hand – well, there was not much to be said about him. A splendid fellow . . . too kind perhaps, certainly too kind. His kindness had got him into much trouble, and he did not now have the courage to stand up to his subordinates, who always got their way in the end. Still, a decent sort.

The chief warder knocked at the door. 'Prisoner Kufalt,' he reported.

The governor looked up from behind his desk. 'Very well, Chief Warder. You may go, I will send the man back myself.'

This was extremely galling to the mighty chief warder, as Kufalt very well knew. Under the former governor he had always been present at every interview, and forcibly expressed his views. But the chief warder gave no sign of his feelings, turned and left the room.

The governor was sitting behind his desk. He had a fresh colour, a couple of duelling scars on his left cheek, and blue eyes. His head was bald, and fresh-coloured like his face, pink towards the forehead and deeper red towards the crown.

'Sit down,' said the governor. 'Cigarette, Kufalt?'

He offered him the box; it was a kind that cost six pfennigs, as Kufalt noticed with awe. And then the governor gave him a match.

His hands were very well kept, he was wearing an immaculate

lounge suit, and his shirt cuffs were so neat and spotless that Kufalt felt hopelessly dirty and uncouth.

'Well, it will all be over tomorrow,' said the governor. 'Now can I do anything for you?'

Kufalt, in his present mood, would have gladly accepted anything the governor proposed, but he had no suggestions of his own, in spite of his need, so he only looked at the governor and waited.

'What plans have you?' asked the governor. 'You must have some.'

'I don't really know. I think my relations will write to me.'

'Are you in correspondence with them?' And he added, by way of explanation: 'I don't read the post, you know. The chaplain is responsible for the censorship.'

'In correspondence? No. During the last three months I've written them a letter on every writing day.'

'And they have not answered?'

'No, not yet.'

'Are they in a good position?'

'Yes.'

'If no answer comes – it may still come, of course, but if it doesn't – would you go to your relations?'

'No,' said Kufalt, quite taken aback. 'No, certainly not.'

'Ah. And you want to settle down to work?'

'I would prefer,' said Kufalt hesitatingly, 'to go to a place where I wasn't known. I thought of Hamburg.'

The governor wagged his head. 'Hamburg . . . A large city . . .'

'I'm fed up with all that sort of thing, sir. It doesn't attract me any more.'

'The temptations of a great city? Ah, well, Kufalt, I don't believe in them either. Or rather, they're exactly the same in a small one. But unemployment is naturally worse in Hamburg. Have you no one there who would help you? Here, perhaps I could . . .'

'No, please, not here. All the faces . . .'

'Very well. Perhaps you're right. But what are you going to do there? Have you thought of anything?'

'I don't yet know. I couldn't go back to bookkeeping or cashier work. And I couldn't get a job very easily, with a gap of five years in my papers . . .'

'No,' agreed the governor; 'probably not.'

'But I can still use a typewriter. I might buy a machine, and type addresses by the hundred? And later on start a proper typing agency? I can type very well, sir.'

'You have no machine? Have you any money?'

'Only my pay for prison work.'

'And how much is that?'

'Three hundred marks, I think. And could you have it paid out to me all at once, sir? So that I won't have to collect it from the Welfare Office every week.'

The governor looked doubtful.

'I'll be very careful, sir,' begged Kufalt. 'I won't waste a penny. I would so hate going to the Welfare Office.' And he added in a low tone: 'I want to be through with all that.'

The governor was easily moved. 'Very well,' he said. 'That's settled. I'll see that what is due to you is paid out in a lump sum. But, Kufalt, you will have to live out of those three hundred marks, for two months perhaps, or even three; you won't be able to buy a typewriter.'

'By instalments, surely?'

'No, not by instalments. You can't reckon on a steady income, your addresses scheme might go wrong. What then?'

'My relations . . .'

'Let's leave them out of it entirely. What would you do then?'

'I – don't – know.'

The governor's voice grew more and more emphatic: 'And how long is it since you have done any typing? Five years, isn't it? Not for more than five years. Well then, you'll find it pretty hard at first, and you won't get through much.'

'I can quite well type a hundred addresses an hour.'

'You could. But you can't now. You tell yourself you're in good health, you have done twice your job of net-making here, and you'll manage all right outside. But there has been nothing to distract you here, Kufalt, and outside you will have all sorts of worries and temptations. You are no longer used to mixing with other people. And then the cinemas, where you can't go, and the cafés you can't afford. It will be very difficult for you, Kufalt; and the difficulties are going to start now.'

'Yes,' said Kufalt. 'Yes.'

'You have been in here a long time, Kufalt. How many have you seen come back?'

'A great many.'

'You will have to be stronger than all of those. You will often think that it isn't worth the trouble – what's the good? I shall never make my way again. But a great many do make their way again. You must be very firm with yourself, Kufalt, very firm.'

'Yes, sir,' said Kufalt obediently.

The prevailing colour in the room was a quiet brown. The windows were not holes in the wall, they had curtains, white muslin curtains with delicate green stripes. There was a proper carpet on the floor.

'You are like a sick man who has been a long while in bed, you must first learn to walk, step by step. When a man's been in bed for a long time, he must have a stick to support him, or someone to help him along. Another cigarette? Good.'

The governor waited a moment. 'You are thinking now: "Let the man talk, I shall be all right." But – it – is – very – difficult. Until you have found your feet outside – you have never been without a settled wage, have you? I thought not. Before you have got used to things, all your money will have gone. And what then?'

'It seems,' said Kufalt, with a wry smile, 'as though a bloke ought to ask you to keep him in here, sir. I'm like a man with his hands cut off.'

'Not cut off,' said the governor. 'But they're paralysed, they're stiff. I want to make a suggestion. There's a place in Hamburg where you might go, they take in unemployed clerks and salesmen, and men just released from prison. There's a typewriting room there, and you do a day's work, exactly as in an office, and for that you get your lodging and your food. If you earn any more, it is reckoned to your account. You don't need to touch your earnings, and they will mount up if you work hard. And as soon as you feel safe, and know of some work of any sort, you can leave the Home. You can leave it any day you like, Kufalt.'

'Yes,' said Kufalt reflectively. 'They're not only ex-convicts?'

'No,' said the governor; 'so far as I know, there are ordinary unemployed too.'

'And I can just go straight into the place?'

'Certainly. You will learn to walk, Kufalt, no more. There will of course be some kind of regulations, and it won't exactly be luxurious, but you have not been spoiled.'

'No,' said Kufalt, with a deep breath; 'no, I haven't. Very well, sir. That's what I'll do.'

He looked before him. The hundred-mark note in his stocking burnt like a sore. He struggled with himself. He would have liked to give it to the governor: 'There, take it, I want to start afresh.' The governor would not ask any questions. But he did not, it seemed too pretentious, as though he meant to pay off his gratitude; he would tear it up when he got back to his cell. He really would.

'Yes,' said the governor; 'then that's settled. And if anything goes wrong, write to me.'

'Yes. And thank you very much, sir. Thank you for everything.'

'Good,' said the governor, and stood up. 'And now I'll take you along to the chaplain. He'll send in your name to the Home.'

'The chaplain?' asked Kufalt. 'Is it a religious home?' He stayed in his chair.

'No, no. There's a clergyman at the head of it. It is quite undenominational. Jews and Christians and heathen.' The governor laughed reassuringly.

'But I don't want to see the chaplain.'

'Don't be a fool,' said the other energetically. 'The chaplain sends in your name, it's a mere matter of form, it might just as well be the police inspector or the post warder. It happens to be the chaplain.'

'But I don't care to see the chaplain.'

'Look here, young man; surely five minutes' unpleasantness with the chaplain is better than throwing in your hand. Now, then – come along.'

The governor was already hurrying along the passage ahead of Kufalt.

IV

Suddenly Kufalt called out to the governor, who had almost reached the door of the chaplain's room, 'Sir, there's just one thing more.'

The governor turned: 'Yes?'

'Bruhn, sir, he's coming out too the day after tomorrow. Could you see him?'

'Yes?'

'There's something wrong. I think he's been promised something and now they want to let him down.'

The governor pondered for a moment, concentrating on the matter, then he asked: 'The foremen?'

Kufalt looked at the governor, but said nothing.

'You won't say any more?'

And Kufalt answered slowly: 'Since the business with Sethe I hardly dare.'

They stood face to face in the office corridor, prisoner and prison governor; and they both thought of that interview when the governor promised the prisoner help and satisfaction. The governor's forehead flushed. He said with great deliberation: 'It isn't all so easy, Kufalt. One has to do just the little that one can, all the time . . .'

Then, with sudden decision: 'Very well, I will speak to Bruhn, and see that he doesn't make a fool of himself.'

And he stepped quickly into the chaplain's room in front of Kufalt.

'I have brought Kufalt to see you, chaplain. He has a request to make.' And to Kufalt: 'Well, I hope you will get on all right. Keep your pecker up – and good luck.'

He gave him his hand, Kufalt murmured something in reply, and the governor was gone.

'Now then, my dear young friend,' said the chaplain; 'you have a request to make. Speak out, tell me all that is on your mind.'

'Don't you wish I would,' thought Kufalt, observing the smooth plump face with ill-concealed dislike.

Chaplain Zumpe's hair was white as snow, he had a fine white smooth complexion, but dark eyes, and over them a pair of bushy deep black brows. It was rumoured in the prison that these eyebrows were false, that the chaplain stuck them on with glue every Sunday before service; and as a proof that this was no mere rumour, it was pointed out that one eyebrow was often higher than the other.

There was friendliness in the chaplain's eye, a rather tepid, almost rabbit-like sort of friendliness, but it was of no avail; Kufalt was perfectly well aware that the man cared nothing about him at all.

'What is the trouble, Kufalt?' the chaplain asked again. 'Are we in need of anything? A nice suit for leaving? That costs a great deal of money, but perhaps it's worthwhile in your case. You have still a chance to make good.'

'No, thank you,' said Kufalt. 'I don't want a suit. But the governor told me I must come to you about a recommendation to a home. That's what I have come for.'

'So you want to go to the Home of Peace? I am delighted to hear it; delighted. It is a great favour to be admitted there, my dear Kufalt. The men have a marvellous life, I can assure you of that. Good food. And charming rooms. And a beautiful sitting room with an excellent library. I have been there myself and seen it all. Admirable.'

'And the work?' asked Kufalt suspiciously. 'What's that like?'

'Ah yes,' said the chaplain, rather taken aback; 'true, the men work, of course. That is excellently organized. There is a large room with a number of typewriters, and there the men sit and type. It looks so – cosy.'

'What does a man earn there?'

'But, my dear young friend, how can I tell you that? You must understand that it is a welfare institution conducted for your benefit. But of course you will be properly paid. I cannot tell you the amount, but you will certainly earn a good wage.'

'All right,' said Kufalt; 'then will you give me a recommendation?'

'Yes. Here are the forms. What is your name? Ah, Kufalt. And your Christian names? Willi? Wilhelm, then.'

'No, not Wilhelm. Willi. I was christened Willi.'

'Really? But Willi is a mutilation. Well, we will leave it. Willi . . . hmm . . . Willi. And when were you born? So you will soon be thirty? It is time, my friend, high time. And for what were you sent to prison? Embezzlement and forgery. And for how long?'

'Do they really want to know all this in the Home? I thought this was all over, I've served my time.'

'But they want to help you, my dear Kufalt. And if they are to help you, they must know you. How long?'

'Five years.'

The chaplain became gentler and more benevolent, as Kufalt's replies grew more abrupt. It was in a tone of something like emotion that he asked: 'And your civil rights, my dear Kufalt; have you still your civil rights?'

'Yes, I have.'

'And your dear parents? What is your dear father?'

Kufalt was now in despair. 'For God's sake, sir,' he said savagely, 'can't you stop this? It makes me . . . what have my parents got to do with this crap?'

'My dear Kufalt, you must control yourself. It is all for your benefit. We have to know from what sort of class you come. The son of a working man cannot be recommended for a post as private secretary, can he? Now then, what is your father?'

'Dead.'

The chaplain was not quite satisfied, but did not pursue the matter: 'Very well. But your mother is still alive, isn't she? You have not lost your mother?'

'Sir,' said Kufalt standing up, 'will you kindly read me the questions succinctly, just as they are printed on the form.'

'But, my dear young friend, what is all this? I don't understand you. Ah yes, yes, it is a sore subject when a man has quarrelled with his nearest and dearest; I should not have touched upon it. But your mother still writes to you, does she not?'

'No, she does *not* write,' shouted Kufalt. 'And you know that quite well. You read the letters, you're the censor.'

'But, my dear young friend, then you must go to her. You must go back to your old mother. You cannot go to the Home of Peace. You must go to your mother, she will surely forgive you.'

'Sir,' said Kufalt, with cold determination, 'what about that bunch of flowers?'

The chaplain was staggered. In quite a different tone, from which all the benevolence had vanished, he said: 'Bunch of flowers? What bunch of flowers?'

'Yes, what bunch of flowers?' said Kufalt, now openly contemptuous. 'What about your bunch of flowers that you took to that poor consumptive Siemsen's cell three weeks after Christmas? What about that complaint that Siemsen wrote against you to the Prison Board? Did it go into your waste-paper basket?'

And Kufalt looked wildly round the room for the waste-paper basket, as though the document might still be lying there three months afterwards.

The chaplain was shaken. 'But my dear young friend, pray calm yourself. That sort of thing does you no good. You are quite wrong, you have been listening to some detestable slander . . . If I took a bunch of flowers to prisoner Siemsen when he was ill, I did so to give him pleasure, but never to . . .'

The chaplain broke off, quite overcome.

'Look, sir,' said Kufalt savagely. 'At Christmas, you promised Siemsen, and his wife, half a ton of coal and a parcel of food. It was granted by the Prisoners' Welfare Association. The woman and her children waited and waited. You simply forgot about it. And when the woman came to see you, you had her sent away. And when she spoke to you in the street you told her not to bother you, as all the supplies had been used up. That is the truth, Chaplain, all the prisoners know it, and all the officials too.'

'Now listen to me,' roared the chaplain in a fury. 'That is all untrue – it's an abominable slander! Do you know I could report you for insulting an officer of the prison? Siemsen's wife is a bad character, who goes with other men, she deserves no help.'

'I suppose she ought to let her kiddies starve, instead of going on the streets! And how is it, sir, that you took Siemsen the bunch of flowers on the very day he had written his letter to the Prison Board?'

'I visited him out of sympathy. The complaint was all rubbish, the Welfare Association is a private body, and the Prison Board has nothing to do with it.'

'And I suppose that's why you were all over Siemsen to get him to withdraw it, eh? And the silly fool did. But I'll write one, when I come out, and I'll see it gets into the papers . . .'

'Do so, by all means,' said the chaplain venomously. 'And see what comes of it. I have been chaplain here for forty years, and I have dealt with many men like you. Is your mother in a position to keep you?'

'No.'

'What is your religion?'

'Protestant. But I shall drop it as soon as possible.'

'Protestant, then. What can you do?'

'Office work.'

'What kind?'

'Every kind.'

'Can you write a business letter in Spanish?'

'No.'

'Then what kind of office work can you do?'

'Typewriting, stenography, American and Italian bookkeeping, by double entry, and balance sheets. The usual things.'

'But no Spanish. Can you use a duplicating machine?'

'No.'

'Folding machine?'

'No.'

'Address machine.'

'No.'

'That's not much. Very well – you have to sign there.'

Kufalt looked over the form. Suddenly he stopped. 'It says here that I accept the House Regulations. What are they?'

'The regulations of the house, of course. Naturally you have to accept them.'

'But I must know what I am accepting. May I see them?'

'I haven't got them here. My dear Herr Kufalt, there won't be any extras for your benefit. All the inmates have agreed to them, and you must do so too.'

'I won't put my name to what I don't know.'

'I thought you wanted to be admitted to the Home?'

'Yes; but I must see the regulations first. You must have a copy.'

'No, I haven't.'

'Then I can't sign.'

'And I can't recommend your admission.'

Kufalt stood there for a moment undecided, and looked at the chaplain. He was sitting at his desk, turning over letters.

'You ought to censor the letters quicker, sir,' said Kufalt. 'It's a disgrace they lie here for a fortnight.'

The chaplain did not look up. 'So you won't sign?'

'No,' said Kufalt, and went.

V

Kufalt looked round the corridor. Over at the Admission Office stood a little group of six or eight men in civilian clothes, newly delivered prisoners. Senior Warder Petrow was in charge of them, and he never noticed what was not pushed under his nose. Otherwise the corridor was clear.

Kufalt went in the opposite direction, away from the cells, away from Petrow, past all the office doors, until he reached the staircase that led to the ground floor. This was a staircase for officers, not to be used by prisoners, but he took the risk.

He met nobody and went down as far as the cellar, where Kufalt found himself confronted by another great iron door that led into the storeman's domain. The chaplain had put an idea into his head: what would his suit look like?

It was five years since he had handed it in, and he tried in vain to recall what he had been wearing at the time. His sole possessions had been what he carried on his person: suit and winter overcoat and hat, and a nightshirt and a toothbrush in a briefcase.

He would have to buy some underclothes. No sooner he got out than his money would dwindle, dwindle. And what will his suit look like now after five years?

He stood there at the iron door and gazed with a troubled expression. His release had certainly come much too soon, nothing was prepared, and above all he himself was unprepared. And now the Home was off, he would have to rent a room . . . Anyhow, he would get his money paid out in a lump sum, he had made the governor agree to that, he had enough to live on for one or two months; and enough to buy a few things. But then?

Warder Strehlow appeared: 'Hello, what are you doing there? Where's your warder?'

'I've had to report to the governor and the chaplain. I am going to the storeman about my things – I'm coming out tomorrow,' he added by way of explanation.

'You category three blokes had better get yourselves a key. We don't seem to be needed. You run around the place as if it belonged to you. Well, it'll go on till one of us gets his head smashed, and then those people at the green table will see how they've messed up the place.'

But Strehlow let Kufalt through; he grumbled, but he let him through, locked the gate behind him, and went up the warders' staircase.

Kufalt was in a long underground corridor, on the right and left of which were the doors of the various store rooms. As he passed he saw vast arrays of plates, armies of buckets, shelves bending under endless piles of laundry. Gradually he approached the Issue Office, which was the storeman's abode. His heart was pounding; all now depended on the state of the storeman's temper.

The storeman was, in fact, a decent sort of man, he never treated a prisoner as a prisoner, just like anybody else: kindly when he was in a good mood, and meanly when he was in a bad one. If he was in a bad mood, he would promptly kick Kufalt out, and probably get him put in solitary for invading his lair by himself.

The manner of addressing him was also a point of importance. There were two factions in the jail: one maintained that he always wanted to be called 'Chief Warder', the other swore by 'Storeman'.

Kufalt had previously belonged to the 'Chief Warder' faction, but, in spite of this, he had twice been thrown out with his request. 'Storeman' had once brought him a reprimand, and that was to be expected because he had asked for metal polish. That, the old man had said, was a most impertinent request: metal polish was only issued to the orderlies, who had to polish the warders' belongings.

He summoned his nerve and went up to the storeman.

'I've come from the chaplain, sir. I wanted to ask, sir, if my things are still all right. Otherwise I might get a little help from the chaplain.'

'Why have you come by yourself?' asked the storeman at once. 'Where's your warder?'

'I was let through,' said Kufalt.

'Who let you through? The chaplain?'

Kufalt nodded.

'Blasted old fool,' said the storeman. 'There he goes again. If we ever suggest some little relief for the prisoners, he's always against it, because he says "the penalty must be paid"; but he's too lazy to walk twenty steps down the corridor. Just let him wait, I'll bring it up at the next officials' conference.'

Kufalt listened politely. The storeman was in a good humour; he was abusing the chaplain, which he enjoyed doing, for the storeman's opinions were Red. And the next officials' conference was not until Tuesday, by which time Kufalt would be well away.

'Well, what do you want?' asked the storeman benevolently. 'Trying to wangle another suit of clothes? Your own is still quite good.'

'I wonder if I might try it on, sir,' pleaded Kufalt. 'I've grown such a belly on all these slops.'

'I don't see much sign of it. Well, all right, though I don't like obliging the chaplains. Bastel, get out Kufalt's things.' He turned over the pages of the register. 'Seventy-five sixty-three. Is the suit back from the tailor?'

'Yes, Chief Warder,' came a voice from the store, and Bastel, the orderly, appeared with a large sack in which prisoner Kufalt's things were neatly arranged on a hanger.

'Wait a bit,' said Bastel to Kufalt. 'I'd rather take your stuff out myself. You'd only crumple it.'

It was the dark blue suit with the white needle stripe, and Kufalt's heart rejoiced, for he had only worn it five or six times at the most.

'A nice suit,' said the storeman. 'What did you give for it?'

'A hundred and seventy-six,' said Kufalt, at random.

'Much too much,' said the storeman. 'Worth ninety at most.'

'But it was almost six years ago,' Kufalt pointed out.

'You're right, suits were dear at that time. It wouldn't be more than sixty-seventy marks today. You can get some for twelve or fifteen.'

'No!' exclaimed Kufalt, in obsequious surprise.

'You must keep on your underclothes. Your day shirt isn't back from the laundress, anyway – we must see about that this evening, Bastel. Yes, you'll be a treat for the girls when we've done with you.'

The storeman was indeed well known for keeping everything in tip-top order; it was his pride that not a thread was ever missing. His assistants had a hard job.

'Very nice. You look a different man, Kufalt. Bastel, come and look at Kufalt for a moment . . .' He broke off angrily. 'What's Batzke doing here? Herr Steinitz, I won't have that bloke down here unless it's absolutely necessary. He does nothing but make trouble. I know you've come to kick up a fuss, Batzke.'

'I haven't opened my mouth yet,' said Batzke, looking round for Bastel. He paid no attention to Kufalt.

'Governor's order,' said Warder Steinitz. 'Batzke may try on his things to see if they fit.'

'This isn't a dressing room. The whole prison will start trying on next. The governor should know better. Well, you clear out anyway, Kufalt. Your shoes? Oh your shoes'll fit all right.' Then in a milder tone: 'Very well, try them on if you like. Bastel, Batzke's things: number twenty-four nineteen!'

Bastel appeared with another sack and Batzke whispered hurriedly to him; he nodded and then shook his head. From the cap that Batzke held in his hand suddenly emerged, one after the other, four packets of tobacco which vanished in Bastel's hands.

Bastel drew back; the two officers stood talking by the window.

Kufalt struggled with his shoes. He just could not get them on, probably because of his thick woollen socks. And his own socks were still at the wash. But surely his shoes had not been as tight as this? Could a man's feet grow when he was nearly thirty?

Suddenly Batzke was heard to exclaim loudly: 'Here's a moth hole!'

The storeman took three steps; then he stopped. 'Ah, Batzke, of course. He's started his games already. A moth hole, indeed! Seventeen years I've been storeman of this prison, and never had a moth hole yet.'

He went back to the window.

'And here's another moth hole. And under the lapel here the stuff's all eaten away.'

'Let me see it – you're crazy . . . There's never been a moth . . .'

'Well, there are moths in my clothes,' Batzke persisted, calmly eyeing the infuriated storeman.

The latter grabbed the jacket and held it to the light. 'It's impossible . . . oh bloody hell . . . Bastel, you bloody idiot, why didn't you tell me there were moths in Batzke's clothes?'

Bastel acted stupid: 'Didn't like to, sir.'

'And why didn't the tailors say anything?'

'Didn't like to either, sir.'

'And why didn't you get it mended?'

'I thought I'd get into trouble.'

'There are moth holes in the trousers too,' Batzke went on, unmoved.

'God damn it! I tell you, I've never had moths . . . But you shan't get away with it, Batzke . . .'

An idea flashed across his mind: 'They were there when you came in. You brought them with you, Batzke.'

'Then it'll be in the inventory. And I must have signed it, sir.'

'And I'll bet you did sign it. Just you wait.' The storeman snatched a bundle of documents out of a pigeonhole. 'How long have you been in? When were you admitted?'

'How should I know, sir?' said Batzke genially. 'I always seem to be in and out. But it's all down in your books.'

The storeman had already found the entry, and was reading it with a frown. He read it again. And a third time. Then he said with ominous calm: 'Very well, I'll have it invisibly mended, Batzke.'

'But I brought a perfectly good suit in with me, sir; I want one to take out with me. A mended one's no use.'

'But no one will notice if it's properly mended. The places will be stronger than they were before.'

'I don't want any stronger places, I want an undamaged suit.'

'But where do you suppose I'm to get you one, Batzke? Be sensible. The tailors couldn't finish one before Sunday.'

'Then let's go out into town, sir, and buy one. I don't mind a ready-made suit.'

'And the money? Do you really expect me to go to the chaplain and beg some out of the Prisoners' Welfare Fund? Hello, you still there, Kufalt? Hop it now, will you!'

'It's my shoes, sir.'

'Well, what's up with your shoes, hey? Got the moth in them, I suppose? Well, Herr Steinitz, let Kufalt pass. That's how my fine gentleman came, all on his own.'

'But my shoes – I can't . . .'

'Nor can I . . . God in heaven, Steinitz, take the man away. Now listen to me, Batzke . . .'

Kufalt was in the corridor. Warder Steinitz let him through into the prison. 'Go straight back to your cell, Kufalt. No, you'd better report first to the chief warder in the glass cubicle that you've come back.'

VI

When Kufalt reached the glass cubicle to make his report, he found it empty. No chief warder to be seen. Kufalt looked up and surveyed the building. There were, of course, orderlies in the corridor, scrubbing and waxing and polishing the linoleum, and warders here and there, but no one was looking in his direction.

Kufalt peered into the glass cubicle. The sliding door was half open. The post must have just come: a whole pile of letters lay on the table, and on top of it a longish yellowish envelope with a white registration receipt.

He looked round. No one seemed to be noticing him. Then he read what he expected to find: 'Herr Willi Kufalt. Central Prison.'

The long-awaited letter from his brother-in-law, Werner Pause; the letter that contained money, or the offer of work.

A quick sleight of hand, and the letter and the registration slip were in his pocket. Slowly Kufalt mounted the steps to his cell.

He stood at his table under the window, his back carefully turned towards the peephole in the door, so that no one could see his hands.

He fingered the envelope. Yes, there was something inside it, an enclosure. They had sent him some money! It did not seem to be a very lengthy letter, but there was a thickish enclosure inside.

So Werner had come to his rescue. In his heart of hearts he would never have believed it. However Werner was a decent sort, all things considered. He had been pretty savage when it happened, but that was natural enough.

Life in the world – how good it was going to be! He would have all he needed, though of course he would be very, very economical. But he could go into a café, perhaps even into a bar . . .

They could not send less than a thousand marks, to give him any sort of start. And in five or six weeks he might ask for a larger sum, three or four thousand, to set himself up in a nice little business, a tobacconist's perhaps . . .

No. No.

The enclosure was not money, it was a key, a flat key, the key of a trunk. Pity . . . And the letter:

HERR WILLI KUFALT.

At CENTRAL PRISON, CELL 365.

By the instructions of Herr Werner Pause, we have the honour to inform you that he has received your letter of the 3.4., together with your previous letters. Herr Pause regrets to state that there is at present no position vacant for you in his office, and furthermore that if one were vacant, he would feel bound from the social point of view to give it to one of the numerous unemployed who have not been in prison, many of whom are in the deepest distress. As regards the financial assistance for which you have asked, Herr Pause regrets that he must refuse this request also. According to information before us you should have earned, during your term of imprisonment, a not inconsiderable sum in wages for work done, which should serve to keep you during the period immediately subsequent to your release. Herr Pause desires to draw your particular attention to the numerous welfare organizations which exist to deal with such cases as yours, and will certainly be glad to do something for you.

Herr Pause expressly requests that you will address no further communications to himself, or his wife, your sister, or her mother. The distress of the past has only been partially and with difficulty overcome, and any action on your part that might revive it would lead to even more definite estrangement. Herr Pause has, however, had despatched to you by passenger train a portion of your personal effects; you will receive the remainder when you have led a respectable life for at least a year. The key of the trunk is enclosed with this letter.

We beg to remain,

Your obedient servants,
PAUSE AND WAHRHOLZ

pp. REINHOLD STEKENS.

The May day was still bright and radiant, and the cell was full of light. Outside, it was recreation period; he could hear the shuffle of many feet.

'Five paces apart! Keep your distance!' shouted a warder. 'And keep your mouths shut, or I'll report you.'

Kufalt sat with his letter in his hand, staring at nothing.

VII

Kufalt remembered very well what had happened when Tilburg had been released three or four years ago. Tilburg had been quite an ordinary prisoner who kept his head down. His crime had not been anything very bad and he had served a normal stretch of two or three years. What he had experienced and thought during that time, no one of course could know. No one in the jail could know, not even the man himself.

The day came when Tilburg was released. He did not do what most prisoners do, he did not get drunk or go with women the first night, he did not look for a room, or for work; Tilburg just went to Hamburg and bought himself a revolver.

Then he came back, surveyed the jail from outside, and walked along one of the streets leading out of the town.

When he had gone some distance and reached the open country, he met a man. Some casual passer-by whom Tilburg had never seen before.

Tilburg drew his revolver and fired at the man. He hit him in the shoulder and broke the shoulder blade, and the man fell. Tilburg went on.

Then he met another man and fired at him too, and this time he hit him in the stomach.

Half an hour later Tilburg saw some policemen on bicycles. He dashed off the road across fields and into a farmyard. He fired a few shots, and shouted that all in the house were to stay where they were. Then he held the yard against the policemen. He had the chance of being what he had perhaps come to regard himself as during those last years: a savage beast. The only explanation that he gave at his trial later on was: 'I just loathed everybody.'

He shot three policemen until they shot him down. But he was patched up again for the trial, and for another sentence: a long one this time, of which he was never likely to see the end.

'It's quite easy to understand Tilburg,' said Kufalt to himself, over his letter in the cell.

And then: 'I'm an idiot. I could perfectly well have left *this* letter in the glass cubicle. What shall I do if it's missed?'

VIII

'You're wanted for final interviews, Kufalt,' a warder called into the cell.

'Right,' said Kufalt, and got up slowly.

'Get a move on, man, there are twenty more to come.'

'Busy man, aren't you?' said Kufalt.

'Hurry along down to the Central Hall. I'll just . . .'

Once more Kufalt passed the glass cubicle. Chief Warder Rusch looked up and gawped at him through his spectacles. His lips moved, but he did not utter Kufalt's name.

'I'll be for it this time. The trunk will turn up, and no key. I've got the key in my pocket, but I oughtn't to have it. And I oughtn't even to know that there's one on the way. What a fool I am. The new life's starting well. How nice and quiet it was in my cell, with a pile of netting on the table.'

'Oh boy, oh boy,' whispered Batzke to him in the Central Hall. 'Did you see the storeman? He really exploded over those moth holes, didn't he?'

'Are you getting a new suit?'

'Well, what do you think? I'm going with him into town this afternoon to buy one. Welfare's paying. And my old one's to be invisibly mended, so I'll have that too.'

'What made him so soft?'

'It was so I shouldn't split about the moth holes. They'd have been livid up there if they'd heard there were moths in the clothing store. They'd give him hell, the commie bastard.' Batzke grinned. 'And he can't find any moths.'

'Can't he then?'

'You didn't believe it was moths, did you? You're pretty green. Moths out of a bottle, they were.'

'Out of a bottle?'

'Didn't you see when I gave Bastel the tobacco? We fixed the job together. I thought it out. The trousers were nearly through, and I wanted to come out in decent togs. So Bastel sprinkled a few drops of acid on the suit, and jagged the edges of the holes a bit with a knife, and rubbed a bit of cobweb into them, and they looked the real thing – take anyone in.'

'But the storeman . . .'

'Oh, him! He's a fathead. He goes over the top when anything goes wrong. I'd reckoned on all that. I couldn't have conned Rusch, he'd have got a magnifying glass and nosed it all out in the end, and I'd have been for the clink again. But the storeman . . .'

'If the category three gentlemen have quite finished their conversation, I suppose we might go along to the cashier, shall we?' said the warder.

IX

'Where do you want to be discharged to, Kufalt?' asked the inspector.

'Hamburg.'

'Have you work there?'

'No.'

'To whom are you going?'

'I don't yet know.'

'Enter him as "on the road", then,' said the inspector to the clerk.

'I'm not going on the road. I'm going to take a room.'

'Perhaps you will let us manage our own business in our own way.'

'But it's not right. I'm not going on the road. I'm not a tramp . . .'

'Off on a little holiday, I suppose. Listen, Ellmers, Kufalt's going on a holiday. No doubt his car will be waiting for him at the gate at seven o'clock tomorrow.'

Kufalt glared suspiciously across the counter: 'You aren't going to date my registration card from the prison?'

'Listen to the man! I suppose you want it dated from the Four Seasons Hotel, eh?'

'I won't accept a registration card with the prison address. It says in the Prison Regulations that the card should not reveal the fact that the bearer has been released from prison.'

'We shall act in accordance with our instructions.'

'But here it is: "Central Prison". I won't accept it. How am I to show that to a landlady? I must have another.'

'This is the only one you'll get. We've had just about enough of your lip, Kufalt.'

'But it says in the Prison Regulations . . .'

'Yes, you've told me that before. Hold your tongue or I'll have you removed.'

'I demand to see the governor!'

'Hold your tongue! Besides the governor's away.'

'That's not true. I was with him only an hour ago.'

'And half an hour ago he went away. If you aren't quiet . . .'

'Batzke, Bruhn, Lehnau – are you going to stand for this? You know it says in the blue book in the cells . . .'

Kufalt's fury rose.

The inspector came round the counter: 'Kufalt, I warn you! I warn you! Your behaviour just now, Kufalt, was mutiny. Tomorrow morning, when your term's up, I'll have you detained on a charge of inciting a riot.'

'You? You! Only an investigating magistrate can do that, you can't. Tell that yarn to the new hands, not to me, Inspector.'

'Well, Ellmers, what do you think of the lads due for discharge?'

'Am I going to get a registration card according to the Prison Regulations?'

'You will get the usual card issued here.'

'Does it say that I've come out of prison?'

'Of course. Where else do you come from?'

'Then I demand to be brought before the deputy governor.'

'Warder, take this man to the police inspector. Now for you, Batzke. I suppose you won't insist on your registration card being dated from the nearest hotel?'

'If my money's all right, sir, you can put me down as a matricide for all I care.'

'There you are, Kufalt,' said the inspector triumphantly.

X

The police inspector was a mild, white-haired gentleman, a fat man, a soft man, a silent man, a man who might almost be overlooked, so soft he was, so silent and so quiet. And yet he was perhaps the most detested official in the place. The prisoners called him Judas.

Kufalt could not forget that the inspector had visited him in his cell during the first month of his sentence; he was sympathetic and kind, and before he went he had said: 'And if you have any request to make, Kufalt, you must let me know personally. I visit your cell every month.'

Kufalt had requests to make, and waited for the inspector. Now it is the rule that prisoners may only make requests once a month, on a certain day and at a certain hour, and if that hour is missed, they must wait another month.

Kufalt waited three months for the inspector's promised visit, so as to make his request by word of mouth. The police inspector did not come. In all those five years he had not come again to Kufalt's cell. He had spoken quite casually, merely to come across as pleasant at the time, and then he had never thought of Kufalt again. He had visited the new arrival once, out of curiosity.

Kufalt had not forgiven him that. He had never brought himself to make any request to the man, so he now merely said: 'Sir, there is a clause in the Prison Regulations that a man's registration card must not show that he has been released from prison. But they want to give me a card headed "The Central Prison", and stamped with the prison stamp.'

The police inspector gazed long at the prisoner before him; he wagged his white round head from side to side and looked into a corner, where there was nothing but a filing cabinet full of papers.

'Again,' he said regretfully; 'again.' And he wagged his head. 'How deplorable!'

Kufalt stood before him and waited, wondering what was the point of this performance. That the police inspector should feel regret at anything affecting a prisoner exceeded his powers of belief.

Behind Kufalt stood the warder who had accompanied him, in a deferential attitude. A clock on the wall, adorned with oak leaves, swords and eagles, ticked out the time very audibly. The police inspector again let his eyes rest on the prisoner. 'And what are we to do?'

'Give me a card according to the regulations.'

'Yes, of course,' said the inspector cheerfully. 'Of course.'

Again he relapsed into gloom. 'Except . . .' – in a soft and confidential voice – '. . . there are difficulties.'

He leaned back in his chair and said: 'There are two kinds of regulations: those that can be carried out, and those that cannot. I say nothing against this regulation; on the contrary, it is humane and sensible, it is in accordance with the democratic spirit of today, but – it cannot be carried out. Consider, Kufalt; I now speak to you not as to a prisoner, I speak to you as a man of sense and education.'

The inspector stopped. He looked mildly at Kufalt. Then he continued in a slow and gentle voice: 'The Central Prison is situated in a town. In the town is a Registration Office. In this office is an index of residents. We provide ourselves, in accordance with the letter of your regulation, with a number of registration cards. We fill them in, we hand them to prisoners on their discharge, and – and . . .'

The police inspector again gazed at the corner. Kufalt waited patiently, he had calmed down; he had his plan. Let the man talk, he would get his card all right.

'. . . And,' said the police inspector, 'the prisoner refuses the card. You smile, Kufalt,' – he was doing nothing of the kind – 'you don't believe me. The prisoner refuses the card. You have not followed me. What is the matter with it? It is not stamped. For what can we do? Either we must use the Central Prison stamp, in which case we violate the regulation, or we leave it unstamped, and then the card is invalid.'

'As a third alternative, you might get a stamp from the local Registration Office.'

'Kufalt! Kufalt! You, a man of sense and education! We are a Central Prison, how could we be in possession of a Registration Office stamp? No,' he went on, in a gloomy tone, 'this regulation cannot be carried out, sensible and humane as it is. Don't you realize this?'

'I ask for a card in accordance with the clause in the Prison Regulations.'

'I would gladly give you one, Kufalt, very gladly. It is impossible. Warder, take this man away, he has had his explanation.'

'If I'm given a card stamped with the Central Prison stamp I shall send it on the day of my release to the Law Officers' Department, with the explanation now given me . . .'

Silence.

'Of course,' said the police inspector, not gently now, but in a sharp and rasping voice. 'Of course. You would run your head through a wall. I never expected anything else from you. You are a fool, Kufalt, you think only of your discharge, you don't think that a time may come when . . .'

He broke off. And Kufalt said: 'When what, please, Herr Inspector?'

'That will do. Warder, take this man away. Tell them that a stamped card is to be got for him from the Registration Office.'

'Thank you very much, sir.'

The police inspector merely coughed in reply.

XI

Kufalt was back in the Discharge Office. The warder had made out his papers. The other discharges had already gone, their business settled.

'Your sentence is up at twenty minutes past one p.m.,' said the inspector.

To which Kufalt replied: 'I ask to be released in the morning, as usual.'

'What do you mean, as usual?' growled the inspector. 'You think you know all about the Prison Regulations. The prisoners are to be released at such time that they may reach their place of destination on the day of their release. You are for Hamburg; so you have plenty of time to reach your place of destination in the afternoon.'

'But all the prisoners will be released tomorrow at seven o'clock,' said Kufalt.

'You leave that to us. You might complain if we robbed you of a bit of your sentence.'

Kufalt stood silent. After all, he might be glad to get clear without trouble. There were many ways of giving hell to a prisoner during his last twenty-four hours.

The inspector began again: 'Your pay for work done comes to 315 marks 87 pfennigs.'

'May I see the account?' said Kufalt.

'Ellmers, give Kufalt the account for his inspection and approval.'

Kufalt looked at the account. It was only the last total that interested him, and there it was – only sixteen units were entered, not seventeen.

He reflected whether he should pipe up again, but thought better of it and was silent.

'I want to apply for an advance on my pay today to buy a pair of shoes. My old ones have got too tight from my wearing slippers.'

'Certainly not,' said the inspector. 'I'll tell the storeman to give you a pair of the working boots used by the outdoor labourers. They will do for you perfectly well.'

'But I can't . . .'

'Then you'll have to, Kufalt . . . You'll need five marks for your fare to Hamburg, and ten marks to keep you for the first week. Fifteen marks eighty-seven will be paid out to you on discharge, and the rest transferred to the Welfare Office.'

'But the governor said . . .' Kufalt stopped and pondered.

'Well, what did the governor say? Out with it, Kufalt. I've nothing to do today except settle your business.'

'The governor arranged that the money I've earned should be paid to me in full on my discharge.'

'Is that so? And why do I know nothing of this arrangement?'

'The governor approved it early this morning,' insisted Kufalt.

'That's a lie, Kufalt. The governor can't have made any such arrangement, it's contrary to the Prison Board's instructions. You want to squander all the money in a week, and then have the tax-payers support you, eh? I don't think so!'

'The governor arranged it.'

'Then it would be entered in your papers. But it isn't.'

'I want my money in full.'

'Right. Fifteen marks eighty-seven. And now you must countersign the account.'

'I demand to see the . . .'

'Well, who's it to be this time?' said the inspector, with a contemptuous grin.

Kufalt had an inspiration: 'The chaplain!'

'The chaplain?'

'Certainly, the chaplain!'

'Warder – but this is the last time I shall send you to see anyone. I'm just about fed up with you! Warder, take this man to the chaplain!'

'What a fuss you're always making, Kufalt!' said the warder disapprovingly, as they went down the corridor. 'Can't you stop spoiling it all? You look as though you've been spat on the wall.'

'They ought to do their duty by us,' said Kufalt.

'You're a fool,' said the warder. 'If you'd sucked up to the inspector a bit, like Batzke, you'd have got all your money in full. But you will go on annoying him!'

'I demand my rights,' said Kufalt resolutely.

'That's just where you're a fool,' said the warder.

'Sir,' said Kufalt to the clergyman, who eyed him angrily, 'I've been thinking it over, and I'll sign the admission form for the Home of Peace.'

'Oh, you will, will you? And suppose I don't think you're fit to be admitted to such an admirable institution?'

'The governor said I should go there.'

'Then the governor did not know you. Very well, sign here.'

Kufalt wrote his name.

On his return he said loftily to the inspector: 'My pay is to be transferred to the Home of Peace. The chaplain has approved my admission.'

'You're going to the Home of Peace? Oh, Kufalt, Kufalt, you *have* got a nerve, my lad.' The inspector quivered with delight.

Kufalt glared at him in fury.

'You're properly for it, my poor little Kufalt! Well, you'll think of me and how I laughed.'

Kufalt was nervous, he did not like the sound of this. 'What's wrong with the Home of Peace?'

'Why, what should be wrong? No, there's nothing wrong. On the contrary. But in that case you won't want fifteen marks, of course. Five marks for your fare are quite enough. Make a note of that, Ellmers: 5 marks 87 to pay out, 310 marks to the Home of Peace.'

Kufalt thought of the hundred-mark note in his sock, and made no further protest.

'There – and now, thank God, we're through with the man, warder. Take him to his cell. Three more like you, Kufalt . . .'

As Kufalt passed the glass cubicle, the chief warder raised his head again and again eyed Kufalt. But again he said nothing.

'There's something up,' said Kufalt to himself; and when back in his cell he twisted the letter and the registration slip into a tiny tube and fastened it to the side of one of the peephole bars so that it was invisible both from outside and in.

Then he took the note out of his sock, rolled it up tight, and pushed it firmly up his rectum.

He did not like the look of things; Rusch had glared at him so strangely.

However, he slammed down his bed and flung himself on it, utterly exhausted.

XII

He must have slept very soundly. When he woke up he saw – his back towards him – a short stocky figure standing by his cupboard, in uniform, topped by a thick close-shaven skull: Chief Warder Rusch.

He held the songbook in his hand. He gripped it by the two covers, shook it – and nothing fell out. Then he peered down the binding at the back.

He put the book back in the cupboard and took out the Bible. 'Have a good look,' said Kufalt to himself, and lay with open eyes.

The chief warder shut the cupboard door, went up to the table, squatted on his heels and looked underneath it. As he rose, he caught the prisoner's eye. But the chief warder was quite unperturbed. He walked up to the bed. 'What. Asleep? Daylight long ago; get up and work.'

'They've taken my work away,' said Kufalt.

'Clean your cell, man. Table's filthy! Get on with it!'

'Very good, sir. And I'll clean underneath the table too,' said Kufalt, and hurried to the table.

'Stop! When did you last get letters?'

'When? Oh a long time ago, sir. Let me see . . .'

'You haven't had a letter today?'

'No. Is there a letter for me? Fine, it'll be from my brother-in-law, sending me money.'

'Indeed!' said the chief warder, surveying his prisoner once again, and he growled: 'Get on with it now! Put your bed up!' and left the cell.

'And my letter?' shouted Kufalt, but the chief warder had already gone.

He attacked the table with great vigour; he had never thought of cleaning the underside of it before. And when he had finished he took down his little cupboard and scoured the back of it.

While he was doing this he noticed an unusual noise throughout the building. On all the landings cell after cell was being opened and something shouted inside; Kufalt jumped up and listened. But he did not catch what it was, until he heard the word 'letter'; then something to the effect that a letter had gone astray; and he grinned.

The disturbance gradually approached his cell; now they were at the cell next door, and now . . .

His door opened, a warder put his head in: 'Have you got a letter that doesn't belong to you . . . Oh, it's you, Kufalt – no, everything is all right.'

'What's up, sir?'

But the man had gone.

When Kufalt had cleaned his cupboard, he saw that he would have to polish the floor of his cell. It was strenuous work. The building was full of the faint suppressed noises of the day: the clink of the net-maker's iron rod, the clatter of a bucket lid, someone started to whistle and suddenly broke off, a few rolls of yarn were thrown down in front of a cell nearby. The sun was now high, and his cell quite light.

He was curious to see what they would do.

It was just before supper time, so after five o'clock, when the door of his cell was again opened. Three men came in: the police inspector, chaplain and chief warder. The door was carefully shut behind them. Kufalt positioned himself under the window, facing the officers, and waited.

The chaplain began: 'Listen, Kufalt, there has been a mistake, we don't yet quite know how it happened. A letter came for you today . . .'

'Yes, I know. The chief warder told me. From my brother-in-law, containing money.'

'I didn't tell you,' growled the chief warder; 'that's a lie. Nothing of the sort. You told me.'

'No, not containing money, my dear young friend. There was a key inside it.'

'Oh?' drawled Kufalt. 'May I have the letter?'

'That's just it. The letter has gone astray. It will turn up again. But you are going out tomorrow . . .'

'Gone astray?' said Kufalt, with an air of surprise. 'But nothing gets lost here. Inspector, the governor gave orders that my pay should be given to me in full, and the Discharge Office will only give me six marks. That's unfair. If the governor gave orders . . .'

'Now, now, Kufalt, keep calm. We may be able to discuss that later. But . . .'

'But the money from my brother-in-law, it's my money. You've got to let me have it. Why won't you give me the letter?'

'Kufalt,' said the chief warder, 'that will do. There was no money in the letter. The chaplain knows that for certain. The letter was taken away from *me*.'

'I had just read your letter,' went on the chaplain. 'Your brother-in-law did not write himself, he wrote through his secretary to the effect that he could not help you. He also refused to send you money, as you had what you had earned in prison . . .'

'But I'm not to get that either!'

'And your brother-in-law is sending you a part of your belongings. You can have the rest later.'

'I have made inquiries, Kufalt. Your trunk has already arrived. As a special favour you may, after the cells are locked, examine its contents today; we will have it opened in your presence. The storeman will stay late on your account.' The police inspector was being very obsequious . . .

'Kufalt,' said the chief warder, 'the letter cannot be found. If you insist, the police inspector will have to write a report, and I shall be held responsible.'

The police inspector said: 'You are a man of education and good sense, Kufalt. Why make difficulties for Herr Rusch? Accidents will happen everywhere.'

Kufalt surveyed the three men: 'And when my socks were pinched when I was having a bath, I got three days' deprivation of warm food, and had to pay for them out of what I earned, didn't I? Those were your orders then, sir. Why should Rusch get off scot-free because he's let someone pinch my letters?'

All three started at the bald reference to 'Rusch'.

Then the chaplain said: 'We must all be able to forgive, my dear Kufalt. You will one day make mistakes and stand in need of forgiveness.'

This was too much for Kufalt, and he turned on the chaplain in a fury: 'Get out of my cell! Get out! I'll knock everything to pieces! And you, Inspector, get out too!'

'Really, this is intolerable . . .' the inspector burst out.

And the chaplain: 'Aren't you ashamed of yourself, Kufalt? . . .'

But Rusch was quite emphatic: 'Please leave me alone with the man.'

And, with angry glares at Kufalt, the others went.

Kufalt stood and looked at the door. He was still beside himself with fury, and he said excitedly: 'Why do you bring those two, Chief? Liars, the pair of them. The very sight of those slimy brutes makes me wild . . . Look, Chief, you've never done me wrong, will you promise that I'll get my pay in full tomorrow?'

'I promise, Kufalt.'

'Give me the form, I'll sign the receipt for the letter.'

The chief warder did not give him the form. He pondered: 'How did you know it was a registered letter, Kufalt?'

'Well, my brother-in-law would hardly send a key in an ordinary letter.'

Rusch still pondered.

And Kufalt added: 'How can a registered letter go astray?'

The chief warder took the form out of his pocket. 'Kufalt, you're a tricky one. Well, sign. You shall have your money all the same.'

XIII

It was the morning of the next day, about eleven o'clock.

Kufalt stood in the discharge cell. The trunk, the large trunk sent by his brother-in-law Pause, lay on the floor beside him. He stood and waited.

Time crept on, he could do nothing. There were books in the trunk, but who could read at such a moment? In two hours, five years would have passed over his head, in two hours he would be a free man; he could go where he liked, he could speak to whom he pleased, he could go out with a girl, drink wine and sit in a cinema . . . it was beyond imagination still . . . the burden of his imprisonment yet lay upon him . . .

No bell in the morning. No weaving of nets. No feuds with other prisoners. No more gruel at midday. No polishing of cells. No worry whether his tobacco would last out. No warders. No stinking bucket, no prison slops to wear . . . his mind refused the thought.

How tight his suit felt across the stomach. Indeed, he had actually to leave the trouser and waistcoat buckles undone; he had grown so fat on the watery diet. There had been times when he had gulped down two litres of gruel and a bit more as well. Against his stomach lay a watch, his silver Confirmation watch. He looked at it; eighteen minutes past eleven.

The others had been out for four hours now – he cursed himself for not somehow getting Rusch to let him go with them. They had gone; and Bastel, the storeman's orderly, had told him when he dressed that Sethe was out too. Early that morning they had asked him whether he accepted the penalty for insulting an official, and he had agreed. It would be added to his probation. After all, they were brutes here. Brutes. And brutes they all became. He had been a brute over the letter on the previous evening, and over the hundred-mark note, and many, many times during the past five years. And what was the point of it all? The straight game would have got him out at exactly the same hour – but with different feelings.

Well, it was over now, anyway. From now on he would do what was right, and sleep in peace at night. No more trouble for him, never again. So long as he could get that hundred-mark note out. That was the last time he would do such a thing.

Kufalt paced up and down, and back and forth. Today, too, the cell was very light. It was a glorious day outside. These last days the cells had been brighter than ever he remembered them for five long years. He hoped the weather would still be fine when he got out . . .

This Home of Peace, though . . . The inspector had grinned so maliciously. Anyhow, he would get his money in full at the prison lodge, and if he could not stand the Home of Peace, he would just clear off . . .

There was a scratch at the door. Kufalt was there in a bound. 'Yes?'

'Hello! Are you Willi?'

'Well, of course, large as life.'

'Didn't recognize you in those fine togs. I'm the landing orderly. Have you got any soap in that bag of yours?'

'Yes.'

'Leave me a bit, mate. Put it under the bucket. I'll fetch it out of the cell the moment you're gone.'

'OK by me.'

'Sure thing, Willi?'

'You can look through the peephole. Here it is . . .'

'Hey, Willi, have you got any baccy too? You can buy some more at once. You might slip us a bit along with the soap.'

'You scrounger!'

'I've got another three years, my lad.'

'That's nothing. I did five, and Bruhn, who came out today, eleven.'

'Oho! Bruhn! Haven't you heard? The whole place is full of it.'

'What? What's up with Bruhn?'

'He's back already. He was outside for three hours, and now he's back again.'

'That's a bloody lie! You don't kid me, mate.'

'The storeman told me himself. When they came out, first thing this morning, they started drinking straight away. Only Sethe went off by train. And one of them knew where the girls were. So they went along to the house. But the women were still asleep, and they wouldn't let 'em in, being drunk. So they started a row, and the boss came along and told them to get out. So they chucked the boss down the stairs and out of his own house. And when the boss got back with the police, they'd got in among the girls. And the girls were all shrieking, as the cops came in, that they'd been raped and the doors had been broken in. Well, the boys had a hunger, sure thing! And now they're all in the lock-up. And this afternoon they'll be back in the clink till the case comes up, the storeman says.'

'I don't believe it. I don't believe it on your life. I could understand the others, but not Emil Bruhn. No, not him.'

'Look out! Rusch!'

Kufalt leapt back from the peephole to the window. Outside he heard the chief warder cursing after the orderly.

'Yes,' thought Kufalt; 'maybe. Emil Bruhn, poor silly fool. It's always blokes like him that get it in the neck. Always quiet, never threw his weight about all those eleven years – and then gets into a mess like this because he's glad to be outside. And even if you only get a couple of weeks' stretch, your probation will have gone west and you'll have to start all over again.'

Willi Kufalt was afraid: he felt that the same thing might happen to him. It is hard for a man to get a grip on himself when he goes outside, there's a trap round every corner . . .

'Once a jailbird, always a jailbird!'

Kufalt pondered. Then he took down from the wall the blue pamphlet of extracts from the Prison Regulations. He turned the pages for a moment, and read:

'In the infliction of punishments, consistently with the strict enforcement of the penalty and the maintenance of discipline and order, efforts are to be made to raise the spiritual and moral level of the prisoners and to preserve their health and powers of work. The aim should be to train them to live an orderly, law-abiding life after their release. The sense of honour is to be fostered and strengthened.'

Kufalt closed the pamphlet. 'So that's that,' said he. 'Oh yes, it's all just fine! Everything is all right as it is! What are they thinking anyhow, these people?'

XIV

The time was quarter past one. Kufalt stood with his watch in his hand. He waited. His heart throbbed. Footsteps – they came nearer, they passed his cell. 'If these scabs forget me, if they keep me just three minutes longer than my time!'

Footsteps – they came nearer, they stopped outside his cell. A rustle of paper. Then the key was thrust into the lock, the bolt shot back, and Senior Warder Feder said wearily: 'Come along, and bring your stuff, Kufalt.'

He went out, and as he went looked back at the hall, towards the glass cubicle. There stood the vast building with its seven hundred cells; this had been his home for five long years. His landing orderly peered round the corner to see whether he could slip into the cell. Kufalt nodded to him.

Then through the cellar corridor to the storeman. Here all was quiet. Something came into Kufalt's mind: 'Is it true about Bruhn, sir? That he's inside again?'

'I don't know. I heard something, just shithouse talk, I dare say.'

'He isn't back again yet?'

'No, he couldn't be. He'd have to go before an investigating magistrate before he could be committed to prison.'

They walked across the outer court. Senior Warder Petrow was standing by the lodge.

'Come along, son; there's a lot of money waiting for you.'

In the lodge Kufalt signed his receipt.

'Put your money away safe, you'll need it. Wait, notes in your wallet. That's a fine wallet; mind it's always full! The rest in your coin purse, silver here, nickel here and copper here. And now come on, lad.'

They stood under the archway. Petrow shot back bolt after bolt. Then he inserted the great key.

'And now, forward march, and don't look round. You mustn't look back at the prison. I shall spit three times at your back, and you mustn't wash it off, that's for luck, so you shan't come back again. Off with you!'

The gate opened. Kufalt saw before him a broad square in blazing sunshine. The grass was green. The chestnuts were in bloom. Men walking; and women in bright clothes.

Slowly and cautiously he went out into the light.

He did not look round.

3

The Home of Peace

I

Firstly, Petrow had spat much too heartily on his overcoat, and Kufalt felt that everyone was laughing at him. So he hung the coat over his arm; the gobs were thus rubbed off, but no matter, he would never come in again.

Secondly, as he looked back at the town from the train, he suddenly saw again between the houses the steep grey concrete walls with their many barred windows – no matter. Anyhow now he was steaming away from the clink: he would never come in again.

But in the train, when he thought it over properly, he found he had already done a lot of things all wrong. He had taken a taxi to the station because people stared at him, he could not bear the way they stared at him. And he had eaten dinner at the station though he had left his jail stew untasted. And ten cigarettes at six pfennigs, the sort the governor smoked. And a newspaper. And, worst of all, a glass of beer with his dinner, though he had forsworn alcohol. An utter waste of five marks ninety, the pay for sixty-three units of work. To earn it, he had had to stand and knot nets for sixty-three days, and at the start he had taken twelve or thirteen hours over a unit. In two hours he had spent the labour of sixty-three days: here was a fine beginning to his new life!

He had not thought his voyage into freedom would be quite like this. He was now passing through sunlit countryside, very pleasant to look at, but had he time to look at it? There was much to worry about, as much as in his cell. And what would that Home be like?

'Can any of you gentlemen tell me which is the right station in Hamburg for the Apfelstrasse?'

Silence. Kufalt was already afraid that none of them would

answer, that he had not spoken loudly enough, when the man in the corner let his paper drop and said: 'Apfelstrasse? You must change at the Central Station, and then go on to the Berliner Tor.'

'Pardon me,' objected the man next to Kufalt. 'That's not correct. There's no Apfelstrasse there. Where do you think it is?'

'Of course it's there. It's just by the public baths . . .'

'I am afraid this gentleman has misdirected you,' observed Kufalt's neighbour. 'You must get out at Holstenstrasse. The Apfelstrasse is quite near there . . .'

A short fat man said decisively: '*This* gentleman is right, and *that* gentleman is right. There is, in fact, an Apfelstrasse in Altona and one in Hamburg. Which one do you want?'

'I was told Hamburg.'

'Then you must go on to the Berliner Tor and change at the Central Station.'

Silence reigned.

Suddenly Kufalt's neighbour began again: 'Where do you want to go in the Apfelstrasse? People often say Hamburg, and they really mean Altona.'

'Excuse me, the gentleman said Hamburg, so he must get out at the Berliner Tor.'

'But was the address expressly given as Hamburg? Or were you just told to go to the Apfelstrasse?'

'I really don't know. I'm going to relations.'

'And how did you write to your relations: Hamburg or Altona?'

'Er, I have never written. Someone always wrote for me – my mother.'

Kufalt's neighbour had a pimply face and blinking eyes. Moreover, he smelt unpleasantly when he bent over Kufalt.

'You want to go – to that place?' he whispered.

'How do you mean? What place?' said Kufalt.

'That's all right, I know. And I advise you to get out at Holstenstrasse, that's where it is. Otherwise you'll have to lug that suitcase of yours halfway across Hamburg.'

'Yes, thanks. I don't know. I'm going to relations in Hamburg.'

'Oh, if they're your relations . . .'

Kufalt cursed himself for having started this conversation. He picked up his newspaper.

'If I were you, I'd go to the Halleluja Brothers in the Steinstrasse.'

Kufalt unfolded his paper.

'It costs only four groschen a night there, too.'

Kufalt read his paper.

'If you like, I'll carry your bag.'

Kufalt paid no attention.

'I'm not going to do a bunk with it. I'll carry it, even if you want to traipse to Blankenese.'

Kufalt got up and went to the lavatory.

II

'Apfelstrasse?' asked the policeman, surveying Kufalt. 'Yes. Down this street and the second on the right.'

'Thank you,' said Kufalt, and walked off. 'He stared at me too. It must be my yellow complexion. I wish I looked a bit different, I can't speak to anybody . . .'

Apfelstrasse. He had been told No. 28. 'City Mission Club-House. Bedrooms across the yard. Bed: Fifty pfennigs.'

Was that it?

In the doorway stood a fat man with a forbidding face. Kufalt approached him nervously. The man was wearing a curious kind of cap. Even before Kufalt had reached him he shouted out: 'What do you want at this hour? The bedrooms aren't open till seven.'

'What can be the matter with me?' thought Kufalt nervously. 'I'm as decently dressed as ever I was, and yet they all stare at me.' He replied: 'I don't mind about that. I only wanted to ask if this was the Home of Peace.'

'Home of Peace? Well, you can call it that if you like – this evening. Tomorrow you'll call it something quite different.'

'The Home of Peace is a home for the unemployed. Is this it?'

'No, it isn't.'

'Can you tell me where it is, then?'

'How on earth should I know?'

The man retreated into the doorway and Kufalt went back into the street. It was useless to inquire further. This was certainly No. 28. The Home must be in Hamburg. He took a tighter grip of his trunk and departed once more in the direction of the station.

In answer to Kufalt's ring at the bell, the door was opened by a girl in a blue apron, young, but very unwelcoming. She glared at him – at least, she squinted violently, Kufalt could only assume that she was glaring at him. 'She's prison rescue, no fear,' thought Kufalt, 'so I've found the place all right.'

'What do you want?' said the girl in an indignant tone. 'Why have you come so late?'

'I am supposed to be received in the Home of Peace.'

'I know nothing about that. You've wasted all your money and now you come here. Are you sober?' She went up to him. 'Stand back, young man, so that I can see whether you're tipsy.'

She pressed him back, step by step, until he was outside again, and then she slammed the door in his face.

Kufalt was once more in the street, or rather in a railed and paved front garden.

'Well, she's a brazen hussy!' thought Kufalt with interest, and looked up at the Gothic lettering of the inscription 'Home of Peace'. 'Can't be much peace about a place if she runs it.'

He heard her raucous voice through the front door. 'Herr Seidenzopf, there's someone there. He isn't drunk. He's carrying a bag. No – come down yourself, he's outside in the garden.'

Then silence.

It was a suburban street, the Apfelstrasse in Hamburg. Thirty little two-storey houses, all like the Home of Peace, most of them with a neat garden and a tree and a shrub; and eighty five-storey tenements.

There were many passers-by. Little people. Kufalt had the feeling that he did not need to worry if they all guessed how he came to be standing there, bag in hand, outside the Home of Peace. They knew what it meant, and they didn't bother any more. He was not repelled by his reception, it was the best sort of reception from the world; there was a familiar ring to it; people also treated you like that in jail.

Meanwhile he awaited the person called Seidenzopf.

He appeared, as though in answer to a call. The door opened abruptly, a little man in a baggy black suit stepped quickly through it, and the door was shut once more.

Herr Seidenzopf stood before Willi Kufalt; he looked rather like a Schnauzer, his face was so overgrown with woolly black hair, large pale nose and black beady eyes. His hair, however, was plastered over his head, and glistened with oil.

Herr Seidenzopf surveyed the young man for a while in silence. Face and hands, jacket and trousers, shoes and bag, collar and hat – all were carefully scrutinized.

The inspection apparently over, the little man cleared his throat, thereby revealing a surprisingly deep bass voice. 'I can wait,' said Kufalt modestly.

'Certainly, but the point is whether it would be any use. You have not been recommended to us,' said the man. His voice was a leonine booming bass; a few children, who were spinning tops, gathered by the railings.

'Yes I have. And the recommendation should have arrived. I signed it early yesterday morning.'

'Yesterday morning?' shouted the little man. 'You understand nothing, you know nothing, you just stand there and say – you can wait.'

'Well, so I can,' said Kufalt, dropping his voice as the little man began to bellow at him.

'Recommendations go to our chairman first, Herr Deacon Doctor Hermann Marcetus. They may possibly get here in four days; can you stand outside the door for as long as that?'

'No,' said Kufalt, who suspected that this was a promising reception.

He reminded himself that Chief Warder Rusch used to adopt that sort of tone; a man did not make so much fuss unless he was going to help you in the end.

'Well then, if you can't wait as long as that, you'll just have to apply very humbly, my young friend.' Raising his voice, he went on: 'There is no shame in humility, as you perhaps think; our dear Lord Jesus Christ was not ashamed to beg humbly of his disciples as well as of his Heavenly Father.'

'I ask to be received into the Home of Peace this evening,' said Kufalt softly.

'There! And whom do you ask?'

'Herr Seidenzopf, if I am not mistaken.'

'Right. But you must call me Father. I am the father of you all.' And in quite another voice, no longer addressed to the public in the street: 'We'll settle the rest inside. Not that I have accepted you yet, but . . .' And again in a booming voice, now directed towards the other side of the street: 'There's no sense in your hanging about here, Berthold. I saw you a long while ago. You won't get a bed from me, and you won't get any food from me – you're drunk again. Go away!'

The swaying figure in the shaggy overcoat across the street raised both its arms and yelled in a high falsetto: 'Take pity on me, Herr Seidenzopf! Where am I to sleep tonight? It's so cold in the parks.'

The figure dashed across the street.

'Come in quick,' whispered Seidenzopf. The door opened, Seidenzopf pushed Kufalt inside, and shut the door again in Berthold's face. 'Disconnect the bell, Minna,' roared Seidenzopf. 'Berthold's at the door.'

The hall was dark, but not so dark that Kufalt could not see two female figures on a staircase leading to the upper floor: one the maid he had already encountered, and the other a voluminous, flabby creature, three steps above.

From the latter came a tearful wail: 'Father! You shouldn't bring a man into the Home so late. He's sure to be drunk, and he's spent all his money on women. Nobody comes out of prison as late as this, Father.'

Then the high, rasping voice of the squinting maid: 'He's not drunk, Frau Seidenzopf. He's just come out of prison; he can't look anyone in the face. His trousers haven't got creased yet, so he hasn't been with women . . .'

'Silence!' roared the lion. 'Get on with your work! Not another word!'

The two figures vanished.

Through the front door could be heard a pitiful whine: 'Father Seidenzopf, where am I to sleep? Father Seidenzopf . . .'

'Hush!' said Seidenzopf, nodding at the door. 'It is sometimes our duty to let the voice of sympathy be silent . . . Come, my young friend.'

Again the voice whined through the keyhole: 'Father Seidenzopf, oh Father Seidenzopf . . .'

They went into a room that was still fairly light. The little man sat down behind a desk in a vast armchair, the sides of which stood out above his head like wings. Kufalt was permitted to sit down on the other side of the desk.

'My wife, young man, hit the nail on the head,' said the little man. 'Where do you come from so late?'

'From the Central Prison.'

'But the Central Prison discharges at seven in the morning. You could have been here at twelve o'clock. Where have you been all this time?'

'I . . .' began Kufalt.

The little man sat up stiffly: 'Stop, my young friend. Do not speak thoughtlessly. A lie soon slips out. You had much better say: I am ashamed to tell you, Father. Then we will be silent for a while and think how weak we, alas, so often are.'

'I wasn't discharged until twenty past one, Herr Seidenzopf.'

'Father,' corrected the other, 'Father. I believe you, friend, but you had better show me your discharge sheet.'

Kufalt took out his wallet, looked into it, picked out his discharge sheet and gave it to Seidenzopf.

The latter was familiar with such documents, and merely glanced at it. 'Good, you have spoken the truth. Still . . . no, leave your wallet on the table. We must have a talk about that. For the moment . . .'

The little man suddenly dashed to the window and hammered wildly against the glass: 'Go away! Will you go away! Am I to call the police? Go away.'

And Berthold's pallid long-nosed face vanished.

Seidenzopf beamed, and said: 'He's afraid of me, did you notice! Yes, we don't put up with any nonsense here. We have to be stern with these unfortunates, stern but kind. And now for your affairs. Even starting at twenty past one you could have been here an hour earlier.'

'I went to the Apfelstrasse in Altona first, and it took me a good hour to walk here with a heavy suitcase.'

'Come round here,' cried Seidenzopf. 'Come round here. Look at your wallet.' He had opened it, and was looking with an air of surprise into an apparently empty pocket.

Kufalt, puzzled and expectant, saw nothing but an empty pocket.

'Blow into it, man. Can't you see the spider?'

Kufalt could see none, but he blew.

Seidenzopf sniffed. 'You have been drinking, my young friend. Though not much. One glass, eh? Yes, but you must give it up entirely. Look at Berthold, such a clever man, a decent and religious man, but drinks. Three times he has signed the pledge at the Blue Cross League – I'm an officer of the Blue Cross, I came from them to take charge of this Home – and broken it each time. Yes, every time.'

'You needn't have gone to all that trouble to find me out.'

'I dare say, I dare say. You're an honest man. I can see that. You will, I am sure, be a pride and joy to us, and do us credit. Now about your money, you must let me look after it for you . . .'

'No. I want to keep my money.'

'Calm down, don't worry; you won't lose it all. You know what kind of guests we have here. We can't be responsible if you keep it. We shall give you a receipt, of course, and if you want any, I'll give it you. Right: 409 marks 77. I'll let you have the receipt at once.'

Kufalt looked angrily at his money. 'But I need money, at once. I must buy some sock-suspenders and a pair of slippers. I'm not used to leather shoes and my feet hurt me.'

'You'll soon get used to them. I'll give you three marks. But you'll spend it carefully, won't you? Three marks are hard to earn.'

'I need at least ten marks,' growled Kufalt.

'Oh dear, oh dear! Are we millionaires? You can always have some more when the three marks are gone. I'll let you have it, my friend. But when you have to go to Father Seidenzopf first, you will think twice about asking. And that's how money is saved.'

The little man was already at the cupboard; the wallet was gone.

'If I had had any notion of this,' thought Kufalt, quite dumbfounded, 'I'd have hidden the stuff. You're always going to get taken in by people like this.'

'And now let us hurry up and sign the Home Regulations and the Typing Room Regulations, and then go upstairs and unpack and make your bed.'

'Can't we turn on the light?' asked Kufalt, looking at the closely printed documents before him. 'I would like to read what I'm signing.'

'Do you want to read them all? My dear friend, what *is* the sense in that? Thousands of men have signed, you needn't mind doing it.'

'But I would just like to know what it's all about. Please let me read them.'

'And don't lose your temper, dear friend. Of course, if you like. There is still light enough by the window.'

There was no longer light enough by the window. Kufalt looked out onto the twilit street and the front garden. There crouched a figure, a pallid white-nosed creature, who grimaced at him. 'There's Berthold!' he cried.

'Where? The miserable wretch! I'll have to have him removed by the police. My dear Herr Kufalt, please be so good as to sign your name at once. I must go down to the unhappy man, I cannot have a scandal. Our house must not attract attention, it must be a true Home of Peace. Ah – thank you. Shake hands, dear friend. You are now my son. May God sanctify your presence here.'

'But the home is undenominational, isn't it?' asked Kufalt with a grin.

'Of course it is. Quite undenominational. Minna, bring Herr Kufalt his sheets and a towel. Minna, this is your brother Kufalt. Kufalt, this is your sister Minna.'

'Oh God – oh God,' thought Kufalt.

'Now shake hands both of you; but mind you don't get too familiar. Kufalt, will you go upstairs now and choose your bed. You are at home here now. You will find a brother there . . .'

'He's crazy, Father,' said Minna, the maid in the Home of Peace.

'Yes, he's ill. Brother Beerboom is still ill, my dear Minna. His long imprisonment . . .'

'He asked me whether I would go out with him,' said Minna with the squinting eyes.

'Did he indeed? It was not necessarily improper for him to want to go out with you, but of course I will warn him. Go now, Kufalt, I must go and speak to our fallen brother.'

A glance through the window revealed to Kufalt that brother Berthold had really fallen; he was now crawling on all fours through the front garden, with his hat between his teeth.

'I must really ring up the police,' said Seidenzopf at the sight of the crowd thronging against the railings of the front garden. He threw open the window and said: 'Don't stand there gaping – go away. Aren't you sorry to see a fellow creature so degraded?'

A coarse voice shouted: 'Don't dirty your shirt, Woolly Teddy!' Kufalt groped his way up the almost pitch-dark staircase.

III

In the passage above there was scarcely a glimmer of light. Kufalt was just able to make out a door. He turned the handle, and the door opened. A dark, apparently large room. Kufalt's hands felt for the switch, found it at last, and the light came on, a dim sixteen-candle bulb set in a deep shade.

Twelve beds arranged in exact alignment. Twelve shallow black cupboards. And a single oak table.

'Not exactly luxurious – the jolly old Home of Peace,' thought Kufalt. 'The windows aren't barred anyway. Otherwise it might be a prison. The beds are no better.'

He then noticed for the first time that the sheets over his arm were prison sheets, blue and white check. 'Must have cadged them from the Prison Department. Well, there's no one living here. Let's try the next door.'

The next door was locked.

The last door led into a lit room where a man was lying on a bed. The man raised his head, looked at Kufalt and said: 'So you've turned up at last, you old jailbird, have you? About time too. How long was your stretch? Has Woolly Teddy left you any money? Got any schnapps in your bag? Have you been among the girls to get the smell of prison off you?'

'Good evening,' said Kufalt.

The man got up and laughed awkwardly. He was thick-set and of average size, with a grey leathery skin, dark dull black eyes and curly black hair. 'You must excuse me. I was trying to be funny. Here we are, in a state of golden freedom, as they call it. My name is Beerboom . . .'

'And mine is Kufalt.'

'My father is a university professor, but he doesn't know me now. Eleven years in prison, for robbery and murder. I've got a little sister, she was a sweet child; she must be a big girl now. Have you got a sister?'

'Yes.'

'Is that so? I'd so much like to see mine again. But I'm not allowed. If I came anywhere near my father, he'd report me to the cops at once – and goodbye to my probation. If I get on your nerves, by the way, there's another room behind, you could sleep there if you like.'

'I'll see,' said Kufalt. 'Are we the only people here?'

'Yes. I've been here for two days. I thought I would be the only idiot to go into this shop of my own free will. Well, I think I'll doss down again. There's still half an hour till supper.'

'I'll just go and have a look,' said Kufalt, to the further room.

'Don't mind me. I understand, I understand everything. Besides I usually cry for an hour before I go to sleep. It would disturb you. In the clink I used to get beaten for it by the others in the communal cell, but I can't drop it. Nice name Kufalt – reminds me of one-fold – simplicity, and three-fold – Trinity. By the way, what does Trinity really mean?'

'Something to do with the Holy Ghost. I don't know either. And now I'd like to have a look . . .'

'Go right along then man, Kufalt, Holy Ghost. Don't you mind me. I always go on like this when I see a new bloke. I picked it up in prison. You don't need to listen. I don't listen either . . .'

'Right, then, I'll go . . .'

'Have you noticed their monkey-tricks with the windows? Worse than in prison. There aren't any bars, but the panes are small and you can open them only ten centimetres. And the frames are all iron. There's no slipping round to see the little girls at night, don't even think about it. Father Seidenzopf has taken care of that.'

'Well, I'll go.'

'Do. You're just as much a bloody fool as I am. When I cry in the evening, I always think there can't be another idiot like me. But there are. There's you, for instance, hanging around here . . .'

'I'm off,' said Kufalt, with a laugh.

The room behind was just such another dismal place – four bare walls, four shallow cupboards, four empty beds; Kufalt chose the furthest, against the wall. He threw his bag on the bed and opened it. The cupboard door was open, and there was no key. The lock was a useless tin affair that could be easily picked with a bit of wire. Kufalt tested it.

'You can stick the cupboard door with spit,' said a voice from the next room. 'You don't need to worry about your things. If I pinched any, I wouldn't get them out of the house, the squint-eyed girl's always on the lookout . . .'

'And you wanted to go out with her?' asked Kufalt, putting his shirts away in the cupboard.

'Why not? A skirt's a skirt. So she told Woolly Teddy. All right, my girl, you wait; I'll rub your nose in something, so I will . . .'

Kufalt unpacked. 'That bloke's done for,' he thought. 'He's crazy. Eleven years in high-security prison, that's pretty well skinned him, he'll never be any use again.'

He went on unpacking. The other man suddenly appeared in the doorway; he had slipped noiselessly down the passage in his socks. 'It wasn't real robbery and murder. I did in my lieutenant, and when the pig was on the floor, I suddenly remembered I hadn't enough money to scarper. Nice things you've got, I must say. They gave me a lot of muck when I came out, my own things were all rotten from being kept so long. Cotton shirts – and the suit, what sort of suit do you call this? Off the peg, thirty marks. But the chaplain, the bogeyman, couldn't stand me. Will you sell your socks? I like them. What do you want for the lilac ones?'

'No, I won't,' said Kufalt; 'but I'll give them to you. I don't much care for them.'

'All right, hand them over if you're such a fool. At first my sentence was "off with his head", then life, then fifteen years. And now they've let me out after eleven years. And no good conduct at that, and no influence. And yet out I got. Why? Because my case stinks, it stinks to Heaven. If I went to the Reds and told them about it . . .'

'But you're out all right.'

'Under police supervision. Loss of civil rights for the rest of my life. Not that I care a damn about civil rights; but I'd like to get my own back on the chaplain. He's coming here in a month's time, the chaplain from the high-security prison. Did you know they're going to celebrate the twenty-fifth anniversary of the Home of Peace?'

'No.'

'They're robbers in this place. That slippery eel, Seidenzopf, he's a robber; but that slimy water-snake, Marcetus the pastor, he's ten times worse, and worst of all is that egg-headed brute Mergenthal, who runs the office. They live on our blood. That's why the grafters have set up this show here, and called it charity, just to sponge off our work. I could tell you a thing or two . . .'

'But you've only been in here two days?'

'What's that matter? Shall we smoke? It's against the rules, but they won't turn us out as long as there are so few people in the Home. Blow the smoke out of the window like we did in prison. As for telling you a thing or two – well, I spot things sometimes – the pastor says: "Get on with it"; or Seidenzopf says: "You're a liar." Then when I lie in bed in the evening and cry, it all goes round in my head, I see through the walls, and I cry because I'm so sorry for myself.'

'But you've got over that now.'

'Oh no, I haven't. I'm right in it, my lad. It's just started properly. If I leave here I shall have to go into some lunatic asylum, or back to prison, there's nothing else. Just listen to that row. Let's listen at the top of the stairs. Don't chuck your fag out of the window, it's the back garden below, and that squint-eyed goat will find it in the morning . . .'

A wild disturbance was going on below. Seidenzopf's deep booming bass, Minna's shrieks, Frau Seidenzopf's tearfully high-pitched protests, and an intermittent and imploring voice . . .

'Leave this house,' shouted Seidenzopf, 'of which you are unworthy . . .'

And the imploring voice cried: 'Take pity on me, Father!'

'It's that drunken brute, Berthold . . .' whispered Kufalt.

'Who's Berthold?' said Beerboom.

'It's a breach of the peace,' roared Seidenzopf. 'One . . . two . . . three . . .'

A heavy fall.

The women screamed: 'Ohgodohgodohgodohgod.'

Seidenzopf: 'You can't deceive me.'

Frau Seidenzopf wailed: 'He's bleeding . . .'

And Minna: 'My beautiful clean linoleum!'

'Herr Beerboom! Herr Kufalt!' roared Seidenzopf. 'Will you please . . .'

In five bounds they were down the staircase. On the floor, in his shabby overcoat, his mouth open, pale, unconscious, with a blood-stained bruise on his forehead, lay Berthold.

'My sons, will you kindly carry this poor wretch to your room? A wet compress is all that is needed for his forehead. Minna, give your brother Kufalt a towel . . .'

It is no easy task to carry an unconscious man, with limbs like lead and slippery as quicksilver, up a steep, badly lit staircase covered with glassy-smooth linoleum.

'Let's put him on the bed next to mine,' said Beerboom; 'then I can always sock him in the jaw if he wakes up in the night, and I shall too, good and proper . . .'

'I'll make him a compress at once.'

'Come off it, he doesn't need a compress for a scratch like that. You should have seen how they knocked me about in the clink.'

'Why have you got such a down on the man? He hasn't done you any harm.'

'I wish I were as well pissed as he is. It's enough to make a man envious. The last time I was drunk was in prison, Christmas 1928. We drank furniture polish from the carpenter's shop . . .'

'Good evening, kids,' said the drunken man, sitting up. 'I seem to have come down with a bit more of a crash than I meant. Well, it made Woolly Teddy take me in again, anyway. The pastor won't half kick up a fuss tomorrow.'

'Then you aren't drunk,' growled Beerboom. 'It's a bloody nerve to let yourself be carried upstairs.'

'Of course I'm drunk. Only I can't get drunk like you young blokes now. I'm free when I drink. You're slaves when you drink. I can do anything when I drink. You can do nothing. Guys, I've got a great idea. One of you – you with the brown hair, you look pretty innocent, go and tell Teddy that you've got to go out again, and fetch a bottle of schnapps.'

'Oh, bollocks,' said Beerboom. 'He won't let us out of the house after eight. And where's the money coming from?'

'Money? Money! You guys are just out of jail, you've got some money. You earn money. I – look at my hands, I can't hold anything, they shake so.'

'Are you proud of it, you old soak?'

'No,' sobbed Berthold. 'It's torture. And now I'll do something to please Teddy. I'll go back to the Blue Cross. I'll take the pledge. And I'll keep it too. A man must be able to do what he wants to do. And if I don't keep it, I'll only begin to drink very, very gradually . . .'

'Tell us,' asked Beerboom; 'were you ever in prison?'

Berthold grinned again. 'No, my boy, I wasn't. I'm just a drunkard and work-shy.'

'Then what are you doing here?' roared Beerboom. 'This place is for discharged prisoners. You won't work, but you want to eat. Do you expect us to work for you?'

'Now don't start a row,' wailed the drunkard. 'I can't stand a row. I'm so glad to be back with old man Teddy. Look, I've got a great idea. Wait, I've got something in my pocket.' He fumbled and produced a wedge of paper. 'Prescriptions. Prescription forms. I pinched them from a doctor today.'

'How did you get to a doctor?'

'I just went along in his consulting hours; you can, you know. And when I got into his room I asked him for the loan of five marks. He said it was impertinence and told me to get out. I said I wouldn't go till I got the five marks. He ran around like a headless chicken, and I just sat calmly. At last he went to fetch some people to sling me out and I pinched the prescriptions and slipped out quietly.'

'Well? And what are you going to do with them?'

'Ah, that's the big idea. We'll fill them in with morphine and cocaine and nice things like that, and then sell the stuff at nightclubs.'

'That's not bad. Do you know how to write them out?'

'I used to know a medical student; that's how I found out. It's a good scam.'

'So that's how you get your money, you drunken pig. Well wait, if I . . .'

A cowbell clanged.

'Supper! Are you coming along?'

'Let me stay here, kids. When I think of what I'd have to eat, my belly turns over; it feels as though it's made of glass.'

'All right, stay where you are. But if you touch our things, you dirty old swine, you . . . !'

'As if! What should I want with them? I haven't needed anything for a very long time.'

IV

Next morning at half past eight Kufalt was sitting in the typing room. He was still idle; the others were at work. Quite a number had arrived – ten, twelve men – and sat down at their tables. They were all hard at it, some writing, and some typing, nothing but addresses. Even the pallid Beerboom was sitting at a table beside Kufalt and writing busily.

'Four marks fifty a thousand,' he whispered. 'I mean to do at least fifteen hundred today. Board and lodging two marks fifty, I shall have five marks over. Not bad, eh?'

'But can you do fifteen hundred?'

'Of course I can. Yesterday I did nearly five hundred, and I'm in better practice today.'

Father Seidenzopf then appeared in his alpaca jacket, followed by a man with a smooth egg-like cranium and a grey pointed beard. Seidenzopf walked up one gangway and down the other, said good morning twice, and disappeared, with Egg-head silent behind him.

Kufalt sat and looked into the garden. It was beautifully green, and the grass looked so fresh.

'Does it belong to us?' he asked Beerboom.

'It does, but we can't use it. It's just there for show, when visitors come . . .'

Kufalt grinned knowingly.

A tall man said in a low voice: 'When the addresses are finished, there'll be no more work again.'

'How many are there left?'

'Thirty thousand.'

'Enough for two days at most. Then there'll be nothing to do.'

'There'll be new work in before that.'

'Wait and see.'

Egg-head appeared again with an envelope in his hand. 'Herr Kufalt, write your address on this. Just your address: Herr Willi Kufalt, Hamburg, Apfelstrasse, Home of Peace. Can't you do better than that? Well, we'll see.'

He disappeared with the envelope and Kufalt again looked out into the garden.

Someone asked: 'What will you do if there's no more work here?'

'I don't know, apply to Welfare, I suppose.'

'I might get a job selling vacuum cleaners.'

'You can ditch that one right away, vacuum cleaners are worse than margarine.'

Another voice: 'There might be something doing with floor polish, or garden sprays.'

'Might have been once. All wiped up long ago.'

Again Egg-head appeared, with an air of huge astonishment. 'Did I hear talking? I must really insist—'

'No one was talking, Herr Mergenthal.'

'I must insist on silence. You all know the consequences of breaking the Typing Room Regulations. If any of you gentlemen prefers the street?' Pens scratched and typewriters rattled. 'Herr Kufalt, Herr Seidenzopf wishes me to tell you that you ought to have been a doctor.'

'How do you mean?'

'Your handwriting, it's quite hopeless. Have you ever in your life been in an office? Indeed? It must have been a funny sort of office. But you can use a typewriter?'

'Yes.'

'So you say. But that's no reason for me to believe it.'

'Of course I can type. And very well too.'

'Ten-finger system?'

More doubtfully: 'Not quite. But six for certain.'

'Just as I thought. When it comes to it you will take two fingers and be lucky if you hit the right key. But first you must put one of these typewriters in order. Take it to pieces and clean it and oil it. Can you do that?'

'Depends on the make.'

'It's a Mercedes. Right, get on with it.'

'I'll need benzine, and oil, and rags.'

'Go to Herr Seidenzopf, he'll give you a penny for benzine. And Minna has rags and sewing-machine oil.'

Half an hour later Kufalt was seated in front of a tin pie-dish, in which all the typewriter levers lay soaking in benzine, his hands coated with violet ink from the ribbon and black grease from the oil.

He was just beginning to brush the levers clean when Minna appeared at the door: 'The new man is to come and wax the floors.'

'No really!' protested Mergenthal. 'He's just on a job he can't leave. Herr Beerboom can go.'

'Frau Seidenzopf says the new man is to do it. Beerboom doesn't do it properly. And if he doesn't come, I'll tell her you won't let him.'

'All right, go and polish the floors,' said Mergenthal. 'Wipe your hands on the rags. You won't be long.'

It took him an hour and a half. Kufalt had to wax all the bedrooms, the hall, and the stairs, under the strict supervision of the maid, Sister Minna.

'Why aren't you doing this?' demanded Kufalt.

'Clean your dirty floors? I only work for the Seidenzopfs.'

When he had finished, Frau Seidenzopf appeared, a slovenly figure in a nightgown, whom Kufalt greeted by saying: 'Good morning, my lady, I hope you slept well.'

As Frau Seidenzopf had no sense of irony, she answered almost graciously: 'Not bad for a beginning. But the man must do the corners better, Minna.'

Afterwards Kufalt sat down to his typewriter levers once more and brushed the joints clean of dirt. He had almost finished this job when Mergenthal, who seemed to oscillate between the manager's office and the typing room, suddenly appeared and shouted: 'Herr Kufalt and Herr Beerboom to see Herr Seidenzopf.'

The Father of them all was seated in his alpaca jacket at a large desk. 'Well, my young friends, we have started work, and I hope it may be a blessing to you. How much money have you, Kufalt?'

'You know quite well. Three marks,' answered Kufalt sullenly, for this was a very sore point.

'Show me your purse a minute. Yes, quite correct. Honesty in money matters means a clear conscience. And you, Beerboom? Show me, don't explain. Empty? Where are your three marks?'

'They dropped down the toilet early this morning.'

'Beerboom! Herr Beerboom! Son Beerboom, am I to believe that?'

'I don't eat money,' said Beerboom. 'And as I never go out of this hole, what should I do with the money? Do you think I gave it to Minna?'

'No; to Berthold.'

For one instant Beerboom was at a loss: 'Berthold? Berthold? Oh, that old fraud? I don't give away my little bit of money to boozers. It fell down the toilet, I tell you. I tried to reach it, you can see for yourself, my arm's all scratched to the elbow by shoving it down the pipe.'

He began to pull up his sleeve.

'That will do,' said Seidenzopf angrily. 'I'm no fool. You won't get money from me again in a hurry. Well, Kufalt and Beerboom, I am going to send you both out into the city alone . . .'

'Yes?'

'Really?'

'It will be your first excursion into freedom . . .'

The door opened and a fair young man appeared.

'Ah, excuse me, Herr Seidenzopf, I am disturbing you . . .'

'No, on the contrary, Herr Petersen, may I introduce you to our two new guests? This is Herr Beerboom, who has been with us since the day before yesterday, and this is Herr Kufalt, who has been our guest since yesterday. Berthold has been here again; I let him in, and again he deceived me. Early this morning, I was waiting for him to turn up to try and borrow a bit of money as usual, and at the moment when I was just – when I had to – in short when I was forced to relieve a natural need – he seized the opportunity and bolted. And, I am afraid, with our young friend Beerboom's money.'

'Do you mean he stole it?'

'My money fell down the toilet.'

'That will do. My friends, this young gentleman, Petersen by name, is your friend and brother, your protector and adviser. He is' – Seidenzopf got into his stride, as though he were repeating something carefully learnt by heart – 'he is a young man of wide social interests, strong convictions and high character, whom you are to receive among you; he will live in common with you, take his meals with you, and act as your friend and adviser in every respect. The evenings and free Sundays he will spend in your company; he will try to inspire you with a sense of good fellowship and, so far as you will allow him, help you to improve your mind. He has passed his qualifying examinations as a teacher in an elementary school and is now in his fourth term as a student of economics, for which he has ample time in addition to his activities in our Home. Shake hands with him, gentlemen.'

They shook hands.

'Herr Petersen, it is my intention to send these two men into the city alone. Do you see any objections?'

'May I ask why they are going?'

'They are to report at the appropriate police station.'

Petersen smiled: 'No, Herr Seidenzopf, I see no objections.'

'And you don't think Herr Pastor Marcetus will have anything to say about it? That I am too trusting?'

'No, certainly not. You may safely let the men go out alone. They will not betray your confidence.'

V

'Do you know,' said Beerboom to Kufalt in the street, 'Petersen, or whatever he calls himself, is just a spy put on to watch us. He can go and get lost, the dirty nark.'

'I rather liked him, there was a nice twinkle in his eye while Father Seidenzopf was saying his piece.'

'Oh, Woolly Teddy can go and clear off too. He didn't believe me about the money.'

'Did you really lose it, then?'

'Of course not. I gave it to Berthold. Do you think I'll get it back?'

'But what did you give it him for?'

'As working capital. He'll buy morphine with it, and we'll share the profit.'

'You'll have a long time to wait for profits.'

'I must have money, Kufalt, I must have money in my pocket. Could you lend me a mark?'

'What do you want money for now?'

'Just for that. I need to have money in my pocket. We might drink a glass of beer out of it, I'll stand you one.'

'But you must have a pot of money with Seidenzopf. After eleven years in the clink.'

'Yes, a good bit, ninety marks.'

'What! Only ninety marks for eleven years in the clink!'

'It was the inflation to begin with, we only got the value of thirty marks for all those years. And then later on I lost interest, I always thought there'd be an amnesty, and then there wasn't, and I cared even less.'

'Ninety marks are soon gone.'

'Ninety marks is a good round sum. I wish I had it, I'd go on the loose. Have you any idea what the girls want here? Not for a whole night, but for a quick one.'

'No idea.'

They walked on. There was a pleasant breeze, and the green of the trees was deliciously fresh. Then they turned down a side street, strolled along the road and looked at the long, lively thoroughfare stretching into the distance. Right in front of them was a petrol station painted scarlet.

'That girl looked at me.'

'Why shouldn't she? You look quite nice.'

'Think so? Do you reckon I'd be popular with the girls? I'm dark really, and people always say that women like dark men. It's only my complexion; do you think I should ask Woolly Teddy for money for some artificial sunlight treatment? They told me in prison that I could alter my complexion that way.'

'I wouldn't do that. You're living quite a different life to what you did in prison, your complexion will alter naturally.'

'That looks like a nice café, Kufalt. There's sure to be waitresses. Lend me two marks, we'll go in. My treat.'

'Let's go and report first,' said Kufalt, feeling very sensible and grandfatherly. 'Two marks won't go very far among the girls in a café like that.'

'But perhaps one of them will fall for us, and we shan't have to pay anything.'

'God forbid!'

'Have you got a girl already? Take me with you when you go to see her?'

'I haven't got one.'

'Then why don't you want one of them to fall for you?'

'Not from a café like that. I think of something quite different.'

'Think! You can think what you like. I want a girl: and as quick as possible.'

In the police station two policemen stood at two high desks and looked at each other. One of them suggested a slightly ruffled bird, with his pointed bristly beard, hooked nose and glittering eyes; the other was small and pale.

'Well,' said the pale man, 'I've got an allotment by the Horn race-course. That's half my life. Gardening's my hobby.'

'Gardening!' said the ruffled bird with disapproval; 'I never heard such rubbish! You aren't a gardener. That's a load of rubbish. And if you did manage to grow a turnip or two, the greengrocer would throw 'em in your face.'

'I don't do it for money,' said the pale man. 'I do it for pleasure, you know.'

'Eyewash,' said the bird; 'just eyewash. Look, I play skat. I do nothing but play skat. Every evening I bring two or three marks home. I know all about skat; I don't mess about with it. No eyewash there.'

'Ah well, if you've got a gift for it,' agreed the pale man.

'And when there's a skat drive for a carp or a sausage or a goose, I'm onto it; I go somewhere different every day. Last winter I won six geese. When the landlords catch sight of me, the beer turns sour on 'em. "You get out," they say; "you just take the money out of our customers' pockets." "What is this place?" I ask. "Is it a public house or not? Can a police officer get his glass of beer here? Is this a public skat drive, or only for regular customers?" Then they dry up, but they don't half look at me, I tell you . . . And what may you want?' he snapped savagely at Beerboom, who had drawn attention to his presence by repeated coughs.

'Excuse me, Sergeant,' said Beerboom. 'We just came in to report.'

'Don't you see the notice? Can't you read what it says: you have to fill in the forms first.'

'That doesn't apply to us,' said Beerboom, with a grin at Kufalt, for he was proud of his way of dealing with subordinate officials. 'The notice doesn't apply to us, Inspector. We aren't like the others.'

'Ah,' intervened the pale man; 'they must be two more from the . . .' He jerked his head round the corner. 'You know . . .'

'Well, hand over your papers and let's have a look . . .'

'But is that the regulation, Mr Secretary sir? Is that the practice here in Hamburg? I never knew that.'

'What didn't you know? What's all this about regulation and practice?' The bird grew more and more furious, his voice rising to a shriek.

'That people like us, from the . . .' – Beerboom mimicked the pale man's jerk of the head – 'may be addressed in this way? I will ask the Station Superintendent about it. I will just go and see him, in his office.'

There was a moment's silence. Then: 'Please let me see your discharge sheet.'

'Certainly, Mr Secretary sir,' replied Beerboom, in high good humour. 'I don't want to stand around here. I don't care for the place. Nor do you, eh? You too prefer skat?'

'I have no time for private conversations.'

'No, certainly not. I just happened to hear you say so.'

'What are you?'

'Murderer. You'll find it on the sheet, sir. Murderer.'

'I want to know what you were before.'

'Nothing at all. Oh yes, I was a soldier, a defender of the Fatherland, Mr Secretary sir. I did in my lieutenant.'

'That does not interest us here.'

'It's only because you asked, Mr Secretary sir. I thought it would interest you.'

The other rummaged in a pile of papers and finally produced a document.

'I have to make you aware – er – that four years of your sentence have been remitted subject to three years' probation . . . You are under police supervision. You have to report here at the station every day between six and seven in the evening. If you change your domicile, you have to report before doing so. If you fail to report daily, you will be liable to instant arrest. Do you understand?'

'But suppose I'm ill, sir?'

'Then send someone here with a medical certificate.'

'No one would do an errand for me.'

'Well, we will keep an eye on you, if we have to come round to your place.'

Beerboom appeared to ponder deeply. 'That isn't correct, Mr Secretary sir.'

'What isn't correct?' demanded the officer indignantly.

'What you've just read to me.'

'It's perfectly correct that you'll be arrested at once if you don't report.'

'No I shan't. And I shan't report either.'

The officer was on the verge of an explosion.

'Why? I've got a permit from the Central Police Office, that I needn't report, because I'm under supervision at the Home.' He fumbled in his pockets, and handed the officer a certificate.

'Why didn't you give me that before? Why did you let me go on talking? Kindly give me all your papers at once.'

'I haven't got them all here. Some of them are at home.'

'Which?'

'My vaccination certificate. And a school certificate.'

The bird's voice was now screeching: 'You're a . . .' Beerboom grinned expectantly. 'Oh well.' And turning to the pale man: 'Have you done with yours? Yes? Right, you can go.'

'Me too?'

'Yes! You too!'

Beerboom and Kufalt both stood outside in the street again.

'Why do you behave like that? What's the point of it?' said Kufalt angrily. 'I felt quite ashamed of you.'

'Those blokes need to have their noses rubbed in it. They're such pricks. It's what I most enjoy. My section warder in the prison, I tell you . . .'

'I don't mind when the bloke's a shit. But to go on like that just for fun . . . No, I shan't go with you to a station again.'

'I won't do it again if you're there, and it annoys you. But what's a man to do all those years in the clink, when nothing ever happens? He must stir things up a bit.'

'Yes, I used to do that too. But now we're outside.'

'I still can't figure it. Do you know, I can't figure it in my mind that I'm outside. And I know it's no use. I'll be in again soon.'

'Maybe.'

'Do you see that girl on the bench with the pram? Pretty, eh? Shall I go up to her and say – Fräulein, would you like me to give you a child?'

'Why? What's she done to you? She's not much more than a child herself.'

'I don't know. I feel so savage. About everything. She's lucky, she is, she doesn't know about anything yet. Why shouldn't she know? It's a foul world. Why shouldn't she be as foul as the rest of it? Oh, Kufalt, I've got such a terrible sore head, I wish I were lying on my bed so I could cry.'

VI

It was the loveliest afternoon in the world, the lunch had been good, two slabs of beef for every man. Kufalt was sitting in front of his enamelled dish; the type-levers were clean, he was now drying them, and wiping the joints with oily rags. He worked in a sort of drowsy quiet; in fact he felt very well.

Beerboom had taken himself off immediately after lunch; he had gone to bed, no doubt to have a good cry. But his flight was soon discovered. The typing room could hear Seidenzopf's booming bass up above, Beerboom's shrill protests, and then he appeared, with Seidenzopf at his heels.

'Office hours are office hours. You signed the agreement.'

'I never read what I signed.'

'Tut-tut-tut, now sit down to your work.'

'I can't sit still for nine hours, my nerves won't stand it.'

'But you want to earn money. Get down to it! Don't you see how much Maack has finished already – and you . . .'

Yes, it did not look as though Beerboom would finish his fifteen hundred addresses that day. Kufalt reckoned up the heap that lay in front of Beerboom. Three hundred addresses, perhaps. Forty-five pfennigs a hundred. No, Beerboom would not earn his board that day.

Maack, on the other hand, tall, lanky, pallid Maack, wrote like a machine. A fleeting glance at the list of addresses in front of him, his hand raced over the paper – and the address was written. Hundred upon hundred were, heap after heap, piled up before him. But he never looked up, he turned out address after address quite mechanically, without moving a muscle of his face.

From time to time, however – as indeed did all the others – he went into the outer room, past the egg-headed watchdog Mergenthal, and dived into the cellar. Mergenthal always growled out something like: 'What, again already? Now watch out! You might have waited a bit!'

When Maack disappeared the next time, after a short interval, Kufalt followed him. Mergenthal muttered: 'There's someone down there now,' but like all the others Kufalt took no notice, and went down into the cellar.

As might have been expected, there was a WC below. And as might also have been expected, it was occupied. And as might also have been expected, it smelt strongly of cigarette smoke.

While he waited, Kufalt rolled a cigarette, and lit it.

The flush gurgled in the pan, and Maack stepped out. He was about to pass Kufalt without a word, but then, as the latter smiled slightly, he said in a low voice: 'Only smoke there in the WC. If

Seidenzopf cops you, there's a fine. Mergenthal just growls, he's not a bad bloke.'

'Thank you,' said Kufalt, and smiled again. 'Thank you very much.'

Maack went. Suddenly he turned: 'If I were you, next time Seidenzopf comes through the typing room, I should ask him what he's going to pay you for cleaning the machine. Otherwise, you won't get a bean.'

'Yes,' said Kufalt. 'Good, I will.'

'Thirty pfennigs the hour, that's the tariff here.'

'Thanks very much. Thirty pfennigs. You don't live in the Home?'

'I must go up now,' said Maack, and disappeared.

No one noticed Kufalt's return. The workroom was in uproar, a revolt was in progress. Beerboom had thrown away his penholder and was shouting that he could do no more, he would go mad, it was worse than splitting canes. It was worse than prison. Why had they let him out, if he was to be imprisoned again in a place like this?

Mergenthal tried to calm him down. 'It's only the first few days you feel like that. You'll soon settle down, and you won't think any more about it.'

'I can't do it. I won't stand it. Let me go out on the street for half an hour. I swear I'll come back. But I must get out . . . I can't be stuck here, I've been stuck in prison for eleven years.'

The wailing monologue went on and on.

Attracted by the uproar, Seidenzopf appeared. 'What's the matter now? But my dear good son, this won't do at all. The other gentlemen want to work.'

'Let me out. Into the open air. Why didn't you leave me on my bed, I'd have cried myself to sleep all right . . . Let me out!'

'But, Herr Beerboom, you are a grown man, you understand the meaning of a regulation. It is a regulation that everyone here must work for nine hours a day.'

'I must get out – I'll smash the place up . . .'

'Beerboom, am I to call the police? You know quite well . . .'

Mergenthal had whispered something into Seidenzopf's ear, and he pondered: 'Very well, I'll take the responsibility. Beerboom, go on writing addresses for three hours, and then you can take the finished envelopes on the handcart to the post. Herr Mergenthal will go with you. In that way you'll get out. No, that's quite enough. You must write as hard as you can, otherwise I shan't give you permission. You have done nothing yet. And the handwriting must be better. Who is going to read that sort of thing? Our addresses must make a pleasant impression, the recipient must be glad to get such a circular. Look, Beerboom, when you write: "Chief Secretary" give a bit of a flourish to the "Chief", so that the man will be pleased to think he has done so well in the world. Writing addresses is an art, and a very interesting one. Excellent, my dear Maack, I like to see a table like that. I will get you a good position very soon.'

'You have promised me that for the last eighteen months, Herr Seidenzopf.'

'And you, my dear Kufalt, that's good, that's a very pretty sight, what a shining, glittering machine. I am sure it gladdens your heart to remove disorder and uncleanliness. It must gladden the heart of every right-minded man.'

'Am I on piece work or a daily wage, Herr Seidenzopf?'

'This is in readiness for your work tomorrow, my dear Kufalt. It is to your advantage, and tomorrow you will get on like greased lightning. Well, ha-ha-ha! Of course it *has* been greased.'

'And how much am I earning? Look at the state my hands are in.'

'We are a typewriting establishment, Herr Kufalt. We undertake typewriting commissions for various firms. They pay for the addresses, but not for cleaning our machines.'

'But I can't work a whole day for nothing. Shall I get today's board and lodging for nothing?'

'I hope, my friend, you are not greedy – greedy about money, I mean.'

'I was told I should get well-paid work here.'

But Seidenzopf had already passed on. 'And you, my dear Leuben, a little slow, eh?'

The tall, pale man looked across at Kufalt, and nodded encouragingly.

Kufalt ran after Seidenzopf. 'I insist on knowing what I'm to get for that filthy job. I've been five hours at it. Thirty pfennigs an hour is your rate.'

Seidenzopf surveyed him with a chilly, evil eye. 'We'll give you a mark. Not another word. It is quite out of order for you to leave your seat and pester me like this. Sit down at once. I am greatly disappointed in you.'

And turning away with a sigh, he added: 'There are so many unemployed, are there not?'

Across the room, seated at his table, the pallid Maack nodded unobtrusively. Kufalt was well satisfied.

VII

Supper was over. It was free time for Willi Kufalt, the second evening of his liberty, after about one thousand eight hundred evenings in prison.

He sat in the common room at the Home and looked through the window down at the twilit street. The window was large, with fine clear panes, and bars on the outside; a bit of arty ironwork, no doubt.

People passed, the evening was mild, some were going home, some were going out. And there were girls among them. The girls' legs in their short skirts were not as impressive in reality as they had been in a prisoner's dreams.

However, there was a large park somewhere in the neighbourhood, and it would be very pleasant to take a walk in it. But a formal permit had to be obtained from Seidenzopf for such an excursion, and Kufalt felt that he was getting fed up with Seidenzopf.

Beerboom slipped like a vagrant spectre through the house, upstairs, downstairs, past the windows, past the doors, but all were well secured. Poor Beerboom, he was waiting for the first share of profits from his three marks. It was not very likely that Berthold would hand them over. Well, when it had grown dark, and all hope had disappeared, he would go and lie down on his bed and cry. That was a relief, it numbed the brain and made it dull and drowsy.

Kufalt switched on the light, went to the bookcase and surveyed the shelves with disgust: the books lay in disorder, some of them with the pages outwards. Kufalt took out a book: *Our U-boat Heroes*. He took out the dark-bound volume next to that saga of the sea: *Hamburg Song-book*. He was about to try a third . . .

Minna appeared in the doorway. 'We don't allow a light for one person only,' she snapped, switched it off and vanished.

'Damn you!' roared Kufalt, and switched the light on again.

He took another book out of the case. *The Sins Against the Spirit*, by Artur Dinter. He opened the book at random and began to read.

From the door came Frau Seidenzopf's whining voice: 'The light must not be turned on here so early in the evening. It is still quite light outside. There's a light on upstairs, and another downstairs. What is our light bill going to be like?'

Frau Seidenzopf switched the light off and went out. She left the door open. Kufalt put the book very quietly back into the cupboard, closed the door and sat down on a chair by the window.

It was almost dark outside.

The light was suddenly switched on. The young man of high character and strong convictions, Petersen, the student, aged perhaps twenty-six, adviser to the discharged prisoners, had come in.

'Sitting in the dark? Do you like it?' he asked.

'Yes, I like it,' said Kufalt, blinking at the tall, fair-haired young man.

Petersen drew the curtains. Then he dropped into a chair with a sigh of contentment and stretched out his legs. 'God, how tired I am! How I have run around today!'

'Is the university far away?'

'Yes, it is. But I wasn't there. I've been to see a man who used to come to the typing room.'

Kufalt looked at him inquiringly.

Petersen was very willing to talk. 'He's living with a girl. And now she wants to get away from him.'

'Well, if she wants to go, she'd better go,' observed Kufalt.

'But she's expecting.'

'And what did you say? What did you do?'

'What can one say? I sat down. At first they were glad I had come. I also brought them a little contribution from us here. Then they started to quarrel.'

'What did they quarrel about?'

'About an eau-de-cologne bottle. He happens to be a very tidy man, everything has to be in its place. And he found the eau-de-cologne bottle in the kitchen cupboard; and it should have been on the washstand. That's what they quarrelled about.'

'What nonsense.'

'They quarrelled pretty badly. Eventually they began to scream. And when they had finished, they were about finished too. Then they cried.'

'It wasn't the eau-de-cologne bottle,' said Kufalt; 'it's because they're down. When people are down, everything comes hard. In prison I used to get excited when the least thing went wrong.'

'Yes,' said Petersen. 'Yes, that is true. But what can one do?'

'What do they live on?'

'He used to work in the typing room. He was quite good. And he suddenly said he couldn't cross the road. That happens to quite a number. When they first come out, you don't notice anything odd about them. It's all new then. But they get like that suddenly . . .'

'Yes, they go a bit crazy. Beerboom's going crazy, by the way. You'd better keep an eye on him.'

'Yes, we must see,' said Petersen dubiously. 'One can do so little.'

'You ought to speak to Herr Seidenzopf. It's madness to make a man in that state sit in an office for nine hours, it will do his head in.'

'It's the regulation, you know, Kufalt, that every man has to do nine hours a day.'

'Yes, "do" is the word!'

The door opened. Minna, with her hand on the switch, snapped, 'Frau Seidenzopf told me to say that the light . . .'

'What's the matter, Minna?' asked Petersen.

'Oh, you're there too,' said Minna. 'One hour's light will be taken off your pay, Herr Kufalt,' announced Minna, and departed.

Petersen and Kufalt looked at each other.

'I'll speak to Herr Seidenzopf,' said Petersen. 'You won't be fined for the light.'

Kufalt half shrugged. 'It doesn't matter. However, thank you.' Then, 'What's the real position here? Can we only go out with you?'

'No, of course you can go out alone too. Still, it is recommended, especially in the evening . . . I'll go anywhere with you, you know.' And he added with a twinkle in his eye: 'I like dancing.'

'What do we do on Sunday?'

'We can go down to the harbour. And afterwards to some nice café, where it isn't too dear. We'll take some sandwiches with us for supper.'

'I've got an appointment on Sunday evening. You'll have to let me go for an hour. I promise I'll be back punctually.'

'You can go alone,' said the student. 'No one can stop you.'

'No,' said Kufalt; 'not alone. I want the people here to think I've been with you all the time.'

Petersen got out of his chair and began to pace up and down. Then he said awkwardly: 'No, my dear Herr Kufalt, I would rather not. It might cause unpleasantness.'

'Right,' said Kufalt. 'It wasn't an important date. In fact it wasn't a date at all. I only wanted to be sure about you. Goodnight, Herr Petersen.'

VIII

Kufalt sat at his typewriter, typing addresses. It was the second day he had done so. Yesterday he had done seven hundred, today he must do better. He was getting on fairly well, though he still made rather too many typing slips, but they passed muster among the many hundred addresses. Every hour or so Herr Mergenthal came in, reckoned up what had been done, and carried it away.

From where he sat Kufalt could not see Beerboom, but during the pauses when he was looking for the next address in his list, he heard him fidgeting with his papers. Beerboom had had a bad day again: three times he had jumped up and tried to escape from the typing room. He kept on hearing Berthold's voice. Mergenthal had then caught him, and pushed and persuaded him back to his place. But Beerboom would not do a thousand addresses that day either; his output diminished every day.

Seidenzopf then appeared and called to Kufalt. The latter got up angrily. No doubt he had not polished the floors properly, he had been in too much of a hurry to get back to work.

But this time it was not the floors. 'Herr Pastor Marcetus wishes to speak to you. Go inside.'

Kufalt knocked; a voice said: 'Come in,' and he went in.

Behind the desk, in the full light, sat a large, heavy man with fine white hair, ruddy face, fleshy nose, expressive mouth, clean shaven. Large white hands.

At the narrow end of the desk sat a lady with a shorthand pad, and near her stood a typewriter. In front of the desk a large chair was placed invitingly for the visitor, but Kufalt was not asked to sit down.

The pastor turned over some papers. Kufalt knew that parcel of papers, it had followed him; it was his file from the Central Prison.

The pastor took his time. Kufalt's 'Good morning' he answered with a brief growl.

Then he turned up one page in the file and said, without looking up: 'Your name is Willi – that is to say, Wilhelm Kufalt, bookkeeper by profession, sentenced to five years' imprisonment for embezzlement and aggravated forgery . . .'

'Yes,' said Kufalt.

'You are a man of good family. How did you come to this? Women? Drink? Gambling?'

It was a cold, businesslike tone in which he spoke to Kufalt. Kufalt knew that tone. The man at the desk had not looked at him for an instant; he did not need to look at Kufalt the man, he had the Kufalt file.

He knew that tone, he knew its echo, and he quivered: it was the old world, he thought it had been swallowed up in those five long years, but it went on just the same. Was it to go on for ever?

People like Seidenzopf or Beerboom could speak to him as they pleased, but this character here, he surely knew better, and he ought not address him in such a way. He's not allowed to.

Kufalt quivered, he felt his face grow pale and cold, but he replied in the same tone: 'Must this be discussed in the presence of the lady?'

Pastor Marcetus looked up for the first time. It was a slow, indifferent gaze that lingered on Kufalt's face.

'Fräulein Matzke is my secretary. Everything goes through her hands. She knows everything.'

'Is the lady an official?'

'What do you mean? Are you here to ask questions? The lady is in my employment.'

'I ask because I do not know whether private persons should be allowed to read my criminal records.'

'Fräulein Matzke is completely reliable.'

'All the same, I am not sure whether it is legal.'

'As you see, your prison authorities sent me your papers.'

'Yes, to you. Is the lady an ex-convict?'

The man behind the table started from his chair. 'Young man . . .' he began.

'Because if she were, I should not feel so uncomfortable.'

For a moment there was silence. Then the pastor said: 'Very well, please wait outside, Fräulein Matzke.'

The woman disappeared; Kufalt stood with bent head in front of the desk.

'Your prison chaplain's report on you is not favourable.'

'No,' replied Kufalt. 'That's because I want to leave the Church.'

'That has nothing to do with it.'

'Perhaps it has.'

Pastor Marcetus returned to the attack. 'And what Herr Seidenzopf tells me about your conduct and work does not sound very encouraging.'

'There is nothing against me.'

'You are continually making difficulties.'

'Continually? I once protested against working for a whole day without pay.'

'A man in your position should be humble.'

'With humble people it is not hard to be humble.'

'You are inefficient. Your handwriting is wretched.'

'I am not a writer.'

'And your typing leaves a great deal to be desired. You make a great many mistakes, and you get very little done.'

'I need practice after so long in prison.'

'That is a mere excuse. Typing is never forgotten, one drops into it again in a couple of hours.'

'Not after five years in prison.'

'Most prisoners are no good at their work. That is why they failed in life and took to bad ways.'

'Perhaps the Herr Pastor would like to look at my testimonials.'

'What for? I can see what you have done. You only find really first-class work among men convicted for crimes of passion. A man sentenced for a crime against property was never any use. Good work will find a market anywhere.'

'Yes, there are five million unemployed to prove that.'

The dialogue quickened as it continued. The fleshy pastor's genial air had vanished; he had flushed dark red. Kufalt's face was pale, it quivered and twitched.

After a pause to take breath the pastor said angrily: 'I am just wondering whether I had not better hand you over to the police at once . . .'

'Do, by all means,' said Kufalt in a fury. 'This is what is called Welfare Work for Discharged Prisoners.'

But something within him warned: there was some purpose in all this talk. He pondered; there was nothing against him. But – the man was no fool.

'In the six hours,' the pastor went on, 'between your discharge and your admission here you have already been guilty of dishonesty.'

'Do you mean I've stolen something? Well, the Herr Pastor would not tell a lie. Clergymen don't tell lies. But I must have been asleep when I did it.'

'You came in here,' said the pastor, fixing his eyes on Kufalt's face, 'with a hundred marks more than were issued to you at the Central Prison.'

Thirteen possibilities whirled in Kufalt's brain, and twelve he rejected, but meanwhile he heard himself say: 'Right. And of course I stole it. The only question is, from whom?'

'You refuse to tell me where this money came from?'

'Why should I? Since the Herr Pastor knows I stole it.'

'Then I shall call the police.' And he reached towards the telephone, but did not pick up the receiver, as Kufalt noted with satisfaction.

'Telephone, by all means, Herr Pastor,' said Kufalt. 'I don't mind. Your colleague in the Central Prison will be glad to tell you about the registered letter from my brother-in-law that was lost. He or the chief warder lost that letter between them. And he'll have to admit it if there's an inquiry.'

'What is all this?'

'Just a thing or two that happened, Herr Pastor. Not everything gets into those papers. Look, you tell them to have a look at the window bars in my cell, they'll find the letter tied to one of them.'

'I thought the letter was lost.'

'And when your colleague censors letters he should look inside the lining of the envelope. That's where the money was. My sister slipped it in; secretly.'

'What on earth is all this?' said the pastor irritably. 'It makes no sense.'

'Everything turns up again sometime,' observed Kufalt composedly. 'Though there's a good many would like to have stolen that money.'

'I don't understand a word. You don't suggest Herr Pastor Zumpe found it in the envelope? The whole affair is quite beyond me.'

'Call the police, and you'll soon find out. Or, why not write to Chaplain Zumpe? He'll tell you Kufalt is a most objectionable man, but this time he's coughed it up.'

'Coughed it up?'

'Told the truth, that means.'

'Very well, I'll write, and you'd better watch out if every word isn't true! I shall communicate with the police at once.'

'And I'll get another stretch for sure, Herr Pastor.'

The pastor shrugged his shoulders helplessly. 'Well, behave yourself in the meantime.'

Kufalt leaned over the desk. Now he was really angry, and no longer afraid.

He hissed into the face of the astonished clergyman: 'Next time you talk to an old lag, say good morning to him. Then, don't ask him in the presence of a pretty girl, if it was trouble over women that got him into jail. Then, offer him a chair. And don't vomit at him. We're used to being vomited at, Herr Pastor, it just cheers us up and makes us keen, it's the salt in our soup, Herr Pastor. Next time try the other key, minor not major, try a little kindness and goodwill. Good morning, Herr Pastor . . .'

'Stop!' roared the pastor. 'You can . . .'

'Leave the Home at once?' suggested Kufalt.

'Oh, get back to your work. You're none of you worth . . .'

'Of course we're none of us worth the pastor's trouble. Good morning, Herr Pastor.'

'Out with you. Tell Fräulein Matzke to come in.'

'Good morning, Herr Pastor.'

'Oh, all right, good morning.'

IX

That evening, Saturday evening, Petersen said suddenly at supper: 'I'm going for a bit of a walk. Does anyone feel like . . .?'

They had reached the stage when they first looked apprehensively at Seidenzopf, but he said genially: 'By all means. Such a delightful evening.'

And Frau Seidenzopf: 'But the house will be shut at ten punctually, and won't be opened for anyone.'

'Then we'll compare our watches,' said Petersen. 'It's twenty minutes past seven . . .'

And Beerboom: 'I'll only go if Herr Seidenzopf gives me some money. I won't go onto the street without it, you can't go anywhere with your pockets empty.'

'I'll soon settle up with these gentlemen, Herr Petersen.'

But their business was not so quickly settled. Kufalt stood at the corridor window and looked down into the twilit garden, while two voices across in the office rose and fell in conflict. The bushes melted into the dark background of the garden walls, the topmost branches of the trees were still tipped with sunlight. From within came Beerboom's pitiful imploring tones and Seidenzopf's booming bass. At last the door opened and Seidenzopf shouted: 'Get out of here, I'm sick of you! Not another penny. Come in, my dear Kufalt.'

Kufalt came in.

'Three working days to your credit. For cleaning the machine on Thursday – well, let us say fifty pfennigs . . .'

'We agreed on a mark.'

A steady look in response. 'Very well, one mark. Friday and Saturday, seven hundred addresses a day – very little, Herr Kufalt, and not at all well typed – six marks a thousand, that makes eight marks forty; total, nine marks forty. Five days' board and lodging at two marks fifty makes twelve marks fifty, so you owe us three marks fifty, which will be deducted from your deposit. All correct?'

'Not a bit of it,' said Kufalt, drawing a deep breath. 'There's more to it than that. How do you make out it's five days' board?'

'The day of arrival counts as a whole day.'

'But I only had supper.'

'That doesn't matter; those are our regulations and you signed them.'

'And the fifth day?'

'Is tomorrow, Sunday.'

'Do I have to pay in advance? Is that one of your regulations?'

'Then it won't come onto your next account. It's to your advantage.'

'So I don't earn as much as I spend here?'

'That will come in time, my young friend, it will all come in time.'

'It isn't possible to do much more typing than that.'

'Oh yes it is. Wait till you've been at it for six months.'

'I want some money for next week, by the way.'

Seidenzopf's brow clouded. 'It was only on Wednesday that I gave you three marks. How much more do you want?'

'Ten marks.'

'Certainly not. Pastor Marcetus would never allow it. Ten marks pocket money a week! That would be just an encouragement to extravagance.'

'Look, Herr Seidenzopf,' said Kufalt darkly. 'It's my money I'm asking for. How I loathe this place. You told me on Wednesday that I could have money at any time. And I'm sure you speak the truth, Herr Seidenzopf.'

'But what do you want the money for? Give me some sort of reason.'

'In the first place, stamps.'

'Stamps? What do you want stamps for? Your relations won't have anything to do with you – to whom do you propose to write?'

'I want to apply for jobs.'

'That's just money thrown away. Who's going to take you? Much better to wait until we know you and can recommend you. What else do you want money for?'

'I must have my laundry washed.'

'Ten marks for that? And what do you want washed? A shirt and a collar. You can perfectly well wear your underclothes for a fortnight, I don't change mine any more often. That will come to eighty pfennigs. What else do you want the money for?'

The voices grew louder and then sank again. After a quarter of an hour Kufalt was beaten, though twice he exploded and banged his fist on the table. He left the office with the sum of five marks.

'You'll soon be through with your savings if you go on like this, my dear Kufalt,' Seidenzopf called after him.

A luminous haze of twilight hung over the city. The soft radiance of the rows of street lamps glittered against the deep blue of the night sky. The streets were full of strolling people. They talked, in voices loud or soft; and now and again a girl laughed.

At Kufalt's side Petersen and Beerboom were engaged in eager conversation. Beerboom was full of bitterness and gall; he was nine marks thirty worse off. Petersen was trying to soothe him.

Kufalt sauntered along beside them. Among the trees in front of the cafés there were people sitting, eating and drinking. Bands were playing, spoons tinkled in saucers. The two others wondered whether they should go and sit in a café. But they could not afford it. Better go to the Hammer Park, where a band could be heard for nothing.

Beerboom was now intent on proving to Petersen that his life was completely ruined, and that it would be just as well to put an end to it at once; while Petersen tried to demonstrate the contrary.

A dark mass rose up before them, the air grew cool and moist – trees, tall trees: the Hammer Park.

They walked along the dimly lit paths, populous with strolling couples. Then they found themselves in the centre of the park, near a brightly lit café. A band was playing in a shell-shaped pavilion, there was an array of crowded tables. Those who did not eat or drink were excluded by a rope barrier.

The three stood for a while among the throng and listened. They could not be prevented from listening, though this would have been done if possible. The onlookers were a cheerful crowd, girls hung about in little groups, young men came up and teased and chased them amid much giggling and merriment. Kufalt was almost knocked over by a bevy of young people.

He longed to get back to the darker paths, but the others wanted to stay. So he pointed to a path and said: 'I'll sit down somewhere over there. Come and fetch me later on.'

He found a bench in the darkness, on which only one couple were sitting. He dropped onto one end of it, rolled a cigarette, leaned back comfortably and gazed into vacancy.

From time to time the night breeze stirred the branches; there was a faint rustle far away which, as it approached, dissolved into a thousand tiny sounds that passed and were lost again in a distant rustle.

The man and the woman on the bench were talking. Kufalt listened vaguely. There was talk of a garden, of an old mother, who was growing more and more trying . . . They were not lovers, Kufalt thought. He wished he had a girl with whom he could sit and talk. But what could he say to her?

Many people passed him by, some of them hand in hand. Not even in prison had Kufalt realized how utterly isolated he now was. He was excluded from all such life as this – would he ever get back to it? Of all that had happened to him in those last five years, he would never be able to speak.

The girl got up and walked up and down. 'It's chilly. I feel so shivery,' she said. The man did not reply. She used the sibilant Hamburg 's' – just then she came into the light of the lamp, a charming, lissom creature, with oval face and fair hair. She slipped again into shadow.

'Let's go,' said the girl.

The man got up.

Petersen and Beerboom appeared. 'We'll go this way,' said Kufalt, and followed the pair. 'Was the music nice?'

The others talked; Kufalt kept his eye on his couple. 'No, we'll go that way. I've got a wonderful sense of direction. I'll take you straight home.'

'But we're going in the wrong direction!'

'No we're not. We'll turn off in a minute. Will you bet I'm taking you the right way?'

'How much?'

'Ten cigarettes.'

'Right. You're a witness, Beerboom.'

It was not altogether easy to follow the couple without attracting their attention. Kufalt kept on the other side of the street and from time to time made remarks that were intended to prove his active sense of direction. 'No, we'd better turn the corner here. Now straight on again – no, better turn to the left.'

And Beerboom was much impressed.

Beyond a railway viaduct the pair suddenly dived down a street to the left, and by the time Kufalt had managed to induce his companions to take this most improbable turning, they had disappeared into the entrance to some house.

Kufalt stopped, and drew a deep breath. 'Well, now I'm lost. Where on earth are we? What's this street called?'

'You're good,' said Petersen. 'Hey, you're going right at last . . . This is the Marienthaler Strasse, and we'll be at the Home in a quarter of an hour.'

And after a glance at his watch, he added: 'Oh Lord, we've only got nine minutes. We'll have to leg it!'

'It can't be as bad as all that,' said Kufalt, running. 'They'll wait five minutes for us.'

'They chuck a man out if he's three minutes late. They won't let him in that night, and next morning he'll have to fetch his stuff and clear out.'

'And we can't afford to get a bed from a girl,' panted Beerboom. 'Oh God, I'm done in, do let's walk for a bit.'

'Nonsense,' snapped Kufalt. 'If you're there, it'll be all right, Herr Petersen.'

'I shan't make any difference,' gasped Petersen. 'I'm only of use as a sort of label. Come on, Beerboom, stick at it. Only four minutes more.'

At the front door there was a violent dispute with Minna as to whether it was one minute past ten, or ten precisely. In any case, she promised to report them to Herr Seidenzopf.

X

In the morning – it was now Sunday – they had to go to church, for the House Regulations stipulated that every inmate had to attend the service of his denomination. Then Kufalt and Petersen played chess until lunch, while Beerboom pressed his trousers with a flat board over the back of a chair. When they went out in the afternoon he had two creases side by side, and he grew quite tearful over the way he always made a mess of everything.

The sight of the harbour cheered them up, and for a while they stumbled along the quays. Then they grew tired. Beerboom complained of hunger and thirst. They didn't get enough to eat – such wretched portions – you got more in prison . . .

They found their way into the gardens by the Bismarck statue, and sat down under some trees. There was a mineral water stall nearby, and Beerboom drank lemonade and raspberryade, ate his supper of sandwiches, bemoaned his lot for a while and went to sleep.

The other two, tired and content, looked sleepily at the stream of passers-by, and now and again exchanged a few whispered remarks about Beerboom, who was clearly heading for trouble. 'But Seidenzopf won't listen, and Marcetus thinks he knows all about discharged prisoners' welfare. It's no use talking to him.'

And they went on watching the passing throng. From time to time they propped up Beerboom when he looked like slipping off the bench.

When he woke up it was already nearly six. He was furious with them for having let him sleep so long; at ten o'clock they would have to be back in the Home of Peace, that was the place to sleep, not here in the gardens.

Then he bought himself a sausage and potato salad, and finished up with a cream puff. After which he stood up and said: 'Let's go.'

The Reeperbahn and Kleine and Grosse Freiheit quarters would help them through an hour. But they had no money, and Petersen also explained that he could not be seen in public with them in such places, or he would lose his job. They might perhaps look in at a café-concert near the Central Station; but they must say nothing about it.

Finally they sat down in a half-empty café. It was the unlucky hour between seven and eight when the band takes a rest. Beerboom cursed and drank beer, Kufalt dreamed and drank a pot of coffee, Petersen's quick eyes were busy among the girls. He drank tea.

As Kufalt was rolling a cigarette, Petersen whispered: 'I don't know if you can do that here. Perhaps you wouldn't mind buying some. We might attract attention. I'll let you off the fifty pfennigs of our bet.'

'All right,' said Kufalt, and got up. 'I'll go across to the station and get them. I won't pay what they'll charge for them here.'

And Kufalt went. He left his hat on its peg. It was just before eight. When he got outside he asked where the Town Hall Square was: round the corner, down the Mönckebergstrasse, barely five minutes away.

Kufalt ran.

There was the Town Hall Square; the clock was just striking eight. He looked round for the statue, and the horse's tail. Not a sign of either.

He asked. 'Yes, it used to be here; but it's been moved. How long is it since you were here?'

Kufalt walked round the square; he walked across it and then back again. He kept on thinking he saw Batzke twenty metres away. Sometimes he caught up with the man, and then it was always someone else, sometimes the man disappeared; perhaps it had been Batzke. What's more, he could not picture to himself what Batzke really looked like; he kept on visualizing a man in blue prison togs and slippers.

The clock on the town hall showed the quarter, and then the half hour. Kufalt persisted in his search. Batzke would come, he would surely come. He would not go back to the Home. That petty nauseating life, those fights over pfennigs, the quarrels with Seidenzopf, the torments at the typewriter, Beerboom, Petersen, Marcetus . . . was that freedom, for which he had waited five long years?

Freedom! Oh God! To do or not to do – just as he pleased . . .

It was after nine when he got back to the café. There was nothing for it, he must return to the Home. Well, he would endure it, he must wait just a little while longer . . . If Petersen dared say anything . . . ! But Petersen was dancing with great enthusiasm and had no notion how long Kufalt had been away. When he came back to the table he began to rave about a girl in blue, who surely must be a better class of girl.

Beerboom drank a second glass of beer and discussed the question whether he should apply to Seidenzopf for more money the next day. On the one hand . . . on the other . . .

Ten minutes after half past nine. 'Now we really must go, or we shan't make it.'

When they got outside Petersen said anxiously: 'We must take a tram.'

And Beerboom: 'You'll have to pay. It's because of your silly dancing . . .'

In the carriage Beerboom suddenly turned yellow and white: 'I feel so ill.'

He staggered to the platform, and was promptly sick.

The conductor was furious. 'Now then, you can't do that here. Get off at once!'

Petersen was in despair. 'Look, we shall have to take a taxi. Herr Beerboom, pull yourself together a bit, don't mess up the taxi.'

Beerboom gurgled.

And when they were in the taxi, in hurried gasps – 'A handkerchief, quick – quick – your handkerchief. Oh, be quick! There! Wipe it up!'

And with a sudden burst of tears: 'What can be the matter with me! I haven't drunk anything! I used to be able to take any amount. Oh God, oh God, see what the bloody swine have made of me . . . can't even have a bit of fun now . . .'

They got back at two minutes past ten. Father Seidenzopf opened the door with a sepulchral countenance, ignored their greeting, and looked sharply at Beerboom.

'Herr Petersen, will you please come to my room. After you have seen your charges up to bed. I wish to speak to you.'

XI

Two weeks, three weeks passed; Kufalt sat in the typing room and typed. He did not get on as quickly as he had expected, and he never reached a thousand addresses. Sometimes it was the fault of the address list, and sometimes the fault was his own.

He woke up in a mood of gloom. Then every sound irritated

him; Beerboom's incessant muttering and whimpering at his back nearly drove him crazy. He sat at his typewriter, but he did not type, he wondered whether he would get up and give Beerboom one in the jaw. It became an obsession; he just sat and listened out for Beerboom! Should he? And yet he had to go on typing.

But it seemed so purposeless to go on frantically tapping out addresses, only to reduce his reserve by five or ten marks at every weekly reckoning with Seidenzopf. Would it go on like this for ever? There were people who had been coming to the typing room for years.

Mergenthal, who was in charge of the typing room, was not a bad man. He often lent a hand when work was urgent. Then he gave away his addresses, mostly to Beerboom, but Kufalt got a hundred once. And he did not mind a little talking provided Seidenzopf was nowhere about. On those occasions Mergenthal went outside. Perhaps he listened, but he did not repeat what he heard.

'How much have you done?' Maack asked Kufalt.

'Four hundred. No, not quite. Three hundred and eighty. Oh God, how I loathe the job! And I do less every day, not more.'

'Yes,' said Maack, and nodded; he had a keen, pale face. 'Yes. That's what mostly happens at the start. It gets worse and worse.'

'Are you . . . ?' asked Kufalt, and stopped.

'Yes,' nodded Maack with a smile. 'So are most of us here. There may be one or two that are just out of a job. No one knows.'

'Has Mergenthal been in prison too?' whispered Kufalt.

'Mergenthal?' Maack appeared to reflect. But perhaps he merely did not like the question. 'I don't know for certain.'

And he went on typing.

Beerboom had another outburst. The evening before, he had delivered some addresses on the handcart, and heard what the firm paid per thousand. 'Twelve marks. Twelve marks! And they give us five or six. Criminals, robbers, exploiters . . .'

But the door opened and Mergenthal reappeared. 'Beerboom, get on with your work. You must not talk. You know if Frau Seidenzopf or Fräulein Minna hears you . . .'

'Fräulein Minna!' sneered Beerboom. 'Did you ever! Fräulein

Minna! That bitch of a skivvy! We have to crawl, and scribble all day so that the women can soak up the rest. They get twelve marks and give us six – well, if that's justice!'

'Herr Beerboom, you must be quiet. I must not listen to you, I shall have to report you to Herr Seidenzopf . . .'

Finally Beerboom calmed down and Mergenthal did not report him. But Minna had been eavesdropping again, and Seidenzopf learnt of it from her.

'I shall hand you over to the police, Beerboom. Your probation will be cancelled. Either or. That is my last word.'

And next day he was arraigned before the pastor. Beerboom was reduced to a pulp; his whining protests were thundered down. He was henceforward to be kept strictly to his task.

That day his total output was sixty-eight addresses.

Kufalt too was again summoned before Pastor Marcetus. 'I understand you are still here?'

'I suppose Herr Pastor Zumpe wrote about the money?'

'Pastor Zumpe?' A negative wave of the hand. 'I did not follow up the matter. You wrote to your brother-in-law?'

'Yes.'

'Your brother-in-law wants to know whether we are satisfied with you.'

'And are you?'

'You often come back late.'

'Always in Herr Petersen's charge.'

The pastor pondered. 'Is your brother-in-law a man of means?'

'He has a factory.'

'Ah; a factory. You asked that all your effects should be sent here. That is of course impossible, we would be responsible if anything went astray.'

'Is that what's annoying you?'

The pastor did in fact look very annoyed. But he expressed himself in more general terms. 'I don't understand the attitude of the young people of today. And yet we are of some service to you.'

'So you'll say you're satisfied with me?'

'Your work is quite insufficient.'

'Let me leave this place, Herr Pastor, and come to the typing room every day like the others.'

The pastor shook his head disapprovingly. 'Too soon. Much too soon. The transition must come gradually.'

'It says in the House Regulations that not more than four weeks are to be spent in the Home.'

'In general, it says, in general.'

'Am I a special case?'

'What are you going to live on outside?'

'On my pay from here.'

'But you don't earn four marks a day. No, no, you have something else in mind.'

'What else?'

But the pastor would have no more of it. He was tired or irritated, or possibly bored. 'It is for me to ask questions, Herr Kufalt. No, I shall write to your brother-in-law that you had better stay with us for the present. In July, perhaps. No, you must go now. And – good morning.'

XII

One Friday at supper Seidenzopf announced in a genial tone: 'Herr Petersen, on Sunday I want my young friends to observe the beauties of nature round the walls of Hamburg. I propose to give you leave off for the whole day. You can set out early in the morning, and, as an exception, you need not be back in the evening until eleven or even twelve o'clock. What do you say to that, my friends?'

And like a shot Petersen replied: 'I would propose an excursion to Blankenese, Herr Seidenzopf. Perhaps we might even swim. And then perhaps a theatre in the evening.'

'Very nice. Excellent,' said Herr Seidenzopf. 'And I will present each of our young friends with five marks out of the Home funds, not to be deducted from pay or reserve.'

'Hooray!' said Beerboom.

'And you, my dear Kufalt, why are you so silent?'

'It'll be very nice, of course. But if we're out for the whole day, what with fares and the theatre, five marks won't be much.'

'I'm sure it can be managed. You will take bread and butter with you, plenty of bread and butter.'

'Five marks are no good,' began Beerboom too. 'You must give us at least another five, Herr Seidenzopf.'

The usual quarrel started. Kufalt pondered.

'Watch out, pal,' said Maack next day. 'I don't like the look of this. There's a jubilee celebration at the Home tomorrow.'

'Thanks, mate,' said Kufalt, and pondered still more deeply.

On Sunday morning the three sat on the shelving beach above the Elbe and contemplated the river, the ships and the countryside. It was oppressively hot, the motor cars sped by in thick clouds of dust and crowds of holidaymakers plodded along every road, sweating and complaining of the heat.

'This is a filthy place,' growled Kufalt. 'It all stinks of sweat and petrol. Let's move on.'

'Where to?' protested Petersen. 'It will be just the same everywhere today.'

'Oh, we'll find somewhere.'

What they found at last was a large overgrown garden.

'Stop, this'll do,' cried Kufalt. 'We can crawl through the fence. It's sure to be cool and quiet inside.'

'But we aren't allowed inside,' said Petersen.

'Of course we aren't,' laughed Kufalt. 'If you don't want to come, you wait outside till we get back. You'll come, Beerboom?'

Beerboom was willing, and Kufalt was already crawling through the wire fence. Beerboom followed, but got caught on the spikes of the wire.

'Hurry up, man,' urged Kufalt; 'there are people coming.'

Petersen, frantic with apprehension, pulled the wire away with a jerk, there was a tearing sound, Beerboom groaned, Petersen crawled after him – and they all three plunged into the bushes.

'I'm sure my trousers are split,' wailed Beerboom. 'It's the sort of thing that always happens to me.'

'They can be mended all right,' Kufalt comforted him. 'Besides it's on the inside of the leg where no one can see, and it'll keep you nice and cool in this heat.'

'And who's going to pay for it? Oh God, oh God, if only Minna would do a bit of sewing for us! When I was in prison I always wanted to be put in the tailor's shop.'

'We really shouldn't have crawled through that hedge, Kufalt. If Pastor Marcetus hears of it . . .'

'Of course we shouldn't. Look there . . .'

They stood behind some outlying bushes and peered into a large orchard, where an old man in a yellow straw hat was walking from beehive to beehive, smoking an enormous pipe. Masses of cottage-garden flowers were in bloom.

'Isn't it lovely and quiet and cool? This is the place; we'll stop here and have a bit of a snooze. God, how lovely and quiet it is!'

They settled themselves; Petersen laid his head on his arm, Kufalt squatted down and waited, looking at Beerboom, who had taken off his trousers and was whimpering softly to himself. However, Beerboom made a cushion of his trousers, laid his head on it and went to sleep.

It was quite still, not a breath of wind in the branches of the trees. The air seemed to be humming with the heat, and the buzzing of the bees in the bee-garden rose and fell.

Kufalt sat up cautiously and looked at his sleeping companions.

He stood up quietly and looked again, holding his breath. Then he slipped across the grass, ran towards the hedge, and as he crawled through the gap by which they had entered, he came out right into a throng of day trippers.

They stopped and eyed him with suspicion. 'Bah!' said he contemptuously, and dashed in wild leaps down the steep slope to the steamer quay.

The next steamer left for Hamburg in a quarter of an hour. The main thing was that they should not miss him before that time. He drew a deep breath of relief when the boat put off from the bridge.

Three hours later Kufalt turned up hot and breathless in the Apfelstrasse. When he caught sight of the Home of Peace, he gave a soft and thoughtful whistle. The Hamburg and the German flags were waving from the flagstaff. Garlands had been hung above the door, in front of which were two great motor coaches.

'The swine,' he muttered; 'the dirty swine. They just wanted us out of the way.'

The door was open, and along the path and up the steps that he had so often scrubbed a handsome red runner had been laid. On the right, in the office, could be heard the murmur of many voices.

He slipped softly upstairs, and opened the bedroom door. He stopped and gasped.

The windows, usually so forbiddingly bare, were hung with bright, inviting muslin curtains; and on the sill stood flowerpots with blossoming plants. Here too was a red runner on the floor. The table was covered with a cloth, a nice bright cheerful cloth. And there were pictures on the walls – pretty lithographs, big and small. And the beds . . .

'Oh God, the beds . . .' whispered Kufalt, quite overcome.

The beds, one and all, were white and spotless, not a sign of the blue-checked prison cotton; fine white linen sheets.

'Well I never!' said Kufalt.

The murmur came nearer and began to mount the stairs.

Kufalt went through the door into his own room. He looked about him for a way of escape, but there was none; he would run right into the arms of the approaching visitors.

Near the table he noticed two comfortable chairs, which had apparently grown out of the linoleum since the morning. But he did not dare sit on them; he wandered helplessly up and down this model bedchamber. Then, when the door of the adjacent room (where Beerboom slept) opened, he sat down resolutely on his own bed.

In the next room, footsteps and a murmur of talk.

Someone coughed and a high feminine voice said: 'How charming!'

And a deeper, masculine one: 'I'm afraid you spoil them.'

'No,' – it was the voice of Pastor Marcetus. 'No, ladies and gentlemen, we do not spoil them, we try to accustom them to an orderly and self-respecting life. The ex-prisoner is meant to find life pleasant here; we want subsequently to inoculate him, so to speak, with a sense of horror and disgust at prison life. When he again falls into temptation, we hope he will think of his pleasant room in the Home of Peace – and the bleak and comfortless cell will seem doubly dreadful.'

The ex-prisoner on his bed, with his head in his hands, thought of the room that he had left early that morning: the beds bare, with their hideous grey mattresses, no curtains, no pictures, no carpets, no comfortable chairs, no flowers . . . In the next room, the orchestrator of this twenty-five years' jubilee said in answer to a question: 'No, no, it's as much as we can do to get the men to leave the Home. You, as patrons and contributors to the Home, know how much support it needs. We are constantly having to appeal to your charity. And we must not limit your generosity to a few. So many come and knock at our door. A month is the longest period for which we can keep any one man. By that time he is acclimatized, and we get Herr Petersen, one of our welfare workers, to find him a room outside. We keep our eye on him, of course, he goes on working with us . . .'

'Is the Home full?' asked a voice.

'At the moment? I cannot exactly say. Pretty nearly so, in any case. But we do not want to provide any more beds. We wish it to preserve the character of a family home. That door leads to a second bedroom, exactly like this one . . .'

Kufalt kept his head in his hands. He heard the footsteps approach. He had intended to remain sitting on his bed, but he got up. Fifteen, twenty people crowded through the door, and all looked at him. Among them was Pastor Marcetus, but Kufalt avoided his eye. He assumed a grave, obsequious expression, as he used to do at cell inspections, and bowed.

A few of the visitors actually bowed in response.

'Herr Kufalt,' said Pastor Marcetus, after a long silence. He cleared his throat and began again in a lighter tone. 'My dear Kufalt, you are not with the party?' And turning to his audience, he added: 'As I have explained, our guests are making a little trip down the Elbe in celebration of this day.'

'I felt ill,' muttered Kufalt. 'It must have been the sun.'

'Did Herr Petersen send you back?'

'Not exactly.'

'Ah. Indeed. I understand . . .' To his audience again: 'Another similar bedroom, you see. Bright . . . quiet . . . just like the one next door.' To Kufalt once more: 'I'm afraid we shall have to disturb you three or four more times, my dear Herr Kufalt. Herr Seidenzopf and Herr Mergenthal are each taking parties round. And I do not know whether Fräulein Matzke has finished yet. I hope you will soon feel better.'

And he turned to go.

The visitors were still looking at Kufalt; perhaps they thought that the only ex-prisoner who had been introduced to them had not been properly noticed. A large man, with heavy lips and the smooth, fleshy face of a parson, said:

'How do you get on here? Do you like it?'

Pastor Marcetus dropped his shoulders in a gesture of resignation.

'I like it now very much,' said Kufalt politely. 'It is now very nice here.'

'And the work?'

'I like that too,' said Kufalt, with a gentle and submissive smile.

'We must all work,' said the large parson, and laughed. 'We aren't all lilies of the field, unfortunately, eh? Isn't that so?' There was some applauding laughter. 'And how long have you been with our brother Marcetus?'

'More than three weeks.'

'Then you will soon be leaving the Home?'

'Yes, unfortunately I shall have to go soon.'

Pastor Marcetus looked meaningfully at Kufalt: 'Herr Kufalt is to leave us at the beginning of next week. He wants to live outside; and we are allowing him to do so. But he will go on working here, until we find him a good permanent position.'

Kufalt bowed.

'Well, that's splendid,' said the large parson. 'Keep your spirits up, my young friend. Do you know that your patron here, our dear colleague Marcetus, has been given an honorary degree for his services to you all? Doctor honoris causa!'

'I heartily congratulate Herr Pastor Marcetus,' said Kufalt, and bowed again.

Herr Pastor Marcetus stepped forward and gave Kufalt his hand. 'I thank you, my dear Kufalt. And as I have already said, we hope very soon to find you a good position, worthy of your great abilities.'

Kufalt bowed; the visitors departed. Kufalt stood by the window and looked down into the forbidden garden of peace. He whistled softly; once again he was extremely well pleased with himself.

4

The Road to Freedom

I

The confidence that Pastor Marcetus had placed in his protégé's good sense was completely justified by Kufalt the moment the last visitors left the Home of Peace. He couldn't have shown more zeal in helping Minna and the ecstatic Frau Seidenzopf take the curtains down, put the pictures away in a chest, roll up the carpets and carry them up to the attic. Then he and Minna laid the white linen, all still nice and clean, back in the linen cupboard, and when they had both hurried across the street to the gardener to return the borrowed pot plants, and when all traces of the well-heeled clerical and charitable visitors had been removed from the freshly polished floors, the rooms resumed their aspect of barren austerity that made them seem to the ex-convict so indistinguishable from prison.

Then, when Petersen and Beerboom arrived, rather breathless, at half past six, there was of course a pleasant little spat with the student about Kufalt's desertion. But the latter was in no mind to have anything more said to him.

'I've got something to say to *you*, Petersen,' he observed. 'When you say you were anxious about me, that's all rubbish; you don't care a thing about me.'

'I beg your pardon!'

'You needn't protest. Not a word. You are only anxious about your job. All this talk about your being our friend and adviser is rubbish. If you were on our side, you would be against Marcetus and Seidenzopf, and they'd give you the sack.'

'Really! That's not true. I can make things easier for you.'

'Oh, yes, you can lick the swines' boots. How is it, when the typing room gets twelve marks for the addresses, we only get six, and sometimes even only four and a half?'

'I have nothing to do with the money side.'

'But that's the first thing you ought to see to. Every week you hear the row with Seidenzopf over the accounts, and how excited they all get, and you say you have nothing to do with it. And you know just as well as I do that it's madness to make Beerboom sit for nine or ten hours in an office, he's getting madder every day . . .'

'Yes,' wailed Beerboom. 'I certainly am.'

'. . . But our friend and adviser isn't going to risk speaking up.'

'Beerboom must get gradually used to regular work.'

'And I went into a tobacco shop yesterday, about ten doors away, to buy half a dozen Junos, and the girl in the shop actually said to me: "Do you come from there too?" "From where?" I said. "Oh, you know," she said. "Is it true that that dark man in your place is a murderer? He asked me whether I would like to go out with him, or whether I was too proud to go out with a murderer. I would have gone," she said, "but Mother wouldn't let me."'

'Oh God,' whimpered Beerboom. 'I only said it because . . .'

'You shut your mouth, Beerboom. You just want to make yourself interesting. But why don't you know all this, Petersen, you – our friend and adviser, eh? You ought to have spoken to Marcetus long ago, about – you know, going soft in the head, and so on. It says in the brochure that you sleep with us, and live just as we do. Then why do you have a separate room and proper sheets, and why don't you polish your floor yourself instead of letting us do it for you . . . ?'

'Why talk to me like this?' said Petersen angrily. 'If you know all that, then you know I've got no influence here.'

'Because you give yourself airs! Because you swank about being anxious about me. Because you're no better than a spy. Because the sight of you makes me sick. Because I wish to God you'd leave me in peace!'

'Herr Kufalt . . .'

'Oh, go away.'

'But please listen, Herr Kufalt!'

'Oh, for God's sake, get out!'

'You are unjust.'

'Do you expect me to be just? Me! Goodnight all.' And he departed to the bedroom, slamming the door in a fury.

But he was not really in a fury at all, he was really jubilant and chanted to himself: 'Freedom! Free! At last!'

And then it was morning once again, a fresh and radiant morning in mid-June. Kufalt had watched the slow coming of the dawn, then he turned over for a little while and closed his eyes; and when he again looked at the window, it was already quite light, the sun was shining and the birds were twittering.

Then, as Father Seidenzopf hurried past his table on his usual morning round, Kufalt said in a low voice: 'I want to stop two hours earlier today, Herr Seidenzopf.'

'Yes, yes,' said Woolly Teddy, impatiently.

'I want to get a room outside.'

'Eh? What? Herr Petersen takes rooms for our people.'

'But not for me,' said Kufalt, eyeing him fixedly.

'Um – um . . . very well, then,' muttered Seidenzopf, and bustled on.

From a neighbouring table Maack glanced at Kufalt, nodded, and went on tapping. Kufalt hammered on his machine: 'Free,' he thought; 'free at last . . .'

In the afternoon he went out. He promptly found his way to the Marienthaler Strasse; indeed he remembered it quite well. But through which doorway had she disappeared? He had not noticed very clearly that night, and now he was uncertain. It was so important that he should find the right house; he had so often thought of that lovely little oval face.

At last he decided to trust to luck, and chose a house at random. 'May I see the room?'

The plump little white-haired woman showed it to him. ('Could this be her mother?')

'Have you any other lodgers?'

'No, none. There's only my daughter living with me, I'm a widow. My daughter goes to work.'

'What price is the room?'

'Thirty marks with morning coffee. We don't clean shoes.'

'That doesn't matter.' Kufalt glanced round. 'Very well, I'll take the room. I'll pay ten marks down. And here are six marks more. My luggage may be coming by goods train in a day or two; please pay the carriage. I'll move in on the first. OK then . . .'

He looked round again, and said suddenly, with unexpected cordiality: 'I hope we shall be good friends, Frau Wendland. Good evening.'

Everything passed off with disquieting ease. That night as he was falling asleep he had pitched battles with Woolly Teddy over his account: 'You have no right to keep my money any longer, it's what I've earned . . .'

And now Seidenzopf just paid him his money down on the table. He did not even offer any comment, it seemed the most natural thing in the world that Kufalt should leave the Home of Peace. The sole remaining inmate, Beerboom, helped him carry his things down.

They walked through Hamburg in the evening light, and Kufalt said to Beerboom: 'Well, you're the next.'

Beerboom happened to be feeling cheerful that day: 'Of course, they can't keep me for ever.'

'I'm so excited to see whether my things have come,' said Kufalt.

Yes, they were there, two boxes and a large trunk, waiting in the bright room.

'The money wasn't enough,' whined the old lady. 'I had to pay three marks ten more.'

'I'll pay you back all right. Now have you by any chance got pliers and a chisel, so that I can open the boxes . . . ? Haven't you? Nothing? But you must have something of the sort in the house? Really not? Then where's the nearest ironmonger's? Right. Ten minutes to seven, I must run. Do you mind waiting, Beerboom, I'll only be a few minutes.'

He ran. His cheeks glowed. Good God in heaven, two boxes, a large trunk, a suitcase, two cardboard boxes – and only six weeks ago his abode had been a bare cell, with no possessions at all. He was wildly exultant: 'This is great!' he said to himself. 'I wonder what can be in the boxes, I'm *so* excited!'

With a hammer and pliers in one hand and a chisel in the other, he dashed up the steps again. He rang . . . he heard whispers behind the door, a whining elderly voice and a shrill young one ('that's not oval-face's voice!'); he rang again, the whispering increased; he rang again, but this time hard.

'So you've come at last; where's my friend? Gone? What do you mean, gone? What's the matter with you? What's up, eh?'

'Oh please,' said the old woman in a quavering stutter; 'please move your things out at once. I'll give you all your money back.'

Kufalt was dumbfounded. 'Move my things out? But why?'

'It's my son,' she stammered; 'my son-in-law – we need the room, he's coming back at once.'

'You need the room? But you've let the room to me.'

'Oh please, do move out!'

'Of course I can't! At this time in the evening . . .'

Then a shrill female voice was heard behind the door: 'If he doesn't go at once, we'll send for the police. We can't let rooms to the likes of him. The friend himself said he was a murderer.' A pause; then raising her voice almost to a shriek: 'And you're an ex-convict too!'

Kufalt stood for a moment, then stepped quickly towards the door. He noticed that he was standing by a mirror. So that was he. There he stood. Darkness was already falling; but there he stood. Odd how the hammer began to quiver in his hand, and his arm swung upwards as though in preparation for a blow. He was trembling with agitation, which was natural enough – he supposed.

Suddenly he saw – also in the mirror – Frau Wendland's dark and anguished eyes and her snow-white face.

'Right,' said Kufalt, taking a tighter grip of his hammer. 'I'll fetch my things away in an hour at the latest. Now give me back my rent. And be quick!'

It was nine o'clock in the evening.

Kufalt stood beside a box wondering whether he dared break it open. Perhaps he would disturb his neighbours, or the landlady. He didn't want another row, that sort of thing got about. Well, if it came out, he would have to move again; indeed he would probably have to shift his lodging a good many times; it would always come out somehow.

He longed to know what was in that box, but he did not dare open it. He did not dare. He stood there; the windows were open, the room was pleasantly airy whereas the Home of Peace had always been like a cell. Now he had plenty of air, a large open window and a white bed. But he did not dare open that box.

It was a large, lean woman who let him the room. A working woman, also a widow, Frau Behn, the Widow Behn. Twenty-five marks, and the room was spotless. A toil-worn woman with an unattractive face, a rather ravaged, evil face, lean and greedy hands and gnarled fingers.

'I'll stay here,' he said to himself. 'I'll stay here quietly for a bit. She actually put a bunch of lilac in the room while I was out fetching my things . . . I hope I shall keep my temper when it happens again. It was unfortunate the girl had such a shrill voice, and I had the hammer in my hand. Ah well, it turned out all right this time.'

There was a knock at the door.

'Come in.'

The door opened. A girl stood in the doorway.

'Would you like a cup of tea?'

She came in, carrying a tray; the spoon clinked faintly against the saucer.

She looked charming and alert, with fair hair and an oval face . . .

'I am Frau Behn's daughter. I hope you will be comfortable here.' And she gave him her hand.

'Thank you,' he said, and looked at her.

'We don't know whether you take milk or lemon in your tea?'

'Yes, thank you,' he said. 'Very nice, very nice.'

She looked at him and blushed faintly. She set her lower lip more firmly against her upper lip. 'Or don't you take anything in it?' she said with a sudden laugh.

'No, nothing at all, of course,' he said, laughing too. Then he looked at her again. 'It's a very nice room,' he said.

He must not go too far yet: 'Have you got all you want?' she asked. 'Mother has gone to bed. Goodnight.'

'Goodnight.'

II

When Kufalt got to the typing room next morning, Beerboom was already crouching in his place, scrawling addresses, with his shoulders hunched up to his ears.

Kufalt gripped him from behind and pulled him up. The tearful, imploring look was again upon his face; Beerboom was unhappy because everything he did went wrong.

'Beerboom, you idiot,' said Kufalt, ignoring the sacrosanct decorum of the typing room. 'If it ever again occurs to you to tell my landlady or anyone in the house that you're a murderer – I'll pick you up and . . .'

He shook him.

Beerboom's body sagged in his grasp, and swayed from side to side as though its bones had melted.

'Psst!' said Mergenthal. 'Herr Kufalt, I really must ask you . . .'

'You're an idiot,' said Kufalt to Beerboom. 'But if you were ten times an idiot, I'd set about you . . . !'

'I won't ever do it again,' wailed Beerboom. 'Oh God, how wretched I am. She was so sympathetic, I thought she felt for us. She asked why our faces were so yellow, and said she supposed we worked in a chemical factory, and so I . . .'

'Idiot!' said Kufalt, giving Beerboom a final shove, and sat down. 'You won't mess up things for me again. I'll kill you, understand that!'

'And now silence, please,' said Mergenthal, 'or I'll call Herr Seidenzopf.'

Beerboom sighed deeply and went on writing. And Kufalt set to work. 'He won't give me away again,' he thought. 'But there are so many ways it might happen. At the police station they might drop a hint to the landlady. Or there'll be a letter forwarded from the prison. Or an inquiry about me . . .' And Kufalt too sighed deeply.

But later, in the midday break – generously extended by Seidenzopf, though Petersen was deputed to go with him – on his visit to a store to buy what was needed for his bachelor establishment, his cheerful mood surfaced again.

'There. Plate, cup, meat dish. What else does a bachelor want, miss?'

'A cheese cover?'

'Cheese cover? Perhaps. What does a cheese cover cost? No. But a butter dish, miss, I wonder you didn't think of that . . .'

Between the three of them a butter dish was bought. But a furnished room is not a larder, it is often hot – what about this earthenware water-cooler . . . ?

'Very dear. And does it really work . . . ?'

The student explained: 'It's based on the principle of evaporation, you know, Kufalt. You must put it in the hottest sunshine, and it gets all the cooler, do you see? The ancient Egyptians . . .'

'Very well, miss; and what else is needed for a bachelor household? Nothing? All complete? Then make out the bill . . . I think the china's really very pretty with that red line round it . . .'

'If I were you,' said the shop girl, looking up from her receipt book with a sly quick smile, 'if I were you I would buy two of everything now . . .'

'Two?' said Kufalt. 'Two butter dishes?'

'No,' she laughed. 'Not butter dishes. But plates and cups. One isn't always going to be alone.'

'I guess not,' laughed Kufalt. 'You ought to know.' And he gazed meditatively at the soft white bosom just visible above the yoke of the black dress.

'I do,' she said, with a half-embarrassed laugh. 'And later on you might not get the same pattern. And it ought all to match.'

'Yes, it certainly ought,' agreed Kufalt, with his eyes still on that breathing bosom.

In his cell, during the five years, the girls of his earlier days had been used up. They had melted away, they had been so often reduced to the simplest physical details that they had become merged into each other. First they became all alike, then they dissolved in a mist – hair and flesh – nothing more . . .

Now, on this glorious June afternoon, as Kufalt put envelope after envelope into his machine, tapped his addresses and flicked them out again, life cheered up once more; already two girls to think about: one with an oval face, and another with a white, rising, milky bosom. Two instead of none.

It all hung together. There was that appointment with Batzke. It would certainly have boded no good: made in a cell, it led back to a cell.

The young, lively greenness of the garden, the radiant sunshine, an oval face and the remembered words: 'One isn't always alone' – can a typewriter sing . . . ? He sang to the rhythm of his tapping keys. 'There's a way out into freedom – one isn't always alone – there's a way out into freedom – where two are better than one . . .'

'It's a good life,' he thought.

Old Widow Behn was in his room, helping her new lodger with his unpacking. As for Fräulein Behn . . .

'Liese,' said the old lady, 'I don't know what's the matter with Liese these days. I can't tell you exactly, but she's out every evening. She says she listens to the band in the Hammer Park – I wonder what kind of band it is she listens to.'

'Old dragon,' thought Kufalt, and he said aloud:

'Is she your only one, Frau Behn?'

'No, thirteen. She could have helped you so nicely with your things – but no, she must go and listen to the band. Do you know, when I was young I worked from four in the morning until ten at night. I was in the country from the time I was fourteen . . .'

'So you have thirteen children?'

'Only two are alive . . . Then afterwards I came to the town. But I was silly. My mistress in the town said to me: "Go and fetch four pounds of roast beef"; she pronounced it ross-bif, and I thought she said horse beef. I stood in the street and thought to myself: eat horse meat! No, I won't begin doing that, not me! I told the mistress it was all gone. Did she make a row when she found out why I never brought roast beef.'

The old woman laughed, and Kufalt laughed too.

'Nowadays girls are cleverer, but I wish Liese would go a bit slower. Out every evening . . .'

'When people are young, Frau Behn . . .'

'I won't say another word! Liese isn't really so bad, she pays her board and lodging regularly. But my boy Willi, he earns a lot of money, he's a chauffeur. But he's a bad lad, he is. He comes along and says: "Mother, have you got something to eat?" He eats all my food, and then says: "Mother, have you got ten marks? You can have them back this evening, but I must fill up quick." And then he goes off and we don't see him for a month. There's no sense in having children, young man, what's the good of them? You wear yourself to the bone to rear them and feed them, and then they go, they're always walking off and leaving you.'

'Not all of them, Frau Behn, you said yourself that your daughter . . .'

'What did I say? Just because she pays her board and lodging? So? No, the real reason is so that when she gets into trouble, she'll push her brat off onto me! That's why! I'm not a fool, I come from the country and I know a bit. Girls are so clever these days, they just laugh. She says: "Mother, it isn't what you think." And I say: "What isn't?" And she laughs: "Oh give over, I mean I'm not going to be the mother of thirteen like you – not me!" But I say . . .'

Kufalt felt hot; he shifted his shoulders uneasily underneath his jacket and looked towards the window. No, the window was open, the curtains swaying in the fresh night breeze.

'Yes, the books,' he said vaguely; 'what about the books? Perhaps you could take the ornaments off the cupboard, Frau Behn?'

'Certainly,' said she. 'I don't mind. One lodger wants the pictures taken down, another doesn't want a chamber pot, you don't want any ornaments – it's all the same to me, we're all picked out of the oven just as we've been baked. There's no sense to be got out of books.'

'No,' agreed Kufalt.

'I know,' said the old woman with a satisfied air. 'You've got rings round your eyes, and when I talk about Liese you can't look me in the face. I know all about it, my dear young man, though I'm past such things. I'll give you one bit of advice, though you won't take it: don't you get mixed up with Liese, she's bad news, she's got no heart . . .'

'Who's bad news? Who's got no heart?' came a voice from the door, and the two started up from the big box as if they had been caught red-handed.

Liese Behn was standing in the doorway. Small: yes. Attractive: yes. Oval-faced: yes. But with a nasty perpendicular wrinkle between the eyebrows. A red, but sharp and narrow mouth.

'Been talking again, Mother, have you? Has she been telling you that I'm half a whore, Herr Kufalt? The sort of girl that'll go with any man? Go, Mother, go and lie down. You ought to be ashamed of yourself – ugh!'

The bent and toil-worn old creature knelt motionless beside the box, silent, her face quite rigid. Then she got up and shuffled, with bowed head, towards the door. She hesitated as she reached her daughter in the doorway, but the girl did not move. The old woman looked at her humbly, and then squeezed past without a word. Her footsteps could be heard shuffling along the passage; a door closed; silence.

Kufalt, who also felt embarrassed, threw an uneasy look at the girl. She was standing in the same position, gnawing her lower lip, and did not look at him. He picked up a pile of books out of the box and carried them to the cupboard, with a sidelong glance at Liese as he went.

She was wearing a white dress with red spots, and her bright little hat was lined with red – the old woman had certainly lied, she did not look in the least like . . .

'Mother's ill,' she said slowly. 'You'd better not talk to her, she invents all sorts of nasty stories about everyone . . .'

'Yes, indeed,' said Kufalt; 'one has only to look at you, Fräulein Behn . . .'

'You're not to look at me!' she cried, stamping her foot. 'Not now. Not after that. Yesterday evening, yes, but not today.'

'I am putting the books away,' murmured Kufalt. 'I am not looking at you.'

For a while there was silence. Kufalt's heart was throbbing; but everything was different, men grow up, and girls; it was an odd world . . .

She cleared her throat, picked up a book, looked at it, put it down, and looked at another. Then she said:

'Well – goodnight.'

She went out of the room without another glance at him, nor did she give him her hand.

III

It had always been whispered in the typing room that the business in the Apfelstrasse was not Pastor Marcetus's only typing firm; there was another in the centre of the city, with all the latest equipment, where there were not only addresses to be typed, but also better work: letters, manuscripts and dictation. But it was no more than rumour; no one knew anything definite. A short, fat, pimply man by the name of Jauch sometimes appeared in the Apfelstrasse typing room, and Herr Mergenthal and Herr Seidenzopf were very polite to him. Sometimes, too, one or other of the workers disappeared; Herr Seidenzopf went out with him, and he did not come back again.

Did this legendary typing room really exist?

A few days after Kufalt's removal to the Marienthaler Strasse, Father Seidenzopf came into the typing room and said: 'Herr Maack! Herr Kufalt! Hand in the work you have done. Put back the address books. Tidy up your tables. Put on your coats and hats, and meet me at the door.'

The others barely looked up and went on with their work; only the inevitable Beerboom began his usual lamentation. 'Oh dear, oh dear, so you're leaving, are you? And when am I going to get out of this filthy hole? Lucky swine. I don't see why they should take you, Kufalt. You never do more than seven hundred addresses.'

Kufalt shook hands with Mergenthal, said a general 'good morning' through the doorway and met Father Seidenzopf outside the door.

'Where is Herr Maack? Ah, there you are, my dear Maack. Let us get along now. But we must hurry, I have a great deal to do today. What a lovely day it is, a truly divine day – it has been a pleasant summer this year.'

He trotted along between the two tall young men – a little elderly man with a black curly beard, babbling as he went.

'Where are we going to, Father Seidenzopf?' asked Kufalt.

'Hush, my young friend,' said Father Seidenzopf, 'you must learn to wait. You are preferred above many; have you ever heard of the Presto Typing Agency, the most up-to-date business in Hamburg? Well, you'll see something worth looking at.'

And when they reached the ticket counter of the overhead railway: 'What is this, my young friends, aren't you going to pay for your own tickets? Very well, I will advance the money, it can be deducted from your next pay. Or . . .' – and he struggled to a heroic resolve – 'I will charge it to the typing room.'

Father Seidenzopf found a seat; Maack and Kufalt stood at the door and smoked.

'I'm glad,' said Kufalt, 'that we're going to be together in the new agency.'

'Are you? Jauch's a crazy brute, I've heard.'

'Jauch . . . ?'

'The fat pimply bloke who often came to our place. That's the Presto office manager.'

'You know all this? Oh Maack, and you never say a word. Is it a typing room like ours? Or will we earn more there?'

'Perhaps, if you're sent to some firm as a temp. Or if you get into the dictating room. But that won't be for a long while. To begin with, you'll go on with addresses. And then you'll do copies of testimonials, and so on. And if you get on all right, and – which is the main thing – Jauch likes the look of you, he'll send you out as a temp.'

'But it says in the rules that we are only to work in the typing rooms for as short a time as possible, and get a business job as soon as we can.'

'I tell you what, mate,' said Maack; 'that's all eyewash, that's just so they can put us into the street if they don't like us or if there's a shortage of work. Look, I've been working in this set-up for a year and a half, and they haven't even taken out my unemployment insurance yet. If I'm ill I have to go to the Welfare Office and beg to see a doctor – so they save their sick benefit contributions.'

'But it's the law that every worker must be insured.'

'Bless your heart, it's a welfare organization. The money we get on Saturdays is charity. We aren't really working!'

'Well, you know . . .'

'I know quite well what could be done by three or four decent blokes with a bit of money. I'm saving hard, but the pastor, old Marcetus, says a man oughtn't to earn more than three marks a day – more only leads him into evil ways.'

'What! Doesn't he earn more than three marks a day, eh?'

'Doesn't he just! Do you ever earn more than twenty marks a week? Twenty-one sometimes, or even twenty-two, if you tap till your fingers drop off; but they'd look pissed off if you do, and they'd want to reduce your pay. I live with a girl: a shop girl, she gets sixty-five marks a month – it isn't much we can save.'

'Do you think a person can live on a hundred marks a month?'

'Of course. Quite well. What do you pay for your room?'

'Twenty-five.'

'Much too much. I could get you one for fifteen; or twelve. What do you want, after all? A bed and a chair, nothing else matters, if you want to get on. Clean the room yourself – an attic somewhere . . . And listen: food morning and evening, fifty pfennigs, and another fifty pfennigs midday . . .'

'But you can't get lunch for fifty pfennigs.'

'Lunch? Do you want a warm meal every day? No one has that these days. Bread, margarine, a dried herring, half a pint of milk – that'll do you all right, and keep up your strength, and' – gesturing – 'he won't get excited. On Sundays you can have a warm meal, and it should not cost more than ninety pfennigs. That's fifteen marks a month for rent, thirty-five marks for food at the most, laundry – five marks, perhaps, and another five for cigarettes and cinema; altogether, sixty marks a month. And perhaps I can find you a girl who earns a bit. Then there won't be any laundry, and the rent's split.'

'So that's what you do,' said Kufalt admiringly, firmly resolved not to do it himself.

'What else should I do? Just think it over and tell me, and I'll find you a room if you like.'

The train stopped, people got in and out. The train went on.

'Look,' said Kufalt slowly; 'hasn't it occurred to you that there's a much easier way to get money?'

Silence.

Then Maack said slowly: 'Yes, my lad, we often think of that, of course. And I wouldn't say I mightn't. I'm not one of the blokes who's always saying "never again". How am I to know what may happen? If my girl clears out because she's fallen for a bloke with a few more beans, or if she gets pregnant – it's a bloody shame that rubber's too dear for the likes of us – then I might do a job again. Otherwise – no, I'm through with that sort of thing.'

'But what do you get out of life? Everything that's nice costs money, and you never have any.'

'I don't say I never will, I tell you, and I don't know whether I'll be able to hold out. But it's possible I might drop into a business job at 140 or 160. I'm going to try this line for the time being . . .'

'Well, my dear friends, did you see the harbour in the sunshine? The *Cap Arcona* was there, wasn't she? What a splendid ship! A sight that makes one proud to be a German.'

'It does indeed, Herr Seidenzopf.'

'And now, my young friends, I'm going to take you to our Presto Agency. Be a credit to the Home of Peace. Show yourselves worthy of our choice.'

They mumbled some reply.

Then they walked up the staircase in a large office building.

Presto Typewriting Agency – Every Variety of Typewriting – Unrivalled for Value – Speed – Accuracy.

'My dear Herr Jauch, here are two young friends of ours who

have already done good work for the Home. Herr Maack, Herr Kufalt. But you have already seen them both at our place.'

'Why two? What am I to do with two? I want one, I told you. This is the sort of thing you always do. You think it's only old Jauch; you can get round him all right.'

The short fat man with the shaven head, dotted all over with pimples, pustules and blackheads, fumed up and down.

'Can they work? They don't look as if they could. You wanted to get shot of them, eh? Now then, you – yes, I mean you – just sit down at the machine. Have you ever seen a machine like that? It's a typewriter, did you know? Used for typing letters, understand? . . . Now then, carbon, normal spacing, take this down . . . God in Heaven above us, what a way to put the paper in! The sheet's at least two millimetres crooked, and it'll go on getting worse. Don't you understand?'

'Yes,' whispered Kufalt.

'"Yes," he said, but he had no idea. Take this: "Hamburg, 23 June" . . . My dear Seidenzopf, what a touch! You can take him away, we want people who know their jobs. Now go on: "Dear Sir . . ." What sort of "S" is that . . . ? It's all shaky, you must strike the keys regularly. Typing ought to sound like machine-gun fire. Were you at the front? No, of course not, how should you know what machine-gun fire is like? My dear Herr Seidenzopf, take the man away with you. I don't run a typewriting school, I need trained staff . . . Go on . . . "With reference to your esteemed favour of the third instant" . . . Oh God . . .'

'My dear Jauch . . . ! Will you please go into the typing room, gentlemen, and have a look round. Now listen, my dear Jauch, Herr Pastor Marcetus wishes . . .'

'What a pig!' whispered Kufalt, short of breath.

'Now don't get rattled; you're a bag of nerves.'

'But if the bloke goes on nagging like that . . .'

'Well, let him, you needn't listen.'

They looked round. It was much the same as in the Apfelstrasse. Only a little larger: twenty machines instead of ten, and not ten but twenty typists.

The door opened into an adjacent room. A girl's head emerged, and then another. They calmly surveyed the new arrivals and vanished once more.

'Inquisitive bits of skirt,' whispered Maack.

'Are they some of our lot?'

'No way. Much too superior to say a word to the likes of us. They're permanent staff; their job is to look after the duplicating machines. Ex-convicts can't be trusted with them.'

The door into the manager's office opened.

Seidenzopf hurriedly departed: 'Well, goodbye, my young friends.'

After a short interval Herr Jauch appeared, in a very bad temper.

'That's your machine. And that's yours. I haven't any work for you today. You'd better have a look at your machines. And you'd better practise that capital "S". I've never seen such typing in my life! Now then, don't look at the machine when I'm talking to you, look at me, please. What sort of script is this?'

'Duplicated typescript,' said Kufalt, after brief reflection.

'Oh God, oh God in Heaven, and this man has come to work here! It's violet script! The colour's violet, isn't it?'

'Yes.'

'Thank God for that, I thought you'd say it was green.'

Herr Jauch bleated with laughter; and here and there in the room a head was lifted from a typewriter, and bleated too. Maack looked round and noted the heads that remained bent.

'There's a box over there,' Jauch went on. 'Do you see that black box?'

'Yes.'

'That's where the ribbons are kept. Find a violet ribbon for your machine – not green, my dear sir; anyhow there aren't any – that exactly matches this script. It must be exactly the same violet, understand? Exact to the tenth of a degree. Is that clear?'

'Yes.'

'Then get on with it.'

Jauch disappeared, and the pair rummaged in the box.

'Have you any idea what a tenth of a degree of colour is?'

'Not the faintest. Hey, you've got off on the wrong foot here. He took a dislike to you from the very start. Well, so much the better for me. Here's a ribbon for you; it's the nearest match. I'll take the other. Now let's go and try our machines.'

IV

No, Kufalt was not very happy. From the day on which he had come out of prison, he had gone forward all the time; he had got over his difficulties, he had learnt to look people in the eye on the street, his efficiency had increased, slowly but steadily; prison, and all its dead, obscene talk, had slipped into the past. He had equipped himself with a room, and possessions of his own, and a modest income, and now . . .

Now, behind his chair, a fat and pimply little creature stood and talked and groaned: 'Oh God, what have I done to deserve this! Look here, my man, you must strike the keys regularly. Don't you see: that "R" is a shade darker than that "E"? That such a man should live – let alone in my typing room!'

Kufalt sat there with a white, sullen face and pursed lips, and tapped.

And while he sat, and tapped and tapped, he thought of many things . . . 'I could get up and leave this place for ever, I don't need to stay, I've got enough to live on for a bit; I would manage all right, and Batzke will soon turn up. Jänsch, who sits in the corner to the left, said if Jauch got too bad we'd watch out for him, and lay into him properly. Jänsch also told me that Jauch himself was one of us, he's done a stretch, and they're always the worst. Oh stop blathering on, you clot,' he said to himself; 'at quarter past seven I'll be back home, and perhaps I'll see Liese Behn; on Thursday evening the kitchen door was open when she was washing herself – oh, her lovely bare back and white, nimble arms!'

He heard nothing more; he always got quite dizzy now when he thought of that particular woman, his heart fluttered as though it were going to stop, and all the blood rushed to his loins . . .

'What I need is a whore,' he thought. 'I must get rid of my obsession, it's making me crazy, and I'll never get Liese anyway . . .'

And he awoke at a shout: 'Have you gone crazy? I've had enough of you, out you go; get up and pack your things! Do you spell *Doktor* with a "c"?'

Yes, there it was: Kufalt looked at the letter, a neat circular addressed to doctors from a laboratory, commending a patent medicine; Kufalt had only to insert the address and superscription: there it was – Herr Doctor Matthies . . . Dear Sir . . .

It didn't look quite right. While he had been tapping on and on in a dream, his mind far away, his first few years at school had come back with their Latin, *docere*, yes that was why, or was it that the continuous nagging had weakened his brain, turned him into another Beerboom, and got him down from seven hundred addresses to three hundred?

Kufalt stood rather helplessly beside his typewriter; it was summer now, nine hours at the machine, the evenings in the streets where he knew no one, and the nights at the open window, he could not sleep; what had helped him for five long years now helped him no more, he couldn't . . .

He stood with a helpless smile, merely wondering how he should set about his departure; he would have to get some papers and a little money, he didn't really mind going . . .

'And you stand there still and grin! *Doktor* with a "c"! I never heard of such a thing in all my life. Must I get legs for you?'

At that moment something happened.

In the large typing room, where twenty people sat, a voice rang out from a corner: 'Mean bastard!'

Jauch swung round, his face paled in an instant to an ashen grey; he stared into the corner and stammered: 'What! What's that!'

Behind him, hardly a couple of metres away, another low voice said: 'Bash the brute!'

Jauch looked at Maack, but Maack was busy putting a fresh sheet into his machine; Maack noticed nothing at all.

And before Herr Jauch could make up his mind, there was another voice, two or three voices, from different parts of the room: 'Shut your ruddy jaw!' – 'We won't half skin you!' – 'Long time since you've heard yourself yelling, eh?'

Yet there were only four or five among the twenty who took the risk, who would not stand the eternal bullying, and cracked sometimes . . .

Kufalt awoke, suddenly realizing that he had almost surrendered without a fight; he shook himself, sat down again at his machine, and rattled on: *To Herr Doktor Matthies. Dear Sir . . .*

Meanwhile Jauch, now purple in the face, lips quivering, looked round the room. But they were all at work, not a sound could be heard but the tap-tapping of the machines; Jauch pattered back into his room. But in the doorway he called out: 'Herr Patzig, please.'

Patzig, a tall, lanky youth wearing spectacles (an obvious pilferer of petty cash), got up, looked nervously round, went into Herr Jauch's office, and Jänsch said: 'If you split, my lad . . . !'

Patzig muttered something feebly, and was gone. Would he blurt out the names of the hecklers?

No, he did not. Nothing happened. They were all afraid, Jauch as much as his blue-eyed boys. Kufalt can go on sitting at his machine; but is it any use?

It isn't even any use that Jauch stops his scolding and nagging. Jauch knew his men; he was pretty sure he would get the right ones if he put five or six on the street; but he was also pretty sure that they would get him in turn, and give him a good seeing-to if he did.

So Jauch went about it more cautiously. He would stand in silence for a good half-hour behind Kufalt's chair, and – every two minutes or so – lay his forefinger on the page, in dumb indication of a typing mistake. And farther on, again and again, that index finger, with its hideous torn nail, that thick, crushed nail, yellow with nicotine . . .

'Can't you pull yourself together a bit, Kufalt?' asked Maack. 'After all, he's right, you do make far too many mistakes.'

'It gets worse and worse,' said Kufalt. 'I try and try, but the more

I try, the worse it gets. And suddenly I seem to slip away, I feel all empty inside, as though I didn't exist.'

'I know,' said Maack with a nod. 'I know all about it. People who've done a long stretch like us have all been through it. You must shake it off as soon as you can. Haven't you got a girl yet? That helps a bit.'

No, Kufalt hadn't got one yet, and it did not look as though he was likely to find deliverance in that respect soon. On the Steindamm there were plenty of girls to be had cheap. But had he been in jail for five years to start that sort of thing again? After all, this was really a new life – was it to begin in that way? No, surely not, quite apart from Fräulein Behn . . .

From that evening in the Hammer Park, leading first to the wrong lodging and then to the right one, from the conversation with the mother about the daughter – until the glimpse of her in the kitchen at night, when she was washing herself – there had been only one girl for him: Fräulein Behn.

It was hopeless, futile, she had other admirers, she was a cold-blooded little bitch, he did not dare to speak to her; and yet he lay in bed at night and prayed in his heart that she might come: 'Come! Come! You must come. I'm dying for you. Come just once . . .'

All this would perhaps have been easier to bear if he could have borne it alone. But – and this was the worst part of it – he was certain that she felt it. He could sense it through three walls and two rooms; she lay in her bed, and knew. It was in her, it was, perhaps, her joy and her delight; but she never came.

The window stood open, the curtains swayed in the fresh summer breeze, suburban trains approached, rattled past the windows and sped into the distance – it was a great and dreadful thing that a man should lie like this tormented with longing and desire. For five years had he lain in a little cell, with its opaque glass window, open slantwise in the wall, and cried aloud: 'Oh let me out, you brutes, just for one night, just for one hour, I shall go mad here.' Who was it that had said to him: 'It's not till a man gets outside that he finds out how bad things can be.'

He was right; they were very bad, and growing worse.

V

Beerboom often came to see him in the evening. Beerboom had not remained the only inmate of the Apfelstrasse Home; fresh ex-convicts had arrived, and he had plenty of company. But he always came along to see his old friend Kufalt, possibly out of affection, in memory of the time when they had been alone together in the Home of Peace.

Beerboom was no better; indeed it was clear from the sight of him that he was worse, much worse. His face was yellow and haggard; thick, greyish-blue, granular pouches hung under his eyes; he had a fearful, dark, darting, stabbing look; and a wild and ceaseless babble of talk without sense or purport . . .

'Yes, Seidenzopf and Mergenthal and that fine-looking pastor of theirs, Marcetus, can go to hell, the whole lot of them. I shan't do any more work; yesterday I did forty addresses; you should have heard what they said!'

He grinned.

'But your money will soon be gone,' said Kufalt.

'My money? It is nearly all gone. I don't care. I shan't need any money at all very soon.'

Kufalt looked attentively at the brooding, sallow face. 'Don't you think of any such thing, Beerboom. You'd get nabbed the very first time.'

'Don't care if I am,' grinned Beerboom in reply. 'I shall have had what I wanted.'

Kufalt thought for a while, then asked some further questions, but on this matter Beerboom, for all his endless babble of grievances, was not to be drawn: 'You'll soon see. Besides, very likely I shan't do it after all.'

Kufalt pondered once again: 'Have you seen Berthold lately?'

'Berthold?' said Beerboom with a contemptuous wave of the hand. 'Yes, he's living in the Langenreihe. Nice little place; he seems to be doing well.'

'Don't you get mixed up with Berthold,' warned Kufalt.

'With a man like that? Not likely! I wanted to get my three marks back, but he stung me for five marks more. He promised on his word of honour that he'd give me twenty marks on the first of the month.' And he added in an entirely different tone, that of the old Beerboom: 'Do you think I'll get them? Do you think he'll give me them? He must give me them, mustn't he? I could sue him for the money, couldn't I?'

'But I thought you weren't going to need any money soon?' said Kufalt.

'Oh well,' said Beerboom, with a sudden return of ill humour. 'Money's always needed. Do you think I'm going to give it to Berthold? Not me!'

No, Beerboom could hardly be regarded as the right company, yet Kufalt found him better than waiting in solitude, until the outer door slammed, a light step tripped across the landing and he heard a soft voice say a few casual words to Mother Behn.

'Be quiet for a minute,' said Kufalt eagerly, and signalled to Beerboom to stop talking. 'Come in, please.'

Yes, she had knocked; just at the wrong moment with Beerboom there, she had come. She stood in the doorway; Beerboom got up nervously and looked at her.

'May I bring some tea for you and your friend?'

She was very polite, there must be something on her mind; perhaps she had had a bad day, and thought of her mother's lodger, and offered to bring him and his friend some tea.

'Not for me, thank you,' said Beerboom hurriedly. 'I must go at once. I have to be back in the Home at ten.'

'Beerboom,' said Kufalt in a fury. 'I told you if you ever again . . .'

Liese Behn stood in the doorway and looked from one to the other.

Beerboom hastily tried to repair his slip: 'I'm not really his friend. Herr Kufalt just lets me come and see him now and again.' And, more eagerly: 'He has nothing to do with me.'

She was wearing a light blue sleeveless dress, cut with a small square yoke at the neck. It was hot, and that might have been why her hair hung loosely round her face. Her mouth, half open, had a childlike expression.

'Well, I'll make you some tea,' she said. 'The water's just boiling.'

But she did not go. Rather she closed the door behind her and said: 'Won't you introduce your friend to me?'

'Beerboom,' said Kufalt; 'Fräulein Behn.'

'What sort of home do you live in, Herr Beerboom?' she asked. She did not look at Kufalt.

'Er – well,' said Beerboom, embarrassed; 'I hardly know how to describe it . . .' And suddenly, as if he had an inspiration: 'It isn't a proper asylum, but I'm not quite right in the head.' He was very proud of this subterfuge, and added, by way of explanation: 'That's why I'm allowed to come and see Herr Kufalt now and again.'

Kufalt felt, from mere despair, an almost irresistible desire to laugh, but Liese did not laugh. She had sat down on the edge of a plush armchair, and surveyed Beerboom with a friendly gaze: 'In what way aren't you right – I mean not quite right – in the head?'

'Well, you know,' said Beerboom; 'that's a long story, and I must really get away now.' He racked his brain to think of something that would not damage Kufalt. 'Well, Fräulein, it's something to do with women. I can't tell you a thing like that, can I?'

'Ah,' said Liese. 'I reckon I know more about it than you think.'

She looked meditatively at Beerboom, and then at Kufalt. Kufalt trembled; it was so easy to see the truth when she had the pair before her. She must know that night after night he lay there and desired her, while still he crept out of her way. Damaged and distorted men, men with a worm in the brain – so easy to recognize.

'Tell me a little bit about it,' she said with a sudden smile. 'I'll be sure to tell you to stop if it gets too bad.'

'Tormentress,' thought Kufalt. And he added, aloud: 'But the water must have been boiling long ago, Fräulein Behn. I only meant . . . you said something about tea . . .'

He faltered under her look, and stopped.

'Yes, there was something I wanted to say to you, Herr Kufalt,' she went on. 'Mother told me a man came here a little while ago, a man in civilian clothes, with a badge, you know, and asked about you. Whether you were out for long in the evening, whether you had much money, and whom you went around with, and so on.'

She paused, no longer looking at Kufalt, but at Beerboom. 'I can't understand . . .' Kufalt was like a man who had been struck on the head.

'I tell you just to let you know,' said Liese. 'Mother and I don't mind. Now then, what's your trouble, Herr Beerboom?'

Kufalt stood motionless. He felt shattered and yet happy, for he could stay where he was; and ashamed, for she had known about it all, perhaps for a long while – and what now?

He looked at her but he had passed out of her mind; she was now talking to Beerboom – her cheeks were flushed and her eyes glittered, so eager was she. She got up from her chair and sat down beside Beerboom on the sofa, and they whispered together; how old was she? Twenty-one? Twenty-two? Certainly not more.

'The fact is,' said Beerboom, 'I can't look at a single woman without thinking of that, and of nothing but that, you see. And if I feel like talking to one, or going out with one, I keep thinking of all the others. I can't make up my mind. It's so long since . . .'

'How long?'

'Eleven years. All those eleven years it was only the one thing, and now there's so much, so many ways – you understand . . .'

He looked at her helplessly.

'And are things still as they were in – in prison?'

She had thrust out her lower lip, she kept her eyes on his face. Like the soft wing of a bird, a strand of loose hair hung over her forehead.

'Prison, no,' Beerboom hurriedly corrected her. 'I'm a high-security man, a lifer; Kufalt was in a regular prison . . .' He looked up guiltily. 'You don't mind, Kufalt? Fräulein knows all about it.'

Kufalt looked at him, but said nothing.

'No,' said Beerboom. 'Or rather – yes. Until quite a while ago. And now it's all different . . .'

He stopped. They sat, the two of them, and waited silently to see if he would speak. The room seemed filled with a dry, sultry haze. They stared into vacancy, neither looking at the other.

'You know . . .' Beerboom began again, and once more came to a halt.

Kufalt ventured a glance. The wizened yellow face had brightened, it was smooth and shining and serene. Like a landscape – with mountains and valleys and broad fields. Was this happiness? Could such a thing be happiness?

'I've got a sister,' said Beerboom slowly. 'When I . . . left home, she was still quite small, ten or twelve years old.'

He fell silent, and then began again: 'I know all about children – I mean about little girls, you know, from having had a sister. It started in prison – always thinking about her. And now . . .'

Once more a pause, and silence. Beerboom got up, paced quickly up and down, sat down again, and said: 'The children, the little girls in the gardens, you understand . . .'

Pause: all stared into vacancy.

Why couldn't someone get up, fling open the window and let in the fresh night breeze to blow away this horror? It was a horror not of this world, it was witchcraft; and there she sat, the witch and the tormentress . . .

'I stand there and look, when I'm allowed out of the Home, I just look. It's awful what a bloke can think of. It wasn't so awful inside, because I thought it was just because I was locked up and it would all be different afterwards.'

Again a long silence. Kufalt made an effort, moved, cleared his throat and said: 'Well . . .'

'Women,' said Beerboom, 'know all about it. Or rather, I know all about them. But these . . . You see, any one of them might be my sister, it's so new to me . . .'

He brooded. His long yellow hand, hairy and lined with thick blue veins, came creeping across the table, extended its fingers and then closed them with a jerk, as though to crush and to destroy . . .

'I thought,' he whispered, 'they'd done for me in prison, once and for all, but now it's all starting over again . . .'

He sobbed, almost for joy: 'The children,' he whispered; 'the little girls with bare legs . . . It's hard for me, I see so few, but perhaps, perhaps . . .'

He stopped and looked at the other two. His lips quivered.

'Go away!' shrieked Fräulein Behn. 'Go away at once!'

She stood quivering. She clutched the chair and muttered: 'You murderer – go!'

Beerboom collapsed. Gone was all his radiance and joy and eloquence. 'I . . .' he stammered. 'You yourself . . .'

'Get out,' said Kufalt; and pushed him to the door.

'With your bloody perverse talk! Here's my house key: clear out at once. I'll come and fetch it tomorrow.'

'But I . . . Fräulein, you asked me to . . .'

'Go away!' Kufalt pushed him out.

The outer door slammed behind him. Kufalt went back into the room and lingered in the doorway . . .

Very likely she was just a whore, cold and rather perverted, perhaps she needed the thrill of corruption and the stench of blood . . .

She had flung herself across his bed and she was crying; as he came in, she raised her tear-stained face and stretched her bare arms towards him. 'Oh come to me, come quickly! He's an awful man, your friend. Come quick!'

VI

Was it deliverance? And did it bring relief?

During the nights when he had tormented himself over Liese, he had thought that everything would be easy and his troubles over if only she would come to him. And now she had come – and was he at ease, or happy? Once again he sat at his typewriter; it was two weeks – or was it three? – since that night, and everything was just as difficult as ever. Or even more difficult?

There he sat and tapped. For a few days, immediately afterwards, he had got on better; so much so that Jauch had given up standing behind his chair; he left him alone.

Then he began to give way again. He pulled himself together, determined he would no longer be treated as a scapegoat; Maack had been called to the dictating room two or three times already. Was he to be kept on these addresses for ever?

But it was as if his strength was paralysed from within; he used to feel alert and energetic and sometimes positively cheerful; now it seemed as though his brain had failed, as though there were nothing but a void within him, and the man called Kufalt had disappeared. Could there be a prison cell within a brain, a narrow room with bars and lock, and within it a formless entity, pacing up and down, up and down, a prisoner that never can escape?

'Look out, mate,' whispered Maack.

It was Jauch. 'Here are five original testimonials, Herr Kufalt. I want copies with four carbons, normal spacing, to be called for in an hour. But no mistakes, please, no corrections, no shaky "S"s!'

'No,' said Kufalt.

'Yes, you say no, of course, but we shall see. Anyhow, it's your last trial.'

Kufalt was much gratified, it was his first skilled work; he would show them what he could do, Jauch would be astonished. And yet Jauch's words – no mistakes, no corrections, no shaky 'S's, every word seemed to set up a barrier in his mind.

He felt harassed at every turn. Four copies: how easy it would be to miscount. Was the carbon paper properly adjusted? Original testimonials – he mustn't make the slightest mark on them – his thumb was a little blackened by the carbon paper, he must go and wash – three minutes' typing time lost. Get on with it!

'Testimonial of apprenticeship. Elmshorn, 1 October 1925. Herr Walter Puckereit, born 21 July 1908, son of Master Baker Puckereit of this place, as from 1 October 1922 has served his apprenticeship in my old-established ironmonger's business . . .'

Etc., etc.

'Will you soon be finished, Herr Kufalt?'

'Yes, very soon.'

'Doesn't look like it. I would rather you said if you can't manage to get it done. I'm sure you can't.'

'Oh yes I can.'

'Well, we shall see. Anyhow, you must type much harder for four carbons – let me look; yes, just as I thought, they're quite faint and grey. You must start again . . .'

While Kufalt was arranging his sheets afresh, Maack whispered: 'Keep your head; don't get nervous, he only wants to confuse you.'

Kufalt smiled an anxious, grateful smile, and began to type: testimonial . . . he found himself wondering if he spelt the word right – oh well, it must be right in the original – Puckereit, not Packereit – oh God! Should he type the 'u' above the 'a'? No, that wasn't allowed. Or rub it out on all five sheets? Or begin all over again? Oh well, start again then. But this time he must get it right!

Maack no longer looked up. Jauch had gone into his room, no one was looking. Or were they all secretly looking at him?

This time he got to the third line of the first testimonial, but the shaky 'S' (it was a shaky 'G' on this occasion) proved his undoing. While he was adjusting the copying paper against the carbons, he glanced across at Maack, but Maack saw nothing, he was typing like a man demented.

He pulled himself together and went on successfully line after line, without a mistake, immaculately neat and regular, the first page would be finished in a moment – when he was seized by a sudden foreboding. He looked. Yes! He had put in the carbon paper the wrong way round; looking-glass writing on four sheets, and the fifth sheet blank!

He sat and stared; it was useless to struggle, there was a devil within him that beat him down. They had fed that devil for five long years, and now he was helpless. 'Go,' they had said to him; 'Do this and that'; they had ordered him about; and now he was on the outside, he simply collapsed, he could no longer cope; it was no use.

It was the third evening after; he had run into the corridor and when the door of the flat opened he had said: 'Oh, my darling, I have so wanted you!' He had flung his arms round her neck – 'What do you think you're up to?' she had retorted, as she broke away and hurried into the kitchen to her mother . . . It was no use . . .

'Chuck that stuff here, Kufalt,' whispered Maack. 'I'll type it for you. Quick! Be careful no one sees you, any of these lads would split. Thanks. You go on with addresses.'

The machine yonder rattled, hammered, ting-a-ling, on again, fresh line, ting-a-ling, on again, fresh line, ting-a-ling . . .

Anxiously he watched the hated door. Eleven minutes more. Maack had just finished the third page – no, the door wasn't opening, barely half a page more . . .

'Now then, hand it in, Kufalt!'

A gasp of astonishment. 'What is this? Why is Herr Maack typing this? Did I give it to him or to you?'

'I . . . I,' stammered Kufalt. 'I asked him to do it, I was so nervous, I made some mistakes . . .'

'In-deed,' said Herr Jauch. 'Indeed! And why didn't you consult me? Am I in charge of this typing room, or are you? In any case I shall report the matter to Herr Pastor Marcetus. I won't stand any tricks of that kind – a man getting credit for work he hasn't done. Give it me, Herr Maack.'

There he had to sit, and tap and tap, as hard as he knew how; it only brought in fifteen marks a week, this week only twelve perhaps, but today was Tuesday, and it was not till Friday that Marcetus held his weekly inquisition in the Presto Typewriting Agency. A man couldn't sit and do nothing, he must go on typing – tormentress!

'Now don't get worked up, Kufalt. I'll have a word with the pastor. And if we do get the boot, I've got a good idea. No, not a bit what you think, but something really solid. Well, we'll see . . .'

'And, Herr Pastor,' said Maack to the white-haired doctor honoris causa, 'it is my opinion that nothing can be done by intimidating people. My friend Kufalt here, for instance . . .'

'One moment,' interrupted Pastor Marcetus, raising a fat white hand. 'One moment, please. You know quite well, gentlemen, that I do not approve of these friendships between ex-convicts. Permission was given to both of you to live outside the Home so that you might again get in touch with respectable society. And here you are saying – "My friend Kufalt."' He looked sternly at the pair. 'Besides, as you very well know, talking is forbidden in the typing rooms. How, then, did you know . . . ?'

He eyed them; they said nothing.

'Intimidation,' growled the pastor. 'I have known Herr Jauch for the past ten years, and I have never found him anything other than kind, conscientious and devoted to his duties. But perhaps it is exactly that of which you complain as intimidation, his insistence on conscientious work . . .'

'But . . .' interrupted Maack.

'One moment, please. When Herr Kufalt came to us, he was far from being a good worker, but – I have particularly noticed this – he earned eighteen, twenty and once or twice twenty-two marks a week. After a certain date his work steadily deteriorated. As I am informed by Herr Jauch, he will barely earn ten marks this week. And so, Herr Kufalt . . .'

Kufalt made an effort. It was not so long since he had stood up to Pastor Marcetus, indeed he had him more or less at his mercy; but at that time he had had energy and courage. Where had it all gone?

'Herr Pastor,' he said in a hesitating voice; 'you think it's because I've left the Home, that there's something else on my mind. But believe me, Herr Pastor, I'm trying, I'm trying as hard as I know how. But suddenly something seems to snap, however hard I try; it's as if I was ill, not really ill, you know, but all this sitting down makes me feel as if I just can't go on any longer . . .'

'Indeed,' said the pastor. 'Indeed. Your suggestion is that now subsequently you are suffering from a sort of prison psychosis – it does not sound very convincing. In fact, we understand from Herr Petersen that your landlady has a very pretty daughter, a young lady of none too good a reputation. Yes, Herr Kufalt?'

Kufalt stood silent. If only Maack would speak! But Maack stood silent too, fidgeted with his glasses and said nothing. He was, of course, furious with Kufalt for not mentioning this daughter, and letting him offer suggestions while the situation had actually been quite different.

'Very well, then,' said Marcetus, after a long pause. 'We will try you for another week. And if your work is not satisfactory – if you don't earn at least eighteen marks a week – we shall have to desist from further employing you, Herr Kufalt. I will also tell Herr Jauch that he is not to worry you in any way, so there shall be no further question of intimidation. Good morning, gentlemen. Ah, one moment, Herr Maack. No, you may go, Herr Kufalt.'

VII

Not until work was over was Kufalt able to speak to Maack again; there were too many spies and go-betweens in the typing room. Slowly they walked down the Alsterdamm in the bright sunshine, crossed the Bell Founders Quay and reached the outer Alster, which was already scattered with a summery array of white sails and small steamers.

'What did he want of you?' asked Kufalt.

'Oh,' said Maack; 'the usual thing; tried to set us against each other; like they all do, those bastards . . .'

'Tell me,' said Kufalt, a bit shaken; then he suddenly realized what the typing room would be like without Maack.

'I'm to go as temp to an export company tomorrow. And if I do well they'll keep me on. So he says.'

'Oh,' said Kufalt; 'I suppose you're glad?'

'Turn round quick,' whispered Maack. 'Quick, quick.'

He gripped Kufalt's elbow and dragged him towards a man who, with his straw hat in his hand, half hidden behind a tree, was contemplating the busy scene at the Hamburg waterside.

'Good evening, Herr Patzig.'

The tall, lanky youth looked up with an embarrassed expression, waved his straw boater and said: 'Oh, good evening . . .'

'The main condition of my getting the job, Kufalt, was that I should give up hanging out with you. It isn't right that criminals should hang out with criminals, they do each other no good, you see.'

The pair looked steadily at the youth, who grew redder and redder.

'I really only came out for a walk,' said Patzig, pilferer of petty cash.

'And now you'll see that Herr Patzig will get the temp job in the export company.'

With a jerk of his forefinger Maack straightened the glasses on the bridge of his nose and rubbed his chin thoughtfully. Though Maack's clothes were old, he always looked neat, he shaved every morning, his hands were well cared for and his trousers creased.

'Well, bum-sucking will get our young friend into trouble one of these days, don't you think?' said Maack.

Kufalt said nothing. He was looking at Patzig; the flush on his face had faded and he was now very pale.

'I really only went for a walk,' he protested again; 'really and truly.'

'Of course,' sneered Maack; 'just behind us, all the way from the office, eh . . . ?'

'Look out!' shouted Kufalt.

But the blow had already landed on Maack's chin, not a bad effort at all for a puny little creature like Patzig.

'You can all go to . . . !' he said, eyeing Maack with satisfaction, who was vigorously rubbing his jaw. Then he clapped on his straw hat, said, 'Good evening,' and was about to go.

'Just a moment,' said Maack. 'Just a moment, Patzig – did you really only go for a walk?'

'Do you want another sock in the jaw?'

'Didn't Jauch or the pastor send you after us, so that you would squeal on us?'

'I'll tell you what,' said Patzig; 'I'll tell you something you don't know. You old crooks always think you're somebody. You spit around the place, just because you've done a five- or ten-year stretch – and because I only did six months . . .'

'Oh, shut up,' said Maack.

'Oh no I won't. Six months, or ten years – it's just as hard for me to get going again as for you; no, it's even harder, for your kind sticks together, and I have nobody.'

'Oh, come on. What about this squealing?'

'Have I ever squealed on you or on that soppy friend of yours, eh? You be careful he doesn't squeal on you, he looks just the sort . . .'

'Look, if you get fresh again, Patzig . . .'

'I'll get another one, eh?' said Patzig, with a grin. 'Of course, I have to crawl to Jauch and the pastor; but squeal, that's what I'd never do. And I never have, neither in the clink nor outside. But you always think everyone's a wrong 'un, and only you old lags know how to stick together. I tell you you're just a rotten little bunch, and you think you're the boss and you can do what you like; but you only know your own little clique, and as for sticking together, you don't know what it means!'

In the excitement of his speech, he had snatched the hat off his head and was brandishing it in Maack's face.

'Well, you needn't poke my eyes out,' said Maack genially. 'But I understand; you want everyone to be happy and you're all for justice, and all that. Can't say I go in for politics much, I look after myself and my girl, and perhaps I'll need Kufalt and a few blokes who can be trusted – I'm keeping my eyes open . . .'

'Keeping your eyes open, indeed. There's a big job on the table, and you've never smelt it, eh?'

He looked expectantly at the pair, and laughed when he saw he had really embarrassed Maack.

'A big job?' muttered Maack. 'I'm never going to touch anything crooked again, and you can pass that on to Jauch.'

'Oh, come off it,' said Patzig. 'This is all OK, a big contract coming along; haven't you noticed Jauch telephoning and running around all morning these last few days?'

'Well?' said the other two, still at a loss.

'Two hundred and fifty thousand addresses, perhaps three hundred thousand. A textile export firm. Catalogues for the autumn and winter season?'

'It would be good if the agency got that. At least a month's work,' agreed Kufalt.

But Patzig laughed. 'If they got it! Jauch is asking twelve marks a thousand inclusive of inserting, and stamping the envelopes, and the Cito Agency in the Grosser Burstah would maybe do it for eleven.

But they're no good. If someone came along and offered to do it for ten or even nine . . .'

He stopped and reflected. 'Three hundred thousand addresses,' he said dreamily.

'Three thousand marks for the job,' said Kufalt ecstatically. 'Just think, guys . . .'

'A month's work for ten men – three hundred marks each,' reckoned Maack. 'Oh boy, Patzig,' he burst out. 'If we could get it, I'd take you in with us. You wouldn't need to go on about sticking together, you'd be earning money.'

'Not me,' said Patzig. 'I just told you so you could see I'm not what you thought. So you could understand what idiots you are, you never notice anything. I'll go back to Jauch, I think the clergy are the safest.'

'All right,' said Maack. 'Every man must know what sort of fool he is. Well, we won't forget you if we bring it off. You can eat your fill for once, on us.'

'Oh yes?' said Patzig. 'Can I really? And you don't even know the name of the firm. And you haven't got any typewriters; or the contract. I'd likely go hungry if I waited for what I'll get from you . . .'

And he turned to go.

What a change in their attitude to little Patzig! They fell upon him, and begged him for the address. 'Just the name and the address, that's a good bloke. We'll give you a hundred marks.'

'You can keep your hundred marks, I'd have to wait for them long enough. Klemmzig & Lange, Hamburger Strasse 128, Barmbeck.'

At last! What a pig to torture them like that! And they made up their minds it would be quite a while before that little brute saw his hundred marks.

VIII

They would have to act at once, and act in secret, so much was clear. They must go on sticking it out in the agency, for they might not get the contract, and they must not lose their only means of support.

They must find out about buying typewriters, on an instalment system of course, and they must look round for an office; and they must work all day at the Presto Agency.

Kufalt and Maack ran around until they nearly dropped; and, on that memorable evening, they had succeeded in mustering five reliable men from the Presto Agency: the explosive Jänsch, Sager, Deutschmann, Fasse and Oeser.

They were sitting in Maack's attic room, on the bed, the window sill, the washstand and the solitary chair. They had turned Maack's girl out. 'You go on the street for a bit, Lieschen, see if you can't once do something for your sweetie.'

'And so I will,' she laughed, her little cherry eyes twinkling under her fringe.

'Here, let's each give her a groschen. You can go to a café, Lieschen.'

'Fat chance! When I've got a day off! When am I to come back?'

'Get along now. You needn't come back at all . . . Say about twelve,' said Maack.

At first they were all dazzled by the prospect of independence and so much money. They all talked at once – of course they were going to succeed; seven men would be quite enough; work would seem quite different when they were on their own; nine hours a day was nothing, they would do twelve, fourteen, and work on Sunday too; Maack must keep away from Lieschen for a month, and Kufalt must pull himself together; and should they share the proceeds, or pay by the thousand as at the Presto?

'But we haven't got the contract yet!'

'Yes, and who will go and get it?'

'You'll have to give notice at the agency, Kufalt, you'll be getting fired soon anyhow.'

'Fired, eh? No, I shall hold on to it. I need the job at least as much as you do.'

Not one of the seven was inclined to let go the bird in the hand for the two in the bush.

'Well then, we'll have to find someone to represent us.'

'But he'll have to look respectable.'

'And not a crook, of course, we all know that.'

'And he'll need to talk properly.'

'And well dressed.'

'Yes, who knows of anyone?'

No one did.

'It will have to be a bloke they can inquire about.'

'Hmmm.'

Rather an awkward business.

It was really absurd: here were seven men who needed someone to act for them, someone with a clean waistcoat, someone from the other – the bourgeois – world.

And they could think of no one.

Plenty of unemployed, plenty of ex-convicts – but such men could not be sent on such an errand.

'Couldn't it all be done by telephone?'

'Of course not. They'll need to trust us with the stamps and circulars and envelopes; there must be someone decent they can interview.'

There were many suggestions, each more fantastic than the last.

'Nonsense! I know your brother-in-law! He stutters when a dog barks at him!'

'Otsche? He never had a decent pair of trousers on his arse, they'd put him in charge at once.'

They sat there and surveyed each other in silence. At last Jänsch got up slowly. 'Well, we'd better go home, lads. We'll never get on anyhow. We must stick at typing addresses for Jauch and the fat pastor for five marks a thousand. Five marks for the two, and the other five for all of us – that's the fair way to split the profits, eh?'

They stood there, still undecided; it was so hard to abandon that dream. Their own work, their own contract, their own money, their own office, their own machines – and prospects for the future, perhaps even a large typing agency of their own . . .

'Well, that's that,' said Jänsch.

'Do you know,' said Kufalt slowly; 'I didn't like to say so, but I believe I know someone. He's an utter soak . . .'

'Well then, he's no good.'

'But he's an educated man, he's been to university, and he might manage it . . .'

'What's his name?'

'How do you know him?'

'Can you get him at once?'

But there were difficulties ahead: Beerboom alone knew Berthold's address, quite apart from the fact that Kufalt had sworn never to have anything to do with Beerboom again: it was then nine o'clock, he would have to go to the Home to check whether Beerboom was there, and then see whether Berthold was in, whether he would come, and whether he was sober enough . . .

'I think we'd better drop it,' said Kufalt, discouraged by so many obstacles.

'What? Drop it? You get along, we'll give you an hour to collect Berthold and bring him round!'

'Go or we'll sling you downstairs!'

'Get a move on! Will you go quietly, or do you want a little help from behind?'

Kufalt went: it was mad, but he went; it was hopeless, but he went . . .

The Home of Peace, the good old carefree Home of Peace, in the Apfelstrasse . . .

'Evening, Minna! Is Woolly Teddy at home? No, I don't want to see him. Petersen there? In the sitting room? No, I don't want to see him. Beerboom there? No, I'm not pulling your leg, I never did, now did I? Beerboom there? Up in the bedroom? Crying? Good, then let me go up to him. You mustn't? Oh, Minna, darling Minna, let your old friend go up, I've just got something to ask him, Minna, I'll go away at once and I'll give you a . . .'

'Who's that at the door, Minna?' came Frau Seidenzopf's peevish tones. 'I'll thank you not to start talking to strange men in my house.'

'It's only Kufalt, Frau Seidenzopf. He wants to see Beerboom, but I shan't let him in, Frau Seidenzopf . . .'

And Minna slammed the door.

Kufalt stood outside.

'Oh God, what am I to do? I daren't go back without Berthold. Shall I ring again? Seidenzopf will tell Marcetus, and I'll be fired at once . . .'

He stood irresolute. Finally he slipped through the front garden, through which Berthold, whom he now so badly wanted, had once crawled, hat in mouth. Kufalt peered through the window bars and rapped on the sitting room window.

It was indeed Petersen who looked out; there were two or three heads behind him.

'Good evening, Herr Petersen. Would you be so kind as to call Herr Beerboom to the window. It's something very important . . .'

Kufalt and Petersen had never really made up their quarrel since the evening of that unfortunate excursion. So Petersen replied with a doubtful look: 'You know the regulation, Kufalt – Herr Kufalt – I will first have to ask Herr Seidenzopf.'

'Oh, please don't do that, Herr Petersen. You know what Father Seidenzopf's like, he always makes such a storm in a teacup. I promise you it'll only take two minutes; and you can all listen . . .' And as he caught Petersen's expression, he added: 'It's very important for me and my future prospects . . .'

Petersen, student Petersen, friend and adviser to the ex-convicts, shook his head. 'No, my dear Herr Kufalt, it's against the rules . . . Of course I'll gladly go to Herr Seidenzopf if you like . . .'

'OK, don't then, you dope,' roared Kufalt in a sudden fury – mainly because he had begged, and begged in vain; and he made off.

Suddenly Petersen called after him in quite a different voice: 'Kufalt! Herr Kufalt!! Listen a moment . . .'

'Damn him!' thought Kufalt savagely. 'He's just such an arsehole as I am. Talks very big, and then he's all over you. If I go back to those blokes they'll sling me downstairs – pot full of soup and no spoon. If I go home, I'll think of Liese – another pot full of soup, and so it goes on . . . but – if – I go . . .'

An idea suddenly came into his head; he turned, ran past the Home of Peace (the sitting room window was still open), jumped onto a tram and went down to the Lange Reihe.

The Lange Reihe is not a very long street, but not a particularly short one, and to inquire at every house would have been something of an undertaking. But there would be taverns of which Berthold was certainly a good customer, especially as his affairs, so Beerboom had said, were prospering.

'Berthold?' asked the man behind the counter in the second tavern he entered. 'I suppose you mean Herr Doctor Berthold? What do you want him for? Money?'

'I also am a doctor of political economy,' said Kufalt reproachfully.

'Indeed, I beg your pardon, Herr Doctor. Herr Doctor Berthold is in the back room; right through.'

'Berthold! Herr Berthold!' said Kufalt imploringly to the pallid, hawk-nosed creature. 'Do try to sober up for a minute. There's money in it! A lot of money. We're talking about three thousand marks.'

'Idiots!' said Berthold, who was very drunk. 'No money. You trying to sting me? If you are, the lad behind the counter'll chuck you into the street.'

'Do listen, Herr Berthold . . .' said Kufalt again; 'it's like this . . .'

And he told the whole story over again, slowly, word for word; Berthold seemed to listen, nodded and said, 'Your health!' from time to time: 'Filling envelopes and licking stamps, eh? Hah! Have a rum grog?'

'So you see, Herr Berthold, we mustn't let a thing like that go, when there's so much money in it.'

'No money at all,' persisted Berthold, and went on drinking.

'But I have explained it all to you, three hundred thousand addresses, perhaps ten marks a thousand, makes three thousand marks. And you'll get your share, Herr Berthold.'

'Morons,' grinned Berthold. 'There's no Hamburger 128 in Barmbeck.'

'But I tell you there is! You needn't go there now, I want you to come round and see my friends to discuss the matter.'

'Hey, Adi!' shouted Berthold. 'Bring a map of Hamburg. This bloke here still believes in print.' And to Kufalt: 'You're an idiot, you're a pack of idiots, you'd fall for any confidence man. Crooks, eh? Oafs, idiots, fatheads, that's what you are . . .'

He stood there, fairly steady on his legs. 'Name of firm?'

'Klemmzig & Lange,' said Kufalt breathlessly, as Adi appeared with a plan of the city, grinning.

'Klemmzig,' said Berthold, gesturing with his hand. 'Klemmzig means snatching, don't you see, you fathead? Lange,' went on Berthold, and made another snatch with his hand. 'Haven't you heard of the famous firm of "Snatch and Grab", idiot? And Barmbeck, everyone knows that's where the crazies are sent, you poor mutt! Give my compliments to the other idiots, with love from Berthold. My best love.'

But Kufalt had long since rushed off, his brain illuminated by ten-thousand-kilowatt lamps.

IX

The seven dupes had only one consolation, and that was a reckoning with Herr Patzig next day. Alas, Herr Patzig was nowhere to be seen.

'He's got your export job, that's dead certain,' whispered Kufalt to Maack.

'That's why he was so above himself, the mean bastard . . .'

'Well, we'll catch him one day,' said Jänsch to the others as he passed them on his way to the ribbon box.

'My ribbon's worn out too,' said Maack to Kufalt, and went towards the box.

'I think I'd better . . .' said Kufalt to himself, and joined them.

'Perhaps he's been talking to Jauch,' said Jänsch to Maack.

'Look, we don't want you as well,' protested Maack to Kufalt. And to Jänsch: 'I hope not. Oh God, here comes Deutschmann. If Jauch sees us all here . . .'

'My ribbon's worn out,' growled Deutschmann. 'And Jauch keeps on telephoning. I can hear it through the door from where I sit. About a big contract. I can't help thinking . . .'

'Nor can I,' interrupted Maack. 'That pig Patzig wasn't pulling our leg at first. It was all true about the three-hundred-thousand contract. It was when we needled him for the address that he got the idea of taking us for a ride.'

'Could be,' agreed Kufalt. 'Perhaps he's after the big contract for himself?'

'But he can't do it on his own?'

'He'll have got someone else on the job.'

'Job? What is this I hear about a job?' Jauch's rasping voice startled the little group. The four men, in their zeal for new ribbons, had not noticed the profound stillness that had suddenly fallen upon the room, broken only by the rattle of typewriters, nor Sager's warning cough.

Beside them stood Jauch, flushed, almost trembling with rage. 'What kind of criminal conspiracy is this, gentlemen? I don't know what the place is coming to, I . . .'

His voice rose to a shriek. The door of the adjacent room opened, the heads of the two girls appeared, and the taller of the two said: 'Not so much noise, please, Herr Jauch. There are customers waiting in the dictating room.'

And they surveyed the scene dispassionately.

'We were talking about Herr Patzig,' said Maack; 'and how well he'd done for himself. *I* was to have had that job in the export company. But what you say about criminal conspiracy and all that – I shall complain to Herr Pastor Marcetus.'

Maack picked up a ribbon and went calmly to his place.

'So will I,' said Jänsch. 'You have no business saying such a thing in the presence of the . . .'

He jerked his head towards the door where the girls were standing, picked up a ribbon and went back to his place.

'I'll bring an action against you, Herr Jauch,' said Deutschmann indignantly, and disappeared to his seat.

'Really, gentlemen,' said Jauch, breathless and bewildered. The eyes of the whole typing room were on him. Kufalt tried to slip away in silence.

'This is all since you've been here, Herr Kufalt,' roared Jauch in a fresh outburst of rage. 'Stop! Come with me! Come into my room.'

'Don't you stand any nonsense from him, Willi,' whispered Maack, in an audible tone.

And Kufalt, helpless and shattered, wondering why every bit of trouble always came his way, shambled obediently behind Jauch into his room, the door of which he politely shut behind the typing room manager.

But the dreaded outburst did not come at once. Jauch paced up and down the room like an infuriated bull. But he soon slackened his pace, looked up, glanced at the figure by the door, went to the desk and picked up a piece of paper.

Finally he stopped by the window and said, to the window, not to Kufalt: 'Hoppensass, the banker, is getting a great many begging letters from ex-convicts. It seems to have got round that it's his hobby to help such men.'

He paused for a while; Kufalt waited.

'Hoppensass, the banker,' said Jauch, no longer to the window, but this time to the desk lamp; 'Hoppensass had an idea on which I venture no opinion. He wants inquiries made, through an ex-convict, as to whether the ex-convicts that apply to him are deserving cases or not. He thinks that such a man would know best. Yes?'

Kufalt faced the pseudo-sympathetic scrutiny of those evil little piggy eyes. 'An excellent job for me,' was his first thought. 'I shan't get it.' 'A sprat to catch a mackerel,' was his second.

'We ought to recommend him some reliable person – yes, Herr Kufalt?'

Silence.

A long silence.

Then Kufalt cleared his throat, and said with desperate resolve: 'We were only discussing why Patzig had got the export job. Patzig's work is hardly any better than mine.'

'Indeed,' said Herr Jauch dryly. 'That's your opinion,' he remarked unpleasantly. 'Now I'll tell you something,' Jauch continued, but he never got to what he was going to say to Kufalt, for the telephone rang. 'Presto Typing Agency. Yes, Herr Jauch himself speaking. What? We must give a definite answer? But of course! Eleven marks is really a very low rate. If it wasn't for the fact that it's for three hundred thousand, we should charge you twelve, as usual. Your address lists are very easy to copy? Yes, but I should have to see them first. Very well, if that's so, perhaps half a mark less, I'll speak to Herr Pastor Marcetus at once. No . . . no . . . we'll let you have a definite decision this afternoon. All right, I'll come at once, I'll be round in a quarter of an hour.'

Jauch hung up the receiver. He had forgotten Kufalt. Suddenly he noticed him by the door, attentively studying the backs of the commercial directories.

'I've no time for you now,' he growled. 'I must go out at once. We'll have a talk later on.'

'May I ask a favour?' said Kufalt, in an unusually obsequious tone. 'I've got terrible toothache. May I go to the dentist at once?'

'I can't write you a note for the Welfare Office now,' said Jauch. 'At lunchtime.'

'I'll go at my own expense, Herr Jauch. I don't want to give you any trouble.' And he added anxiously: 'It doesn't cost more than one and a half marks to have a tooth pulled out, does it?'

'I must go,' said Jauch.

'I'll be as quick as I can,' said Kufalt. 'I really can't bear it any longer.'

'Very well,' said Jauch, and ran out of the room.

X

Kufalt slipped like a weasel through the typing room, as he passed whispering to Maack: 'It was true what Patzig said,' and was outside in an instant. Maack had not caught his hurried whisper.

Coat and hat – what a time it all took! Jauch's step was no longer audible on the stairs; it all depended on whether Jauch walked, and did not take any transport. Kufalt had to walk, he knew the state of his pocket too well. A few pfennigs – good for three cigarettes. Better not take any more or he might be tempted to spend it.

The street. A glance to the right, a glance to the left. Not a sign of Jauch. No good to stand and hesitate: to the centre of the city? Or the suburbs? To the centre, surely, for a textile house. Kufalt ran.

At the next street corner there were three alternatives. Kufalt dashed blindly round the corner to the right. A wild goose chase; it was futile.

Not a sign of Jauch; not a sign. A throng of people. No Jauch. Should he go back? Yes.

Kufalt ran back to the crossroads again; the traffic light was red, but he dared not wait. He slipped round cars and trams, until suddenly he found himself wedged in; someone cursed, he doubled back onto the pavement he had left, and as he looked round a figure emerged from a tobacconist's puffing away on a cigar. Herr Jauch!

'Well, Kufalt, where are you off to?'

'Over there.' And he pointed. He hardly knew his way around Hamburg. What if Jauch should ask the name and address of the dentist!

But he did not ask.

'You'd better hurry up. You know you have to make eighteen marks this week. Toothache or no toothache. Do you understand? No excuses accepted.'

'Yes,' said Kufalt humbly, took off his hat, and dropped behind.

Then he followed Jauch, under cover of a couple just in front. Jauch went on his way, walking with the bouncing, tiptoe gait of fat men, puffing contentedly at his cigar; and if he looked round occasionally it was certainly not at Kufalt, but at the girls in their light blouses, with their bare arms and lissom legs.

'Damned pimply old goat,' whispered Kufalt, and for safety's sake crossed to the other side of the street, the better to conceal himself.

Jauch likewise crossed over. Kufalt dodged back again, and saw Jauch disappear round an opposite corner. Kufalt went after him – what an unpleasantly empty street! It would be awkward here. He must keep some way behind. Jauch turned the corner, Kufalt trotting in pursuit. And Herr Jauch vanished – how does the phrase go? – as though the earth had swallowed him.

Kufalt stopped, panting. So the chase had been in vain. He had vanished, vanished for good, into one of these houses.

At last Kufalt came to his senses and realized that a textile firm must have a shop, or at least a plate on the door, and that it must be one of not more than ten or twelve houses; and he began to search.

There were no shops. As to firms: on fifteen houses there were only two plates, either of which might be what he wanted: 'Lemcke & Michelsen, Children's Clothing, Wholesale' and 'Emil Gnutzmann, Successors to Stieling, Textile Distributors'.

'That was an easy one,' thought Kufalt to himself with relief, planting himself behind an advertisement pillar; and sure enough, twenty minutes later, he saw Jauch come out, stop, look up at the sky, take a cigar out of his pocket, cut it, light it, walk down the street, and turn back . . .

Herr Jauch came back, straight towards Kufalt's pillar; Kufalt dodged nervously round it. 'Which side will he come? Suppose I ran bang into him! Did the brute spot me?' But Jauch disappeared into a quiet little café, and Kufalt suddenly understood. 'Jauch has practically fixed it up, he's just got to telephone Marcetus.'

There Kufalt stood, still behind his pillar, and thoughts raced through his head: 'We'll lose it, we'll lose it! And such a chance, a contract like that only comes twice a year . . . I ought to have a try. I'll be on the street in a week, I can't make eighteen as long as Liese . . . If he's sitting behind the curtains, he's bound to see me cross the street. It's madness, I'll slip round the corner and go back to the typing room, Berthold ought to be here, perhaps I'll make eighteen . . .'

But he risked it and ran, stood in the entrance of Gnutzmann, Successors to Stieling, and looked across at the café to see whether the door would open, or Jauch's angry fist appear from behind the curtains . . .

Slowly Kufalt mounted the stairs. It was, at any rate, encouraging to know that he was wearing a good suit, his blue one with the white needle stripe, and a decent shirt, so that no one would smell an ex-convict, if he behaved properly; indeed he looked as well as the old Kufalt looked in his heyday.

'Can I see the boss?' he asked in that tone of forced cheerfulness that he used to hear in days gone by in many an office from many a commercial traveller.

'What about, please?' asked the pretty, fair-haired young woman in the reception room in that tone of metallic courtesy which every clerk in every office can produce at will, for every uninvited caller.

'The address contract,' said Kufalt, listening in the direction of the stairs on which he could hear a step.

'Herr Bär is dealing with that,' said the girl. 'But I think the contract is already assigned. Just a moment. Would you kindly take a seat?'

The step passed, but Kufalt did not dare sit down; Jauch might appear at any moment. He paced up and down, the blood began to throb in his throat, the coward's courage had already vanished.

What – oh, what – had he let himself in for?

'Herr Bär will see you,' said the young woman, and led the way. The door of the disconcerting reception room shut behind him, and Kufalt then felt safe.

'What is it?' asked Herr Bär curtly.

Kufalt bowed. He had imagined Herr Bär as an elderly, careworn, corpulent personage, and he saw before him a young man, athletic and well dressed.

'We heard,' said Kufalt, recovering from his bow, 'that you had a large address contract to award. My firm is very anxious to get it. We are quite a new firm, and we would offer you discount prices, the lowest you could possibly get.'

'What would they be?'

'If the address lists are fairly straightforward to copy – ten marks a thousand.'

Young Herr Bär's face darkened: 'The contract is as good as given. I have more or less promised it.'

And he looked inquiringly at Kufalt.

'Well,' said Kufalt hurriedly, 'we would do it for nine fifty.'

'Nine marks,' said Herr Bär, 'and I'll see if I can get out of my promise.' Kufalt hesitated, and Bär said: 'It would be rather unpleasant for me, so you would at least have to make it worth my while.'

'Nine marks twenty-five,' added Kufalt, as the door opened, the pretty reception clerk looked in and said: 'Herr Jauch is here, Herr Bär.'

Kufalt glanced anxiously at the door . . . it would open in a moment . . . the manager of the typing room, and here he was trying to compete against him . . . a mere ex-convict . . . besides which, he was at the dentist . . . but it was against the law to reproach a man publicly for having been in prison . . . or perhaps in a case like this it was permissible . . . ?

'Tell him to wait,' growled Herr Bär. And to Kufalt: 'That's your competitor. He'll do it for eight and a half.'

'Not under ten and a half,' said Kufalt. 'I know him.'

'Ah,' said Herr Bär. 'By the way, what is the name of your agency?'

Kufalt's brain cut out . . . a name. Quick! A name!

'Cito . . . Presto,' he said breathlessly. And then more calmly – it was a sort of short circuit in his brain: 'Cito-Presto Agency.'

'Well,' laughed Herr Bär, 'that's certainly one up on your competitor! And when can you begin?'

'Tomorrow morning,' said Kufalt, feeling dizzy. (No typewriters – no office – and they would need a telephone too.)

'And how many can you deliver daily?'

'Ten thousand.'

'Right. That makes a month. No, five days more, not counting Sundays.'

'We'll deliver the three hundred thousand in a month.'

'Right,' said Herr Bär meditatively, surveying Kufalt, but his thoughts were obviously elsewhere. 'You can fetch the envelopes and the address lists first thing tomorrow. Where is your office, did you say?'

'We are moving at the moment,' said Kufalt hastily. 'We haven't got into our new place yet, and we have left the old one. As soon as we are settled I will give you the address.' And he cursed himself for being a fool – after all, he must know where they were going!

But Herr Bär was still absorbed in his own thoughts. 'Right,' he said pensively; and then added abruptly: 'Listen . . .' – he stopped; 'I don't yet even know your name, Herr . . .'

'It may go wrong,' thought Kufalt; 'why should I put both feet in it? There's Jauch outside . . .' And he said hastily: 'Meierbeer is my name. Meierbeer.'

'Any connection with the composer? Or with me – at the tail end? Ha-ha!' Herr Bär laughed. 'Now, Herr Meierbeer, I dare say you won't mind if I send you away by the trade staircase. You see, your competitor, Herr Jauch . . . I've more or less promised him the job . . . I must fix it somehow; you understand?'

'Of course,' Kufalt laughed with relief, and the throbbing of his heart began to subside. He suddenly realized that this was his lucky day. 'I wouldn't care for the competitor to see me pinching his contract.'

'That's all right then,' said Bär. 'Come along.'

'How much printed matter is there to be in each envelope?' asked Kufalt suddenly.

'Oh, not too much,' said Herr Bär encouragingly. 'One eight-page prospectus folded, and an order postcard inside.'

'Putting in order cards makes extra work.'

'Not as much as all that,' said Herr Bär cheerfully.

'I beg your pardon – when there are three hundred thousand of them. It means at least four, or five, working days extra.'

'Well, nine marks then,' said Herr Bär, holding out his hand.

'Nine marks fifty is the lowest,' said Kufalt, with his hand behind him.

'Excuse me,' said Herr Bär indignantly; 'you have already said nine marks twenty-five.'

'Not with a reply postcard,' said Kufalt. He was standing on the top stair, and Herr Bär on a mat outside the door.

'Then we'll call it off,' said Herr Bär, withdrawing his hand. 'Herr Jauch is still waiting.'

'We have to live,' said Kufalt, certain that Jauch would not do it at the price; 'and we will do them much more neatly than any other firm.'

'That's what they all say,' growled Herr Bär; 'and then half of them come back undelivered.'

'That can only be the fault of the address lists.'

'Not here; our addresses are all correct.'

'That's what all firms say,' smiled Kufalt.

'Oh, do talk business, Herr Meierbeer,' said Herr Bär, with a smile, attracted again by his visitor's name. 'Do you write it with an "ä" like me?'

'No, with a double "e",' said Kufalt. 'Nine fifty.'

'Let's say nine twenty-five, and here's my hand on it.'

'Well, I'll meet you,' said Kufalt coming down. 'Nine forty.'

'Herr Jauch says he can't wait any longer,' said the reception clerk.

'Herr Jauch can go to . . .' shouted Herr Bär furiously; then, composing himself, he added: 'No, no, Fräulein, he can't. Tell him to wait just three more minutes.' To Kufalt he proposed 'Nine thirty.'

'Nine thirty-five,' said Kufalt; 'and that's my last word. But cash down on delivery of every ten thousand.'

'Agreed,' said Bär. 'Confirm it in writing; and I'll send you an acknowledgement.'

'Right,' said Kufalt. And now the hands met. 'Then early tomorrow morning . . .'

'In the name of my firm I thank you very much for the contract,' said Kufalt, suddenly becoming very formal. He shook the other's hand again. 'I hope we may do further business together.'

He descended the stairs with dignity, while Herr Bär reluctantly applied himself to wriggling out of his option to Herr Jauch.

XI

It was shortly after the half-hour's midday break, and a scorching summer's day. The typing room was stifling and sultry, the white-washed windows did not even admit the solace of blue sky and sunshine: just a room full of hot and choking air.

Fingers danced limply on the keys; when the carriage clicked it was pushed back by slow and weary hands, a second's pause, and the fingers began again.

Hot, moist foreheads, blank drawn faces, not a word, not a whisper; just limp and grumpy men, typing.

In the next room, the women at the copying machine were gossiping. They had nothing to do; it was now three or four days since they had had any work. But they got their pay just the same, they did not need to worry; food drops into some people's mouths, but it's not much good licking lips on an empty belly.

Twenty typewriters were rattling, but above it could be heard the door in Jauch's office being flung open and then slammed with a thunderous crash.

The building quivered.

Kufalt glanced at Maack. Maack glanced at Kufalt. Maack dropped his eyelids to indicate that he had understood.

Hurried footsteps in the office, a window was thrown open, and Jänsch burst into suppressed merriment, for within Jauch could be heard cursing himself. Then silence fell; the door opened, Jauch thrust a purple face into the room and roared: 'Fräulein Merzig! Fräulein Merzig!!'

'Yes, Herr Jauch?'

On the further side of the typing room the door opened, Fräulein Merzig (the tall one) also put her head through. 'Yes, Herr Jauch, what is it?'

'The Hamburg address book – quick, please.'

'Certainly, Herr Jauch.'

Everyone noticed that a storm was brewing, the lightning had begun to flash. Fräulein Merzig hurried from seat to seat in the typing room, in search of the Hamburg directory.

Jauch, his face still purple, followed her with his eyes. 'Who the hell has got it? Can't he speak up!'

She found it on Sager's table, and took it away.

'Look here, Fräulein, I've got a job to do,' protested Sager feebly.

She ran with it to Herr Jauch, who announced in a menacing tone:

'Several pushy gentlemen will soon find themselves without a job.'

He grabbed the directory and vanished.

'You might at least say "excuse me", or "please", Fräulein,' moaned Sager.

'I don't speak to you at all,' said Fräulein Merzig, and she meant not merely Sager, but everybody in that room. She departed to her colleague, carefully leaving the door slightly ajar. 'There's something up today, I've never seen Jauch like this; he's certainly going to sack one of those men.'

He was still cursing in his room, savagely turning the pages of the directory; then he appeared again in the door; the whole of him, this time.

'May I have my directory back, Herr Jauch?' asked Sager obstinately.

'Has anyone heard of the Cito-Presto Typing Agency?' asked Jauch, advancing into the middle of the room.

Silence.

Then a voice was heard: 'The Cito Agency, Herr Jauch . . .'

'I said Cito-Presto, you fool!' roared Jauch; he was already in the next room, where he repeated his question.

'The Cito Agency . . .' said Fräulein Merzig.

'Fool!' roared Jauch, controlled himself, and said more mildly, 'Beg pardon,' but slammed the door behind him.

He swung round; before him sat the entire typing room like a class of schoolboys, all with their faces turned towards him. He leaned against the door, thrust his hands into his pockets, rattled his keys in one of them, jingled his small change in the other, frowned darkly and gnawed his underlip.

'Someone get the cigar out of my ashtray . . .'

He pondered, looked along the ranks, his eye resting balefully on Maack, who was typing. Jauch pondered once more, then darted at the man behind Maack, and shouted: 'Lammers!'

Lammers jumped up nervously, almost ran into the office, returned with the stump of a cigar and handed it to Jauch.

'Match!' said the latter.

Lammers felt in his pockets, found some matches, struck one, and lit Jauch's cigar, quivering nervously all the time. Jauch drew on the cigar and puffed out smoke. 'You know quite well that smoking is forbidden here. If I see you with matches again . . . !'

'But I haven't been smoking, Herr Jauch,' faltered Lammers.

'Hold your tongue! Do you want to be sacked, or will you hold your tongue!' roared Jauch to Lammers, who was now ashen.

Lammers stood for a moment, then tottered to his place, crouched down into his chair and started typing.

For a moment there was silence. Jauch snorted. Everyone felt it was the first gust before the breaking storm. Jauch was on the look-out for his next victim, and his eye fell on Kufalt, who was typing desperately. Jauch's lips were moving, when a powerful bass was heard from the back of the room, 'Stinking monkey cage!'

Jauch turned sharply, his lips parted in amazement, and he gasped, like a man winded by a blow in the stomach: 'What? Who said that?'

Jänsch stood up behind his typewriter and raised one finger like a schoolboy: 'I did, Herr Jauch.'

He stood for a moment waiting, and watched Jauch working himself up for an outburst; then, just as Jauch was about to explode: 'I said that this monkey cage stinks, Herr Jauch. It always does on a sweltering hot day like this, doesn't it?'

'Come with me!' shrieked Jauch. 'Come with me to my room and get your papers. You're sacked, you ungrateful swine. Take your papers!'

'And my money,' said Jänsch imperturbably, and walked beside Jauch to his room.

They were nearly through the door when someone else got up in another corner of the room, Deutschmann this time, and shouted: 'Herr Jauch, I too think the monkey cage stinks.'

Jauch stood dumbfounded; his lips moved but no words came. He thought for a moment, then raised his hand. 'Come with us, Herr Deutschmann, you are both dismissed.'

'Good,' said Deutschmann; 'that's all right by me.'

But before they could get into Jauch's office, Sager got up and said in a polite and quiet voice: 'May I have my Hamburg directory back, Herr Jauch? I must get on with my work.'

'Be quiet!' roared Jauch in reply to this polite inquiry.

'In that case I am also of the opinion that this monkey cage stinks,' said Sager, with the same smiling politeness. And added rather more quickly:

'I would like to join the others, Herr Jauch, I will do so at once.'

'This is mutiny!' shouted Herr Jauch. 'This is . . .'

'You have forgotten, Herr Jauch, mutinies only occur in prisons,' said Maack coolly, also standing up. 'We are not, I think, in prison here?'

'Herr Maack, of course,' said Jauch slowly, and his fury had now evaporated. His face was no longer red, it was sickly pale. He was still very agitated, but he had got a grip on himself. 'May I, to save time, ask which of you considers that this – er – monkey cage stinks? Do speak freely, gentlemen.'

Kufalt, Fasse and Oeser stood up.

'And myself,' said Maack.

'Well, of course. Herr Fasse, Herr Oeser. And our friend Herr Kufalt. But I know all about it, gentlemen, though you may think I don't. I know . . .'

The hearts of the conspirators stood still: if the brute really did know all about it, and managed to spoil their game . . .

'It is a conspiracy, and our dear good humble friend Kufalt is at the bottom of it. I heard you at the ribbon box today making arrangements about a job, as you called it. I shall report it to the police, I shall . . .'

'I also consider that the monkey cage stinks,' said a clear and ringing voice. Another had got up, a tall, slim, fair-haired pretty boy called Emil Monte . . .

'You sit down, my lad, you don't belong to us,' shouted Jänsch, not thinking.

'There is the proof,' said Jauch gravely; 'that it was a premeditated plan. Come into my room one by one and get your papers and your money. I shall discuss the matter with Herr Pastor Marcetus. You'll soon see the result of this day's work.'

5
The Cito-Presto Typing Agency

I

Here was glory!

One of them cried: 'Let's go and get some grub first; I'm famished.'

'So am I.'

'And I.'

The inner remonstrating voice, 'Hot dinners on weekdays!' died away unheeded, and all eight of them marched into a beer cellar. From the economical Maack, who ate sour lentils at thirty-five pfennigs, to the voracious Jänsch, who disposed of a goulash and a dish of pigs' trotters, not to mention two beers (three marks sixty), all tastes and temperaments were represented.

'I'll stand you all a beer,' shouted Monte, in his high falsetto. 'Thank God I'm out of that monkey cage.'

'Refused with thanks,' growled Jänsch. 'I pay for my own beer.'

'You can drink in a month's time,' said Maack, 'when the job's done.'

'Ugh!' said Monte. 'Don't be so goody-goody. I'm so-o-o glad that all that damned envelope addressing is over. It made me puke. I did enough work in the clink.'

The seven others sat, knife and fork in hand, looked at Emil Monte, and then seriously at each other.

'Now then, what ideas have you guys got, eh? Out with it, I'm game for anything.'

'But we aren't,' cried Fasse, and got a stern look from Jänsch.

It was already clear that there were two who would compete for leadership. Maack replied for Jänsch: 'What ideas we've got, Monte? Address-writing!'

'Yes,' said Jänsch quickly, making his view known; 'and such address-writing as hasn't come your way yet. Fifteen hours a day, and if that don't suit you, a whack on the arse.'

He raised his great spade-like hand and held it threateningly under Monte's nose.

'I doubt whether we should take Monte at all,' said Maack in a quick, level voice. 'He's not one of us.'

'Oh God, oh God, oh God,' said handsome, fair-haired Monte, quite overwhelmed, 'you're going to do real work, are you? Then what a fool I've been!'

'We must discuss all that,' said Jänsch. 'I've finished. Waiter – bill!'

'Waiter – all the bills!'

'We'll go to your place, Kufalt, it's the most handy.'

II

Here was glory!

To begin with, by a majority of two votes, calm Maack was elected manager of the typing agency.

'I gratefully accept your choice,' said Maack in a quick, firm tone, with a little jerk at the spectacles on the bridge of his nose; 'and I shall always do my best to promote your interests. Now you lot have all got to toe the line,' he said more rapidly, as he caught a jealous growl from Jänsch. 'I shall give as few orders as possible, but those I do give must be obeyed without question. Anyone who objects . . .'

'Whack on the arse,' growled Jänsch.

'Yes, Jänsch, something of the kind was in my mind,' said Maack with a smile. 'And now about Monte. I have thought over the case again. I am now of a different opinion . . .'

'So am I,' growled Jänsch.

'You are against keeping him?'

'Yes, I'm against keeping him.'

'I am,' said Maack, 'of a different opinion. We have to deliver three hundred thousand addresses in one month. Two men must be continually folding the prospectuses and putting them into envelopes. That leaves, including Monte, six men for typing. Six times ten is sixty, six times six is thirty-six, nine thousand six hundred . . .'

'What sort of bloody sum is this?'

'Even if Monte stays, each man will have to type from sixteen hundred to seventeen hundred addresses per day.'

'Blimey!'

'That's a bit stiff!'

'I can do two thousand,' said Jänsch.

'So can I,' said Maack. 'And I'm sure Deutschmann can too. But there are several that can't. So I propose we should put Monte on to folding, and sticking into the envelopes, with Kufalt to help. Otherwise we shan't manage it.'

Hostile silence. One said angrily: 'And what's he to be paid?'

'But I don't want to come in with you,' Monte butted in. 'It wasn't for this sort of job that . . .'

Jänsch stood up and marched across the room to Monte. He took him by the shoulders, held his arms against his body, and shook him. 'You little pansy,' he said; 'you little pansy.'

'That will do, Jänsch,' said Maack. 'So now you know, Monte. In one month you can do what you like. Until then . . .'

'See,' said Jänsch. He picked up Monte and set him down with a thud on the nearest chair.

Monte produced a handkerchief, wiped his forehead, rubbed his arm, looked from one to the other with a sort of camp indignation, and suddenly began to giggle like a girl . . .

'What a fine strong man,' he giggled.

'Before we come to a division of work,' said Maack, 'we must find out what money we have available as working capital. We must buy six typewriters on the instalment system – say thirty marks each for the first payment; hire a room – thirty marks; tables and chairs – sixty marks . . .'

'But we can get these things' – with a movement of the hand – 'like that.'

'Tables and chairs, sixty marks . . . And that will be all. A hundred and eighty the machines, thirty the rent; grand total – two hundred and seventy . . . How much can each of you put down?'

Silence.

The silence deepened. Each man was staring fixedly into space.

'There are eight of us,' said Maack. 'That makes forty marks each. Anyone got that much?'

Silence . . . silence.

'Well, I'll put down forty marks,' said Maack. 'What about you, Kufalt?'

'But I got the contract,' said Kufalt dismally. He was afraid that if he produced forty marks on the spot, and the others saw he still had three hundred and forty marks in his wallet, he would have to pay the whole amount.

'And you, Jänsch?'

'My money goes on food, as soon as I get it,' said Jänsch sullenly. 'Anyhow you're the manager, Maack.'

'And you, Fasse? Deutschmann? Sager? Oeser? Monte?'

'You expect me to give you money?' yelled Monte. 'After being treated like this?'

Long and gloomy silence.

'It's up to you – you're the manager,' said Jänsch once more.

'Kufalt got us into this, anyway,' said Oeser angrily.

'Bloody fools we've been. Seventeen hundred addresses a day indeed!'

'Shit!' shouted Sager, and banged on the table.

'Shit!' shouted Fasse likewise.

And suddenly they all shouted 'Shit!' They were like wild men, they hammered on the table and fell into a paroxysm of despair; that dear old typing room they had so lightly given up!

'One moment,' said Maack; and they gradually subsided.

Maack – who really was a compelling figure, with pale, composed face and neat gold spectacles – said: 'Supposing we can find the money . . .'

'Balls!'

'Excuse me! I am convinced that you all have money – except perhaps Monte.'

'No, I've got none,' said Monte. 'If I'm to come in I must have an advance.'

'Very well then; supposing the money can be collected, and we start work tomorrow, the firm will pay us on the day after tomorrow ninety-three marks fifty for the first ten thousand, and a further ninety-three marks fifty every day for work done . . .'

'Yes – if!'

'I now propose that for the present we should pay a weekly wage of twenty-five marks only to each man, until the contributors have got back their deposits. And every contributor shall take fifteen marks from the earnings for every ten marks advanced, as compensation for his risk.'

Deep breaths and silence.

'If this proposal of mine is accepted,' said Maack briskly, 'I am prepared to put up a hundred marks.' A moment's silence – and Maack added, in an absent voice: 'I shall then get back a hundred and fifty.'

'A hundred marks, eh?' growled Jänsch. 'And why should *you* put up a hundred marks? I'll subscribe a hundred marks too.'

'So will I!'

'And I!'

'We don't want as much as that.'

'A hundred and fifty here!' shouted Kufalt.

'And I haven't got more than forty marks,' wailed Monte. 'Why should I be the one to make so little?'

Roars of laughter.

'Look! The pretty boy has twigged it too!'

'Wants payment before, the little pet! No, after, my sweety.'

'Well then,' said Maack, 'the money question is settled in the sense that each of us pays forty marks . . .'

'But we get back sixty!'

'Of course . . . So will everyone please go home as quickly as possible and fetch the money? There's a lot to do today.'

They all hurried out.

'Monte my lad, if you don't come back – we'll find you!'

'I'll come all right,' said Monte; 'if I'm to get sixty marks for forty!'

Kufalt and Maack stayed behind. Maack ruled a sheet of paper, wrote the names of the eight men in a column, with his own on top, and against each the figure 40. Then he took two twenty-mark notes out of a battered red wallet, laid them carefully in front of him, and wrote his own receipt: 'Received, Peter Maack.'

Then he took Kufalt's forty, wrote the receipt, smiled at Kufalt, and said: 'You aren't very bright, you lot! You think you will make twenty marks each and you don't realize it's all going to be equally deducted from what you earn.'

'Wow!' gasped Kufalt. 'And you knew that all the time. Suppose the others find out!'

'I've only told you,' said Maack. 'I hope it won't occur to any of them before they've brought along the stuff.'

III

And then the hour of glory really came.

It seemed that all of them – apart from Oeser, whose clothes were always dirty, and Monte, who was always dressed to look like what he was – had grasped the dignity and gravity of the hour; they had not merely brought the money, they had changed their clothes. Even the uncouth Jänsch looked almost smart, and he had shaved; and Deutschmann, in spite of the burning summer afternoon, came in a morning suit and a stiff black felt hat.

They stood round him and struck up a students' song:

'The bowler!'

'And the pork pie!'

'Oh, your sweet little, stiff little black one' (of course from Monte).

'With your trilby, you naughty boy.'

Deutschmann endured this noisy admiration with smiling composure. Maack, as a token of appreciation, said: 'You, Deutschmann, go with Fasse and rent an office. As near the firm as possible – what's the name of it, did you say?'

'Emil Gnutzmann, Stieling's successor,' interjected Kufalt.

'Right. One room will be enough. An attic will do. Must be a good light. Not more than thirty marks . . .'

'You leave it to me.'

'Not more than thirty marks at the outside! Here's your money; sign the receipt; and mind you get one from the landlord . . .'

'That's all right,' said Deutschmann. 'I'll see to it. What about lamps?'

'Wait a bit. You, Herr Jänsch . . .'

'Look, drop the Herr! When we've all pooled our money, we don't need to call each other Herr.'

'Thank you, Jänsch,' said Maack politely. 'Well then, will you go with Sager and Monte and see to the furniture? You may be able to hire some; if not, buy some plain trestles, so that we can nail boards across them. And three to four second-hand oil lamps. Here's the money; sign the receipt. And please bring back the bills.'

'OK. No need for all this backchat.'

'I'll go with Kufalt and see about the machines. At half past seven we'll meet here again at Kufalt's and report.' And he added, with an air of serious concern, 'But now, lads, we must get everything in order at once; tomorrow, without fail, we must sit down and start typing.'

'You look after the machines, I'll get the furniture.'

'And I'll rent the office.'

'And what am I to do?' asked Oeser.

'You?' said Maack with a sort of embarrassed gravity: 'I've got a special job for you . . .'

'Well, cough it up then. It's the dirtiest job of the lot, that's quite clear.'

'Oh no it isn't. But I don't know whether you'll like it. Now I want to ask you something – I was told – er . . .'

'Out with it, Maack,' said Jänsch.

'I'm listening,' said Oeser. 'I'm not going to blow up yet.'

'Well then, Oeser, I've been told,' Maack began again, 'but of course it may have been just gossip . . .'

'Oh get on or *I'll* blow up,' said Jänsch.

'Counterfeiting, wasn't it?' said Maack.

Oeser was a tall, lanky man in his middle thirties with an angular, sharp face, foxy red hair and long, curiously gnarled hands.

'Drone on,' he said. 'I'm listening . . .'

'Tomorrow, as you know, Kufalt has to produce a statement of the agreement between our firm and theirs. Well, we haven't any headed paper, and can't get any so soon, and anyhow we don't yet know what our address is going to be. Now I wonder if you could fix up a few sheets of paper, by hand, of course, so that they will look exactly as if they had been printed. Did you notice the Presto paper?'

'Go on, I'll sock you one in the jaw when the time comes.' But Oeser grinned.

So Maack continued, more eagerly: 'We must have headed paper, otherwise it will make such a bad impression. And the stuff ought to look specially neat, and a bit modern; a girl, perhaps, sitting at a typewriter: Cito-Presto Typing Agency – the Most Up-to-date Firm on the Continent; Quick – Cheap – Accurate; and perhaps a flash of lightning running through it all, to signify how quick we work. But it must look absolutely as though it were printed . . .'

'Arsehole!' roared Oeser, but with enthusiasm. 'You foolish dog. I've made twenty-mark notes, with the watermarks, that no one can imitate; but I imitated them, and no one noticed, and the Reichsbank took them – and do you suppose I can't make a few sheets of poxy notepaper?! Don't think much of the lightning idea, though. You clear out all of you, and leave me alone, and this evening at half past seven I'll deliver the goods. Hand over five marks, I'll sign for them and give you the bills later . . . Now you all clear out, don't gawp so, this is a job for an expert. I'd always thought – don't look at me like that! I'd never get a decent job to do, I always seem to stink of the clink . . . now then, out you go, and leave the worker to his work . . . Get out!'

'The bloke's quite above himself!'

'Well, make a good job of it, Oeser!'

'Don't put any twenty-mark notes on the firm's paper!'

And they departed laughing.

IV

None of these tasks was easy, but Maack and Kufalt were agreed that theirs was the worst. To borrow, hire, or buy six typewriters for a hundred and eighty marks – that was going to be difficult.

They set their hopes on Herr Louis Grünspohm.

Louis Grünspohm advertised regularly in the Hamburg papers, inviting inspection of his enormous stock, comprising the most modern machines of every variety. Monthly instalments of ten marks upwards.

It turned out that Herr Grünspohm's business was situated in a rather remote and dark alley of second-hand dealers; that Herr Grünspohm was a tall, pale man with a stubbly beard who controlled an array of typewriters of every sort and model, ever since typewriters were invented; but that a man had to produce at least a prime minister or a bank director as a referee before taking possession of a typewriter at a monthly instalment of ten marks.

Grünspohm surveyed both his customers with his quick, bleary, little black eyes, and said: 'Here's one that will do for you. A lovely machine! Ninety marks, two-thirds down, the rest on a bill at three months, with a good sound endorser.'

They both eyed the lovely machine; on the front of it was a sort of indicator-table set with letters; a needle tapped the desired letter and a cylinder began to rotate shakily against the paper, and lo and behold on the paper the letter appeared. Kufalt and Maack shrugged their shoulders.

'A lovely little machine,' urged Herr Grünspohm. 'It writes like a dream, just like a dream.' (And this was no lie.)

'The fact is,' said Maack, 'we are starting a typing agency, we are quite a new firm, but we have very good contracts on hand, very good contracts indeed. But within the next three hours we need six machines, large, modern office machines, you understand. We'll pay thirty marks on each machine, and the rest in monthly instalments of thirty . . . What do you say?' – turning to Kufalt – 'Forty marks, then.'

Kufalt nodded agreement, Herr Grünspohm shook his head thoughtfully: 'From whom have you got these excellent contracts, may I ask?'

Kufalt and Maack exchanged a glance.

'One of them,' said Kufalt, 'is from a textile firm. Emil Gnutzmann, Stieling's successor.'

Grünspohm nodded appreciatively. 'A first-class firm. A sound firm. Uses Adler machines, buys direct from the agent. I bought from them a couple of second-hand machines – Herr Bär's a keen hand at a bargain!'

'You may say so,' laughed Kufalt. 'I found him pretty tough. I had to sweat to get that contract!'

Herr Grünspohm seemed more cheerful and his gloom began to vanish. 'And what is the amount of the contract, may I ask?'

'It will bring us in about three thousand marks,' said Maack with gravity.

Herr Grünspohm pondered. He paced up and down, and then, having made up his mind, he stopped in front of the pair.

'As you are young and energetic, and look honest and respectable, I will make you an offer; tomorrow morning at ten I will deliver you six machines as good as new . . .'

'Not as good as new – new,' said Maack.

'As good as new,' said Herr Grünspohm immovably. 'Good reliable machines: Mercedes, Adler, Underwood, AEG . . . You will pay me three hundred marks down, and bring me a note from Herr Bär authorizing me to collect fifteen hundred marks off what will be due to you, a month from today . . .'

'Certainly not!' shouted Kufalt. 'What are we going to live on?'

'Three hundred marks each for old machines! Are you out of your mind?' protested Maack.

'You are trying to do us down just because we've got the contract and have no machines.'

'Well,' said Grünspohm, 'it's an offer. I doubt if anyone else in Hamburg would make you such an offer.'

'No,' sneered Kufalt. 'No one would dare.'

'Well, think it over, gentlemen,' said Grünspohm. 'A nice little note from the firm of Gnutzmann signed by Herr Bär, and I'll . . .' – he shook himself – 'as a favour to you, I'll say two hundred down.'

'Don't you wish you'll get it,' said Kufalt.

And Maack, with sudden politeness: 'Good day then, Herr Grünspohm. We will consider your offer.'

'Maack . . . !' said Kufalt.

'Good day, gentlemen,' said Grünspohm, as he escorted them to the door, 'you will come back, I am sure. And I will give you really good machines . . .'

They sat on a bench and smoked.

'I don't understand you, Maack,' said Kufalt. 'If we deduct twelve hundred marks, then, reckoning in the three hundred and twenty marks that we have put aside for expenses, only about thirteen hundred marks are left; and that comes to – per head?'

He calculated.

'A hundred and sixty marks, and one typewriter, paid for,' said Maack. 'Not so bad, when you've got your own machine.'

'But we are eight, and there are only six machines,' objected Kufalt.

'Oh, Monte can go and put his head in a bag; why does he foist himself on us?'

'What about me?'

'We'll pay you your share in money.'

'I'll have to wait a while for that; I suppose I can put my head in a bag too,' said Kufalt bitterly.

For a time there was silence.

'And I won't go to Bär with a note like that,' said Kufalt suddenly. 'He'd simply kick me into the street when he finds out I've agreed the contract and we haven't even got machines. I shan't go. I won't do it!'

'Well, you needn't,' said Maack slowly.

'How do you mean?'

'I say – you needn't.'

'But . . . ?'

'Oeser can fix the note for us.'

A long, long silence. They avoided each other's eyes.

There they sat on their bench; they were neatly dressed and looked presentable young men on that fine summer afternoon. They were smoking decent cigarettes; men of brains and efficiency, capable men; outwardly no one could see anything wrong.

'Oeser . . .' Maack said.

But no, they are men with a handicap, blighted men; in them lies the feeling – it was born of a crime, it was fostered in prison and came to fruition on release – that they can never achieve anything in the normal way, that they will never, ever return to the peaceful life of the ordinary citizen. They live on the edge of existence; they shrink at every casual word, at the sight of any sort of policeman; letters, prison companions, a word let slip in sleep, the official at the Welfare Office – all may bring ruin on them: but the worst menace of all is their own selves. They have lost faith and belief in themselves, everything they do inevitably fails; once a jailbird, always a jailbird.

'Oeser,' Maack had said.

And he added hurriedly: 'Please understand, we aren't going to do old Grünspohm down. He'll get his money at the end of the month, but from us. It's all the same to him where he gets his money from. Or we'll give him the machines back. A month's a good while, we can look around a bit.'

'But why?' asked Kufalt. 'We can have another try in other shops.'

'No,' said Maack obstinately; 'this is the best way to fix it. We will know where we are, and we can do as we like.'

'That's what you say,' said Kufalt. 'Look, Maack, you said you weren't going crooked, and the moment we get a job, off you start again. I don't understand you.'

Maack lit a cigarette. He blinked slightly, but he said quite quietly, 'Well, I'm not going crooked, you fool. I just want to see how things are at the end of the month.'

'I'll tell you what you're after,' shouted Kufalt in sudden inspiration. 'You're going to sell the machines and bolt with the money.'

Maack was not in the least offended. He jerked his spectacles into place, spat out a little tobacco and said: 'And I'll tell you something about yourself; you've got a girl here, and that's why you have no guts.'

'Well, and what about your Lieschen?' asked Kufalt excitedly, thinking of the pretty creature with the bright cherry eyes and cork-screw curls.

'Oh, women!' said Maack. 'There are women everywhere.'

He fell silent and then added: 'Mine's going to have a baby, by the way.'

Kufalt, shocked by the news, said nothing. This was bad luck for Maack, as little Lieschen would lose her job – and how would they manage with three of them? But – and he began to think more and more rapidly – why had Maack given up his job at the typing agency just at this very moment; it was at least safe, as he was such an excel-lent typist?

And suddenly an idea shot through his brain, and he said excit-edly: 'Oh Maack! I know all about it now. You were going to pinch all the money. I don't yet know how; that's what you meant to do, and then clear off with it.'

'I'd have left you a bit,' said Maack with a grin.

'And why are you telling me this?' asked Kufalt, bewildered.

'Because I'm sick of it all,' burst out Maack, usually so quiet and self-controlled. 'Because I'm fed up to here. All my life outside has been just hell. Look, Kufalt, I pretend I'm no end of a crook, but I only did three months, even less than Patzig – and that's four years ago, and I work like a horse, and don't spend a penny – and I never get any farther, never. Just one problem after another, and that brute Jauch, and that old hypocrite Marcetus – they all trample on you; twice I've had a job, and I thought I'd got back to a respectable life. But then someone found out, and it all started again – the odd looks and sneering talk; and then someone said he'd lost his rubber, it must be Maack that had it; and somebody else's money was missing out of his overcoat pocket – Maack, of course, Maack, only Maack . . .'

He had stood up and was almost shouting. Passers-by stopped and stared; Kufalt pulled him back onto the bench and tried to calm him down.

Maack took off his spectacles and wiped his forehead.

'And then the boss sent for me and said: "You see for yourself it's no good. I'm not going to say anything against you, but you see for yourself, don't you?" And now my girl's going to have a baby, and she says she won't have it taken away, she's even pleased, the silly fool, because it's mine – mine!'

Maack swallowed; Kufalt said nothing.

'And yesterday morning, when I was going to get that job in the export company, I was as pleased as Punch and I thought, it'll be all right now, I can slip away somewhere with Lieschen and we can have a baby just like other people . . .'

He swallowed again; and then he added: 'And when it was all off with the job, for only bum-suckers get on, I thought, nothing mattered, I'd just collect a bit of money, I didn't care how, and hand over a bit to Lieschen so that she'd get something out of it when I went back to jail.'

He sat huddled on a bench in the park, the sun shining through the trees of the zoo.

'I'll tell you what, Peter,' said Kufalt, 'let's look up the typewriter firms in the commercial telephone directory. I'll go and talk to them myself, and you'll see; at seven o'clock I'll have those machines . . .'

Maack shook his head.

'I will,' protested Kufalt eagerly. He smiled.

'I don't imagine it's so difficult. We made the mistake of trying to get all six at once. We'll soon have that typing agency fixed up, and we'll get more contracts, and you'll be a proper manager on a salary, and glare at us all just like Jauch. And Lieschen shall have her baby – you'll see.'

V

It was a radiant summer morning, about nine o'clock, when the whole Cito-Presto Agency descended on the firm of Gnutzmann. Fasse and Monte were pulling a handcart lent them by their new landlord, while Oeser was pushing it from behind.

On the pavement, in front of the cart, walked Maack and Kufalt. Jänsch, who directed the handling of the cart in traffic, walked a little in front of Sager and Deutschmann.

As they marched along scarcely a word was spoken, except that Jänsch called out from time to time, 'Put out your right arm when you're going to turn a corner to the right, Monte, my lad.' It was a relaxed enough journey, but they were all conscious of the significance of the hour.

'Smart lot, eh?' said Deutschmann.

And Sager, crafty fox, always just a little too polite – in huge delight at the cavalcade – replied, 'I don't think!'

They drew up in front of the textile house, and Manager Maack rapped out his orders.

'Fasse, Monte, each of you to a street corner. If you catch sight of Jauch or any of the Presto people, whistle as agreed, and take cover.'

'Sager, you wait in the entrance hall; if you hear the whistle, run upstairs and warn us.'

'Jänsch, Deutschmann and Oeser, come with us to carry down the envelopes and the address lists.'

'Kufalt, you will introduce me to Herr Bär, and we will hand him our letter of confirmation.'

'Do let me be there,' begged Oeser, 'just to see, Maack.'

'Right,' said Maack, 'come on!'

The young woman in the reception room knew all about them already. 'There are the envelopes; a hundred thousand to begin with. The addresses are on index cards in these drawers – mind you keep them in good order!'

'Of course, Fräulein,' said Jänsch. 'We are very careful people.'

'Mind how you carry them down,' said Maack.

'Card index addresses – they're really good for typing out,' said Deutschmann.

'May we have a word with Herr Bär, Fräulein?' said Kufalt.

'One moment, I'll go and see,' and she vanished.

'Take me with you,' implored Oeser.

'If I can,' said Maack.

'Will you come in, please?' said the young woman, returning.

Kufalt was in front, Maack behind, and Oeser squeezed in after them.

'May I introduce our manager, Herr Bär? Herr Maack, Herr Bär . . .' Hoarse whispers from the rear. 'Oh, yes, Herr Oeser, one of our assistants . . .'

'May I hand you our confirmation of the contract you have been good enough to give us?' said Maack, and took out of a wallet a spotlessly white envelope, which he handed to Herr Bär across the desk.

Bär took it nonchalantly, held it in his hand, and said:

'Nobody seems to have heard of your typing agency, Herr Meierbeer.'

'We are quite a new firm,' said Maack.

'In six months all Hamburg will know our agency,' announced Kufalt proudly.

'Indeed,' said Herr Bär dryly, and unfolded the letter.

Oeser said nothing at all, but with burning eyes – eyes that almost dropped out of his head, they bulged so much – he watched Herr Bär and the sheet of paper in his hand.

But Herr Bär had not yet looked at it. He said with a smile: 'I know all about you young fellows.'

The hearts of the three stopped beating; at last Kufalt pulled himself together and said, in a strange hoarse voice:

'How so – Herr Bär?'

And Herr Bär said pleasantly, 'Come, you must forgive me, I see you are quite upset. But I have twigged in the meantime that you are unemployed men, who have somehow got wind of our contract, and that, incidentally, I could have got you at eight marks a thousand.'

Three hearts beat again.

'Well,' said Herr Bär in conclusion; 'that's no business of mine. The main thing is that the work should be done without the slightest cause for complaint. May I assume that it will?'

'Certainly, Herr Bär,' said three happy voices.

'And that I shan't have any trouble with the Unemployment Office over fraudulent benefits and illegal stamping?' said Herr Bär, turning to the letter.

'Out of the question, Herr Bär,' said Maack. 'None of us are drawing anything.'

'Very attractive indeed,' said Herr Bär, looking at the letter. 'Really charming!'

Oeser blushed dark red with gratification.

No, he had not put in the flash of lightning, which he said suggested a firm of lightning conductor manufacturers. The heading 'Cito-Presto Typewriting Agency' was handsomely printed at the top; beneath it, in smaller lettering, 'Every kind of office work undertaken'; under that, in rather larger lettering again, 'Cheap – Quick – Accurate – Discreet'; and then the place and date, in the usual manner; but down the entire left-hand margin there were designs – on top, a girl at a typewriter, who has typed a letter and is handing it to a young man standing a little lower down the page. And he, with his other hand, is handing a packet of letters to a tall, broad, bearded man, who – a little lower still – is standing behind a sort of packing table.

'Very attractive,' said Herr Bär again. 'I shall keep this letter when it has been dealt with.' He could not put it down, and mused: 'But surely I know the lady, the girl at the machine. And the young man too – and the man with the beard! Tell me, where did you get them from?'

'I really don't know,' said Maack. 'Some man did the design for us.'

'Odd,' said Herr Bär; he put down the letter, and pushed a bell. 'I shall find out somehow. I'm certain I've seen them.'

And when the young woman came in: 'Write a confirmatory letter to the Cito-Presto Typing Agency, here is the format for it. Now careful, please; a nice neat letter . . . "With reference to your communication of the 15th inst., we beg to confirm etc. Yours faithfully." Very well; thank you, gentlemen, I hope it will be a satisfactory transaction.'

The procession with the handcart made its way back to the Cito-Presto Agency; a hundred thousand envelopes and prospectuses, index cards for three hundred thousand addresses, and eight happy men.

'Oeser, come here a minute,' Kufalt called out suddenly.

Oeser came. 'Well?'

'Look, Oeser, Maack and I have been racking our brains, we know those people on your notepaper, and we just can't think who they are. Who's the girl, anyway?'

Oeser, again beaming with pride, merely answered, 'Elizabeth Holbein, née Schmidt, of Basle.'

'What?' said the others slowly, bewildered at first. 'Wasn't she a beauty queen?'

'Let me explain,' said Oeser innocently. 'And the young man is Dietrich Born, merchant, and the man with the beard is Hermann Hillebrandt Wedigh, of Cologne.'

'Never heard of them. But how is it that we know them?'

'You silly dopes!' burst out Oeser in sudden triumph. 'The girl is the girl on a twenty-mark note. The young man is on the ten-mark note. And the man with the beard is from the thousand-mark note; I just took off their caps and hoods, they're all after pictures by Holbein – and no one spotted it!'

He dug his two open-mouthed companions in the ribs. 'Oh, guys, fancy pulling all your legs like that . . .'

'You're a piece of work, Oeser,' said Maack sternly. 'It isn't your job to be pulling people's legs. It's your job to be writing addresses.'

'But surely I know the girl at the machine,' said Oeser mimicking Herr Bär's high-pitched tones. And all three burst into roars of laughter.

VI

It was about ten o'clock in the morning.

In the Cito-Presto office stood the six typewriters, ready for work. Beside them lay piles of blue envelopes; and open drawers packed with blue, red, green and yellow index cards, from each of which a number of cards had been taken and lay ready to be transformed into addresses. At the six machines sat six men, their hands still resting idly on the table, or on their knees.

At a table in the corner sat Kufalt and Monte; before them lay heaps of prospectuses and the reply cards still neatly arranged in bundles, the folding-knives ready to hand.

An expectant silence reigned.

Maack got up, straightened his glasses, and began:

'Gentlemen . . .'

Then he stopped, and blushed slightly as he corrected himself:

'Comrades!'

He looked at them all in turn, and they all returned his look.

'Comrades,' said Maack, and his voice freshened. 'We are just going to begin to type what we have been typing every day for years – addresses. And yet today we are starting a new and hopeful task: we are working solely on our own account.'

He paused.

Then he went on: 'If we are to carry out what we have undertaken, we must all keep hard at it. Every one of us can earn a lot this month. Comrades, save it up. No girls, no cinemas, no drinks, all through this month. And then perhaps we shall manage it.'

Again a pause . . .

Maack hesitated, smiled, and said: 'We are on a sort of month's probation, we're being given another trial, and we're going to try once more . . .'

He stopped and smiled again. Then the smile slowly faded, he looked round him and said: 'I think we might start work now.'

'One moment, please,' Jänsch called out; 'I have a proposal to make.'

'Yes?'

'I propose that talking should be forbidden during working hours. Any man who talks to be fined ten pfennigs for a common fund.'

Maack looked inquiringly round him; 'I think that's a very sensible proposal. Is anyone against it?'

'But . . .' said Monte.

'You hold your tongue, Monte, there's no need for you to talk,' said Jänsch.

'If I'm to work, I'm going to talk,' said Monte defiantly.

'Shut your mouth, I tell you,' said Jänsch menacingly; 'or . . .' and he raised his hands.

'I rule that the proposal is accepted,' said Maack. 'Anything else?'

'Yes,' said Deutschmann. 'I propose that smoking should be forbidden under the same conditions.'

A gloomy silence, for nearly all of them were passionate smokers.

'Smoking not only costs money,' said Deutschmann persuasively, 'it interferes with work; and the room isn't big enough for eight men to fill it with smoke all day long.'

'This is going to be a right little prison,' said Oeser peevishly.

'If I can't smoke, I'm not going to get much fun out of this lark,' observed Fasse.

'But it's quite a sensible suggestion,' said Deutschmann.

'I agree,' said Maack. 'After all, anyone who wants a cigarette can go out to the lavatory and have a smoke.'

'But that wastes working time,' objected Sager. 'Much better smoke while we're working.'

Reluctant silence.

'Shall I put it to the vote?' said Maack hesitatingly.

'I've got another suggestion to make,' said Kufalt eagerly. 'Every two hours, or, if you like, every hour and a half, we can each smoke a cigarette. Maack will give the signal. Then we shall all enjoy it, and work all the quicker.'

'Good idea! That sounds all right,' said one of them approvingly.

'That's sensible.'

'Every hour would be better.'

'Every half-hour!'

'Why not every ten minutes, you fathead.'

'Well, I think – every hour and a half,' said Maack. 'Anyone against, hold up his hand. No one. Deutschmann's and Kufalt's proposal is accepted. Any other proposals?'

A moment's silence, then Jänsch said: 'I propose that we should start work now. It's twenty past ten already.'

'Right,' said Maack emphatically. 'To work, friends, to work.'

And in an instant the room was filled with the sharp metallic rattle of the machines, bells tinkled, carriages clashed back, envelope after envelope – the work began to fly.

Kufalt folded and folded. 'German Products of the Highest Quality, from Emil Gnutzmann & Co., Successors to Stieling. Textile Distributors,' he read on the prospectus.

He wondered whether he would ever manage to read the contents – Monte folded pretty well, at least as quickly as he did himself; however, it was bound to take a bit of time to get the knack of it. How well he had managed all this; it was really his own achievement, both the contract and the hire of the machines. Well, at worst he would return them at the end of the month . . .

Monte leaned towards him and whispered: 'Doesn't half throw his weight about – Maack; fancy all that talk about a mucky job like this.'

'Maack,' said Kufalt loudly; 'Monte wants to give you ten pfennigs for whispering . . .'

Monte was about to protest, but Jänsch said: 'Hold your tongue, pie-face.'

Whereupon Maack said: 'Jänsch, a groschen from you, please.'

Laughter. On and on. The first few hundred were finished. Kufalt collected them, noted each man's share (they each worked on their own account), and the process of putting the folded prospectuses into the envelopes began. At first there was only a small heap in the corner of the room, then it grew and grew and spread, and rose into a pile.

'Ten minutes to twelve,' said Maack. 'Cigarette break.'

And then once again typewriters rattled, prospectuses were folded and inserted. Outside the sky was blue. And the sun shone . . . They were sitting in a large attic room, which grew hotter and hotter. Without a word Maack opened the window, and later on Deutschmann left the door ajar. Jänsch was the first to take off his jacket, then the others did so too. Jänsch was the first to take off his collar and tie, then the others did so too. Jänsch was the first to slip out of his shirt, and type bare above the waist, to roars of laughter; then the others did so too.

Typewriters rattled, prospectuses were folded and inserted.

'Twenty past one,' said Maack. 'Half-hour midday break. Break for talking.'

They were all in high excitement; they reckoned up how much

they had done, and how late they would have to work, to get ten thousand done that day.

'It will be twelve o'clock at least,' said Maack gloomily.

'Nonsense,' replied Jänsch. 'We have only to get properly into the swing. Not later than eleven.'

'This is quite a sight,' laughed Deutschmann. 'Jauch ought to see us sitting here half naked!'

'It's good for work.'

'Quite a sight for little pretty boy,' shouted Fasse.

'I won't have you say that,' screamed Monte.

'To work!' cried Maack. 'No more talking.'

At twenty past nine Kufalt announced with much solemnity, 'Ten thousand, friends, the first ten thousand.'

'Hurrah!'

'All hail!'

And Monte squeaked: 'Kufalt owes a groschen.'

'So I do,' said Kufalt; 'and I'll pay it.' And he added, with outstretched fingers: 'Guys, this is great.'

'Tomorrow morning at eight,' cried Maack.

'All right,' shouted Sager.

'Good evening, friends.'

'Absolutely OK.'

VII

'You're becoming quite a playboy, Herr Kufalt!' said Liese.

She was standing on the dark landing; it was ten o'clock in the evening, and he divined rather than saw her face. But he could hear the mockery in her voice.

'Yes,' he said shortly, and went into his room.

'I suppose you're still angry with me,' she laughed, and followed him.

He switched on the light, put his briefcase down on a chair, and took off his jacket.

'I am tired, Fräulein Behn,' he said. 'I want to go to sleep at once.'

He ventured no more than a fleeting glance at her as she stood in the doorway. She had certainly been in bed; she was wearing a bright white and yellow bath robe, her legs were bare and on her feet were little blue slippers.

'Men,' she said, 'are funny. They think when they've slept with a girl once they can sleep with her whenever they like.'

He flushed. He felt it again; a sort of glowing cloud wafted from her to him. But he would not. What had Maack said? A month without girls. A month's probation. And of course she would come on the very first day of that month. Tormentress!

'I don't think anything at all,' he said angrily. 'I'm tired. I have worked hard all day, I want to go to sleep – alone.' He hesitated, and stopped; then the red wave swept over him again, and he looked at her: 'Besides, you didn't sleep with me, you slept with Beerboom.'

'Why don't you get undressed?' she said. 'You needn't mind me.'

'No,' he said; and sat down in a chair by the window, so that she was no longer in view.

Silence. Not a sound.

Outside, the rails of the overhead railway glittered, the lights flashed red, then green, the shutter of an advance signal clicked down and an express swung gracefully past, its couplings clanking and all its windows lit. It was night, a velvet night of summer, there were the trees below, so richly green; the sap of life surged up and came to fullness and burst forth, as though there were never any cold, decay, or death – wasn't there a song: 'This is the night of love' . . . ?

No, no, no, no, she was the evil thing. She was the tormentress. Never two days the same. No hand could hold her . . .

He heard a faint rustle once or twice – she must have come farther into the room; wasn't that the click of a closing latch? Perhaps she was standing behind him, perhaps she was reaching out a hand towards his hair, to bend his head back for a kiss, perhaps she was coming to him; where was she?

This night, through which the trains kept speeding past, was very still. The world seemed to hold its breath, in a sort of vast expectation. Poor, wayward, feeble heart – was this a new life? Why had she gone into the Hammer Park that night, and sat on the same bench as he, beside another man?

But he had not gone to her. He had taken a room from someone quite different. And then, in frantic haste, from someone else. And there she was – was that chance? And could you ever escape a chance that laid its snares so well? Was all defence in vain?

Silence; and a quiet cell. Work quota, extra food, a pot of dripping fried for him by the tailor, two books a week. He could go out onto the Mönckebergstrasse, for instance, where there was always a policeman, smash a shop window, grab something – a handbag, a camera, or whatever it might be – and land himself in jail; then peace would descend once more; no problems, no cares and no more struggles.

Wasn't that her voice calling – 'Come'?

No, he would not. Not yet; perhaps never again.

Other people did not have this resource, they did not realize that there was a way out. They turned on the gas tap, hanged themselves with a clothes line or swallowed poison and passed out, with swollen bellies, distorted eyes, foul with their own excrement; he could simply go and steal something, and find himself in peace, in eternal patience, where all winds were stilled, on the other, sheltered, side of life.

Maack knew about this, Monte knew about it, so did Jänsch, Oeser, Deutschmann, Fasse – every one of them. The rest would never understand. They could not realize why convicts were like that, that the prison air had changed them, that something in their blood had decomposed, and altered their brains. All this life outside was something to which they could withdraw consent; and any instant they might do so.

He might kill Liese, or her mother. For others, such a thing was unthinkable and monstrous; for him it was perfectly in order. For five years he had lived with such people, with pimps and murderers and thieves – he knew it was quite possible to do, it was no more difficult than a thousand other things in life, it was certainly easier than hanging yourself.

They were so odd, these people outside; somehow they could not understand the things that every convict knew. A warped and useless citizen, a menace, an enemy to society – no doubt. Here he sat, Willi Kufalt, a man of about thirty, but as determined as any adolescent of fourteen to run away from any difficulty. Was he really like that? No, he had become so, he had been made so. And thus they had finished him off. There was an old expression from prison life that was still used of a man when his brain was weakening under the strain; he was said to be 'spinning'. Probably at one time they actually used to spin in prison, and it would have been a normal enough occupation except when undertaken in prison air. There it ate into a man's mind. In Kufalt's case one should substitute 'net-making'. For five years he had made nets. Now he was 'net-making'. And it would go on all his life. All – his – life.

Wasn't that her voice whispering: 'Oh do come now'? Ah well, he would come, or perhaps he would not come; of course he would come. He did what lay to hand, what was expected of him; he would always do what he was told. So much had been taught him, and it stuck: 'Go out of that door . . . Write your letter today . . .'

Ah well . . .

But for the time being he was sitting here comfortably, looking out of the window. Let her wait; he too had had to wait, first for five years, and then three or four weeks for the young woman who was now visiting his bed.

Smoke and hair and flesh.

Good. Smoke and hair and flesh.

All this scheme of setting up a typing agency of their own was absurd; he had got round Maack, he could make a sudden effort, such as persuading six typewriter dealers in succession to sell a typewriter by instalments on the sole security of the same police registration card – but he could not deceive himself. It had got him. He spelt *doktor* with a 'c', he just needed a nice ordinary girl, and here he was running after a girl-woman like Liese . . .

'Hi! – Liese,' he said.

No answer.

No doubt – as before – she had crept into his bed, perhaps she was already asleep. Ah, that soft curved neck of hers, the vertebrae barely showing beneath the skin . . .

'Liese – dearest Liese . . .'

He looked round.

Of course the bed was empty, the room was empty, the door had been shut from outside.

And he had known it, he had of course known it all the time, he had been purposely deluding himself. Wasn't it really just as well that she had gone? Desire is better than fulfilment – a lesson from prison; to covet a woman is better than to possess her – lesson from prison; fulfilment in the mind is better than fulfilment in the flesh – ditto from prison.

For a moment he stood irresolute in the centre of the room; then he began slowly to undress. He laid his underclothes neatly on a chair, hung his coat and waistcoat on a hanger, and put his trousers in a press. He washed his face and hands, and cleaned his teeth . . .

. . . And he took blankets and pillow from his bed, slipped barefoot across the landing to the door of her room, and there deposited his bedclothes; once more he went back to his room to turn out the light. Then he settled himself outside her door, wrapped in his blankets.

It was already dark in her room, not a glimmer of light could be seen through the cracks in the door; she was surely asleep, not a sound from within.

There he lay, he did not sleep, his brain and heart thrilled within him: 'Here I lie, please don't come for me. It's so lovely to lie outside your door and be despised . . .'

And at last he too went to sleep . . .

He was awakened by her eyes upon him. She was kneeling at his side, she had slipped an arm under his neck and laid his head against her breast.

'Oh, my dear,' she whispered, 'my dear – is it so hard?'

'It's lovely,' he whispered, still half in dream and sleep. 'It's so lovely.'

'But it's so late, my dear,' she whispered. 'You'll have to get up soon. And I must go to the office straight away. But this evening, won't we – this evening?'

'Leave it like this, Liese, and don't torment me.'

'It'll be lovely,' she whispered again. 'I'll make it so lovely for you. You'll be back early, won't you? I'll wait for you.'

'Oh, leave it like this . . .'

'You'll be back early? Quite early?'

Oh, the fragrance of her bosom!

'I'll see . . . I'll try to manage . . . as early as I can . . .'

'Oh, my darling!'

VIII

'Seems all right,' said Herr Bär; 'quite all right.'

He was sampling the first ten thousand, taking out an envelope here and there from the packets and surveying it. 'If you keep on like this, we shan't quarrel.'

Kufalt bowed and said: 'We'll do better than that, when we've got into our stride.'

'All right, Herr Meierbeer,' said Herr Bär once more, with a friendly glance at Kufalt. 'Then good morning.'

But Kufalt did not move, and Monte looked at him reproachfully.

'May we have a little money, Herr Bär, just a small amount?'

'Certainly, certainly,' said Herr Bär. 'You would like to be paid daily? That will be quite all right. What is the amount?'

'Ninety-three fifty.'

'Right. Here is an order on the cashier. He'll give you the money. Good morning.'

'Thank you very much. And good morning.'

They made their way out into the street, and there was joy on their faces; that came to about twelve marks a head, a nice little sum for one day's work . . .

'Stop! There's someone looking round that advertisement pillar. After him, Monte – run!'

They ran, one each side of the pillar: nothing.

'Odd how you can be mistaken. I could have sworn it was Jablonski; you remember, the bloke who limped a bit, from the Presto . . .'

'You must have been dreaming.'

'Seems so. It's strange how you always see something when you've got a bad conscience. And yet I don't need to have a bad conscience, do I?'

Shithouse gossip is not confined to the army and to jail: when the pair came back the room was full of it. The firm of Gnutzmann could not pay; would not pay; Kufalt would come back without money; with a worthless bill; an uncovered cheque; with empty promises; no, with the news that the contract had been withdrawn.

They had got quite heated and abusive over it and, in spite of the protests of two or three of them, the embargo on talking had been lifted. They had been smoking, Jänsch had sent out for three bottles of beer, Oeser for a pickled cucumber, and hardly a thousand addresses had been typed between eight o'clock and half past ten . . .

And now came Kufalt, with money – crisp, crackling notes.

It was almost a disappointment.

'Well now – who on earth started all this?'

'You did, man, we could do with a little less of your lip, for Christ's sake.'

'You said that if the blokes didn't pay up . . .'

'I . . .'

'That will do,' said Maack. 'Now we must get on. We've got two hours to catch up, otherwise we'll be here till ten again. Jänsch, put down that beer. No more talking.'

'If I drink beer, I don't talk,' growled Jänsch, but started typing again.

They all began, some hesitant and half-hearted for a moment or two, but they were soon drawn into the common rhythm and the eternal routine; and they had reached the stage when they could type and think the while, type and dream themselves into a world of heart's desire . . .

A man could dream, too, when folding prospectuses, and slipping them into envelopes, and even when counting addresses. Kufalt dreamed himself into the hours that were to come.

If only they might not be so late that evening! She would wait for him – what had she called him? Dearest? Darling? Perhaps all would still be well, perhaps that was what his life had lacked all these long years: something to which a man could look forward with pleasure.

He longed for the evening, she had been so different that morning, so gentle. She would surely be sitting in his room, waiting for him . . .

But who was this, waiting for him? Who was it sitting in the corner of the sofa in the dim room, who was it that did not even get up but merely looked at him, that evening just before ten? Not Liese, it was Beerboom!

Kufalt switched on the light. He was so furious that he hardly looked at his visitor and merely said: 'What are you doing here? I said you were not to come here again.'

Beerboom was the evil spirit, he was the dark, disastrous star that had brooded over their first night of love, and now, by some mysterious fatality, he was to be present at their second. The door opened and Liese came in. She was wearing a white dress with a bright flowered pattern, and looked very cheerful; she gave him a frank and friendly hand and said: 'Good evening.'

'Good evening, Liese.'

His sole idea was to get Beerboom to go; if Beerboom had not been there, he could have taken her in his arms at once.

'Herr Beerboom asked to be allowed to wait here. It's very important, he says.' She stopped for a moment, and added cautiously: 'I let him sit here alone. I even forgot to turn on the light.'

'Well, what is it, Beerboom?' asked Kufalt.

'Oh, nothing,' said Beerboom. 'I'm just off.'

But he did not move.

The tone of Beerboom's voice had so changed that Kufalt looked closely at his whimpering companion of a little while before.

Beerboom had always had a pallid, leathery skin, but that evening it seemed to be lit by some sort of inner glow. His hair was matted as though with sweat, his eyes flickered and gleamed . . .

He could not keep his hands still, they darted incessantly here and there, sometimes tapping on the table, sometimes fumbling in his pockets, sometimes fingering his face, searching for what he could not find . . .

'Well, what is it?' asked Kufalt. And, with a glance at his watch: 'You'll be late back to the Home, it's ten o'clock already.'

'Oh no, I shan't be too late.'

'How's that? Have you left there, eh?'

'Left it? I've been chucked out!'

'Oh, indeed,' said Kufalt slowly, and then: 'Where are your things?'

'Still there. I tell you they chucked me out, ten or twelve men set on me and chucked me out.'

'But why?' asked Kufalt. 'How did it happen? I can't see them doing that sort of thing.'

'I smashed up my typewriter,' said Beerboom. 'I couldn't stand the sight of the thing grinning at me any longer; a hundred addresses, five hundred addresses, a thousand addresses.' He got up, looked round for a moment, sat down again and said: 'It doesn't matter. What will be, will be.'

'Now listen,' said Kufalt firmly. 'That doesn't make sense at all. You don't tell me that the others chucked you out because you smashed up a typewriter. Seidenzopf might, but not the others. What did you smash it up with?'

'A hammer.'

'Where did you get the hammer?'

'Pinched it. No, I bought it.'

'It's no good,' said Kufalt. 'I don't believe you. The others would be only too glad if you'd smashed up one of those stinking pigs' typewriters. I can understand that Woolly Teddy would chuck you out for it, but the others – no!'

'I did in all their work, too – squirted a fire extinguisher all over it. So they chucked me out. Beat me and chucked me out.'

'And Father Seidenzopf?'

'I landed him one in the jaw.'

'But he wouldn't just let you go after a thing like that, he'd call in the cops.'

'I was off before he could.'

'Oh, then you weren't chucked out, you did a bolt.'

'Well, it doesn't make much odds,' muttered Beerboom; he got up and went to the open window. Suddenly he asked eagerly: 'Would it kill a bloke to hop onto those rails?'

And he put one foot on the window sill.

'No nonsense now,' said Kufalt. 'I don't want any trouble on your account.'

He held Beerboom firmly. But if the man had really meant it nothing could have held him back. It was Liese who stopped him, with her slender fingers.

'But why did you cause all that trouble in the typing room, Herr Beerboom?' she asked.

'He put on a fit of rage, I know that from prison,' said Kufalt.

'I got fed up with it all,' said Beerboom. He looked at the girl and returned so far into the world as to take his foot off the window sill. 'Nothing but typing – typing, all day long, and everything gets more and more topsy-turvy in my head.'

'But,' said Liese, 'you must have been fed up a long while ago? Why so suddenly?'

'Because it got to the limit, Fräulein,' said Beerboom. 'One reaches the limit, then the courage comes.'

'What limit?'

'Ah,' replied Beerboom, with an evil look. 'You don't want to hear about it, Fräulein. You'd just call me a murderer again.'

Silence fell.

Then he said: 'I thought they'd put me into an asylum, but they just called up a flying squad. So I thought I'd better clear out.' He burst into a sudden shriek of laughter. 'I gave Minna one on the nose as I went, I'm pretty sure I smashed it.'

Liese had moved away from him; she was standing in the door as though ready to escape, but she did not take her eyes off him.

Kufalt stood near him – he was still leaning against the crossbar of the window.

'And what are we going to do with you?'

'Ah—' said Beerboom slowly. 'I might jump . . .'

And he leaned right out of the window.

'Stop!' shouted Kufalt.

But his fears were groundless. Beerboom brought his head back into the room. He grinned. 'That's exactly what they'd like – all these people who have done me down: my parents and the investigating magistrates and the public prosecutors and the clergymen and the officials in the clink. How pleased they'd all be if I pushed off quietly like that, eh? I'm sure! Nothing doing . . . !' His voice rose as he went on. 'I'm going to make a hell of a stink first; I'll give them something to remember me by. I don't mind going out, but I'll have a big case before the courts anyway, with two columns in the papers every day . . . I'll show 'em . . . I'll get them all sacked, the grafters, and Woolly Teddy first!' Once more he burst into sudden laughter, which shook him like a convulsion. 'I tore half his beard out, he yelled just like a cat!'

The other two looked at him with grave and disapproving eyes; but their gravity and disapproval completely passed him by. 'Have you got a cigarette, Willi?' he asked. 'I haven't got a bean left.'

Kufalt gave him a cigarette. 'Well, and what's to be done now?' he asked.

'I'm not worrying,' said Beerboom, smoking greedily.

'Listen to me a minute,' said Liese, after a pause.

'Yes?' said Beerboom, and looked at her with an evil grin. 'You're only a bit of flesh even if you wash every day, Fräulein. You stink too.'

Liese acted as though she had not heard. 'You said just now you thought they'd put you in an asylum, didn't you. Why not go into one of your own free will?'

'That's not a bad idea, Beerboom,' agreed Kufalt.

Beerboom thought for a while. 'But suppose they won't take me, suppose they just hand me over to the police?' And he went on doggedly: 'If the police are going to get me, I'll see that it's for something worthwhile. Three months for damage and assault is no good to me.'

'We can put one across them all right,' said the resourceful Kufalt. 'We'll say you live with us, you suddenly started raving and attacked us. You're quiet now, but you're afraid it might happen again. They need only keep you one or two days.'

'And then?'

'By then you'll have talked to the big cheese among the doctors, and any fool can see that you're a complete nutcase, if you really tell him all about it. You mustn't forget that business with your sister.'

A glance at Liese.

A glance from Beerboom at Liese.

There she stood, fair-haired and radiant, so delicate, so pink and white, a child . . .

'Am I to tell that too?'

'Of course. Especially that.'

'You think that sounds so crazy?'

'Then let's get going,' urged Kufalt. 'You can't stay the night here. I don't want any trouble with the police. Which is the nearest, Liese?'

'Friedrichsberg,' she said, half in a whisper. 'You haven't got far to go.'

'Listen, Fräulein,' said Beerboom. 'I'll only go if you take me there.' His voice rose into a scream: 'So help me God, I'll stop here if you don't go with me.'

Kufalt and Liese Behn looked at each other.

'All right,' said Liese. 'I'll go with you. But you must promise me that you really will go into the asylum.'

'Look, Kufalt,' said Beerboom, 'lend me twenty marks and I'll clear out. There won't be any trouble, and you can go to bed with your girl straight away.'

'In the first place I haven't got twenty marks,' said Kufalt angrily; 'and, secondly, I wouldn't lend them to you if I had. You'd go and get drunk, and do something, and I'd get into it for giving you money.'

'All right,' said Beerboom. 'Then let's go. I don't yet know where. Perhaps we might really try the asylum after all.'

IX

'Look, old chum . . .' Beerboom began in quite a different tone when they had reached the street.

It was a relief to be outside in the street with him. Here a wind blew, people passed, lamps shone, all had suddenly grown more real, life had become normal and straightforward; all that had been done and said in the half-darkness of the room now faded into the distance and seemed quite fantastic.

Liese had attached herself to Kufalt. They walked like a genuine pair of lovers, clasping hands with fingers intertwined.

Beerboom shuffled along beside them. Up above he had been a figure of ill omen; what was left of him now? They could call a taxi and leave him standing; they could approach a constable, and he would bolt – there needn't be any Beerboom – Beerboom was an accident, a detestable, warped creature, spoiled by prison . . . they would get rid of him somehow. Then they would be alone together. And love and work, and work and love . . .

Beerboom was at ease out in the street. He began in an entirely different tone: 'Look, old chum, you seem to be in a bit of a mess too. They want your blood as well. Marcetus and Jauch were at the Home this morning, and had a long talk with Woolly Teddy, and most of it was about you . . .'

'How do you know that?' asked Kufalt.

'Because I listened,' said Beerboom proudly. 'I was going to the WC and I listened at the door of Seidenzopf's room. But they were so suspicious, it wasn't three minutes before they'd slung open the door and banged me on the head with it.'

'Well, and then?'

'Then they all went for me and blackguarded me, one after the other – that's what made me give out like I did this afternoon.'

'And what did they say about me?'

Beerboom pondered. Then he said rapidly: 'Give me twenty marks if I tell you?'

'Not fifty pfennigs,' laughed Kufalt. 'You come along to Friedrichsberg instead of getting drunk.'

'But you'll get pinched for sure if I don't tell you what they're up to; they talked about the police too.'

'I know,' said Kufalt. 'I can imagine it all. The fact is I'm through with Presto.'

'Well, and—?'

'I thought you knew all about it. They can't do a thing to me.'

'Oh, OK then,' said Beerboom, offended, and relapsed into his former malignant silence.

'What are you doing then, if you've given up the typing office?' asked Liese.

'I've got a new job, a much better job,' whispered Kufalt.

'With Kutzmann's or some such name,' said Beerboom.

'Eh?' said Kufalt, pricking up his ears at once. 'And what do you know about Gnutzmann?'

'Twenty,' said Beerboom.

'No, nothing doing,' said Kufalt. 'Not only because twenty marks is a lot of money, but because you'd do something foolish and get me into trouble.'

'I'll do something foolish anyhow,' said Beerboom.

'Yes, but you won't get me into it. Now please, Beerboom, tell me what they said!'

'You oughtn't to treat a friend like that,' added Liese. 'And Willi's trying to help you.'

'Willi,' thought Kufalt ecstatically.

'Yes, helping to get me into an asylum. Nice sort of friend that is. No, I shan't say.'

'OK then, don't,' said Kufalt savagely.

And he thought aloud to himself: 'Even if they do know, they can't do anything. There's no law against competition, and Herr Bär's a decent sort. If we put it to him, he'll let us do the work, even though we have been in prison.'

'There's Friedrichsberg already,' said Liese.

For most of the way they had been walking through gardens – shrubs, and smooth lawns, and beds of roses, and beside a little stream.

The night was still and soft, and pairs of lovers sat on the benches. There was a whispering among the foliage, a rustle and a murmur, and the air was rich with fruitfulness . . .

But beyond lay the squat, dark entrance buildings of the Friedrichsberg asylum. Blank and entirely dark.

'They're all asleep,' said Beerboom, and stopped. 'Give me five marks anyway.'

'There's always a nightwatchman in an asylum, just as in a prison. Come along.'

'And it's just like a prison inside,' said Beerboom scornfully. 'Fräulein, give me three marks. Give me two marks; give me one mark anyway.'

But Kufalt suddenly lost his temper: 'You bloody twerp, you – you're always butting in. You've messed up my whole evening. Are you coming, or not?'

He grabbed Beerboom by the arm and dragged him to the gate.

'No, no,' said Liese; 'not like that, be careful.'

But Beerboom suddenly became docile, he even laughed: 'Don't hold me too hard, Kufalt, if I really hit out, I'd soon put you down . . .' He had shaken himself free and stood with his back towards the gate of Friedrichsberg, looking over at the gardens and benches.

'There they sit,' said he. 'They cuddle till they get what they want, but the likes of us . . .' He waved an arm at Kufalt: 'Does he get what he wants, Fräulein? He'd like us all to think so, but does he?'

'Don't talk rubbish,' said Kufalt. 'Are you coming or not? Otherwise we'll go home.'

'Of course I'm coming,' said Beerboom, suddenly becoming tearful. 'What else can I do as you won't give me any money?'

But once again he stopped, in silence. This time he did not look down at the park, nor into the faces of his two companions. He was feeling for something. He passed his fingers carefully over his body and produced – Liese uttered a faint shriek – a knife: an open razor.

Beerboom held it up; it did not close, he had clearly tied something round it, and . . .

And they both looked at him – the wicked, drawn, defiant face of a child that may not have its cake – dark hair and bushy brows . . .

'Away with it,' said Beerboom suddenly, and flung the knife into a bush. It gleamed and flashed through the night like a ribbon of silver. They heard it fall.

'I'm done,' said Beerboom, with a gasp of relief. 'I thought I could. But they've spoilt me even for that. Come on.'

They walked in silence towards the building, Liese clinging closely to Kufalt. He felt the weight of her, and felt her quiver inwardly with fear and self-abandon.

Of course there was a night bell. They rang; still all was dark. They rang once again; still all was dark . . .

But Beerboom did not again say that they had better go, nor did he ask for money; he waited patiently.

At the third ring a light appeared, a sleepy keeper shuffled out, and said through the grille in the gate: 'What is it?'

'Excuse me,' said Kufalt hurriedly. 'My brother-in-law here went raving mad this evening, he smashed up everything and tried to kill us too. He's quiet now, but he has a feeling that it will come on again – could you possibly take him in for one night, please?'

The keeper behind the gate was a tall, lanky, pale man, with a skull-like, fleshless head; he looked remarkably like an inmate of the establishment himself.

'Don't give him anything more to drink,' he said, after brief reflection. 'Let him sleep it off.'

'He hasn't drunk anything,' said Kufalt. 'He suddenly started raving.'

Beerboom stood by in silence.

'Who is his doctor?' asked the keeper suspiciously.

'He hasn't been to one yet,' said Kufalt eagerly. 'It came on quite suddenly, I tell you.'

'That never happens,' said the keeper. 'What is the man's job?'

'Unemployed – at the moment,' said Kufalt.

'Good evening,' said Beerboom quietly and calmly, and turned to go.

The keeper looked after him intently through the grille.

'My dear sir,' he said to Kufalt, 'I'm sure you mean well by the man, but if you knew how many unemployed come along here and think they can get a meal and a good bed by acting like lunatics . . . What's he doing there? What's he looking for?'

'Oh God!' cried Kufalt as he swung round; 'Keeper, come along quick, he's looking for his knife, he's just thrown it away . . .'

'Hurry up . . .' screamed Liese.

'I can't come outside,' said the man doubtfully; 'I'm the night-watchman . . .'

But he unlocked the gate. The other two ran off, and Kufalt said – to whom did he say it? – 'He's been in jail eleven years, or thereabouts, and he's only been out six months . . . and he's mad . . .'

The dark shadow in front of them sped across a stretch of grass, and slipped round a bush . . .

'Quick, Liese! Where's the keeper? He knows how to deal with madmen . . .'

'You run and fetch a policeman, sir. I can't leave the door, it's open . . .'

They came to a path; beside it sat a couple.

'Did you see a man run past you?'

They started apart . . . 'Eh? . . . What? . . .'

At that moment they heard a shriek. It was a crazy, high-pitched shriek that suddenly broke off, followed by a deep, choking gurgle.

'There! There . . . !'

It came from behind a bush – even in that night, at that second, they smelt the fragrance of the garden . . .

They pushed the branches apart . . .

It was something white that lay there, a white bundle of clothes, so white, so very white . . . above it there was darkness, from the head, from the neck, darkness welled forth – streaming darkness, thick and clotting blood . . . a stain, a larger stain – so dark . . . so dark . . . And that strange gurgling . . .

'Help! Police!' a shrill voice screamed.

And Kufalt saw the face of Liese Behn, the shorthand typist Liese Behn, her panting parted lips, her head thrown back—

And he was filled with horror at this thing called life.

'Come along quick,' he whispered. 'Quick! We don't want to be mixed up in this . . .'

'Let me see . . . I must see . . .' she whispered breathlessly.

He dragged her through the throng of people running up from every side.

X

There are good days and bad days in every life – everyone knows that. Kufalt knew it too. He had the feeling that this 16 August was to be a dark and evil day for him; what lay hidden in its womb?

He had begun by telling Liese at once that he would give up his room, on the first of the next month at the latest.

He could not forget her face, her lovely face, with the panting parted lips, and thrown-back head – and those greedy eyes!

'Oh,' Liese had said. And once more: 'Oh.' And then after a pause: 'I'm sure I don't care . . .'

She had gone out of the room, and the door had shut behind her. Well, that had come to an end, he wanted no more of love like that. She would certainly have been willing to sleep with him, under the patronage of Beerboom the sex-murderer: declined with thanks.

It was all over.

Then Kufalt had bought a newspaper on the way to the office, a morning paper, and in it he saw a long and detailed account of Beerboom's case. He found a good deal to amuse him, as for example the statement that Beerboom had now really been admitted to Friedrichsberg (provisionally, as being the most effective method of rescuing him from the infuriated crowd, who wanted to lynch him); Friedrichsberg, where Kufalt had so vainly implored that he might be taken in . . .

'And there he would stay – for the rest of his life,' said Kufalt to himself.

Farther on, however, Kufalt found a paragraph to the effect that Beerboom's victim (who had died in the night) was a thirty-seven-year-old seamstress, an old maid in fact, who had very likely visited the Friedrichsberg gardens every night, to get from the spectacle of those kissing couples that little share of love for which Beerboom too had yearned . . .

Beerboom – the great evil and savage sex-murderer!

No; a poor wretch, damned for ever to futility, a crazy dolt, inflated by the newspapers into the semblance of a bestial and diabolical murderer – this hopeless freak from the shadow side of life!

Parted, while unhinged by adolescence, from his little sister, for eleven long years he had been turned into a monk against his will, with all his instincts perverted and only the flesh still alight; he had then come out into the world, incapable of sleeping with a woman and so finding deliverance, his brain filled with the wildest fantasies, and had bemused himself in a mad desire for girls and children, in dreams of naked children's bodies . . . and then, of his own free will, he had been willing to surrender, to crawl with his unfulfilled imaginings into a madhouse, a cell, and there remain, unsatisfied, all his life long . . .

But he had been rejected, and, almost against his will, flung back into a desperate life that offered him no home, no work, no food, no chance of happiness, not a kind word, nor a friend, and had no place for him at all . . .

And so he dashed out, knife in hand, to seek the one, the *one* remaining fulfilment of his life . . .

And he had come upon his counterpart, no virgin child, but a desiccated old maid, his female counterpart . . .

And Kufalt pictured to himself how this poor fool Beerboom would spend the rest of his long, or short, life in a barred stone cell, and how his mind would circle round and round one sole point: 'If only I had found something young that night . . . if only it had been a child . . . if only I could have found happiness once in my life!'

Happiness. And in the hot August sunlight, on his way to the Cito-Presto Typing Agency, Kufalt shuddered: happiness, what men call happiness, what is truly happiness in this world . . .

Happiness: instead of an old maid of thirty-seven, a little twelve-year-old girl, in socks . . .

That was happiness.

XI

At the Cito-Presto no one knew anything about all this. Newspapers were not among the needs of ex-convicts, and even the most alluring headlines could hardly tempt them to sacrifice the ten pfennigs that would buy three cigarettes – not likely!

'Pack up what's finished and take it along,' said Maack to Kufalt and Monte.

'And don't bring back twenty-mark notes this time – how are we to share out the money?' said Jänsch.

'No, we'll bring it back in thousand-mark notes,' replied Monte, and both went out, each grappling a load of five thousand addresses . . .

'Here are the next ten thousand, Fräulein,' said Kufalt. 'We don't need to disturb Herr Bär, it's all perfectly in order. Just a little order on the cashier, if you will be so kind.'

'No, Herr Bär wants to see you, Herr Meierbeer,' said the young woman. 'You can leave the addresses here, and the other gentleman can wait. Herr Bär wants to see you personally. You know the way.'

Yes, Kufalt knew it, and as he went along the corridor his heart was heavy.

Perhaps it had really been Jablonski yesterday . . . and all this talk of Beerboom's about what he had overheard . . . perhaps they ought to have given him twenty marks. Was he never again to be at peace!

Herr Bär was sitting at his table smoking a cigar and turning over papers; he did not look up when Kufalt came in and politely said, 'Good morning.'

He did not even answer . . . Yes, at last he answered. 'Good morning, Herr Meierbeer. Your name is Meierbeer, isn't it?' he asked.

Kufalt stood, and said nothing. But his heart sank.

Bär threw a fleeting glance at his visitor. 'Your name is Meierbeer, isn't it?' and there was almost a menace in his voice.

'Yes,' replied Kufalt obediently.

'And your Christian name?'

'Willi.'

'Ah, Willi Meierbeer, not Giacomo. Right.'

Herr Bär looked thoughtfully at his cigar. 'And if I rightly understood you, you are unemployed.' He corrected himself: 'I mean you were unemployed until you got this work from us?'

'Yes.'

A long, meaningful pause.

'And that's all? Only unemployed?' asked Herr Bär, suddenly.

'That's all,' answered Kufalt obediently.

It is right and proper that men behind desks should sit and ask questions, and that men in front of desks should stand and answer them. It was quite unthinkable that Kufalt himself should start asking how and why it was any business of Herr Bär's.

He had to stand and wait until Herr Bär had slowly looked him up and down and said: 'Everything you have told me is quite correct, Herr Meierbeer?'

Kufalt stood for a moment, silent. He wondered – but what was the sense in a confession? None at all; every old lag knew that from all his interrogations by the police.

'Quite, Herr Bär,' said Kufalt.

'Very well,' said Herr Bär, and returned to his papers. 'All correct. All exactly as you told me, nothing to add!'

'No,' said Kufalt. 'Nothing.'

'Right. Thanks. You will get your money at the cashier's office, Fräulein Becker has the order. Good morning, Herr Kufalt.'

Not until the door was shut and Kufalt was already ten paces down the corridor did he realize that Herr Bär had addressed Herr Meierbeer as Herr Kufalt. What should he do? Perhaps Herr Bär had actually meant it kindly, as a sort of warning. Now he must keep his chin up, the bomb was ready to explode . . . and yet . . . and yet, they can't do anything to us.

The worst of it was that he could not talk about these things to Monte. There he was, trotting along at Kufalt's side, really quite a handsome lad with his wavy, fair hair, but nothing in his head except his own nasty little notions. He did not share in anything, he hated regular work, he was always trying to shirk for one reason or another . . . Kufalt slouched along beside him. A grim, disastrous day; what did it still have in store?

When he opened the door of their attic office, he stood dumbfounded – who was it, in the middle of the room, with the typewriters rattling all round him?

Who else but Father Seidenzopf, their beloved Woolly Teddy!

He swung round as the pair came in. 'Ah, there you are, my dear Kufalt, I've been wondering when you would come back.'

He dashed up to Kufalt, holding out a hearty hand.

'Don't you shake hands with him,' roared Jänsch.

'No talking there,' said Maack warningly.

Kufalt could just withdraw his hand, which had nearly touched the tips of Seidenzopf's fingers. He went with Monte to his place, sat down without looking up, and started folding prospectuses.

On . . . and on . . . and on . . . without a pause . . .

'My dear young friends,' began Woolly Teddy, standing quite undismayed in the centre of the room . . .

And the typewriters rattled and tinkled, and once again Jänsch was wearing neither coat, nor waistcoat, nor shirt . . .

'My dear young friends, I think it greatly to your credit that you are devoting yourselves with so much energy to honourable labour. I have heard some unpleasant suggestions, especially against you, Kufalt . . . But I am thankful to know that they are unfounded – quite unfounded . . .' Father Seidenzopf stood in the middle of the room and rubbed his hands slowly and with relish. He looked round to see whether anyone was looking at him, but no one was doing so. They were all typing, or folding, or inserting.

The master of the Home of Peace stepped behind one of the typists. He looked over the man's shoulder, across the clicking keys, and said reflectively: 'All new machines. Fine new machines . . . Mercedes . . . Adler . . . Underwood . . . AEG . . . Remington . . .

Smith Premier . . . A pleasure to use, eh? . . . Wonderful, wonderful . . .'

Maack's and Kufalt's eyes met for an instant.

Seidenzopf went on: 'Three hundred thousand addresses – a very good commission – a lot of work, six weeks or so, I suppose – and what then?'

No one answered.

'A commission like that comes along in Hamburg twice, or maybe three times a year, and the rest of the time? Oh, my dear young friends' – his voice swelled until it boomed like a bell, his black beard was matted and dishevelled – 'oh, my dear young friends, we of the Home of Peace, we of the Presto, took you in when you came out of prison, when you were helpless and in despair, and almost penniless. We gave you food, good plentiful homely fare, a roof over your head and a decent life.'

Warming to his work: 'We of the Home of Peace first taught you to work, with unwearied patience we trained you to the habit of regular work once more – and is this your gratitude?'

His voice shook with anguished emotion, and in that moment – God knows – the old Pharisee may really have believed in what he was saying . . .

Seidenzopf paused. And as he began again, a profound and honest indignation filled his heart: 'And at what rate have you undertaken this work, I ask you, at what rate? Ten marks, I dare say, perhaps only nine fifty, perhaps only . . .'

He scanned their faces: '. . . perhaps only nine – and we would have got two marks more; six hundred marks in all, flung away through your inexperience. I do not reproach you, but what a calamity! This will bring prices down for years.'

His audience was growing uneasy, but Seidenzopf went on undeterred: 'And what is to become of you at the end of these six weeks? No work – and the care associations, the welfare offices and the homes, if you apply to them you will find yourselves dealing with *us*; *we* work in conjunction with them and they come to *us* for the information and details that they need . . .'

He shook his head, and suddenly roared like an infuriated lion:

'You'll come whining to us on your knees: give us shelter, Father Seidenzopf, give us a warm meal! For God's sake help us, Father Seidenzopf, you can't let us starve! But then we shall . . .'

What they would do was lost in a general uproar. Almost all of them leapt up from their work, yelled at him and flung abuse into his face:

'You, you lived on us!'

'Four marks fifty a thousand was what you paid us!'

'We could take it or leave it – plenty of unemployed, eh?'

'Sock him in the jaw, the sneak!' (Jänsch.)

'Hang him out of the window by the legs!' (Oeser).

'Yes, then he'll do a bit of whining!' (Kufalt.)

'Be quiet!' shouted Maack, and then repeated once or twice – 'Be quiet!'

He shouldered his way through the gesticulating throng that had gathered round Seidenzopf, who was pale but did not seem much alarmed. 'Now go, Herr Seidenzopf!'

'Oh no, I shan't,' bellowed Woolly Teddy. 'I must bring you to your senses. You must realize what you are doing; come back to us and all will be forgiven . . .'

'Come on,' said Maack to Jänsch.

And they both took Father Seidenzopf by the arms and ran him to the door. But Seidenzopf went on bellowing: 'Whoever comes back to us within three hours will be received without questions asked. And the first will be made assistant manager of the typing room under Herr Jauch!'

The door slammed, and only a confused roar could be heard on the stairs. Then Maack and Jänsch came back.

'Well, that's that,' said Maack, his white face twitching. He looked round him, and said, 'To work. We must do our ten thousand. Get on with it! No talking!'

He looked round the room once more. He looked at Jänsch and nodded. Then he said softly, but there was menace in his voice: 'Or does anyone want to accept Herr Seidenzopf's offer? If so, will he please speak at once?'

They all returned to work.

XII

Of course they inevitably discussed this momentous event in the midday break. They were very proud of having ejected the great Herr Seidenzopf, who had, such a short time ago, been master of their destinies . . .

'He'd have been delighted if we'd let ourselves be drawn into a row!'

'Thinks he can say just what he likes!'

'He can wait till we come.'

'Whine, indeed – I know who'll start whining first!'

'You ran him out properly – couple of cops couldn't have done it better.'

'He won't come back.'

'Don't you believe it. Of course he will. Three hundred thousand – he'd wear his heels out for that.'

'Perhaps Jauch will come next.'

'Oh God, when he starts bellowing, I laugh fit to burst.'

'Marcetus won't send Jauch, he knows he's only a windbag.'

'Suppose Marcetus himself comes—?'

Long and gloomy silence.

A rather uncertain voice said, 'No, he's much too grand.'

'Possible, though.'

'Everything's possible, but I don't believe it.'

'We'll just sit tight, he'll soon go if no one answers him.'

But there was misgiving in their faces: 'Marcetus – hope not, he's a sly bugger.'

'To work, gentlemen,' said Maack. 'No time to lose, we'll have to work like fury.'

The tap-tap of the machines began, rattled on, faltered and – stopped.

They all looked round at one seat, a seat at one of the typewriters, and it was empty.

They all looked round the room, but there was no one to fill that empty seat.

Someone whistled – a long-drawn-out whistle.

'Ahoy! Ahoy! Man overboard!'

'Where's Sager?'

'Gone out to fetch beer.'

'Assistant typing room manager!'

'Typing room assistant manager!'

'Bloody swine – we'll show him!'

'Ahoy! Ahoy! Man overboard! Ahoy! Ahoy!'

'Comrades—' Maack began, and swallowed painfully.

'Comrades, my arse!' shouted Jänsch brutally. 'There's no comrades here. This is a bunch of old lags and crooks. There's the door! Kufalt, open it, and leave it open – wide open. Right; now all of you go and stand against the wall with your backs to the door. Wide apart, so you aren't touching. Now put your arms up to your eyes. Anyone that looks will get a sock in the jaw from me; now!' he roared. 'Get along out, you blinking crooks, you cowardly scabs – out with you, no one's going to see your nasty mugs, you can clear out, nobody's looking, go on tiptoe. Go!'

A pause, a long pause; they stood unseeing with their faces to the wall. Was that a plank creaking? Was someone creeping to the door? Oh vanished childhood, vanished faith in fellow men! Jänsch snorted: 'Are you off, Monte? They'll give you a nice cushy job, I dare say.'

'Stupid old brute!' squeaked Monte.

So he was still there, at any rate.

And Jänsch growled in his deepest bass, but with an intonation of relief: 'Do you want me, pretty boy?'

Roars of laughter – eyes opened, looked once more into the sunlight, and into each other's faces: they were all there.

'Ah,' growled Jänsch. 'We'll see what happens in the morning, when you've all slept on it. I don't trust one of you.'

'Trust? I never did.'

'All men are shits.'

'Look,' said Maack to Jänsch. 'I think you'd better take charge of the agency from now on. You manage it much better than I, Jänsch.'

'You're too nice a bloke, Maack,' said Jänsch disapprovingly. 'Nice blokes are sure to be weak, I always think. Well, what's the bloody odds? All right then. Kufalt, you've got to type, do the best you can, eh?'

'Yes,' said Kufalt.

'And what about me?' wailed Monte; 'I can't fill ten thousand by myself.'

'Why didn't you nip out just now?' said Jänsch. 'Now then, my lad, don't you get worked up about nothing. We'll all help you this evening. Get down to it!'

And they did.

Kufalt, once more at the machine, a fine new machine, was happy. Happy, but uneasy.

Happy, because his fingers danced upon the keys; scarcely had his eyes caught the address than they danced on, with no mistakes. Where was last night? Swallowed and forgotten; he would simply move his lodging, and so farewell to Liese. That was the best of life; something else always came along, there was no need to cling to the past; let it go.

As with the others, packets of envelopes were piled in hundreds at his side. He tore off the band of a bundle; his neighbour, Fasse, had broken into his bundle three or four envelopes before him; but when Kufalt was through with his hundred, Fasse was still a few envelopes behind. Kufalt was at the top of his form; it's an odd thing, you never can tell, it looked like being a bad day – but it was a good one.

Still, he was uneasy. And all the others were uneasy too. They kept on clearing their throats, pausing in their work, whistling meditatively and humming tunes in a way they had not done before. True, Seidenzopf had been there and thundered on, but that did not mean that the storm was past; the lightning had not struck. Sager was no lightning. Nor was Seidenzopf . . . The storm was still overhead – when would the lightning strike?

At exactly thirty-five minutes past five the thunderbolt fell. At exactly thirty-five minutes past five there was a violent knocking at the door. Maack (Maack, of course, as though he were still the manager), called out, 'Come in,' all turned their faces towards the door, and Pastor Marcetus entered.

'Good evening,' he said, advancing three or four steps into the centre of the room.

'Good evening,' said one or two in an obsequious undertone, swallowed, and were silent.

Four of them (Maack, Kufalt, Jänsch and Deutschmann) turned to their work again, the machines began to rattle and . . .

'Stop!' said Marcetus. 'Stop!'

Three (Maack, Kufalt, Jänsch) went on typing.

'Stop!' said the pastor a third time. 'You will have the decency to stop, while I speak to you for five minutes.'

One (Jänsch, of course) went on typing, made a slip, stopped and started off again; but the tap-tap sounded very faint and desolate in that large room, so recently filled with the rattle of machines. 'Oh shit!' said Jänsch savagely; and his machine fell silent too.

'That's right,' said the pastor sharply to Jänsch; 'you have described it quite correctly. You have indeed got yourselves into a pretty mess.'

He was silent; Jänsch growled. The pastor looked round the room and said, very politely: 'Herr Monte, lend me your chair for five minutes – I am an old man.'

Monte jumped at once, blushing slightly; Jänsch growled again, but he did not prevent Monte putting the chair in the middle of the room.

'Thank you very much,' said Marcetus genially, and sat down. He sat down quietly and looked about him. It seemed to Kufalt that he was singled out for especially intent and frowning scrutiny.

'Well . . .' said the pastor slowly.

But nothing followed.

The pastor held his hard black felt hat in one hand, and a fine large linen handkerchief in the other, which from time to time he passed lightly over his face. A ruddy, full face with an expressive mouth and a strong chin. (The men sitting round him all had weak chins, excepting Jänsch, who had another sort of strong chin, more of a boxer's chin.)

And it was Jänsch who at last murmured angrily: 'Beg pardon, Herr Pastor, we must work, we haven't as much free time as you have.'

The pastor ignored this and merely replied: 'Are you in charge here? Or is it Herr Maack?'

'Sager lied,' grinned Jänsch. 'I am manager here.'

'Ah,' said the pastor meditatively. And once again: 'Ah.' And he seemed to ponder deeply. Then he said; 'So you are responsible for everything here: payments, accounts, and so on?'

Jänsch also pondered. He glanced quickly across at Maack, but the pastor followed the look with such attention that they could not reach an understanding.

'Yes,' snapped Jänsch, 'I am.'

'Then,' said the pastor softly, 'I assume that this business is properly registered with the police.'

Silence.

'And that the deductions for income tax have been duly calculated.'

Silence.

'And that notice has been given to the health insurance authorities, and the stamps stuck on, eh?'

A longer silence.

The pastor was no longer looking at the faces round him, he was gazing thoughtfully and mildly at the blue summer sky, now tinged with gold.

The seven men threw a fleeting glance at each other – there was something in the air.

'We are much obliged to you, Herr Pastor,' said Maack politely. 'There is still time to deal with all that. Today is only our third day.'

'Ah,' said the pastor.

'Three days' grace are allowed,' said Jänsch politely. 'And without your reminder I might perhaps have forgotten.'

'Ah,' said the pastor once again. And it was noticeable that he did not look quite so pleased.

'My business,' began the pastor once again, 'is a thankless one. Every one of you is always imagining that he has been imposed upon by me. You merely observe that we take eleven and give you only six . . .'

'Four fifty,' said Jänsch.

'Four fifty,' agreed the pastor. 'You never remember that we have to pay the rent of the office, the heating and the light, and that typewriters wear out, and that we carry you through lean times – your earnings, God bless my soul!' he laughed bitterly. 'You think I do nothing but come and bellow at you once or twice a week. And I am sitting all day writing begging letters for you, I collect patrons and founders and members. One gives five marks, another ten – eight hundred or a thousand such contributions every year – that's how the work is kept up . . .'

'And the pastor too,' added Jänsch.

'And the pastor,' agreed Marcetus. 'You who insist so strongly that all work shall be paid for at its proper value, would surely not have me work without reward?'

'Listen, Herr Pastor,' said Maack slowly; he was very pale, his glasses had slipped and he jerked them back onto the bridge of his nose. 'That's all very fine, what you've been telling us, and we don't want to quarrel with you, but . . .' and Maack grew warmer; 'but why don't you let us go our own way? We have got our own work, we bear the risk, and we certainly shan't come running to you again – so leave us alone. We are now enjoying ourselves, which is what we never did with you. So don't come along here and threaten us; we've heard "Halves, or I'll split" just a bit too often. Let us go our own way, we aren't doing you any harm.'

'That's right,' said Jänsch, and one or two others murmured approval.

'I will not refer to the fact,' said the pastor, 'that it was we who trained you to become efficient typists. I will not mention how unfair I think it of you to have spied out our customers' addresses; nor how reprehensible it was to underbid our tariff prices. I will merely tell you that not one of you will achieve his object; that for all of you this act of ingratitude will only lead to ruin and further crimes . . .'

'And how?' sneered Jänsch, unimpressed.

'Because you . . .' Here the pastor broke off and stood up. 'These are beautiful new typewriters . . . How were they bought, hey? How were they bought?'

A moment's silence.

'On the never-never system, I think,' said Jänsch.

They nearly burst out laughing, but the pastor burst out in a fury: 'By fraud, that's how they were bought, by common criminal fraud.'

There stood Kufalt, the eyes of the others turned on him – flaming, evil, anxious, deadly eyes . . .

Then the pastor continued: 'When Herr Seidenzopf came back from here with a report about these new typewriters, we naturally put the matter into the hands of the police at once. The inquiries are not yet complete, but it has already been established that several typewriters have been bought by the same destitute young man, and three of the dealers have already decided to prosecute . . .'

A long, long silence.

The pastor glared at Kufalt. 'Yes, you're frightened now, you would like to escape, but it is too late. I warned you, Kufalt, I have always warned you.' And he called out: 'Herr Specht, please – Herr Specht!'

The door opened and through it came a man, a broad, squat figure of a man, with a greyish white policeman's moustache, thick, bushy, white eyebrows and a completely bald head.

'That is Kufalt, Superintendent Specht,' said Pastor Marcetus.

'You come along with me, Herr Kufalt,' said the superintendent pleasantly. 'I'm sure you'll come quietly and not give us any trouble.'

He grasped Kufalt lightly by the forearm, the pale faces of his companions looked into his, then they vanished, and the door came nearer and nearer ('Would none of them speak?') – the door opened, the door closed, then the staircase – and from within boomed a strong, firm voice: 'Now, my young friends . . .'

The game was over: he had lost.

XIII

When Kufalt awoke, he at first thought he was in a dream. A loathsome, evil dream that had come to visit him. All night he had been pursued, and he had fled and hidden himself foolishly, where all could see him. Or he was accused of something, and had to defend himself, and as he grew more and more imploring, they just sniggered and did not listen . . .

Kufalt felt as though he had been weeping, as though his bolster were still wet with tears, and . . . and hadn't he shrieked 'Let me go, let me go!'? Yes. Yes, he had. But now he was awake, a pallid grey light glimmered in the narrow cell, and right in front of him, almost above his face, he saw two terrible, primeval beasts, armed as though ready to attack him. Brownish-red, their bodies encased in flat shells, their antennae and their greedy beaks outstretched towards him, they crouched above him like beings of another world, like threatening demons – and his mind, just emerging from the dark abysses of dream, strove to understand; what could they be . . . ?

Then he felt a burning itch all over his arms and legs, he moved his head a little, the coverlet slipped, and the beasts upon it vanished . . .

Bugs, he thought. Bugs, of course, that was the last straw. All was as it once had been – was there ever a police cell without bugs?

He jumped up and washed. He inspected his body, which was once more marked as it used to be . . . he began to reckon . . . how long had he been outside? A hundred and two days. A hundred and two days, and now inside again. Better so. What was the sense of struggling?

He paced up and down in the grimy police cell, its walls stained brown by squashed bugs. He could now start hunting bugs, so that his next night would at least be quieter – but what was the good of hunting bugs? What was the good of a quiet night?

None – poor fool.

Herr Specht, Superintendent Specht, had taken down a brief statement the previous evening, grinning as he did so: 'Yes, of course, my boy, you had no criminal intent – eh? What was that? Six typewriters, and you were going to pay 180 marks every month out of what you earned . . . I believe you, I believe every word of it! Like a cigarette? Well, you can hardly expect one, if you tell me that sort of yarn; you'll have to cough up a thing or two, my boy, if I'm to give you a smoke. You know that from old days, when you got that five-year stretch. Cigarette? Nothing comes of nothing, eh?'

Yes, he knew it all by heart – and now it was beginning all over again – very likely Beerboom was locked up here too, ten cells away, and he too would be brought before the investigating magistrate, he too would be tormented by bugs, and be hanged or get life . . . and be quite pleased about it all, the poor fool . . .

And Liese. They were certain to have searched the house long ago and turned all his cherished belongings upside down, and she had probably thought they had come about the other business. And she would have given it all away; but they hadn't come about that, but on his account, and she would have poured out the whole of Beerboom's story. Then *that* hullabaloo would all be out, and they would keep him here and question him for ever . . .

And God Almighty, it's enough to make a bloke crawl up the walls, or hang himself from the leg of a bed, I never thought I'd have to endure all I've had to suffer these last four months; when a bloke swallows a spoon so as to get into hospital and have a nice little operation, and it hurts like hell – I can understand it. When a man's yelling with a pain in his belly, he can't have any troubles in his head . . .

How dry his eyes were, and how they burnt.

The bolts clashed back; three times the key clicked in the lock.

He leapt to the window and stood there alert.

A grey warder's face.

'Your name?'

'Willi Kufalt.'

'Wilhelm Kufalt.'

'No, Willi Kufalt.'

'Come with me.'

The corridors and the iron staircases and the iron doors, the clashing locks, the hurrying warders and the orderlies scouring and polishing – just like old times!

A large, gloomy room, with whitewashed windows and hideous yellow shelves for files. At a desk sat a large, powerful, fresh-faced man with a couple of duelling scars on his cheek, a stiff, fair hairbrush growing on his head, smoking an enormous black cigar.

'Thank God, not a bully like Specht,' thought Kufalt. 'Thank God, the investigating magistrate himself.'

'Wilhelm Kufalt, under arrest,' reported the warder.

'Right,' said the large man. 'I'll ring later on, Warder. Sit down, Kufalt.'

Kufalt did so.

The man turned over some papers. 'You know what you are charged with, Herr Kufalt. And now tell me how a practically penniless man like yourself came to buy six typewriters in six different shops, on the security of your registration card. What did you want six typewriters for?'

And Kufalt began to tell him. He spoke falteringly at first, and with difficulty, he had to keep on going back; he realized that he must begin right at the beginning, from the time of his discharge, and even before that, to make the whole matter clear.

But here was a man to whom he could talk. In the first place, he made no notes, he listened. Secondly, he really did listen; Kufalt observed that he had not yet made up his mind. Specht had already been convinced that Kufalt was a criminal; this man – not yet.

So he warmed to his tale and felt quite at ease to be sitting there and telling it. But suddenly he came to a halt, as though he had run dry, and he looked at the investigating magistrate with a helpless and expectant expression.

'Hmm,' said the latter, contemplating the cone of ash at the end of his cigar. 'Well, that's one way of telling the story. But Herr Marcetus and his friends don't tell it quite like that.'

'Oh!' said Kufalt contemptuously, suddenly feeling very superior. 'They're just mad because we snaffled their job.'

'We will not suggest,' said the magistrate sternly, 'that these gentlemen deliberately deposed falsely about you because you were their competitors. We will refrain from that, if you please.'

And the magistrate looked coldly at Kufalt.

Kufalt suddenly felt small again. What a fool he had been; the investigating magistrate and the pastor were both university men. And university men start by believing the best of each other. Especially when confronted by an insignificant ex-convict.

'Now listen to me, Herr Kufalt,' said the large man. 'You know all about this kind of thing. You have been long enough in prison to know how easily a man gets into trouble.'

'Yes,' said Kufalt, with conviction.

'And you know equally well that a man like you must be doubly careful. Doubly? A hundredfold!'

'Yes, I know that.'

'Now even if I assume that everything you have told me is true – you must admit you have been excessively thoughtless? You pledged yourself for the money, you alone, on your own signature, for all six machines – and you had not nearly the means, nor any prospects even, to guarantee such a sum.'

'But we agreed that an equal deduction should be made from the earnings of all the others.'

'Ah! And now that your agency has collapsed and there is nothing more coming in from which deductions can be made, how are you going to pay?'

Kufalt writhed. 'If the Herr Pastor is so mean and makes it impossible for us to work . . .'

'Don't be a fool,' said the investigating magistrate sternly. 'Use your common sense. What is that to the dealers? You have to pay 180 marks a month for twelve months, how are you going to do it?'

Kufalt had an inspiration. 'I'll simply give the machines back. It is in the agreement that I am to give the machines back, if I don't pay punctually.'

The magistrate leaned forward. 'And suppose the machines are gone? You understand me, suppose they have been stolen?'

'But our machines won't be stolen,' said Kufalt incredulously.

'Last night,' said the magistrate significantly; 'last night there was a burglary at your attic. The thieves took four machines . . .'

Kufalt crouched on his chair, his brain working frantically. 'The bastards, it can only be one of us – who can it have been? Fasse? Oeser? Monte? Oh God, or perhaps the assistant typing room manager, Sager? And these people of course think I'm in it. The game's up . . . the game's up . . . !'

He looked wildly at the magistrate.

'And what are you going to do now, Herr Kufalt?'

'I . . .' said Kufalt, straightening himself. 'I will go back to prison. It's no use, I see that quite clearly, I will go back . . . What do I care, it doesn't matter to me . . .'

The investigating magistrate looked at him sharply: 'And why did you tell Gnutzmann & Co. that your name was Meierbeer, Herr Kufalt? A man doesn't give a false name if his business is above board.'

'So that the Presto people wouldn't know I had the contract,' said Kufalt, and got up. 'But there's no point in all this, sir. Let me go back to my cell. I always have bad luck.'

'Bad luck, indeed,' snapped the magistrate. 'You have a great deal more luck than you deserve. A man in a position like yours shouldn't get himself into such a mess. You're stupid and reckless. You'll do no good if you carry on like this. Always discontented, always whining, always after what you haven't got. You had quite a good, safe job at the typing agency, and after all it wasn't so bad, even if they did bully you . . . But of course, you wanted adventure, you wanted to make a lot of money . . .' He was very contemptuous. 'A silly young fool like you—!'

Kufalt stood before him, an uneasy feeling in his mind: this was a proper dressing-down, certainly, but he had an idea that behind all this there was something different, something of good-will . . .

'Couldn't you have made yourself a little more pleasant to Superintendent Specht?' asked the magistrate. 'He told me that when he questioned you, you behaved just like a hardened old criminal.'

'Herr Specht treated me just as a police officer does treat a real criminal. Not like you've treated me, sir,' said Kufalt artfully.

'Nonsense! It was Specht who saved you, and Specht alone. Yesterday evening he was looking for those purchase agreements, and as he couldn't find them in your lodging, he went along to that attic of yours in the night, and there he found them, but not till later. He found something else first – what do you think it was?'

'The burglars . . .'

'And who do you think the burglars were?'

'I don't know,' stammered Kufalt.

'You know perfectly well. Now just show me if you've got an idea who are your friends and who are your enemies . . .'

'I . . .' began Kufalt, and stopped.

'Out with it,' said the investigating magistrate.

'Fasse,' said Kufalt.

'Oeser,' said Kufalt.

'Monte,' said Kufalt.

'Sager,' said Kufalt more eagerly.

'Maack,' said the magistrate.

'Jänsch,' said the magistrate.

'There; so now you know. It was lucky for you that Specht chanced upon it all. And it was lucky for you that the agreements had been kept in your office, and that Maack had carefully drawn up a sort of table showing the payments to be made by each of you . . . He seems to have changed his mind afterwards . . . your friend's a rogue, Kufalt, a pitiable rogue.'

'His girl's expecting a baby,' said Kufalt.

'I'll tell you what,' said the magistrate, and this time he was really angry. 'This whole business was a piece of flat, futile idiocy on your part. Either you want to get straight again, or you don't, eh?'

'Yes,' said Kufalt.

'Very well, then,' said the magistrate. 'The typewriters will be returned to their owners by the police, and then the prosecutions will be withdrawn. You will have to wait until that has been done. But I think we can let you out this evening or tomorrow morning.'

6

On His Own

I

A young man was walking along the Mönckebergstrasse. With a large cardboard box under each arm, he pushed his way hurriedly through the throng that, on this lovely autumn afternoon, were strolling, stopping, staring into shop windows, walking into shops and out again. He hurried with bent head past them all.

At the Karstadt store he caught a sidelong glimpse of a great window display of brilliant dresses, the silky sheen of women; a vision of bright-coloured loveliness.

The young man quickened his step, looked straight in front of him. Three blocks farther on stood the big office building that was his destination. He mumbled to the porter: 'China-Export,' spurned the lift and escalator, and ran up the staircase.

The showroom, full of glass, fabrics, Buddhas and porcelain, was still very quiet at that hour of the morning. A single apprentice, a small, undersized urchin with prominent ears so raw and red that they looked as if his boss had just been pulling them, was flicking a feather duster about.

'Yes?' said the apprentice.

'Herr Brammer,' said Kufalt. And: 'Thanks, I know the way.'

He walked through two offices, where girls were sitting at typewriters, and entered a third. There Herr Brammer had his domain, behind a long, rattling, tinkling bookkeeping machine, and surrounded by all manner of brightly coloured cards and invoices.

'The last two thousand, Herr Brammer,' said Kufalt.

Herr Brammer was himself quite a young man, with a fresh face, fair hair and the rather short Hamburg upper lip.

Herr Brammer pressed on a couple of keys, the carriage slid back with a rattle and a ring, and spat out a card. Herr Brammer read it with a wrinkled brow and said: 'Will you put them down?'

Kufalt did so.

'The total is quite correct?'

'Quite,' said Kufalt.

'Right,' said Herr Brammer; he put the card on his table, fished about somewhere in the background for a receipt form, filled it in, handed it to Kufalt along with a pencil; and Kufalt found a ten-mark note in his hand.

'Thank you very much,' said Kufalt.

'Thank *you*,' said Herr Brammer with emphasis. He looked down at his machine, then at Kufalt, and said with a polite smile: 'Good morning, then, Herr Kufalt.'

'Good morning, Herr Brammer,' said Kufalt with equal politeness. But he did not turn to go, though this was plainly expected of him; he said hesitatingly: 'There won't be anything more?'

'Nothing,' said Herr Brammer.

'No – no,' said Kufalt hastily.

'The boss doesn't intend to send out any more catalogues at present, you understand; in such bad times—'

'I understand,' said Kufalt. He had noticed the cashbox in the background; there seemed to be quite a lot of money in it, an improbable amount of money, not for immediate expenses, but just for any emergency that might arise.

'Yes . . .' said Herr Brammer, observing Kufalt with close attention.

Under his gaze Kufalt slowly flushed. He noticed himself getting redder and redder, and said awkwardly: 'You couldn't perhaps recommend me to another firm?'

'Certainly, certainly,' said Herr Brammer. 'Only . . . You know . . .'

'Yes,' said Kufalt hastily, 'of course.'

He tried to free himself from Brammer's steady gaze, and get another glance at the cashbox. It was such a pleasant sight; but no, the other's eyes held his fast.

Moreover, Herr Brammer seemed to have grown annoyed about

something: 'Besides, Herr Kufalt, you are too expensive. Five marks for a thousand addresses! Every other day we have a man in who will do them for four, or three. I can't answer for it to the boss.'

'No,' said Kufalt suddenly. He had not had another look at the cashbox, and he knew he would never see it again. 'No,' he said, 'I can't do it cheaper than that, Herr Brammer.'

'Ah,' said the other. 'Then good morning.'

'Good morning,' replied Kufalt, and left.

II

The shortest way from the Mönckebergstrasse to the Raboisen takes barely five minutes. But Kufalt did not take the shortest way. He had typed for two days, and half the nights as well, hardly looking up from his machine. Now he had all the time that God had made; he was again without work, and could stroll along in peace. But though he had no work he had money, ten marks just received, and one mark twenty cash in hand; eleven marks twenty in all. A nice little sum. A substantial barrier between himself and the void. He would, however, have to pay his tiresome old landlady at least three marks on account, or she would put him on the street.

What a lovely morning for a walk!

No, Kufalt no longer lived in the Marienthaler Strasse; he lived in the Raboisen, in a dingy lair at the far end of a dark backyard; however, he was not going there now, he was going to take a walk by the Alster on this fine morning, like a gentleman of leisure . . .

'Besides, you are too expensive, Herr Kufalt. Others will do it for three marks . . .'

Nasty little ape! Nasty little long-tailed ape. So he had lost that work too, just because he had stared at the cashbox like that, and now he had no work at all. Was his belly less empty on that account? It might not sit well with any man in these hard times, but he would give himself a little treat first.

And Kufalt bought four rolls and a quarter of liver sausage; twenty-five pfennigs, leaving ten ninety-five.

Well, why shouldn't he? Just for a picnic? And why not?

The pleasant room in the Marienthaler was a matter of the past. No more fluttering curtains, clanking trains, obscene mothers, perverse Lieses. He had simply gone, and gone without a word. When Kufalt got back from the police station, there was no one at home. And as there was no one at home, Kufalt quietly and silently packed up his things and departed. Leaving no address.

To tell the truth, there might have been another chance; there had been a moment of waiting or, more precisely, a full half-hour, while Kufalt had paced up and down. He could have got a taxi and been spirited away at once, wherever the driver might suggest; no, he had paced up and down, and waited.

Is she coming?

No, she is not coming.

There had been one shameful night when we lay outside her door – shall we venture in now? Yes, we are mad, the blood surges to the brain, we smell her clothes and sniff at her bed . . .

But then a door opens, and we dash out on the landing, our heart throbbing with fear, lest it may be she. But it is only one of the neighbours' doors.

That was the end; we could really stand no more, the last days had been a little too much, what with Beerboom, Cito-Presto, arrest by the police, and his good friends Maack and Jänsch – let's get a taxi and depart.

It was not enough to have found a room at last in one of the backyards of the Raboisen, a dark, dirty, stinking hole with tarnished windows, next door to a hovel of a kitchen, about the size of a towel, inhabited by countless cockroaches and an old and crazy landlady called Dübel – a proper lodging for the broken, discouraged, desperate Kufalt; a dark lair where he could lie in the folds of a lumpy eiderdown and doze for hours and hours; but that was not enough.

For at times there came a flash within him: hope – ambition; all – oh God! – might yet be well.

An idea sped into his brain: had he not paid money on his typewriter, and should that money all be lost?

A little flower blossomed in his dreams; a typewriter of his own was something significant, not merely an object of steel and iron, composed of wheels and springs and cylinders and rubber – a typewriter was a hope, with a typewriter a man might hack his way through life, it was a draft upon the future. No more three hundred thousand contracts but, as he lay there on his bed, apparently dazed by the extent of his collapse, while his thoughts turned in the eternal dismal, grinding round of self-reproach: 'If only I had . . . if only I had not . . . !'; in his mind's eye he saw himself going from office to office and asking, 'Have you got some typing for me to do?'

Surely it must be possible to earn enough in a great city like Hamburg to keep a man from starving?

And he had succeeded; he had been allowed to give his kindly friend the investigating magistrate as a reference, an equally kindly firm had listened to his appeal, and he had got a typewriter. Not a new one, but one that had been very carefully treated; 150 marks – 30 marks up front and the remaining 120 in cash.

How delighted he had been with his old Mercedes in the first days he had it, how he had scoured and polished it, brushed away the faintest speck of dust, tested all the keys and listened for the tinkle of the bell at the end of the line.

And yet – he was not now living in a room, he was housed in a hovel, a burrow into which one crawled and lay. There stood the draft upon the future under its oilcloth cover; hadn't he better get up and collect orders?

Very well. He got up and went out, and occupied a long-distance telephone box at the Head Post Office for an hour and a half, while he copied out half the commercial telephone directory . . .

Then he went on his way, rang twice, had two interviews, and was twice sent about his business; and so home, to his hovel and his hideous bed. There was no sense in taking off his boots, he had no idea whether he would feel like putting them on again . . . so he flung himself on the bed in his boots and lay and brooded . . .

'I was a convict, I am a convict, I shall always be a convict. It's no use.

'I couldn't even make a decent crook; I suppose I may get a few orders, but how am I to live on that?

'And the money goes, however frugal I am, it goes and goes, ten marks ninety-five between me and nothing – and what then?

'I can pawn what I've got left, I can pawn the machine – and what then? I can give up this hole, and get somewhere to sleep, I might even doss at the Hallelujah Brothers – and what then?'

Oh Kufalt, Kufalt, make up your mind!

But when it is made up, what then?

III

So Willi Kufalt sat on a bench by the outer Alster and tried to make up his mind. And in the process he consumed his four rolls and his quarter of sausage, and very good they were; he did not need to worry about his appetite – if only all his affairs were equally sound!

Strange: in these last few gloomy weeks, the memory of the Central Prison in that little town seemed like a blessed island emerging out of the grey and misty ocean of his life. Hadn't it been a glorious peaceful time when he lived in his cell and did not need to think about money, food, work or lodgings?

He got up in the morning and cleaned his cell, he went out at the recreation period and talked with the companions of his destiny, he stood at the net and wove – the hours went by, there were peas for dinner and he was glad, or there was gruel and he was angry, but he could look forward to lentils next day – truly, a blessed island.

No wonder that, with the island, appeared the vision of a fair-haired seal-like head, little Emil Bruhn, with his pale blue eyes. Emil had been right; he ought to have joined him instead of going to Hamburg.

There had been two alternatives before him then: Batzke – crook he was, and crook he would remain; and Bruhn – 'never, never again'; but he, Willi Kufalt, fool that he was, had never said yes, and never said no, and here he sat, his talents wasted.

Of course there was still the possibility of deciding on one or the other; he could write to Bruhn and say he was coming, or he could inquire about Batzke at the Registration Office. But that was exactly what Batzke had warned him not to do; it was too late. All his money had gone, he had no longer any working capital with which to plot, arrange and finance any proper scheme; he would have to take action hastily, and that always spelt failure. And he had no longer even had the money to up sticks and travel to Bruhn with all his things, and to part with them now . . . had things really got as bad as that?

The October sunshine was warm-hearted, and in its grateful warmth the world did not look altogether hopeless; there would surely be some way out, only he must really make a decision.

A decision was essential.

One solution, which commonly strolled by the Alster at this hour when the day was fine, Kufalt already knew. It was a parallel decision to Batzke, and its name was Monte.

Both the prospectus-folders from the late Cito-Presto Agency had met here once again. But latterly they had not known each other any more, they exchanged no greeting, they regarded each other with contempt.

On the first occasion it had been a very cheerful encounter; they had so much to tell each other – Kufalt about his experiences at the police station and the final triumph of innocence, Monte about the break-up of Cito-Presto and how they had gone on their knees to Marcetus, Seidenzopf and Jauch and begged to be taken back to Presto and the Home of Peace, even at half pay. What in all the world were they to do, poor Deutschmann, Oeser and Fasse, led astray as they had been by Kufalt and Maack?

And after much hesitation, stern refusals, savage vituperation of their behaviour, Herr Pastor Marcetus finally took pity on them – they could not be allowed to go to ruin in the cesspit of a great city. And now, when they ran into Monte, they once more bemoaned the yoke of Jauch, who never gave them a moment's peace: 'Another word, and you will find yourself in the street. Now be careful . . .'

As for Jänsch and Maack, they were still under provisional arrest. The robbery, which had hardly been a burglary, had become rather a complicated case – for each of them had paid an instalment on the typewriters they had been intending to carry off. They boldly maintained that it had been their intention to keep up the instalments, and as they were both in possession of a fair sum of money, it could not be denied that they might have intended to carry on the payments. How did Monte know? Monte knew everything.

Monte had not crawled to the foot of the cross. Monte had, as he often said, worked hard enough for a longish period of his life; Monte had gone back to his old profession.

And it was this old profession of his that led him, nearly every fine morning, through the more populous streets of Hamburg and the parks and gardens chiefly frequented by foreigners. Monte was on the lookout for customers, in the form of dignified, elderly gentlemen, who were as coy and bashful as young girls, or horse-toothed Englishmen who, when the business was over, haggled over every mark with the savagery of a bulldog.

It was on this account that these two last pillars of the late Cito-Presto had fallen apart, and were no longer on speaking terms; Monte had wanted someone – Kufalt – to extract the cash for him.

In fact, however, their difference really arose out of a quarrel over tobacco, the source of so much contention both in prison and outside. On every other point they could have reached agreement, but on the tobacco question Monte had rather narrow and even petty views; hence the disagreement.

At their first meeting all of course went swimmingly. They had chatted away amicably, Monte had constantly offered Kufalt his large silver cigarette case, and he had naturally noticed that Kufalt was hard-up. For in the first place Kufalt only had Junos at three and a third, while Monte smoked Aristons at six, and secondly Kufalt had only three cigarettes, while Monte said indifferently: 'When they're all gone, there's plenty more in the nearest shop.'

So all was very cordial and friendly, Kufalt had felt better for his smoke, and they arranged to meet again in the same place next day.

But the next day Monte started to say how difficult it was to get the cash out of his customers. He needed someone who would snip the money for him, as he called it; in other words, in return for 25 per cent of the incomings, his companion was to stand by, and when the gentlemen were half undressed, just rifle through their wallets.

Pinch the wallet?

Oh my God, no! Nothing of the sort! Merely slip out a ten-mark note or so, just to ease the transaction. And a fifty-mark note of course, if the wallet was specially well lined.

Up to this point everything had gone very well; Kufalt had taken full advantage of Monte's generosity in the matter of cigarettes, and had helped himself liberally out of the silver case. But when the decisive moment arrived, the proposals had been made and the answer was expected – Monte thought he could detect a certain hesitation, something like the hint of a refusal, on Kufalt's features.

He had at once explained that there was no risk in such little encounters; there was a Clause 175 in the Criminal Code, for which Monte's customers had a remarkable respect. Besides he would soon train Kufalt up, so he could tell at once if there was any risk or not.

And while he was explaining all this, he had looked dreamily into his cigarette case, taken one out, looked at Kufalt, lit it, looked at Kufalt again, gone on talking, puffed at his cigarette, and gone on talking . . .

Now Kufalt was one of those people who can only bear to see other people smoke when they have a cigarette between their own lips. He had smelt the delicious flavour of the Ariston, and he had quite well understood why Monte had looked at him like that.

It was not, in fact, such a bad offer, though hardly in Kufalt's line; still, he would in any case have to think it over carefully – but if this little rascal who sat there and puffed smoke into his face thought he'd got him, he would find himself mistaken!

A brief exchange of views followed: Kufalt regarded Monte's way of life as low, Monte considered Kufalt a fool, and they finally parted, in opposite directions – and knew each other no more.

That had been in August; it was now October, and in two months much may be forgotten. As Kufalt munched his liver sausage sandwich and surveyed the passers-by, Monte might have found him very ready to listen to reason. If Monte had only had a little more sense in his curly-haired cranium at the time, and understood that there was nothing to be gained by blackmail by cigarette, they might have done a nice bit of business together.

But Monte did not come.

Someone else came in his stead: a large, dark-haired man with a leathery, grey skin and piercing, powerful, dark eyes, wearing an extremely loud check suit.

'By God – Batzke!' shouted Willi in amazement.

'Hello, Willi,' said Batzke, and sat down beside him on the bench.

IV

'I was just thinking of you, Batzke,' observed Kufalt.

'Then you must be up shit creek,' said Batzke with emphasis.

'How about you?' asked Kufalt.

'Ditto, thanks, ditto,' answered Batzke.

There was a brief pause, and then Batzke shifted about on the bench as though he were going to get up. So Kufalt said hurriedly, 'Is there nothing doing, Batzke?'

'There's always something doing,' said the mighty Batzke.

'But what?'

'You don't suppose I'm going to put you up to a job, do you?'

A long silence.

'Why didn't you meet me at the horse's tail that time?' Kufalt began.

'Oh, drop it,' said Batzke.

'I suppose you'd gone to see your ship-owner's widow at Harvestehude?' persisted Kufalt.

'Oh, come off it, Willi,' said Batzke. 'Got anything to smoke?'

'No.'

'Nor I.'

They grinned.

'Got any money?' asked Batzke once again.

'No.'

'Anything to pawn?'

'No.'

'Then let's go to Ohlsdorf.'

And Batzke stood up, and stretched his great horse-bones until they cracked.

Kufalt remained seated. 'And what am I to do in Ohlsdorf?'

'In Ohlsdorf,' said Batzke, 'is the most up-to-date churchyard in the world!'

'What do I care about that?' asked Kufalt. 'I don't intend to get buried yet.'

They both grinned again.

'Well, come along, man,' urged Batzke.

'But what am I going to do there?'

'I thought you wanted to do a job with me.'

'But how, in the most up-to-date churchyard in the world?'

'You'll soon see.'

'I'm not going to pay your fare,' said Kufalt dubiously.

'Who asked you to, you dosser? I've got a few pence.'

And they departed, to the Central Station.

There, at the ticket office, although the whole fare came to a few nickels, Kufalt noticed that Batzke's wallet was stuffed with twenty- and fifty-mark notes. But although Batzke seemed to be anxious that his new pal should be aware of this fact, he was careful not to pay for Kufalt; he watched with satisfaction the bewildered expression on Kufalt's face.

The train was full and they could not talk on the journey. But scarcely had they got out at Ohlsdorf when Kufalt said:

'Hey, Batzke, you're stuffed with money!'

'Well,' said Batzke; 'what if I am? There's the churchyard.'

'Yes,' said Kufalt. The churchyard did not interest him. He felt easier in his mind. He could surely touch Batzke for twenty marks. That was four thousand addresses; and a good step further into safety. He was now quite ready to put himself under Batzke's orders, and he said, 'Shall we go along to the churchyard?'

'Do you want to?'

'Don't *you*?'

'I asked whether you wanted to.'

'I might have a look at it.'

'Ah,' said Batzke. 'I don't much care for churchyards.'

'Well, let's go somewhere else then.'

And Batzke turned down a street that led away from the churchyard.

'Where are we going now?'

'No need for you to know everything.'

'Look, Batzke,' said Kufalt. 'You might buy a few cigarettes.'

'Oh might I!' said Batzke, and thought for a moment. 'But I haven't any change.'

'But you've got plenty of twenty-mark notes,' said Kufalt.

'I don't want to change them now. You get them, I'll give you the money back this evening.'

'Right,' said Kufalt, and looked round for a shop.

He saw one and made towards it.

'Stop!' said Batzke, and took a note out of his wallet. 'Here's twenty marks. Get fifty. I'll walk on slowly. Down there.'

'Right,' said Kufalt, and went on.

The bell in the little suburban tobacconist's rang for quite a while, but no one came. Kufalt could easily have filled his pockets from the stacked boxes of excellent cigarettes, but that wasn't his style. It wasn't worth the risk.

Kufalt went back to the door, opened it and shut it again, making the bell ring a long tinkle. As no one came, he called out several times, 'Hello!'

At last a little withered old woman with rolled-up sleeves and a blue apron appeared from the back room.

'I beg your pardon, sir,' she said, in her cracked old voice. 'I was scrubbing and then it is difficult to hear the bell.'

'Yes,' said Kufalt. 'I want fifty Aristons.'

'Aristons?' said the old woman. 'I'm not sure whether we keep them.' She looked doubtfully round at the showcases. 'You see, my daughter had a baby last night, and I'm just helping in the shop.'

'Then give me one at five,' said Kufalt with resignation. 'Only please be quick. I am in rather a hurry.'

'Yes, yes, I quite understand, sir.'

And she fished a cigarette out of a package and held it out to him.

'I said fifty,' said Kufalt irritably.

'But you said one at five,' said the old woman.

'Then give me fifty. Yes, fifty of those, please.'

'I know I'm very bad at serving,' sighed the old woman. 'And people are always so impatient. Here you are,' and she handed him the packet of fifty.

'Thanks,' said Kufalt, and gave her the money.

She held the note at some distance from her eyes. 'Twenty marks?' she said. 'Haven't you anything smaller?'

'No,' said Kufalt.

'I don't know whether we've got that much change'; and she went into the back room.

'Hurry up!' Kufalt called after her; and waited.

She soon reappeared. Three five-mark pieces, one two-mark piece and fifty pfennigs – 'Is that right, sir?'

'Yes, yes,' said Kufalt, and hurried out.

Batzke was no longer visible, though Kufalt ran after him along the street. Not a sign of him – then he suddenly emerged from a side street.

'Let's go along here,' he said. 'Have you got the cigarettes?'

'Here they are,' said Kufalt. 'And here's the change.'

'OK,' said Batzke. 'And here's ten cigarettes for yourself.'

'Thanks,' said Kufalt.

'Who was in the shop?' asked Batzke as they walked along.

'An old woman,' said Kufalt. 'Why?'

'Because it took so long.'

'Oh,' said Kufalt. 'It took so long because she didn't know anything about anything.'

'No,' agreed Batzke.

'How do you mean?' said Kufalt.

'Because it took so long,' laughed Batzke.

'You seem very odd, Batzke,' said Kufalt suspiciously. 'Is something up?'

'What could be?' laughed Batzke once more. 'Do you know where we're going?'

'No,' said Kufalt, 'no idea.'

'Then you'll soon see,' said Batzke.

And they both walked on, smoking silently.

The square to which Batzke led Kufalt was dominated by a large building with a whole complex of brick galleries, cement partitions, high walls and small, square, barred windows . . .

'It's a prison,' said Kufalt in a disappointed voice.

'It's Fuhlsbüttel,' said Batzke in an almost solemn voice, and then added in a different tone: 'I did seven years in there.'

'And did we come out here to see where you were in jail?' asked Kufalt, half indignant and half disappointed.

'I wanted to have another look at the old place,' said Batzke, quite unruffled. 'A great time it was – when I think of the bloody life I lead now . . .'

'What are you getting at? All that cash – what have you got to moan about . . . ?'

'Come round the other side. I'll show you the carpenter's shop where I used to work.'

Kufalt went with him.

'Do you see? At the back there. That's it. It was a fine place, that shop, I can tell you, all first-class work, not rubbish like in Prussia.'

Kufalt listened.

'I used to make roll-top desks,' said Batzke dreamily, and surveyed his hands, now carefully kept and manicured: 'You know, Willi, it was fun when we got the slats so they didn't stick, and you could rattle the cover back and forth!'

Kufalt listened. Batzke was lost in his memories: 'And then we made some built-in cupboards for the governor – I often used to be at his house. Wait, we'll go round and I'll show you.'

They went round.

'No,' said Batzke irritably. 'You can't see the cupboards from the outside, but they were a neat bit of work, I tell you. And the governor, he used to buy old furniture, he was fair crazy about it, you know. "You come along to my place, Batzke," he used to say to me, "I want you to look at an old bit I've just picked up – see if you can put it to rights." '

He drew a deep breath: 'And I always managed it. Worn-out inlay and so on – all sorts of old pieces I fixed up for him so they looked first-rate.'

'Well?' said Kufalt disapprovingly. 'You can always get back there if you liked it so much. They'll take you there gratis from the police station, you won't need to pay any fare.'

'Ah?' said Batzke, and looked at Kufalt with a flash of anger in his eyes. 'Ah? Think so? I'll tell you what, Kufalt, you're plain stupid!'

So saying, Batzke swung round and hurried on with long strides. He walked round the whole building, once, twice, and Kufalt ran in silence by his side, trembling lest he might have frivolously thrown away the favour of so powerful a patron.

'Well, you can do what you like,' said Batzke suddenly. 'I'm through for today. I'm going to trudge back home.'

'So am I,' said Kufalt eagerly. 'So am I.'

So they walked together all the long way home; Batzke quite dropped his sullen manner and the pair of them fell into a sensible and friendly talk. They had a great many memories in common and could enjoy a good laugh when they recalled all the fools they had got the better of in prison, warders and convicts too.

And when Kufalt's ten cigarettes were gone, Batzke bought him another five: 'But you must make do with those.'

When they reached the city, Batzke hesitated for a moment outside a restaurant and said suddenly: 'Come along in, Kufalt, I'll stand you supper.'

'Thank you very much,' said Kufalt.

It was not much of a restaurant; indeed, it was a smoky, dirty little hole, close by the Alley Quarter. But the food tasted good, so did the beer, and Batzke said after a while: 'Are you game for a job, Willi?'

'All depends,' said Kufalt, who had eaten his fill for once.

'I've spotted something,' said Batzke.

'Yes?' asked Kufalt.

'At the Post Office,' said Batzke.

'Can't be done without a gun,' said Kufalt, with a professional manner.

'Don't be an idiot! Snatch and grab!' said Batzke angrily.

'What's the idea?' asked Kufalt.

'Every Wednesday and Saturday,' whispered Batzke, looking round him, 'there's an old bag comes and gets six or eight hundred, and toddles off with it halfway across Hamburg to a shop on the Wandsbeker Chaussee.' Pause. 'Well, what do you think?'

Kufalt pulled a face. 'It isn't so easy.'

'It's perfectly easy,' said Batzke. 'By the Lübeck Gate one of us will give her a tap on the head, and the other pinch her bag, and bolt in opposite directions.'

'That's no good,' thought Kufalt to himself. 'He'd be off with the cash and leave me to be caught by the cops.'

And he said: 'I don't understand, Batzke – when you've got a pocket stuffed with dosh.'

'You just stop talking about my money!' shouted Batzke angrily, and then, more calmly: 'Well, then; yes or no. There's plenty who'll come in with me.'

'I'll have to think it over,' said Kufalt.

'Tomorrow's Saturday,' said Batzke.

'Yes . . . yes . . .' said Kufalt meditatively.

'Then it's – no?' asked Batzke.

'I don't know,' said Kufalt dubiously. 'Seems a bit silly to me.'

'Silly? Can't do anything without risk.'

'But not so much risk for so little money. I don't want to do another stretch.'

'But you will, anyhow,' said Batzke slowly. He stopped and added: 'If I choose.'

'What do you mean?' asked Kufalt in bewilderment.

'That's a crazy-looking bloke, that waiter,' said Batzke irrelevantly.

'Why should I have to do a stretch because you choose?' persisted Kufalt.

'Will you pay the bill?' asked Batzke with a sudden laugh. 'I'll give you another of my notes.'

'Of – your – notes—?' Kufalt stared at him, wide-eyed.

'Don't you understand, you idiot?' burst out Batzke. 'They're dud notes – inflation money; and you go and buy fifty cigarettes with one of them!'

The scene that afternoon suddenly unfolded before Kufalt's eyes. The wrinkled, flustered old woman with the cracked voice; in the back room the woman who had just had a baby, perhaps their last money – and what a dreadful risk he had run! Batzke had slunk off down a side street, the bastard. And if a salesman had been in the shop, who had been a little more wide awake, Kufalt would have been in a police cell at that very moment with a nice long stretch in front of him . . .

But Batzke had just laughed in his face, he put all the change in his pocket without even forking out a share . . .

'Batzke!' shouted Kufalt, 'I'll . . .'

'Waiter! My friend's paying the bill,' cried Batzke, grabbed his hat, and before Kufalt could protest, he was outside.

Kufalt paid three marks eighty.

That left him seven marks fifteen.

V

On that eventful, fateful Saturday Kufalt woke up early, very early. He lay in his bed and thought; in that dirty, shabby room with the lumpy eiderdowns, on which hundreds must have slept before him, with or without their girls, for old Dübel did not mind – indeed she rather liked that sort of thing. He looked at the window, the dawn had surely come, but hardly any light found its way into that narrow yard. Suddenly he had a feeling that the sun was shining outside; he could not see it, but he felt its presence.

He got up slowly, washed himself with great vigour and thoroughness, shaved carefully, put on clean underclothes and his best suit, and went out with his beloved Mercedes under its oilcloth cover. Outside, the sun was really shining.

His first disappointment was that the pawnshops did not open until nine o'clock. No one could predict at what hour the old goat would appear at the Post Office. He took his place in the queue, many of whom had eiderdowns; one man had a pendulum clock under his arm. The people waited motionless and silent, all staring in front of them, all isolated in their own distress. Only when some newcomer joined the ranks did they throw a quick glance at him to see what he had brought to pawn. Then they stared ahead again.

When the door opened at last, the proceedings were very quick.

'Twenty-three marks,' said the official, and as Kufalt hesitated, thinking of his hundred and fifty, he said at once:

'Move on, please.'

'No, no,' said Kufalt, 'I'll take it.'

He had to wait a little while at the cashier's desk, and when he got his money he ran, rather than walked, to a bicycle hire shop which he had discovered the previous evening. Here, too, there were difficulties. The man thought twenty marks too little as security for a brand new machine. Kufalt did his utmost to talk him round. Finally he deposited his registration card, and the pawn ticket, and then rode away.

He had been used to bicycling, but it was not so simple, after six years, to steer a course through the traffic of a modern street. But he must do it, and do it skilfully. For today everything depended on speed, decisiveness and presence of mind.

The Lübeck Gate (which is no longer a gate, but a square) is a very confusing place. Many streets lead into it, foot passengers hurry across it from all sides; you have to keep your wits about you. There are booths that break the view, and the passing trams hide the people on the opposite pavement.

But suddenly – and Kufalt and his bicycle took cover in a flash – he saw a face looking out of the public lavatory on the other side of the square, a well-known face. And he knew that, although the clock showed fifteen minutes past eleven, he had not come too late.

There he stood. He may have been thinking of many, many things, perhaps even of his childhood, when his mother had come into his dark bedroom after supper, bent down over his bed and said: 'Pleasant dreams. But go to sleep at once!'

There he stood, and the people hurried past; prison was very present in his mind, he knew he would go back there sometime. But when? That very afternoon? Or not for five years?

Batzke's head kept on popping out, his hard, evil face and blinking eyes peered like a watching fox across the street, and then vanished; once more Kufalt was free to jump on his bicycle and ride home. And then what should he do? Find some shelter, honestly and decently, beg, humiliate himself and yet die like a dog.

Kufalt gripped his handlebars more firmly – how was he to know what this elderly bookkeeper looked like?

He knew. There she came with a quick, angular stride, her brown skirt was a bit too long, she turned her toes in as she walked, her face was faded and very pale with the sickly pallor of office rooms. She wore a small felt hat and her hair was bobbed.

She came, and his heart beat quicker and quicker, and he heard a beseeching voice within him say: 'If only he might not have the courage, I could ride home – if only he might lose his nerve!'

Nothing at all was noticeable in the first few moments. Batzke was behind her, he seemed to brush against her as he slipped past her, just as casual passers-by brush against each other in the street; then Kufalt heard the faint sound of a suppressed, bewildered cry. With a brown briefcase in his hand Batzke dashed down a side street, the woman suddenly burst into a shriek and people came running up. Kufalt merely saw the gathering throng, he could no longer see Batzke, and then, with a tremendous effort of will, he jumped onto his bicycle, a policeman's whistle blew, motor cars stopped, a tram pulled up abruptly with a rasp of wheels, he pedalled across the square and down the side street; no Batzke. Down the next side street, straight on; no Batzke. Was it all to have been in vain?

It was senseless to ride on. He must have encountered Batzke long ago. The game was lost. And yet he rode on. His mind revolted; he must take care the game was not lost, that it had not been in vain.

Kufalt suddenly realized that what he had planned that morning was not to start a new life of crime; it was to have been the start of an honest, quiet little existence, in the small town back there, perhaps with a pleasant wife, and children in the years to come. Just a bit of working capital for the start – and this was to have been the start. He must see that it had not been in vain.

He had reached a district of villas and apartment houses, the noise of the Lübeck Gate having long since faded into the distance. He was riding along the Maxstrasse and the Eilbecker Riede. And then, after about fifteen minutes, he came out onto a broad, wide road. It was the Wandsbeker Chaussee. He was barely five minutes from the Lübeck Gate. And there – at the fork of the Wandsbeker Chaussee and the Eilbecker Weg, where there was a small traffic island, and on it a police post, where all was quiet and at peace – he saw Batzke; yes, it really was Batzke. He braked, dismounted, surveyed him from a distance, and said to himself: 'It's no good, I'm afraid of him.'

A constable went into the police post, glancing casually at Batzke as he entered, but Batzke did not mind; couldn't a man stand here waiting for his girl, with a briefcase under his arm?

Slowly and thoughtfully Kufalt leaned his bicycle against a tree and left it standing there; if it was lost it was lost, and anyhow if all went well it wouldn't matter.

Batzke was looking in a different direction. Kufalt came to within a few paces of him, then the tall, dark man turned his head and looked at his companion of the day before. Ohlsdorf cemetery, the dud notes and the supper bill.

Batzke frowned and his face looked black enough to frighten anyone. And Kufalt was certainly frightened.

Nonetheless, he knew that everything now depended on his tone of voice, on his demeanour, on what Batzke thought of him.

He said, with a glance at the window of the police post, through which a constable could be seen: 'Halves, or I'll split!'

Batzke looked at Kufalt. He said nothing. Kufalt watched him raise his free right hand, a huge carpenter's fist – and then he saw something in Batzke's face that gave him courage.

'Look, mate,' he said. He uttered the words in quite a friendly manner. Suddenly he realized that they stood on equal terms. He had got Batzke by the short and curlies. Batzke was naturally furious, but crooks devour each other; that is part of the game. It is a natural phenomenon; that's all there is to it.

Batzke said, also with a glance at the window of the police post: 'But not here!'

'Just here!' said Kufalt.

Batzke stood irresolute.

A police car came dashing down the Wandsbeker Chaussee from the Lübeck Gate and stopped in front of the police post. A constable jumped out without so much as looking at the pair; what crook would be likely to take his stand under the direct shadow of a police post? Batzke was a cunning devil!

And he proved it by opening the briefcase without further ado, fumbling inside it, extracting a crumpled handful of paper and giving it to Kufalt.

But Kufalt had lost his nervousness. He smoothed out the notes, six fifties, and said with mild composure: 'I said halves; let me look into that bag.'

Batzke again hesitated. Then he once more plunged his hand into the bag. Again he produced a little wad of paper, this time eight fifties. He gave them to Kufalt and said: 'But now that's it, Willi; or I'll chuck the whole business right here by this post. But first I'll fix you so your own mother wouldn't know you.'

Now it was Kufalt's turn to hesitate. For a moment he stood, looked at Batzke, who was shutting the briefcase, looked at him again, slipped the notes into his jacket pocket and said, with a laugh: 'You still owe me the three marks eighty from yesterday, Batzke!'

'So long,' said Batzke.

'So long,' said Willi Kufalt.

And they parted. Each in a different direction across the road, Kufalt towards his bicycle, which was indeed still there.

'Hello!' shouted a voice abruptly. 'Hello, Willi.'

They turned, and again approached each other.

Batzke laid his hand on Kufalt's shoulder and gripped him until it hurt. 'But if you cross my path again in the near future . . .' he said.

Kufalt shook off Batzke's hand. 'Till we meet again in the clink, Batzke,' he said, and laughed.

Then he walked to his bicycle, mounted and rode away. He had to hurry. In two hours at most he would have to get himself and his belongings out of Hamburg; Batzke might well change his mind. Kufalt was registered with the police so Batzke could find his address, and the backyards on the Raboisen don't pay much attention to screams.

He pushed with all his weight on the pedals.

VI

The little Schleswig-Holstein manufacturing town was a stopping place for express trains and possessed a canal harbour. It lay in the centre of a flat, treeless plain, a limitless expanse of fields, diversified only by the hedges that enclosed them – low ridges overgrown with bushes.

It was a busy little town, of which the most prominent feature, more noteworthy than the churches or the factories, was the tall cement and red-stone structure of the Central Prison.

It was a sight at which Kufalt did not greatly care to look. He was a sort of prisoner, who had come of his own free will back to the place of his imprisonment – whenever he turned a corner he ran into a warder who grinned and said: 'Good day, Herr Kufalt.' And he kept on catching glimpses of the walls, the brick battlements, the rows of little barred windows.

We all come home to our own selves; always, in the end. There is no greater folly than the talk of a new life that is about to start. We are what we are and remain so. There he was, in his little room on the Königstrasse, on the outskirts of the town.

When he stepped out of the door and walked away from the city he was met by the November wind, and the swirl of leaves, and the bleak, interminable roads that led somewhere that was just the same. And the mouldering reek of the ditches, laden with death and decay; and solitude, that gets one nowhere; all, all was as it had been: a futile life, without hope, without courage, without patience.

He sat there in his room on the Königstrasse; it was a good, lower-middle-class room; Bruhn's was worse. Bruhn had a workman's room, a mere sleeping place. But Kufalt's was adorned with mahogany and plush and knick-knacks and pictures; a list of addresses lay beside his machine, and he was typing letters. A great many letters for a man who hardly saw a single person, about ten or twelve; he finished the last, signed it, slipped it in its envelope, stamped them all, all local letters at eight pfennigs, and then put on his coat and hat. He picked up the letters and stood in the doorway.

It was eleven o'clock in the morning. He had, in a sense, done his day's work. The beggar's daily task of hopelessness; and a man cannot be always sleeping, nor can he be always brooding. A man has his troubles, even though he is a man of means, with more than four hundred marks still in his wallet.

He stood in the doorway and hesitated. It did not matter in the least whether these letters were posted at midday or in the evening, when it was already dark, nothing would come of them. It did not matter in the least; but there was little Emil Bruhn, always so concerned for his friend Kufalt, who had said the evening before: 'The clergy, try the clergy, they *must* do something for you.' He had emphasized the 'must', and Kufalt was to meet Bruhn that evening, and Bruhn would ask whether he had remembered the clergymen and applied to them. Bruhn was a persistent man; Bruhn would never leave him be until Kufalt had done what he thought he ought to do. So Kufalt had to leave his room at eleven o'clock in the morning and get the addresses of the five or six clergymen who were to be found in the little town.

Kufalt still stood in the doorway and hesitated. Suddenly he made up his mind. He went to his trunk and opened it; in it was the *one* reply he had received to all his letters of application. It was from a man by the name of Malte Scialoja. He was the chief editor of the bigger local paper. The chief editor of the other paper had not answered. Even so, it was not a very promising answer. However, he had better go and see the man. Kufalt read the letter. It was not long, only a few lines; it ran:

Dear Sir,

Distressed as I am to learn of your sad story, I do not think I can do anything to help you. The testimonial from your prison governor is certainly excellent, but you must yourself realize what a responsibility it would be for a managing editor to take you onto his staff. However I should be glad to see you any day between eleven and one.

Yours faithfully.

Kufalt sighed as he read the letter. 'Hopeless,' he whispered; 'utterly hopeless. But when I get the addresses I might go and see this bloke too.'

He held the twelve letters of application in one hand; with the other he slipped Malte Scialoja's note into his pocket. And then he went out into the street.

Malte is a Low German Christian name, Scialoja is an Italian surname. The man who bore both these names was the famous Holstein author, a man devoted to his native soil, who wrote books about peasants, whose speech was the Low German dialect that he himself preferred to use. The story was not as complicated as might be supposed. A hundred years before, an Italian sailor had put down roots in one of the little harbour towns on the coast. He had married a Frisian girl, and it was his grandson who sat behind a desk in the editor's office, shuffling papers, listening to the wireless and really doing nothing. He was no more than an advertisement for the paper, astutely engaged by the proprietor for this purpose. Once a week, on Sunday, a sapient article by him appeared in the vernacular.

But he was an important man. He had to be handled with kid gloves by everyone in the editorial department; the people believed in their dreamy, enraptured author. The public wanted him. There he sat among his papers, though he really might as well have sat at home. He listened to the great linotype machines rotating; at half past twelve the evening edition was ready; but that was no affair of his. For that, the little reporters had written their little pieces; and they were no affair of his.

Scialoja was a pale man with faultlessly parted dark hair, wearing an alpaca jacket. He listened to the dance music, read a few lines from the manuscripts in front of him, and then contemplated his nails. He was a great man, and quite aware of the fact. It was not a simple matter to live the life of a great man. It carried its obligations. That he had always understood.

There was a knock at the door of his office. He growled: 'Come in.' He always growled, 'Come in.' He did not like to be disturbed. He was a very busy man, with an intense and active inner life.

The messenger stood in the doorway. 'A Herr Kufalt to see you. He says you know about him.'

Scialoja had a pencil in his hand and was writing. He barely looked up as he said: 'I'm busy. I have never heard of Herr Kufalt. I know nothing at all about him.'

The door closed. Herr Scialoja was again alone. He had laid the pencil down and was listening to the wireless music. They were playing dances. Those corrupt and evil dances that did the people so much harm. There were such pretty peasant dances, all of which had been pushed aside by this urban kitsch. Still, he listened. It did not sound so bad, bad as it was.

There was soon a further knock at the door. Once more the messenger appeared. 'The gentleman says,' he announced diffidently, 'you gave him an appointment between eleven and one.'

The chief editor replied: 'I have so many things in my head; I must work, don't you understand? I made no appointment. Send the man away.'

The door again closed. Once more the music and the papers and all the tiresome manuscripts by other hands than his.

Was the messenger really coming back? Would he dare? Yes, he did! This time he had a bit of paper in his hand – a letter. 'The gentleman won't go away, he says you wrote him this letter.'

The messenger stood in the doorway with the letter in his hand. Scialoja was writing. He said abruptly: 'One moment, please, I am busy.'

And he wrote for quite a while.

Then he put down his pencil with a sigh. 'Show me the letter,' he said.

He read it through, once, twice; he carefully examined the signature: signatures of great men can be forged, so he examined the signature. Then he said: 'Bring the man in. But tell him I can only spare him a minute. I am busy.'

Kufalt stood in the chief editor's office in front of the white-faced man with the black parting, who was writing and did not look up.

Half an hour before, in his own room, Kufalt had still been doubtful whether he would use the letter. But resistance breeds resistance: 'What thou hast written, little friend, that do.'

'Well – what is it?' asked Scialoja, and went on writing.

'I gave full particulars in my first letter to you,' said Kufalt in a hesitating tone.

The chief editor looked up. He smiled. 'I have so many things in my head,' he said. 'Hundreds come to me for help. I am known all over the country. What is it you want?'

'A job,' said Kufalt. 'Some work to do. Any kind of work.'

And he added in a low tone: 'I mentioned in my letter that I had been in prison. I can get no work. I thought that just you, sir . . .'

That was really the right appeal to the great man: just you, sir; on the other hand the great man could not admit that there were cases that he had not met before. So he said:

'Dozens of ex-convicts come to me for help – dozens, I tell you.'

He had stopped writing and eyed Kufalt with friendly detachment. Kufalt stood expectant.

'Yes,' said the great man; and once again, 'Yes.'

Kufalt still did not know what to say. So he stood and waited.

'You see,' said the great man, 'I have to work; I represent the people, the simple people, you understand? Blood and soil, you understand?'

'Yes,' said Kufalt patiently.

'I have to conserve my energy,' went on Scialoja. 'I belong to my vocation. Do you understand what a vocation means?'

'Yes,' said Kufalt again.

The chief editor surveyed his visitor as though the matter was settled. But Kufalt did not agree; there was no need for him to be asked to call between eleven and one, merely to be informed that another man had a vocation, whereas he had none.

He stood and did not move.

'Look,' said Herr Scialoja. 'You might inquire again later on. As I said, I feel very sorry for you. The governor of the prison gave me an excellent report of you.'

His memory seemed to be coming back to him, in spite of the thousand things that went through his head. So Kufalt tried once more.

'Just a little work,' he said; 'one or two hours a day.' And he added persuasively: 'I have my own typewriter.'

Scialoja's face assumed a sympathetic expression.

'I really don't know,' he said hesitatingly. 'I live only for my own work. Perhaps you had better see our business manager.'

'Would you recommend me to your business manager?' said Kufalt.

'But, my dear sir, I don't know you at all.'

'But you had a talk with the prison governor about me.'

'The governor of the prison,' said the chief editor, suddenly returning to earth, 'naturally recommends all his discharged prisoners, so as to save himself trouble.'

'But why did you tell me to come and see you?' asked Kufalt.

'Now look,' said the great man with a sudden inspiration. 'We have a sort of fund here, I'll give you an order on it for three marks if you'll promise not to come back again.'

Kufalt stood silent for a moment. He thought it over. Then all his diffidence departed, and he said abruptly:

'You live in the Dottistrasse, don't you, Herr Scialoja, in a villa?'

'Yes,' answered the chief editor, looking puzzled.

'Ah,' said Kufalt. 'That's fine. Office shuts at six, I suppose?'

'What do you mean?' asked Scialoja.

'Because it's pretty dark around there,' said Kufalt, and laughed. And, still laughing, he walked out of the editor's office.

He left an agitated man behind him.

VII

The laughter with which Kufalt had left the office did not last very long. The Dottistrasse was certainly dark about six in the evening, and it was certainly pleasant to know that for some time to come Herr Scialoja would go home in a state of nervousness and would probably get some sub-editor or compositor to see him home – but what was the use of that!

Four hundred and thirty marks was not a great deal of money, and the end of it could be easily reckoned. Well, he would go to the six clergymen whose addresses he had looked up at the counter of the newspaper office, though he was sure that nothing much would come of that either. Among the six clergymen there was one whom Kufalt knew. That was the Catholic priest, whose altar Kufalt had had to look after in the prison; a stern man, advanced in years. Kufalt had often fallen out with him. Perhaps the priest made Kufalt pay for it, that the officials had foisted a Protestant on him for this work.

However, as Kufalt walked along the street and thought matters over, the man did not seem so bad. He had done his best for his prisoners, and though he snubbed and scolded them he was always there when they wanted him. Perhaps he would be there now that Kufalt wanted him.

Kufalt made up his mind at once; after that bloody Scialoja, he would go straight to the priest.

A nun, or someone who looked like one, opened the door to him, her white face almost hidden under a great coif. Kufalt had to wait a while in the hall; the house was as still as death. He had to wait a long while; but, after all, he had nothing else to do, nothing at all.

At last the priest appeared. The tall, powerful figure went slowly up to him, and asked him, in a slow and gentle voice, what he wanted. He had not recognized Kufalt, and Kufalt had to remind him of the prison.

'Ah, yes,' said the priest, still not quite remembering his visitor. 'But you look quite different now. So neat.'

'That's the different clothes,' Kufalt reminded him.

'To be sure,' said the priest, 'yes, different clothes.'

He still spoke in a slow and gentle voice; he was certainly a peasant's son from the coast, where the men have just this gentleness and strength.

'And what can I do for you now?'

Kufalt told his story, the priest listened, even asking a few questions, and Kufalt noticed that he understood how a man might feel.

In the end the priest said briefly: 'I will give you a note for the manager of a tannery. I don't say that it will be any use. But I will give it to you.'

He sat down and wrote; then he looked up and said: 'But you are not a Catholic, are you?'

It occurred to Kufalt to lie, but he said in a low tone, 'No.'

'Good,' said the priest, and went on writing.

'Go round at once,' he then said. 'The man is sure to be at home for his dinner.' He shook his head. 'But don't be too hopeful, there is much worse distress than yours. Have you any money left?'

'Yes,' said Kufalt.

'And clothes?'

'Yes,' said Kufalt.

'Well, perhaps you will come and see me again if this is no good. I will see what I can do . . .'

He gave Kufalt his hand.

Kufalt handed in the letter at the manager's house and waited at the door. His heart throbbed a little – the kind old man had told him not to be too hopeful – but what if something came of it?

The maid came back, slipped some money into his hand and said: 'You need not call again.' Then she shut the door.

He stood gloomily on the steps and counted the money; it was thirty pfennigs. He could hear the maid moving about the kitchen, dropped the thirty pfennigs through the letterbox, and ran down the steps as he heard them drop into the box.

Then he made his way home, downcast and miserable. In a shop on the Königstrasse he bought two dried herrings; there was bread in the house and milk, so his daily lunch, à la Maack, was complete. Then he could sleep after his food or not, just as his head felt disposed, and then came the bright spot of the evening, the visit to Emil Bruhn. And, if Emil Bruhn had done well at his timber works that week, they might even go to a dance hall. Such were the fantastic plans that hovered in his mind. Grasping the herrings in their greasy parchment paper, Kufalt opened his door and stood still.

A lanky, red-faced man with a long nose was sitting by the window, reading a newspaper, which he proceeded to fold up.

'Herr Kufalt, I take it?' said the man. 'Pardon my making myself at home like this. Your landlady didn't seem to mind.'

'Not at all,' said Kufalt, rather taken aback.

'My name is Dietrich,' said the man, looking amicably at Kufalt with quick, mouse-like eyes set strangely near the bridge of his nose.

'Mine is Kufalt,' said Kufalt quite superfluously. He still did not know who his visitor was.

This the stranger realized at once.

'Ah,' said he. 'I see you don't remember. You wrote to the *Town and Country Messenger* about a job; and about your unfortunate position. There was some talk about your letter in the office, but of course none of the big people will do anything, and that's why I'm here.'

He smiled affably, and seemed to regard the matter as explained.

The *Town and Country Messenger* was the smaller competitor of the more important paper, upon whose editor Kufalt had already called.

'Yes,' said Kufalt doubtfully, putting the herrings down on the washstand, 'and have you a job for me?'

'Possibly,' said Herr Dietrich. 'That remains to be seen.'

'And what must I do about a possible job?'

They had both sat down and were surveying each other with friendly eyes.

'I may tell you,' said Herr Dietrich, and leaned so near to Kufalt that he became very aware that Herr Dietrich had been drinking brandy; 'I may tell you that I am not on the staff of the *Town and Country Messenger*. I am on my own.'

Kufalt recoiled slightly: as much at his visitor's breath as at his announcement.

'*But*,' said Herr Dietrich, drawing out the word, 'I am a very busy man. I have a great many things in my head.'

Kufalt thought he had heard that remark once before that day, and sat silent and expectant.

'First,' said Herr Dietrich, laying his hand softly on Kufalt's, 'First, I am subscription canvasser for the *Town and Country Messenger*.'

He raised his hand and observed it meditatively. He did not seem to notice that the short and bitten nails looked rather dirty. After a pause, he laid it down again on Kufalt's.

'Secondly,' said Herr Dietrich, 'I am advertisement canvasser for the same paper.'

Again the same manoeuvre with the hand. And again the hand returned to Kufalt's.

'Thirdly,' said Herr Dietrich, 'I canvass for voluntary health insurance and collect the subscriptions.'

The hand again hovered in the air and again came back to Kufalt.

'Fourthly, I collect the guild subscriptions for the local publicans' union.'

Kufalt was convinced that Herr Dietrich had been collecting the publicans' subscriptions that very morning. He did not know how long Herr Dietrich had been sitting in his room. But the room smelt decidedly of spirits.

'Fifthly,' said Herr Dietrich gravely, 'I also collect the membership subscriptions for the Old Oak Sports Club.

'Sixthly, I am the business manager of the local Commerce and Transport Office, and I provide all the information which would otherwise have to be supplied by the entire staff of a Central European travel bureau.'

Kufalt waited to see if there was any more to come, but the hand remained in the air, then found its way to Herr Dietrich's pocket and rattled his small change.

'Well, he's not going to sting me for a loan,' thought Kufalt.

'I was utterly overcome by your story,' said Herr Dietrich confidentially, 'I assure you – utterly overcome.'

Pause.

It was really time for Kufalt to say something; but he said nothing. Herr Dietrich suddenly turned and looked straight into his interlocutor's face. 'And what do you imagine I can do for you?' he asked.

'I don't yet know,' said Kufalt dubiously.

'I can't pay you a salary,' announced Dietrich with decision. 'But I can offer you prospects.'

'Ah,' said Kufalt non-committally.

'Look,' said Herr Dietrich, 'I'm going to be quite candid with you. I am, as a matter of fact, a very candid man. My candour has done me harm a thousand times.'

He looked at Kufalt with a friendly smile, and appeared to be at a loss how to go on.

Then he had an idea.

'By the way,' said Herr Dietrich, 'there's a man called Lemcke has a public house just at the corner here. Can I offer you a glass of beer and a schnapps? We'll get on much quicker like that.'

Kufalt hesitated a moment. Then he said: 'I never drink anything in the morning. It doesn't suit me.'

'Nor me either,' said Herr Dietrich; 'but you understand, owing to my connection with the publicans' union . . .'

Kufalt took refuge in silence. Herr Dietrich fidgeted a bit, looked uneasily at his cigar and then said, more or less to the cigar:

'We must come to a decision.'

'Yes,' said Kufalt politely.

Suddenly Herr Dietrich got going.

'Now look, my dear Herr Kufalt,' he said, 'after all, you don't know me, and I've drunk a little brandy this morning. You go to the editor's office tomorrow morning at twelve; there you'll find our head honcho, Freese, and he'll tell you the sort of man I am. Then I'll let you collect the cash from all the associations and the union, on a percentage basis. And you can canvass for advertisements and subscribers, and if you do any other work for me I'll pay you extra. Now what about it?'

'What would that bring in monthly?' asked Kufalt cautiously.

'That depends entirely on you,' said Herr Dietrich. 'If, for example, you get a hundred subscribers in a month, at one mark twenty-five per subscriber, that makes a hundred and twenty-five marks, of which a quarter goes to me – well, it's pretty easy money.'

'Ah,' said Kufalt. 'And what about the job of collecting it? People don't like paying their subscriptions these days.'

'That's so,' said Herr Dietrich. 'You won't become a millionaire. But it's a living. Will you take it on or not?'

'I'll go and see Herr Freese,' said Kufalt.

'And there's one more thing, my dear Herr Kufalt,' said Herr Dietrich, leaning so close to Kufalt that he got the full benefit of the aroma of half a dozen brandies. 'When you're collecting the cash, you see, you'll have hundreds of marks in hand, for which I shall be responsible.'

He eyed Kufalt with an air of grave concern.

'For which I shall be responsible,' he repeated.

'Yes,' said Kufalt, and waited. He knew quite well what was coming, but he did not want to make it too easy for the other man.

'Well now, my dear Herr Kufalt,' said Herr Dietrich; 'you mentioned it in your letter. That was what landed you in jail – I mean, that was how you came to fall into such misfortune.'

'Then I can't go round collecting money,' said Kufalt.

'Oh, yes you can,' insisted Herr Dietrich. 'We can fix it somehow. You come from a good family. A security . . .'

'Then I'll go and see Herr Freese tomorrow,' said Kufalt, and got up.

'You mean that there's no question of a security? I would of course give you every possible guarantee for it.'

'What can you be thinking of?' cried Kufalt. 'Do you suppose I would need to be writing begging letters if I could put up a large security?'

'But what about a small one?' asked Herr Dietrich. 'You could settle up with me every day.'

'Not even a small one,' said Kufalt decisively. 'In any case I would have to see Herr Freese.'

'There's no point in that,' said Herr Dietrich, carefully stalking the door. 'Freese is the rudest pig in the world. Besides,' he said, as he succeeded in clutching the door handle; 'besides, I only came to you because I was overcome by your story – utterly overcome.'

'Yes, yes,' said Kufalt vaguely, and gazed at his long-nosed visitor thoughtfully. Suddenly he had an idea. 'I wonder if you could lend me twenty marks?' he said. 'I'm pretty well cleaned out.' He laughed.

And then a wonderful thing happened. Dietrich, half drunk, jingling in his pocket the silver he had collected from the publicans' union, produced a handful of money, counted out four five-mark pieces, thrust them into Kufalt's hand, and said:

'Never mind a receipt. We shall be working together.'

And he disappeared, with the soft and cautious step of the habitual drunkard who knows he must be careful going down the stairs.

VIII

Emil Bruhn lived in the Lerchenstrasse, also some way outside the town, not far from the timber works, where he knocked nest boxes together on piece work, just as he had done in prison.

He had a room with green-washed walls, of which he was not the only tenant.

He shared it with the nightwatchman of a tannery, who went out about eight in the evening and did not come back until eight in the morning, an hour and a half after Bruhn left the house. They slept in the same bed. They had most things in common, and when there were disputes – and there often were – they were aired on Sundays, when the nightwatchman had his free night.

Kufalt, who had been in the little town only a fortnight, knew all about these disputes. How the bastard never used his own soap, never hung up his clothes and came back drunk with a girl every Sunday evening and wanted Bruhn to sleep on the floor. 'Just for a little while, Emil. We shan't be long . . .'

Bruhn used to open his heart on all these matters. But Kufalt minded that much less than the presence of Krüger, who had formerly shared the room with Bruhn.

Krüger had – fortunately – long since departed from the scene; he had pilfered from his fellow workmen. Pitiable, nasty, stupid little thefts of tobacco and cufflinks. He was now in jail once more, unlamented by Bruhn.

If Emil Bruhn had altered in one respect, it was that young men no longer played any part in his life. He was now after girls, but somehow he never succeeded. Either he was too shy, or too forward. Or they guessed that there was something not quite right about him, and it came to nothing. And he ran around and ogled them with his kindly, blue, seal's eyes, sweated his heart out in the dance halls, bought them two, or even three glasses of beer out of his pitiful little earnings, and then they let him down. They vanished into the night, or departed quite openly with other men, leaving Bruhn to watch them go.

Perhaps that was why he had been so glad when Kufalt came back. A smart lad like Kufalt, always well dressed; they'd be sure to click now. The girls always went out in pairs. Well, Kufalt would take the pretty one – there was always a pretty one and a plain one together, but however plain she was, she had what Emil Bruhn wanted.

He stood in front of his mirror and struggled with his white collar, and told Kufalt what fine girls would be coming to dance that evening in the Rendsburger Hof. He had such pathetic confidence in his friend, quite unaware that Kufalt's luck with the girls was just as bad.

'Isn't it too dear?' said Kufalt.

'Dear?' said Emil. 'I do the whole evening on one glass of beer. But of course if you have to get the girls tight first . . .'

'There's no question of that,' said Kufalt.

'Well then,' said Emil, 'I always said you had a way about you.'

'And what did you earn this week?' asked Kufalt.

'Twenty-one marks sixty,' said Bruhn. 'They keep on deducting more and more, the swindlers, they know they can treat me as they like. They've told the foreman I was in for robbery and murder. And he's only got to pass the word to the other blokes and I'll be on the street. They wouldn't work with anyone like me, if they knew about it.'

He was standing in front of his mirror, having adjusted his collar and tie at last. He looked at Kufalt.

And Kufalt looked at his young friend Emil Bruhn.

In that look was the flicker of a fire gone out. A faint memory of old days, when they slipped each other notes by the orderly, when they stood under the same shower; when they made love.

Here they were; together once again. They looked at each other. Life had gone on, much had changed, and above all they themselves had changed. But here was redolence of old days, the memory of close intimacy and of fulfilment, so ardently desired, so seldom achieved.

No, they did not even shake hands now. Life had gone forward. It was another body than the one immured in prison walls, and a different desire to what it then had been. There were girls in the streets, skirts swirling round their legs, and rounded breasts . . . A fine life, or at least it should have been . . .

'I suppose nothing was done about your savings bank book?'

'Nothing,' said Emil Bruhn. 'They did me down, the bastards. But if I ever go back to the clink . . .'

'If you're ready, let's go,' replied Kufalt.

No, it was over. Another world and other companions, you cannot hold it, you cannot call it back; but over in the Königstrasse, here in the Lerchenstrasse, stands the lonely bed, with its brooding dreams and lonely satisfactions.

Must it be always so?

IX

On one side of the smoky dance hall, from the ceiling of which still hung the paper garlands and lanterns of the Venetian night of the last carnival – on one side stood the girls, and on the other stood the lads.

The girls wore the usual little factory girl's short frock, and many of the men wore caps. Several were in shirtsleeves. When they wanted to dance they beckoned to a girl and the girl came across and stood before her man, who calmly brought his conversation to a close before he put his arm round her waist and moved off with her.

Kufalt and Bruhn sat at a table and drank their beer. The other lads went to the bar between dances and drank a glass of schnapps or beer while standing up. Or they drank nothing – what had they paid thirty pfennigs admission for? The band played very loud and the girls joined in for all the popular songs. And when the dance was at an end, the young louts left the girls standing just where they were and joined their fellows.

'Let's go to a better place,' said Kufalt.

'A better place would cost a lot of money,' said Bruhn. 'And one woman's as good as another.'

Kufalt was about to make some reply when he saw her. She was quite tall, with a frank and cheerful face, a lively mouth and a snub nose.

Her dress was perhaps a little prettier than those of the others. But perhaps Kufalt merely thought so.

'Who is she?' he asked Bruhn, with sudden eagerness, quite forgetting his suggestion that they should go.

Bruhn, of course, could not at first make out whom Willi meant, but then he said:

'Oh, that girl – she's no good to you. She's got a baby.'

'How do you mean?' asked Kufalt, puzzled.

'Well, because no one will pay for the child.'

'All the more reason—' began Kufalt.

'No, no,' said Bruhn. 'She won't have anything to do with a man now. She's had enough of that. She's been beaten so often by her father, a glazier called Harder in the Lütjenstrasse, she won't look at a man ever again.'

'If that's so . . .' said Kufalt slowly.

And then he sat still and watched her. The music seemed to grow louder and louder, and from time to time she too danced and laughed. She was Hildegard, Harder the glazier's daughter in the Lütjenstrasse. She had probably given him the slip that night. And he was Kufalt, from the Königstrasse, with no prospects at all. But he had a little money, and a decent suit – and now and again she glanced at him.

When the girls went, he could run after them. Never mind if he made himself ridiculous, because they had not really gone away, only to the lavatory. He stood outside and waited, indifferent to all the laughter; the stranger in the neat blue suit, who went about with the little seal from the timber works, had fallen for a girl. Well, what was the harm in that? Some time, surely, a man must follow his fancies. The others had gone, and he watched her; she had a little habit of putting her hand to her hair and sort of holding her head while she danced. And she had a child, she had already slept with other men. That would make it all the easier . . .

. . . And the way she bent her head down to her glass, so that her hair tumbled all over her cheeks. 'Go soon,' a voice within him whispered, 'so that I can speak to you . . .'

But she went on laughing and dancing and talking, and did not look at him, for now she knew that he had seen her . . .

'Please go!'

He was thankful for those solitary nights that made this possible; that it could come to him like this, as happiness, as the greatest happiness of all. And she could not say no; she would not say no. Let them laugh at him as they liked. Next Saturday he would dance with her, he would get a job and would marry her and they would have a child.

Oh, Liese of a little while ago – what a different world!

These were the small, badly lit, narrow streets of low houses. And the spaces of the sky above his head seemed deep – deep and very near. The wind whistled round the corners, and the two girls clung closer to each other. And he walked behind them. A pace or two behind them, and he had not yet uttered a word. They reached the Lütjenstrasse and she opened the front door and chatted to her friend for a minute or two, and he stood quite nearby, and a voice within him prayed that she might come to him.

And the front door shut, and the other girl passed him and laughed and said: 'You yob!' and went on. And he stood there alone. It was very dark, and he was afraid of his own room.

It was not for a while that he discovered that there was a yard behind the house, that the yard door was not fastened, that he could get into the yard, and that a light was still burning in a window on the ground floor.

And, however it happens, well, once in a while a man's courage rises. He softly scratched on the window pane, and then tapped gently, and again a little louder. The window opened; she was at the window. And a voice said softly: 'Yes?'

'Oh, please!' said Kufalt.

And the window shut again, and it was dark. And he stood there, in that strange yard, and suddenly he looked up, in his solitude he looked up. And he saw the stars; they came so strangely near and seemed so full of meaning. And a hand was in his. And a voice whispered: 'Come.'

Again there was a light in the room, but it was not her bed that he saw. It was the child's bed, and the child was asleep. He was lying huddled up, with his knees under his chin, just as he may once have lain in his mother's womb. And his cheeks were rosy, and his hair all tousled over his forehead . . .

Both of them looked down at the child.

And then they looked at each other.

'Oh, dear, dear face!'

He raised his two hands and laid his fingertips against her cheek and drew her head to his. He thought he could hear the blood murmuring in her veins. They looked into each other's faces, and her eyelids quivered over her brown eyes; and her face came nearer and grew larger.

Gone were the stars, gone was the night and the solitary vigil in the yard. The face of such a girl could stand for a whole world. Mountains and valleys and deep, deep lakes of eyes . . .

Oh, dear, dear face!

There was her mouth – but it was firmly closed. It did not yield to the pressure of his lips.

Suddenly her shoulder slipped away from him, and then her face. The child was still asleep. There they stood, in a strange world.

'Go,' she said, and led him by the hand across the yard into the street.

And he went home.

Thus it began.

X

There were many things you could not mention to Emil Bruhn. In prison their comradeship had seemed complete – but now there were many things of which you could not speak.

'Where did you get to last night?'

'I was so tired and it was so boring . . .'

'Oh yes – because Hildegard Harder went away.'

'Her, indeed!'

'And you let yourself be called a yob by a girl like Wrunka Kowalska from the tannery?'

'Rubbish,' said Kufalt. 'Rubbish!'

And as Bruhn said no more, he went on: 'Nothing doing with the clergymen. They say they can't help and tell me to go to the Welfare Office. As if I didn't know that!'

'Yes, and you never even got into her room.'

'Look, Emil, I've been thinking about your situation,' said Kufalt, taking an interest. 'That timber works of yours is no good in the long run. And you're a first-rate carpenter . . .'

'I certainly am,' Emil agreed. 'When a man's done eleven years in the carpenter's shop in prison . . .'

'Suppose you passed your journeyman's test, and got a job with a good employer, in Kiel or Hamburg, where no one knows anything about you?'

Bruhn again grew surly. 'And the money, my friend, the money for the test, and all the time when I shan't be earning anything? . . . No, you made a right fool of yourself before the whole town yesterday. I shan't go out with you again in a hurry.'

Could he tell him? Yes, he could; after all, he had been to her room at night, after twelve . . . But the child's bed, and that dear face that had come so close to his . . .

'Supposing I went to the governor, and talked to him about you?' said Kufalt. 'There's a fund for discharged prisoners. And it couldn't be better used than in getting you a decent job.'

'It would be no use,' said Emil, rather mollified. 'The whole Prison Board will be against you.'

'Well, I'll go,' said Kufalt. 'I've always got on with the old man. You'll soon see!'

For Emil the past night was forgotten, and the friend with whom he had been anxious to show off, and who had allowed a Polish girl to call him a yob without smacking her face for her pains . . .

'If I could get to be a carpenter journeyman,' said Emil dreamily. 'You've no idea how sick I am of this job. For eight years I've been making nest boxes. I know every hammer-blow. But if I could make a cupboard again, or a table, with the legs properly dovetailed . . .'

'I'll tell the governor,' said Kufalt. 'But it will be some time till it's fixed up.'

'I've got plenty of time. I can wait,' said Emil.

'Right. Tomorrow, then,' said Kufalt. 'I must see how I can fit it in. I've got so many things to do tomorrow . . .'

'What have you got to do?' asked Emil. 'You've got nothing at all to do.'

'I've got a great deal to do. I have to run around all day.' He paused and coughed. He looked down the street, it was autumn weather, cold, windy and damp, about six o'clock in the evening; it was just possible that Hildegard Harder might be walking down the road.

No, she was not. Kufalt added casually: 'From now on, I shall be earning my ten or twelve marks a day.'

'Balls,' said Bruhn briefly.

'What do you mean, balls! Nothing of the kind,' said Kufalt indignantly. 'I went to see Freese this morning . . .'

'Don't know him,' said Bruhn. 'Never heard the name. And what did you have to slip him in advance for a job like that?'

'Nothing,' snapped Kufalt. 'Not a penny. There was a lanky fellow came to see me first by the name of Dietrich. He wanted a security; and he wanted a quarter of all earned. Well, I soon put him in his place, and he lent me twenty marks before he went!'

Kufalt burst out laughing, and so did Emil, though still rather mystified. Then Kufalt had to tell him about Dietrich. 'A beer and a schnapps at the corner, and he thought he could get out of me the last money I had, the poor idiot . . .'

And Emil laughed too. 'That was the stuff to give him. And then you went behind his back to Herr Freese?'

'I did,' said Kufalt, becoming noticeably curt. 'And I am to canvass for subscribers and advertisements, and get the commission myself.'

'Good for you, my boy!' shouted Bruhn delightedly. 'And if you go to the governor and bring that business off we shall both earn so much money that we'll be able to go to decent places where there's decent women, and all the Wrunkas and Hildegards can go to hell.'

It was at that moment that a voice nearby said: 'May I speak to you for just a moment?'

Embarrassed silence.

Then Kufalt said: 'I dare say I'll come round this evening again, Emil.'

'Right,' said Emil; 'and don't forget the governor.'

'Don't you worry about that, my lad,' said Kufalt.

And his voice sounded unnaturally hearty.

Then Hildegard Harder and Willi Kufalt walked towards the public garden, on the outskirts of the town, where it was dark.

XI

It was not for nothing that Kufalt had deliberately said little about his interview with Editor Freese. The *Town and Country Messenger* might well be a smaller paper than the *Friend of the Fatherland*, but Herr Freese was certainly quite as big a man as Herr Scialoja.

There was no difficulty about admission, no waiting . . . 'Go right through,' said a tall, bony, horse-faced man, pointing to the door. 'But it's one of his bad days.'

So Kufalt went through.

There sat a fat, heavy, shabby man behind a desk; he had a greyish-white walrus moustache and wore a very pendulous pince-nez.

On one side of the desk sat Herr Freese, on the other side stood Kufalt. Between them on the desk lay a litter of papers, beer bottles, a flask of brandy and glasses. Herr Freese's complexion was grey, his eyes were red and angry.

He blinked at Kufalt, opened his mouth as though about to speak and then shut it again.

'Good morning,' said Kufalt. 'Herr Dietrich suggested I should call.'

Freese coughed and gasped a little, until his throat was clear enough for him to ejaculate: 'Get out!'

Kufalt reflected for a moment; he was no longer the Kufalt of a while ago, when he came out of prison with the hope that everything would be easy; he knew a man had to stand his ground and not be browbeaten, just as in prison – so he reflected, and then said: 'As a matter of fact, I really came against Herr Dietrich's advice.'

He stood and watched for the response.

Herr Freese looked at him angrily with his little reddened eyes. He coughed again and cleared his throat, then he looked at the brandy flask, shook his head gloomily, coughed again and said slowly: 'You are an artful young man. But not quite artful enough for an old one like me.' He broke off suddenly: 'Don't you find that stove a nuisance?'

Kufalt was taken aback; he looked round at the great white-tiled stove, glowing with heat; he could not guess what answer Herr Freese wanted (for that was the one he would have liked to give), so he said: 'No, not at all.'

'I do,' said Herr Freese wearily. 'Too cold, much too cold. Put three briquettes on it – no, five.'

There was a scuttle of briquettes beside the stove, but nothing with which to pick them up. Kufalt looked round and had an inspiration; he took a scrap of paper from the desk, a manuscript probably, picked up the briquettes, pushed them into the fire and the paper after them . . . and turned to Freese.

'Artful,' muttered the latter; 'very artful. But not artful enough.'

He sat huddled in his chair, looking very grim and old. Through the window came a faint ray of autumn sunshine, slanting across the grey ravaged face, the flushed forehead and the shabby locks of grizzled hair.

Kufalt wondered if he were asleep.

Far from it. 'You've just come out of prison,' said he. 'I know that complexion. Manicures his hands, the pig, and still hopes to get a decent job.'

He wearily raised his own hand and surveyed it; it looked as grey as if it had not been washed for weeks.

Freese shook his head, again surveyed Kufalt, and said: 'It's no good, my lad, no good at all. The Trehne flows through the park, there's a nice little pool by the tannery, the water's cool and damp – that's the place for you.'

'And what about you?' said Kufalt breathlessly to that ghost of alcohol and gloom.

'Too old,' said Freese. 'Much too old. If a man's got nothing more to expect, he always goes on living. You've got something to expect, so – chuck it!'

They were both silent.

'Cold,' said the old man, and shivered, glancing at the stove. 'Never mind, it's no use trying to do anything. How did you come across Dietrich?'

'He came to see me where I live.'

'What did he offer you?'

'Every sort of work, 25 per cent to him.'

'Did he sting you for money?' asked Freese.

'No,' said Kufalt proudly. 'I stung him.'

'How much?'

'Twenty marks.'

'Kraft!' roared the old man. 'Kraft!!'

The door of the outer room opened and the horse-face appeared. 'Well?' it said.

'This young man will begin with us tomorrow, canvassing advertisements and subscribers. Usual rate. If he doesn't make six a day, he's fired. And see that Dietrich is fired at once.'

'But . . .' began Kraft.

'Dietrich's fired; he let himself be stung for money,' snapped Herr Freese. And then: 'Get out!'

Herr Kraft got out.

'Tomorrow morning at nine,' said Herr Freese. 'But I tell you at once, it's no use. You'll never do six a day and I shall fire you, and then there's the river . . .'

As he sat there he surely saw it, with his very eyes. 'The river,' he said; 'grey and cold and damp. Water . . .' he said. 'Damp,' he added, and shuddered.

This time he poured himself a glass of brandy.

He shuddered again as he drank.

Then he said in a clearer voice: 'And how about those twenty marks you got from Dietrich? He still owes money here. Hand them over.'

'B-but,' began Kufalt.

'Ha!' said the old man. 'You don't know what you're going to live on for the next few days – and you're going out to canvass for subscribers!! Good morning.'

'Good morning,' said Kufalt, almost at the door. Once more he heard Freese say 'Water . . .' and he saw the grey, bloated face, the grizzled hair, the genie of the brandy bottle . . .

'Water . . .' said Freese.

XII

'How do you like him?' she asked.

'Nice. Very nice,' he said hastily.

'His name is Willi. Wilhelm,' said she.

'That's my name,' said he.

'Yes, I know,' said she.

The night was very dark. Over the leafless branches of the trees hung the canopy of sky – starless – a presence more to be felt than seen. First they walked side by side through the lamplit streets, then arm in arm along the road, and then embracing through the leafless copses. They came to a bench surrounded by young pines, and there sat down. The wind was above them; at their sides it seemed more distant; they sat together and were warm.

He saw her face as a bright shimmer, in which the eyes were darkling pools – gleaming out of that silken darkness.

'Children ought to have a father,' she said.

'I have been so long alone too,' he said, and leaned his head on her shoulder; it was very soft.

She drew him nearer, with one hand against her breast. 'Oh, so have I!' said she. 'When the child came, and everybody stared at me and I was suddenly like dirt, and Father was always beating me and Mother always crying . . .'

She sank into her memories.

'I haven't got a father,' said he.

'I wish I hadn't,' she cried. 'Then I could take a room and work for the boy . . . But as it is . . .'

'But why don't you?' he asked. 'You're of age.'

'That wouldn't do at all,' she said quickly. 'Father is well known in the trade, and until this happened he was master of the Glaziers' Guild. Everybody knows me here. No; I shall have to stay at home until someone marries me.'

There was silence for a while. The hand that held the head against the warm, soft breast loosened its grasp. But the other came to join it, and together they lifted the head; lips met, and this time the girl's lips parted. Soft lips seemed to swell and blossom under his kiss.

Hilde's mouth drew back for an instant and a sound came from it, a gasp of relief – water after long, long thirst – then her mouth swooped down upon his from the darkness and drew his lips into hers, burning with desire – fuller and tenderer . . .

No lovers' talk, no uttered word; two thirsty beings that at last, at last could drink. Silent, never-ending kisses; and between them Kufalt could hear the night wind in the trees, the creak of a branch, a sudden swirl of autumn leaves, the hoot of a motor horn, far, far away . . .

And while Kufalt drank, and held his breath, a vast melancholy filled his heart. 'At the very moment I am kissing it is over . . . In the beginning is the end.' And, 'Children must have a father . . . his name is Willi . . . until someone marries me . . . it is over, as I kiss, it is over . . .'

Sad earth that brings sorrow with fulfilment, planet barely warmed by the sun's rays before it turns to ice . . . passion quickly chilled . . . poor Kufalt . . .

They kiss and kiss, they fling their arms around each other, their breath comes quicker, their brains swim, their hearts throb, there is a fire before their eyes like a spurt of flame from ashes – and while their kisses grow more frantic and devouring, an evil thought flashes through Kufalt's brain. If she was crafty he could be more crafty still . . . If she meant to catch him, perhaps he could catch her . . .

And his hand slid from the shoulder beneath the cloak, over the blouse, down to the breast and grasped it. And he pressed his leg against hers.

She flung herself away from him, wrenched her body out of his embrace, like iron from a magnet.

For a moment they both stood swaying. She – he could guess the gesture in the darkness – put her hand up to her hair, as she had done in the dance hall the night before.

'No,' he heard her whisper. 'Never, never again.'

'I only wanted . . .' he began hurriedly.

'If that's what you want,' she said, 'we had better go now. Once is quite enough.'

She shivered; and felt for his arm. 'Come along. It's getting cold. Let's go for a little walk.'

They went. No, she had not been offended; but . . . that was the end of that, thought Kufalt. She had really had enough. She was afraid.

And he said aloud, 'You needn't go home yet? What will your father say?'

'It's one of my father's skittle evenings,' she said.

She found every path in the darkness. The park was large, but she knew them all. 'We must turn left here – now over there, where it looks quite dark. That's the way to the hut.'

'She must often have been here with the other man,' thought Kufalt. 'Or with the others. There's no father, no one to pay for the child. And now I come along when she's had enough of it. Just my rotten luck.'

'The little plump man who was with you in the Rendsburger Hof – is he a friend of yours?'

'Bruhn? Yes, he's my friend.'

'I should be careful of him, I've heard he's a thief and a murderer.'

'A thief and a murderer . . .' said Kufalt angrily. 'What do you know about thieves and murderers? He's a fine young man.'

'But he's been in prison,' she said. 'I know that for certain.'

'Well, and what if he has?' said Kufalt aggressively. 'Do you think that's so very dreadful?'

'It's a question of taste,' she said. 'I don't like such people any more than I like the unemployed. Fancy living on the dole, and the man in the house all day! I could get plenty like that if I wanted them.'

'Yes,' said Kufalt.

It seemed as though she were gradually receding from him; it was good to be with her when they were silent, but now that they began to speak, they fell apart.

'Yes,' he said curtly.

'Where do you work?' she asked. 'Are you in an office or a shop?'

'No; on a newspaper,' he said.

'Splendid!' said she. 'I'm sure you get lots of cinema tickets. Can't we go to the cinema one of these days?'

'I don't know,' he said doubtfully. 'I must see how I can manage. There are a good many of us on the *Town and Country Messenger*.'

'So you're on the *Messenger*,' she said in rather a disappointed tone. 'I thought you were on the *Friend*. We always read the *Friend*. It's a much better paper.'

'But how do you know if you don't read the *Messenger*?'

'Oh yes we do. But we've got used to the *Friend*. Perhaps the *Messenger* has improved,' she said encouragingly. 'I don't really know it, we only see it now and again. Come along, there's the hut. I expect it'll be warmer inside.'

'No,' he said, 'I must go home now.'

'Oh dear, and now you're cross,' she cried in despair. 'Because I said that about the *Messenger*. I'll never say anything against the *Messenger* again, never!'

'No, I'm tired. I want to go home now,' he said.

They stood and faced each other. In the clearing, by the little rustic hut, there was a bit more light. He looked at her face; her hands were raised imploringly to the level of her breast.

'Oh, Willi,' she said, calling him for the first time by his Christian name. 'Don't be angry with me. Please come.'

'I'm not angry,' he said, in what sounded a very angry voice; 'but I'm really tired and must get to bed quickly. I've got a great deal to do tomorrow.'

She let her hands fall, and was silent for a moment.

'Then go,' she said tonelessly. 'Go.'

He hesitated, murmured a goodnight, and turned away.

'Goodnight,' she answered, also in a low tone.

And then: 'Give me a kiss, Willi, please.'

He swung round and took a step or two towards her.

And suddenly he flung his arms around her. This was the woman, the very woman he had longed for all those years, his vanished happiness, the fulfilment that had always slipped out of his grasp . . . Here was the female creature, the bosom that brought happiness, the greatest happiness of all . . . Must he toil back to his room, to his lonely bed?

And he fell upon her with a storm of kisses. He dazed her with the avalanche of his caresses and his quick, questing hands. He blurted out broken, incoherent words: 'Oh my dear, have I found you again . . . You are mine . . . I love you!'

They swayed in each other's arms. The little hut came nearer, a door creaked. It was very dark inside, and chill and dank, odorous of rotting wood . . .

Stillness had fallen. The quick breathing had grown calmer and was now quite calm. Hilde wept softly. He lay with his head on her lap, and she stroked his hair, but it was probably other hair of which she thought: silkier, lighter, younger.

In his little bed, a kilometre and a half away, slept little Willi. She can go to him, but will she be able to stay with him? 'Never, never again,' she had said to herself, and now it had started, just as before.

'Don't cry any more,' he begged her. 'Nothing can possibly have happened.'

She wept.

And then she whispered: 'Do you like me just a little, Willi? Please say you do!'

XIII

He said it, and he thought: one can say many things. And she believed it or did not believe it. And then they parted, in the light of a street lamp, and her face was wet with tears.

One can say many things.

But now he lay alone in his own bed; indeed it was good to lie alone in his own bed between the cool, smooth sheets, with no strange warmth beside him. He lay in bed alone, the room was not quite dark, light from a street lamp was reflected on the opposite wall, and he gazed at it.

He pondered: yes, one can say many things. She had tried to catch him; well, he had caught her.

He closed his eyes; it was now dark. But in the vast abyss of darkness appeared a small, bright vision: Hildegard, the evening before, by her child's bed. She had bent over him – and that night too in the hut she had made one sudden movement . . . not repulsion, nor despair, nor tears; and in that brief moment he was hers, she had taken him in her arms – him, Willi Kufalt, and she had wanted him, for one fleeting moment. A flash of tenderness, a quickened, more ecstatic breathing, a sigh of joy . . .

He must see her again and treat her quite differently, much more kindly. After all, she didn't mean any harm. And the child? It was all for the child's sake! She was right, children must have a father (how he slept there – all huddled up, and his hair so tousled), and she was quite right to try to get him a father. Why shouldn't he marry her? Something might come of the newspaper; perhaps he might really earn some money . . . Later on, when they were married, he would tell her he had been in prison . . . All might yet be well . . .

And he smiled. He thought of that gesture when, in her joy, she had drawn him closer into her arms. Had that ever happened to him before?

He was not wholly bad; there were traces of his earlier days; now he had come from a cruel, selfish, dog-eat-dog world, foul . . . A little kindness, a little loyalty and love, and something would stir inside, all that was good in him was not yet wholly buried . . .

'Dear Hilde,' he whispered. 'Dearest Hilde.'

It did not ring quite true as yet, but it almost did.

Next morning he dashed into Linsing the jeweller's shop, just after eight, when it was still being swept; and he bought a gold wrist-watch for sixty-seven marks.

XIV

Punctually at nine o'clock Kufalt entered the editorial office of the *Town and Country Messenger*. He was wearing his best suit – the blue one with the white needle stripe – a black overcoat that was still quite decent, and a hard black hat. In his hand he carried a brown briefcase, and in the briefcase was a parcel containing a lady's wrist-watch; one never knew whom one might run into on the way.

Behind the counter in the despatch room sat the tall, gaunt, horse-faced man, and opposite him a girl at a typewriter.

'My name is Kufalt,' said Kufalt.

'I know that already,' growled Kraft. 'I've heard enough of it.' And as Kufalt looked at him with consternation, he added more mildly: 'You can imagine the shindy I've had with Dietrich on your account!'

'But that wasn't my fault,' protested Kufalt. 'Herr Freese did it, and I don't in the least understand why.'

Kraft eyed him up for a few moments.

'Come along with me,' he said. 'And I'll put you up to the job.'

Kufalt was taken to a little cubby-hole, a sort of lumber room for buckets and brushes, with shelves full of piles of newspapers yellow with age. On the table stood a battered oil lamp, in one corner a shabby, battered sofa, and in the other corner – bottles, an array of empty bottles, with some champagne bottles among them.

'You must get this place cleared up sometime so you can work here.' With a glance at the sofa and the bottles: 'This was where the old man used to entertain his little ladies' – a glance at the adjoining room – 'while he was still up to it.'

Kufalt shuddered at the thought of that bloated alcoholic spectre in the company of women.

'Here are lists,' said Kraft, 'of all the important members of every trade. Pick out each trade in succession. Always take a union one by one, say the bakers or the butchers, and so on; work through each trade systematically. The syndic of all the trade guilds is a contributor to our paper. Every week he writes a long screed about trade questions. You must use that as a lever: "We support you, so you must support us." You collect the first contribution against a receipt from this book. That's your commission. In the evening you come and report the new subscribers to me, so that they get the paper next morning. That's all . . .'

Kraft walked to the door. Then he said in a bored tone: 'You won't come to anything here even if you did get Dietrich the sack.'

And he pushed off without giving Kufalt time to reply.

Kufalt cleared the table, pulled – after looking round – the loose cover off the sofa, dusted the table and began his day's work. He made lists of the masters of each trade; it was a great temptation to start with the glaziers, but he resisted, and began with the painters.

He decided not to begin with the bakers or the butchers; he would have to go into a shop, and he remembered from old days how a travelling salesman was cut abruptly short when a customer entered and had to wait, with a solemn and obsequious smile, till the customer was satisfied. The painters are difficult enough to begin with.

He had made his list and was now looking up the addresses on a plan of the town and sketching out a round – which seemed likely to lead him all over it; he would get to know it pretty well in the next few weeks.

He was still thus engaged when the door opened and Herr Freese appeared, grey, dishevelled, with bloodshot blinking eyes. He had some sheets of newspaper in his hand. 'There,' he croaked. He cleared his throat, several times. 'From our syndic. Pile of crap! But you'd better know what you're going to tout for.'

'Yes,' said Kufalt politely, and took the sheets.

'Right,' said Freese. He looked at Kufalt; it was an evil, bitter face, with cold, fishy eyes.

'Young,' he muttered. 'Too young.' And he added, with a sudden air of concern: 'Do you think you'll manage it?'

'Manage what?'

'Six subscribers a day.'

'I don't yet know, I've never done it before.'

'He doesn't know, he hasn't done it before, he won't manage it, and the other rag's circulation going up and up . . .' There he stood with bowed head, his thick blue lips quivering under his walrus moustache.

Then he remembered: 'By the way, where are those twenty marks you got from Dietrich?' he asked. 'Have you brought them?'

'I haven't got twenty marks now,' said Kufalt.

Freese looked at him for a while. A glint of mockery flickered in his eyes. 'Won't trust me with twenty marks, and goes out canvassing for me . . . How they struggle to keep above water!' he whispered, chuckling.

The spark went out. An evil, querulous man remained. 'That cover belongs to the sofa, young man, do you hear?' he said savagely. 'It's a very important cover, you see! I can dream of it, ha!'

He screamed out the 'ha!' with unnatural violence, it was like the screech of a bird; and then he slammed the door.

Kufalt settled down to an article on the effects on the smaller bakers of the prohibition of night bakery. Then he fell to reading the serial.

XV

It was now eleven o'clock, and the time had come; Kufalt had no excuse for dallying any longer. He picked up his briefcase and said to Herr Kraft in a professional tone: 'Well, I'm off on my round,' and departed.

The round as planned began ten houses away from the *Town and Country Messenger*, at Retzlatt's paint shop, but at the last moment Kufalt changed it; he would pay his first call on Benzin's, in the Ulmenstrasse, on the outskirts of the town. That would postpone the fatal moment, and he would also have time to memorize his speech on the way.

However, it proved impossible to memorize the speech. In the street he met Dietrich. Three houses away from the *Messenger* office he came up to Kufalt and said: 'Good day, Herr Kufalt.'

'Good day, Herr Dietrich,' said Kufalt, lifted his hat and walked on. Dietrich walked with him. Dietrich had lost his wholesome, ruddy complexion of the day before; he looked blotched and dissipated, and the tip of his long nose was white.

'You'll get some shocks when you start canvassing,' said Dietrich.

Kufalt did not answer and walked on. It was foolish, the man had done him no harm; indeed, the man had lent him twenty marks, but he felt furious with him.

'I wouldn't walk about with a briefcase like that,' said Dietrich dubiously. 'It always suggests a travelling salesman. Just put the receipt book in your overcoat pocket, and they'll all think you're a new customer, and bow you into the shop.'

'Thanks,' said Kufalt politely, and walked on. But he could not restrain his curiosity, and said: 'Why did Freese fire you? Over the 25 per cent you tried to get out of me?'

'Look,' suggested Dietrich, 'I'll give you all the tips, especially over the advertisement canvassing, and you give me 25 per cent in return. I'll leave the accounts to you.'

'Without security?' asked Kufalt.

'Without security,' agreed Dietrich.

'I don't need any tips,' said Kufalt.

'Just as you like,' said Dietrich equably. 'You never know; sometimes people are more stupid than you think. However, I'll get one up on Freese. I am going now to the *Friend*.'

'But this isn't the way to the *Friend* office,' said Kufalt.

'Listen, Herr Kufalt,' said Dietrich, 'you needn't give me back that twenty marks yet. I told you we will work together, and so we will. But you won't give it to Freese either, will you? Just tell Freese you've paid it back.'

Pause.

'He'd only buy brandy with it.'

Pause.

Dietrich laughed, a rather rueful laugh. 'And I would only buy brandy with it too, anyway.' At this point a large smile came over his face. 'Why, here's the Pine, my old friend Schmidt's place. Shall we have one to buck us up? Me for the *Friend*, and you for your first customer?'

'I don't drink . . .'

'Oh no, oh yes; you don't drink in the morning,' said Dietrich hastily. 'It's an excellent principle, but I'm going inside . . .'

He stopped and contemplated the windows of the tavern. 'Tell me, when you've drunk too much, do you feel you need to start again at once next day? . . . If not, my stomach heaves.' He smiled, then added gloomily: 'But the effect doesn't last, it heaves quicker every time . . . Well, I'm going to have one now, or I'll vomit.' He wondered: 'I'll just see if old Schmidt's beer has come up the pipes yet. If not, I'll vomit.'

He reached out a hand. 'Well, best of luck.'

'Thank you, thank you,' said Kufalt, and shook the hand. His anger had gone; he was even a little touched. 'How about laying off drink today, Herr Dietrich . . . ?'

'Look,' said Dietrich; 'even if they have sacked me, I'll have to go on reading the old *Messenger*. Write me out a receipt: Dietrich, Wollenweberstrasse 37 III.'

Slowly Kufalt produced his receipt book and pencil.

'The money, eh?' laughed Dietrich. 'Of course you will get your mark twenty-five. Here . . .' He fumbled in his pockets. 'One mark twenty-five. Exactly right.'

Kufalt wrote. 'Thank you very much,' he said, and gave Dietrich the receipt.

'Not at all,' said he. 'Not at all. We will be working together, as I told you.'

And he vanished into the tavern, slipping the receipt under his hatband.

XVI

Kufalt's heart throbbed within him as he stood at the door of his first real customer. He waited a while before he pulled the bell, until it quietened down a little, but it only thumped the harder.

At last he made up his mind to ring; steps came along the passage, the door opened and a young girl stood before him.

'What, please?' she asked.

'May I speak to Herr Benzin?' asked Kufalt.

'Certainly,' said she.

She led the way along the passage and opened a door. 'Father, here's a gentleman for you.'

In the room sat an elderly, pleasant-looking woman at a table, slicing cabbage into a bowl. Herr Benzin, a bearded gentleman, was standing at the window with another man.

'What can I do for you?' said Herr Benzin.

Kufalt, in the centre of the room, bowed. His heart contracted; he wondered with horror whether he would be able to utter a word.

Then he heard himself speak. Good day. Yes, he came from the office of the *Town and Country Messenger*. Might he be permitted to ask whether Herr Benzin could not be persuaded to subscribe to the paper, to begin with, perhaps, on trial?

'We,' said Kufalt, warming to his work, 'are primarily the paper of the industrial middle class, and more especially represent the interests of trade. The syndic of your trade, Herr Benzin, is our regular contributor. In the last few weeks we have published articles by him on trade questions which have attracted the attention of the Chamber of Commerce. In these hard times friends must stand together, and as we are specially active on behalf of trade . . .'

Here he became involved; but soon extricated himself. With a sidelong glance at the wife, he proceeded: 'As regards our serials, they are by the top authors and are exceedingly popular in family circles. We have a serial now running, of which today's instalment is the hundred and sixty-seventh. It deals with the conflict between gamekeepers and poachers . . .'

He stopped abruptly. He had run dry; he had thought to make a final effort, a really pressing peroration – no, the words would not come. He stood and looked rather confusedly round the room.

They all looked at him; the pendulum clock on the wall ticked incredibly loudly, and he could hear the children shouting in the street outside.

'Perhaps we might give it a trial, Father?' said the wife finally. 'How much is the *Messenger*?'

Then Kufalt got under way again, the receipt book appeared, money changed hands; a polite 'Thank you very much. Good morning.'

And Kufalt was again in the street, five quarter-marks the richer. Five quarter-marks in five minutes. Two hundred and fifty addresses! At least three hours' typing!

Kufalt walked on air as he went to call on Herr Herzog, also in the paint trade.

XVII

'How many?' the girl at the typewriter called out to Kufalt as he dashed through the despatch room.

'How many?' asked Herr Kraft, who was standing in the editor's room beside Freese's chair and looked attentively at Kufalt's face.

'Well?' asked Freese, blinking.

'Guess!' cried Kufalt, and flung his hat on the table and his brief-case on a chair, as though he were quite at home.

But he did not wait. 'I took the paint shops today. I thought they would be the best to begin with, Herr Kraft; tomorrow I'll take the upholsterers, saddlers and decorators . . .'

'And how many?' asked Kraft.

Freese merely looked at him.

'Yes, how many? There are twenty-nine paint shops on this list, five were not at home – I'll fix them up next time. I interviewed twenty-four . . .'

'And how many?'

'Anyhow, twenty-four are far too many on one day. From tomorrow I shan't try more than fifteen. I was much too tired when I got to the last, and I could only reel it off. One must convince people . . .'

'Of what?' asked Freese.

'Well, that they ought to take the *Messenger*.'

'Have you read the *Messenger*, by any chance? Today you can only have convinced people of the fact that you are very hard up.'

'Maybe,' laughed Kufalt. 'Now just you guess, gentlemen, out of twenty-four I . . .'

'Six,' said Kraft, who was getting tired of all this. 'Show me your book.'

'No, not six,' cried Kufalt. 'Nine. What do you think of that! Nine out of twenty-four, almost 40 per cent!'

He beamed.

'Nine,' said Kraft; 'nine – yes, that's pretty good . . .'

'Nine,' croaked Freese; 'nine new subscribers on one day . . .'

His hand reached across the table towards the brandy bottle: 'We'll all three of us have one on that . . .' He broke off; his hand did not grasp the bottle, it picked up a pen. 'No we won't. Kraft, I think I'll go on with my series of articles about the history of the town . . . People are still interested, I think. Nine – let's call it fifty new subscribers a week . . . The *Friend* will throw up . . .'

'Dietrich's going to the *Friend*,' announced Kufalt. 'He's going to canvass for them.'

They merely laughed.

'Fat chance of them taking him! The man's a good-for-nothing; he never kept accounts and only went out to work when he hadn't a penny in his pocket.'

'I got a subscription out of him,' boasted Kufalt. 'He actually paid in cash . . . Dietrich . . . Wollenweberstrasse . . .'

'Get out!' said Freese. 'I want to work. Kraft, take that brandy, and pour it down the WC.'

Kraft grinned, and clasped the brandy bottle tenderly under his arm.

'Well, well. Lock the bottle up in your desk; the man's full of himself today; but I dare say he'll only get two tomorrow. Or none at all.'

Freese sighed, and looked sceptically at Kufalt over his pince-nez.

'Besides, I'm playing skat this evening. I can start writing tomorrow. We must first see how it goes. One swallow doesn't make a summer. Put the bottle on my table again, Kraft; it won't get fuller in your desk. Good evening, gentlemen.'

XVIII

Many prisoners like to go back to their prison – on a visit. It really seemed a little bit like home as Kufalt rang the bell at the prison gate, especially as Senior Warder Petrow, from Posen, opened it.

'Hello, Kufalt, old chum! That's right – coming back to us now winter's started. Are you on remand, or have you got another stretch . . . ?'

'No, it's not that, sir, I just want to see the governor.'

'Oh indeed! Worn out your pants, I suppose? Want a little help from the Benevolent Fund, eh? Well, the governor's your man; he's always good for a bit. It makes the other officers wild; but I always say: you let the governor be, money always goes somehow – on booze, or girls, or pants – old lags can't keep money . . .'

'Is the governor in?'

'Go right along, old chum. You know the way; I needn't ring.'

It was only the office building, and not the prison proper, but he could already smell the old familiar odour of whitewash, of a rather musty cleanliness. The linoleum shone like a mirror; it looked too spotless to walk on with rubber heels.

It was the quiet time of the day and Kufalt had chosen it on purpose; no prisoners were interviewed at that hour, and the corridors were empty. The officials were at breakfast. For a moment he listened at the old man's door, but there seemed to be no visitor within. So he knocked, heard the clear voice say, 'Come in,' and entered.

It was now late autumn, almost winter; December beckoned, but the governor was still wearing a light sports suit and a very neat shirt. Kufalt could see a good deal of it, as the governor was pacing up and down the room in his shirtsleeves.

He stopped for a moment and looked Kufalt up and down. Three or four hundred prisoners had been discharged since that day in May, but he had Kufalt's name in an instant. 'Good morning, Kufalt. I heard you were back in these parts. What's your job? Or haven't you got a job?'

So saying, he shook hands. And, as before, he said, 'Cigarette?' and, as before, it was a good cigarette. Except that Kufalt was not as impressed by such a cigarette as he had been then.

'So you have left Hamburg for good, eh? We had an inquiry from the police about you, but I never heard any more of it. Did you get into trouble there, or don't you want to talk about it?'

But Kufalt did, and he told the story of Cito-Presto.

The governor shook his head. 'Pity – but perhaps it's not such a pity, it wouldn't have gone well, with all you ex-convicts together. And what are you doing now?'

'I'm canvassing subscribers for the paper here, sir – the *Messenger*.'

'Can you live on that?'

'I'm certain to make two hundred a month, sir,' said Kufalt proudly.

'Indeed! I heard the paper was as good as bankrupt. I've never seen it. And now you want to get a subscription out of me?'

'No, indeed, sir,' said Kufalt hastily, in a rather injured tone. 'I really don't need to do that. I'm getting quite a nice lot of subscribers.'

'Well then . . . ?' said the governor. 'Old debts? A winter overcoat? Though yours still looks pretty good. What is it?'

Kufalt was quite offended. Couldn't a man go to the governor without wanting something for himself, just to pass the time of day, out of gratitude and friendship?

No, he had to admit that he too wanted something from the governor; no one came here who did not want something.

'Well, Kufalt . . . ?' asked the governor once more.

'Bruhn,' said Kufalt. 'Do you remember Bruhn, sir?'

'Bruhn?' said Governor Greve, and thought. 'I'm not quite sure, we often have men called Bruhn in here. Which was the one in your time?'

'Emil Bruhn, sir, the little man with the round head, in for robbery and murder, sir, but it really wasn't robbery and murder . . .'

'Oh yes,' said the governor. 'I remember now, eleven years, or something like that. And a period of probation.' He frowned. 'Surely that was the ruffian who got blind drunk on the day of his discharge and started a brawl over some women. Are you living with him, Kufalt?'

'No, sir, I'm living alone; I have my own furnished room. But I often see him, sir, he really is a very good fellow and a hard worker . . .'

And Kufalt reflected that the governor had a very much better memory than he had. He had quite forgotten to ask Emil what had happened on the day of his discharge.

'That business of Bruhn's on the day he came out of prison was very bad,' said the governor. 'They threw the landlord downstairs, and the chaplain had to go to a great deal of trouble before the prosecution was withdrawn. Otherwise your friend Bruhn would have had his probation cancelled . . .'

'I knew nothing about that, sir,' said Kufalt with dismay.

'Very well – never mind,' said the governor; 'and now what about Bruhn?'

And Kufalt told the governor what an excellent carpenter Bruhn was, how he had done nothing but carpentry all his years in prison, and how he could make no use of it outside because he had not passed the journeyman's test. And that he, Kufalt, had thought it might be possible to send Bruhn to a master carpenter as an apprentice; the employer would do well to have such a first-rate workman as an unpaid apprentice, and then Bruhn would have a proper trade in which he could make some progress . . .

Kufalt spoke eagerly and the governor listened to him with deep attention. He paced up and down the room, said, 'Yes,' from time to time, sighed now and again, and gave Kufalt a second cigarette.

But when Kufalt had finished, he stopped and said: 'In the first place you will have to find an enlightened employer, who doesn't object to robbery and murder. Very, very difficult. Yes, yes, I know, you're going to tell me it wasn't anything of the kind, but it stands so in the records, and that is what he served his sentence for and he never applied for the case to be reopened . . .

'And then he would have to be kept during the long apprenticeship, when he was earning nothing. The Benevolent Fund would have to pay out fifty marks a month at least, for three or four years. That will be all the more difficult, as we don't know how much money we shall have at our disposal next year, and whether there won't be very many more needy cases.'

Kufalt was about to make some objection, but the governor said: 'No; let me finish. And then I would have to bring the whole matter before the Prison Board and, apart from other difficulties, I would have to persuade all the other officials that Bruhn was deserving of such very particular assistance. And really, my dear Kufalt, I don't see much chance of doing so; not to mention anything else, that affair on the day he was let out of prison . . .'

'Oh but, sir,' said Kufalt, 'you know yourself that no one is normal on the day he's discharged. Everyone is all worked up when he comes out. I was too.'

'Yes,' said the governor; 'we know that of course. And that is why we did our best for him, to get the prosecution withdrawn. But it's not a recommendation; you must admit that, Kufalt.'

'When he was inside Bruhn never once got into trouble. And he worked harder than anyone.'

'Well, we must see,' said the governor. 'If he really is as good a man as that . . . perhaps . . . But no, Kufalt, I really can't take the responsibility of granting so much money to a person . . .'

'But he really deserves it, sir, he's such a nice boy.'

'Indeed?' said the governor, suddenly speaking with great deliberation and emphasis, and looking very hard at Kufalt. 'Indeed? A nice boy, is he? By the way, have you got a girl, Kufalt?'

A blush spread over Kufalt's face, slow but very red. 'Yes, I have a girl, sir. And it's not what you think, sir, at all. I won't deceive you, four or nearly five years ago it was so, but never since then. That's absolutely true, sir. I'm not appealing for him because he's my pal in that way.'

'Very well,' said the governor. 'Then why are you appealing for him, Kufalt?'

Yes, why was he? Hurriedly Kufalt asked himself, and he did not know. What was it . . . ?

And the governor went on: 'You are no longer spokesman for category three, Kufalt. Just you let everyone speak for himself; Bruhn can perfectly well come to me alone, I understand what he wants, even if he doesn't speak so fluently as you do, Kufalt.'

And when he saw Kufalt looking so abashed, he added: 'Yes, yes, I quite believe you; it wasn't merely self-importance, there was friendship in it too. And now tell Bruhn to come along and see me in a day or two, Wednesday or Thursday at twelve. Goodbye, Kufalt. Another cigarette? Goodbye.'

XIX

In the dirty, squalid little hole where he slept, Bruhn sat at a bare, unvarnished table with his head on his arms, and howled. He raised his head, answered, 'Evening,' shamelessly displaying a red, ravaged face, glistening with tears – and went on crying.

'Hello!' said Kufalt lightly. 'What's up?'

But at the bottom of his heart he was genuinely shocked, for he recalled that in all his five years in jail he had never seen Emil cry – on the contrary, the lad had always been jovial and cheerful; and prison is a pretty hard branch on the tree of life.

He was now crying quietly to himself; the tears ran down onto the sleeves of his old field-grey working jacket until they were wet. He wept like a child, let the tears run down his cheeks and wailed: 'Oh God! O-h-h God!'

'What on earth is the matter, Emil?' asked Kufalt.

No answer but a groan.

'Have you got the sack?'

A burst of tears.

'Is it about a girl?'

'Oh-h-h! . . .'

Kufalt thought for a while, sat down on the edge of the bed near the table, laid his hand on Bruhn's arm and said: 'I earned a lot of money today, shall we go to the cinema?'

For a moment the wailing seemed to stop, but then continued.

Kufalt began to feel nervous.

'Bruhn . . . Emil . . . are you ill?'

No reply.

Kufalt got up gravely. 'Well, if you won't speak to me, I'd better go . . .'

Pause; not a word of protest.

'. . . And I was going to tell you about my interview with the old man . . .'

That did it!

With an abrupt snuffle the weeping stopped, Bruhn stiffened and sat up straight, blinked his eyelids, above which his white brows had turned an angry red, and said breathlessly: 'Have you been to see him? Will he do it?'

'Gently, gently,' said Kufalt. 'Do you suppose we could fix all that up in half an hour? The man must have time to think it over first.'

'Then it's no good,' said Bruhn, and his face fell once more. 'If the governor needs to think a thing over, it'll always be no – I know that from the times he used to send for me.'

And with a gesture of despair he was about to let his head fall onto his arms again.

Kufalt caught him by the sleeve. 'Stop, Emil, don't start that again. You've got to go and see him on Wednesday or Thursday at twelve, he wants to talk to you himself.'

'But there's nothing more to talk about,' said Bruhn sullenly. 'Either he's going to do it or he isn't. Talk's all eyewash.'

'Now don't be a fool, Emil,' said Kufalt sternly. 'Of course he must talk to you first. To begin with, he's got to find an employer for you. That isn't so easy; perhaps you can help.'

'Yes,' said Bruhn, sniffed, went to the washstand, opened the drawer, looked into it and muttered: 'Has that bastard of a nightwatchman taken my handkerchief!' and used his sleeve.

'That's better!' said Kufalt. 'And then he's got to arrange about the money. It would be no good if he started the business and then couldn't give you any money after six months.'

'Oh,' said Bruhn sceptically, 'he's always got money when he wants it.'

'No, he hasn't,' said Kufalt firmly. 'You know what the boys are like: they want a new suit out of the fund, or boots, or they need tools, or there's a trunk that has to be got out of pawn – no, he hasn't always got money, he has to arrange for it.'

'And when he's got the money and found an employer – will there be anything else?'

'Then the whole Prison Board has to agree that you are a fit and proper person.'

Bruhn heaved a sigh of relief. 'Well, if that's all! There'll be no trouble about that. No one's got anything on me, not even the chaplain.'

'We-ll . . .' said Kufalt slowly. 'Think so? But surely you have . . .' Then he stopped. Why should he tell Bruhn? He would only start crying again.

'What have I?' asked Bruhn.

'No, nothing. I only thought . . . Did you always go to church, then?'

'Of course I did – and to Communion as well.'

'Then it's all right,' said Kufalt cheerfully. 'You go and see him tomorrow at twelve o'clock.'

'I have to be in the works at twelve.'

'But surely you can take an hour off?'

Bruhn did not answer, and for a moment it looked as though he were going to burst into tears again. But he did not; the mood of gloom had passed and anger took its place.

'Take an hour off . . . ? They'd chuck me out for good and all, and glad to do it. Just because I made the remark that a timber works would make a fine bonfire.'

'Bruhn!'

'Well, what of it? They've done me down all round. First they swindled me over my savings bank book. They promised to take me on as a foreman at a foreman's wage, and I do the job and get an unskilled wage. And they keep on knocking a bit off my wages, just because they think Bruhn can't get another job, Bruhn's been in prison – we can squeeze him all right.'

And he looked bitterly at Kufalt – his friend – as though he were Herr Steguweit of the timber works, and into Bruhn's gentle, watery blue, kindly eyes came an expression of fury – uncontrolled fury . . .

'Well, so what?' said Kufalt. 'You're used to all that long ago, Emil!'

'I tell you I won't stand it,' burst out Bruhn. 'Why should I work the skin off my hands and get less than a clumsy lout that can't even knock in a nail! And just because I've been in prison, and never hear the last of it, though I've done my stretch!'

'Why not go a bit slow?' asked Kufalt.

'I've tried it,' said Bruhn more calmly. 'But I can't, it isn't in me. I'm a grafter, I have to get on with the job and do it.' He took a breath.

Then, 'No; I got at some of the lads, and we did our jobs so that complaints kept on coming in – a nail was sticking out, a board was loose or a door wouldn't work. And when they came along and started bleating about all the stuff coming back and what were we up to, we said we couldn't do any better for that kind of wage, and mistakes were bound to happen when we had to turn the stuff out so quick . . .'

'Well, and then . . . ?'

'The fat cats!' said Bruhn contemptuously. 'They put an inspector on the job, though the pittance they paid him would have been all we wanted. He looked over the stuff and kept on throwing it out as not up to standard.'

Bruhn snorted with fury.

'Go on! Go on,' urged Kufalt.

'Well, so then I made sure that everything was absolutely shipshape. Not up to standard, eh? Just you wait, my lad, says I. And when it was all brought out and ready for despatch, I went along at night, every third or fourth night, with two or three of the lads – and we mucked the stuff up again.'

'The things you get up to!' said Kufalt.

'Why wouldn't they treat me properly, eh? What would you have done, Willi?'

'I don't know,' said Kufalt. 'Go on. That wasn't what you were crying about?'

'No; but the blokes of course thought I was in it somewhere, and the lads that helped me, well – they were a rotten lot, of course – and one of them split. And because they knew I said a timber works would make a fine bonfire, they fixed it so that I would have to chuck the job in myself.

'And when I came along this morning and showed Stachu how he always nailed the roofs on too loose, he waved his hammer at me and shouted that he wouldn't be spoken to by a bloody murderer – the lousy Pole. And when I'm quietly doing my own job, someone asks what the time is, and whether the murderer won't take a look at his pocket watch. And in the midday interval they stole my tools and I had to go around all afternoon looking for them and couldn't do a stroke of work, and had to listen to them saying they didn't fancy working with a murderer. And the foreman said every man had to look after his own things, and the firm couldn't be responsible . . .'

Bruhn was silent and glared into vacancy.

'Make an end of it then, Emil,' said Kufalt. 'There is no sense in staying on. You will have enough to live on for a while. And perhaps the governor will be able to fix you up, and then the others can go to hell.'

'No, Willi, no,' said Bruhn slowly. 'You don't understand. Are they to be always in the right, and I in the wrong? If I go, then!'

He was silent.

'But if something comes of this business with the governor, you'll go, won't you?'

'I often think,' said Bruhn, 'that we're done for. It seems sometimes as if something is going to turn up, but it never does.'

He went on in a more subdued voice: 'And then you think of prison, where no one accused you of anything, and you got your grub, and were glad to work . . .'

'Now that'll do, Bruhn,' said Kufalt warningly. 'Perhaps you'll be working with a carpenter in a few weeks, and laughing at these lousy nest boxes.'

'And what if it's just the same with the carpenter . . . ?' said Bruhn slowly. 'They'll smell a rat when they see a man of twenty-nine coming in as an apprentice, won't they?'

XX

The Lütjenstrasse lies in the centre of the city; Kufalt needed to cross it four or five times every day on his rounds. He actually crossed it ten or twelve times.

A reflector had been fixed on the first and only storey of the six-windowed house. Every time he passed, Kufalt thought, 'Perhaps she's looking into it this very moment and sees you.'

Then he stopped in front of the glazier's shop window and for the thirtieth time he gazed at the showpiece, 'Fighting Stags', displayed as being suitable for the autumn season. Couldn't she make a sign to him? No, she remained invisible.

The lady's watch in his briefcase, wound up every morning and then carefully wrapped up again, ticked in vain. No opportunity . . .

But he came again and again. It was now December and the stags were replaced by a picture called 'Little Sister's Christmas Dream'; but his visit was always in vain. The watch would have been such a fine present on the day after the event; but now, ten days later, it looked like an attempt to establish a claim on her and carried an unpleasant suggestion of remorse, or bribery, or surrender.

And yet it must be given to her!

The following day, and the day after that, he had been sorely tempted to put the glaziers on his list, but he postponed them again and again. Kraft had already said: 'You seem to have forgotten the glaziers?' But how, in her presence, could he possibly produce his little speech about subscriptions, and hear her old bullying father merely growl out No.

'Aren't you going to try the glaziers?'

'Yes, tomorrow.'

But tomorrow there were some bakers left . . . There was one baker, by the name of Süssmilch, a young man with a smooth and mealy face and thick black eyebrows, who kept on making appointments for Kufalt to call. 'I would be very glad to subscribe to your *Messenger*, but I'm not quite convinced. Perhaps you could think of another really cogent reason, and come back on Friday . . . ?'

Kufalt knew very well he was being fooled; but at the end of his round he found himself quite glad to call on Süssmilch again. The baker shuffled sleepily out of his bake room covered with flour, his bare feet in floury slippers, and said: 'Well, young man, do you think you can convince me today?'

'The best reason is my receipt book,' said Kufalt. 'Look how many bakers have ordered our paper today again!'

And Süssmilch looked and rubbed his face and Kufalt thought, 'I really might be standing in Harder's shop.'

No, Süssmilch did not give an order this time either; he certainly would have done, but that day he had to pay for his flour. However, by Tuesday he would perhaps have collected enough money to be able to order the paper; 'Till Tuesday, then, young man.'

Therewith the baker shuffled sleepily back into his bake room and Kufalt trudged back to the office, carefully avoiding the Lütjenstrasse.

There would certainly have been enough money for two cinema tickets; besides, Freese had told him he could just walk into a cinema and take his fiancée too. He had only to say he came from the *Messenger* . . . A fiancée, how so? He thought that Kufalt had made a mental note about the River Trehne. A fiancée wouldn't make the water any warmer . . .

Drunk again, he had not started writing yet, though the prescribed total of six new subscribers was exceeded nearly every day; but there was plenty of money for two cinema tickets.

'Little Sister's Christmas Dream' – the jack-in-the-box on the edge of the bed. How fine he was. He had a real nutcracker face like Kraft. The shop door was fitted with an opaque pane in the middle; round it were brightly coloured bullseye panes with red, blue and yellow glass knobs . . .

Heavens, what was all the fuss about? He had been into many shops and houses, why didn't he dare enter this one?

Here he was at the nearest corner, by the co-operative shop, and though he kept on urging himself forward, it was no good . . .

Was he to carry this damned sixty-seven-mark watch around with him for ever, or should he use it to get himself another girl?

But she was so sweet!

About turn! Quick march, into the storm of bullets, bombs and shells; perhaps she can see you in the reflector, don't shake your briefcase, it won't do the watch any good . . .

Well, however hard you try, you will only stop dead outside 'Christmas Dream', or bolt past to the office . . .

'Only five today, Herr Kraft. But I'll do the glaziers tomorrow, without fail.'

Had he passed it? No! Yes! No!

How the bell clanged. He flashed into the shop like a comet. Well, well; Harder, the daughter-beater, looked quite different from the way he had imagined him. A little man with a paunch and a black beard, almost like a brother to Woolly Teddy . . .

'Yes, what is it?'

'I represent . . .'

At that moment he saw her in profile at the far end of the shop. She was busy, she did not look up, her face was very pale.

He pulled himself together, otherwise he would never finish his sentence.

That pale and stricken face . . . 'Never, never again.' We know not what we do. We never know what we may do.

He pulled himself together.

'Herr Harder – glassware?'

'Yes – what is your firm?'

'Might I speak to you in private for a moment?'

'My daughter won't disturb us.'

'In this case I'm afraid she will!'

'Very well, go upstairs, Hilde.'

'Couldn't we go upstairs? What I have to say can't very well be said in the shop.'

'What is all this? I'm not buying anything.'

'It's quite private.'

'Hilde, look after the shop,' said the little man. 'You can call me at any time.'

He emphasized the words 'at any time'.

Kufalt looked at her as they went up, her lips moved, he didn't understand what she wanted to say, but her face and her whole body were an unuttered prayer – please don't!

As they walked upstairs Kufalt noticed that the windows were glazed with beautiful designs: ground floor, Trumpeter of Säckingen; first floor, Lorelei. There was no second floor.

The room with the reflector was the living and dining room. By the reflector sat a withered woman with skin so transparent that her face was almost blue.

'Well?' said Herr Harder, and there was menace in his tone. Suddenly Kufalt understood that this little man might have a heavy hand.

The woman, her mother, half rose from her chair at the sight of the visitor and quickly sat down again when she heard that angry 'Well?'

He was not asked to sit down. They stood facing each other. Herr

Harder said 'Well?', and Kufalt answered calmly (it was odd that he was so calm; he was by no means always calm when canvassing):

'My name is Kufalt, Wilhelm Kufalt. I am at present employed as a canvasser for subscribers and advertisements on the *Town and Country Messenger*. I earn from two to three hundred marks a month . . .'

'Well, sir!' roared the little man, advancing on him with blank fury in his eyes. 'What has all this got to do with me? I'm not going to take in your filthy rag!'

Kufalt drew a deep breath. 'I ask for your daughter's hand,' he said.

'What . . . ?'

There was a long silence.

The frozen woman at the window had turned and was staring helplessly at the visitor.

'I ask for your daughter's hand,' he said once more.

'Sit down!' said the beard, looking at the chairs round the dining table and at the man in front of him. 'Sit down, sir,' he repeated decisively. And then suddenly leapt to his feet.

'But if you're trying to make a fool of me . . . !'

'Eugen!' said the woman in a warning voice.

'What is your name?' said Herr Harder, and sat down again.

'Kufalt,' said Kufalt; 'but without an "h", just "u-f".' And he smiled reassuringly.

'Kufalt, yes. And what did you say you earned?'

'Two to three hundred marks a month. But that can be easily increased.'

'. . . Easily increased,' murmured Harder. Then suddenly: 'How did you meet Hilde?'

'Eugen!' said the woman in a warning voice once more.

'That is our affair,' smiled Kufalt.

Herr Harder ran his fingers through his beard, stood up, sat down again, threw a quick glance at his wife, at the door, and whispered, his head appearing to sink into his shoulders: 'And you know—?'

'About Willi? I do. Besides, my name is Willi too.'

The hand in the beard stiffened. The little man stood up, planted himself in front of Kufalt and grew visibly taller and more menacing: 'Then you are the blackguard—'

'Certainly not,' answered Kufalt quickly. 'I've only been in the place six weeks. But I don't mind.'

'He doesn't mind,' said the bewildered glazier, looking appealingly at the window.

'And now suppose we ask Hilde whether she agrees?'

'Whether she agrees!' shouted the little man. 'I'll soon show you!'

He rushed to a desk, rummaged in a drawer, pulled out a sheet of spotless white cardboard, scrawled something on it and waved it triumphantly: 'There!'

'Closed for family reasons,' read Kufalt.

'I'll put it up on the shop door at once,' whispered the little man gravely. 'And I'll bring Hilde up with me.'

XXI

He had expected nothing, for he had not known that he would agree to this.

She had stood there at the table, very pale, and when her father started to speak and she gradually understood what was happening, she cried out: 'No! No! No!'

Then she dropped heavily onto a chair, laid her head on the table and burst into a flood of tears . . .

He stood at her side. He had not intended this, and he did not even now believe they would ever be married. No, it should not be said that he could wilfully hurt a human creature weeping so helplessly over her deliverance. But nothing would come of it, things always turned out otherwise. The Batzke affair would be brought to light, and how long, in a little town like this, could his identity be concealed? Oh, if only she were not so ecstatically happy!

'What's for dinner today, Mother?'

And Mother herself went out to get some black pudding for the lentil soup, so that Hilde could stay with her betrothed. And two-year-old Willi was brought in and made to say 'Papa', and there was some sweet wine, Malaga at eighty-eight pfennigs the bottle, a really good, sound wine . . .

But all the time, while they were eating and drinking and talking and laughing, Kufalt had a feeling that this was a dream; when she felt under the table for his hand, it was as if the chief warder would soon be knocking his key against the bell . . .

But he did not, and Kufalt went on dreaming, and in his dream he said he would have to go back to the office so that the new subscribers would get their papers next morning, and for the first time he had got only five new ones . . .

And, laughing in his deep bass voice, Harder the glazier, Lütjenstrasse 17, subscribed to the filthy rag, and so went back on his word. But he left his son-in-law without the one mark twenty-five: 'I'll deduct it from the dowry, Willi' . . . and Hilde was allowed to walk back with him to the office . . .

But there, when Kufalt excitedly told them what he had done and asked them to keep mum and give him a good reference – he would tell her himself at a suitable moment – there he was near to an awakening, for they both looked at him so oddly and Freese for no reason said: 'Doesn't the stove worry you? Isn't it too hot?'

But the dream continued, for Hilde was clinging to his arm, and in the meantime it had occurred to her that she had something to say, and she said it: 'You are so kind! You understood, didn't you, why I cried so, that time?'

And the watch was handed over, and rings were bought at Linsing's. And then the evening came, and the relations were there, and there was a very quiet and affectionate betrothal party, and many a side glance from Aunt Emma to Aunt Bertha . . .

And at last he went home to his bed, and the dream was over, and he awoke and wept and said: 'What have I done?'

XXII

But – in spite of all the tears – this December was the happiest and the most enchanting in Willi Kufalt's whole life.

One day Herr Kraft said to him: 'I don't know how it is, the

Christmas advertisements don't roll in as they used to do. You must get on to the advertisements, Kufalt.'

And Kufalt got on to the advertisements.

By eight o'clock in the morning he was knocking at the doors of the big shops – ready-made clothes, jewellery, underclothes, house linen, beds, cutlery, groceries, wines. He sold sixteenths and thirty-seconds of a page. Three or four times he sold a whole page, quite often a half; and on Saturday he had a reckoning with Kraft, and drew his 180 or 200 marks' commission: 'You earn double what Freese does, Kufalt. Not to mention myself.'

Kufalt had indeed tapped into a vein of success, and prison training now proved to be not without its uses. In prison he had learnt to ask and keep on asking, he was not easily deterred by a refusal; in pestering the warders with all sorts of requests he had proved himself a persuasive wordsmith, and this now stood him in good stead.

When he made it clear to Herr Lewandowski, the proprietor of a small general store in the northern suburb, that he could not possibly be outdone by his competitors, and that an eighth of a page was a scandal for so enterprising a business, while a sixth or quarter of a page would mean a doubled Christmas turnover –

When he trudged on, surveying every window and reading every shop sign, and suddenly dropped in on a blind chair-caner, to whom he sold a sixteenth of a page, on the ground that everybody wanted their chairs mended for Christmas –

When he appeared, panting, in the composing room at half past ten and, against the noisy protests of all the compositors, insisted that three-quarters of a page of fresh advertisements must go in (the paper came out at half past twelve) –

And when he waited in quivering agitation for Fräulein Utnehmer, who brought in the opposition paper, and they all three leapt at the advertisement pages, and Kraft said reproachfully: 'They've got a quarter-page from Haase and we've got nothing!' and he answered crossly: 'I was there first thing this morning, and the old prick told me he wasn't advertising – I'll go round to his place again this afternoon; but we've got Löhne and Wilms, and they haven't . . .'

In those days he was possessed by an exaggerated sense of power and confidence. Prison was at last a matter of the past. Kufalt was fit and capable; no alcoholic ghost like Freese, with his jibes about the River Trehne, could prevail over him now . . .

Money clinked in his pockets, and when the Christmas business was over the New Year came along, with advertisements from bakers and wine merchants and restaurant owners organizing dances. And in January came the stocktaking sales, and so it would go on through a long and busy year, in which he would earn good money.

But when the clock struck six he dashed home, put on his best clothes and sped through the streets on air, a free man. Then he went into Godenschweger, the butcher's shop, and bought an anchovy and liver sausage for his mother-in-law, or ten Brazils for old Harder at the tobacconist's, or a tin toy for the kid, and all the shopkeepers were extremely polite to him and said: 'Good evening, Herr Kufalt. Thank you very much, Herr Kufalt.'

He never visited his in-laws without bringing them a present, and old Harder might well say to his wife that the world these days was turned upside down; and that a girl like Hilde, who had run around with all sorts of men, should get a husband who earned such good money, and was so presentable as well, was really a sin and a scandal, and a violation of God's commandment.

But he liked his son-in-law, did old Harder, and the two of them spent the entire evening chatting away; the women sat in silence, sewing the trousseau. But Harder told him all about the various tradesmen, how he must ask Thomsen about his diabetes and admire the cacti in Lorenz's shop window.

He introduced him to the life of the town. He knew all the scandals of the last hundred years, carefully passed on from mouth to mouth. He could explain exactly why the young Lävens had had a feeble-minded child, Grandfather Läven having been involved with Frau Läven's mother, who was born a Schranz . . .

Kufalt was an avid listener to all this local history and anecdote; he lapped it all up eagerly, while Harder's satisfaction with his son-in-law steadily increased. No, although Hilde had not really deserved it, he would see she had a proper outfit for her marriage, and yet . . . and yet . . . A dark shadow hung over old Harder's mind. There was something wrong about this bright young man. He could not persuade his wily old self that a man like Kufalt should actually want to marry a girl with a child, especially when she wasn't even particularly pretty. Great love? No, they weren't as much in love as all that!

In the twilight hours he sat and watched the two Willis, big and small, gambolling and rolling over each other on the carpet, laughing, fooling around, singing and playing horses – two children, two silly, high-spirited children. But the child cried, 'Papa,' and Kufalt heard, and did not mind or make a wry face – it was not right, there was something wrong.

For many an hour at night old Harder lay in bed and brooded; he would have liked to get up and go across to the living room and bang on the table and shout: 'In God's name, tell me what's the matter with you!'

But he did not; he lay awake until he heard the door latch click, and the two of them go downstairs and the front door close. Perhaps she had really sent him away, but perhaps she had merely made the sound of locking the outer door and taken him with her to her little dark room in the yard, where she had been made to live since she had had her brat. It was all the same to old Harder, she would have learnt to take care of herself by now, and after all she was engaged – but the worst of it was that he was firmly convinced his son-in-law did go home, and not to her room; which was the most uncanny part of it all.

He was right; she did not take him to her room, and if she did from time to time, it was merely to stand by the child's bed, as they had done that first night, and look down at him. Hand in hand, her head on his shoulder, they made a picture straight out of a colour supplement; but outside the window hung the canopy of night, and the town was silent now, just as life was silent – patiently, so patiently enduring. Heart against heart, in the softly breathing night, and silence.

'And now I must go home.'

'Sleep well, Willi.'

'Thanks – ditto.'

A quick kiss and the tramp home through the bleak December streets, where the glass panes of the street lamps clinked as the wind caught them; and three or four schnapps at a bar, so that he might fall asleep quickly and not lie awake and think.

And then, next morning, up and out again after advertisements, on the merry hunt for money, chattering and cajoling and standing about in shops and then, through the twilit streets, to Hilde . . .

Father's picture was all wrong, of what they said and did in the sitting room; they did nothing at all.

On one occasion Harder asked his daughter how they had come to make such a noise and Hilde answered: 'Willi was reciting poetry to me.'

'Poetry?!' cried Harder; and again he wondered how his daughter could be such a monstrous little liar.

And yet Hilde had spoken the truth; Kufalt had really been reciting poems.

The hut in the park on that wild November night lay far behind them, a shameful memory that they must not dwell on. Here they were, sitting in a real, respectable, well-warmed room, side by side on a sofa, like a real engaged couple; he told her what he had been doing that day, all about Freese and Kraft and Fräulein Utnehmer, the shorthand typist, whom he had again seen out with another man. But he soon exhausted his material; he had already used most of it for his father-in-law's benefit.

And when they had talked about their future home, and how they would furnish it – one and a half rooms and a kitchen – there was nothing left to say.

Side by side they sat in silence on the plush sofa, hand in hand; he very stiff and straight, with his eyes turned towards the lamp, she longing to fall on his shoulder and be loving.

Then he kissed her once or twice and said in an encouraging voice: 'Yes, dear, it's nice to be sitting like this, isn't it?' He tried hard to think of something to talk about; her bosom was so near – he could have done what he would with her in that moment. But no, the little hut was an affair of the past. Their object now must be order, respectability and a steady income. An open, upright life – moreover he did not want to be put to shame by Harder, Freese and Kraft. He had breathed again when she indicated that nothing had happened on that occasion; so they would not marry before Easter in any case. If anything did happen, they would all count nine upon their fingers and say: 'Aha, that's why!!'

No; that should not be why!

She was very pale, with dark rings under her eyes; it was quite clear she understood nothing.

Once she did burst out: 'Willi! Willi! Why do you want to marry me? Just because I didn't come again? You don't love me a bit.'

But he soothed her, he rocked her in his arms, he told her he was acting for the best and one day she would understand it all.

Then they relapsed into silence, side by side, the lamp burned noiselessly and again they did not know what to talk about. And then his boyhood came back into his mind.

It fitted in with this homely room, this decorous betrothal. It fitted in exactly with this passage of his life: his offence, and trial, and imprisonment – all were blotted out. Where the old life had stopped, he now started it again.

Poems indeed, but not only poems. They would often sit together and hum a song, quite softly, so as not to disturb the parents in the bedroom: 'Oh ye far-off valleys, oh ye heights . . . Little Anne of Tharau . . .Who hast thee, thou lovely forest . . .'

Their faces lit up, her little foot in its shabby slipper tapped out the rhythm, the drawn curtains were so white and peaceful; then he said: 'Now let me sing by myself . . .' And he sang 'Beatus Ille Homo' and 'Gaudeamus Igitur' . . .

His few school years were his once again; and her eyes never left his face.

Then came Christmas Day, and the betrothed pair duly stood under the lighted tree, and little Willi at their feet duly played with a toy railway. Herr Harder gave his son-in-law a calf-leather wallet with a bright new pfennig inside it on which he had spat three times, 'so that your money will never run short'; and Frau Harder gave him a scarf.

There was nothing from Hilde, but Hilde smiled, her cheeks were flushed with happiness, and all was so astonishingly peaceful and secure, with the sugared Christmas cake and carp stewed in beer, as though there were no world of perils, nor crime nor misery nor prison; nor men who had been in prison.

XXIII

Was it strange that in such happy times as these Kufalt hardly thought of little Emil Bruhn; indeed, he kept out of his way?

He never went to see him, and when Bruhn visited Kufalt he was always either out or hurriedly changing his clothes and on the point of going out again.

Once, however, shortly after Christmas, Bruhn had plumped down into the plush armchair and watched Kufalt change his clothes. He looked even smaller and rounder than usual, but very worried. Kufalt remembered that stress led to overeating for some people, and Bruhn was clearly one of them.

'Is it true you're going around with Harder's Hilde?'

'Yes, Emil.'

'That you're properly engaged to her?'

'Yes, Emil.'

'On the level?'

'On the level, Emil.'

'And the kid?'

'He's a nice kid, Emil, I like him very much.'

'Do they know about you?'

'No, Emil.'

'Are you going to tell them?'

'Not yet, Emil.'

'But you told me a bloke ought to tell at once.'

'You never know how it's going to work out.'

'Then it's not on the level!'

'Yes it is.'

'Then why don't you tell them?'

'I shall tell them sometime.'

'When?'

'Soon.'

Kufalt was shaving very carefully, which was probably why his answers were so curt. But now he had finished shaving and had tidied his shirt and collar and tie, he could begin to ask questions.

'Are you still at the works, Emil?'

'Eh—?' said Emil with a start.

Kufalt laughed. 'What were you dreaming about, Emil? I asked you whether you were still at the works.'

'Yes,' said Emil briefly, and again was lost in thought. Then he said: 'Supposing someone tells the Harders you've been in prison?'

'Who's likely to tell them?'

'Oh, anyone – a warder, for instance.'

'Warders are forbidden to tell, it's a rule of the service.'

'Well – an old lag, then?'

'Why should he? He's got nothing to gain from it.'

'Perhaps he'd get a tip from old Harder for warning him?'

Kufalt thought deeply; he thrust out his underlip, examined his face in his shaving mirror to see whether his chin was quite smooth, and thought.

Emil Bruhn got no answer for some while.

And when Kufalt did speak, the answer was not an answer, but a question: 'Did you go and see the old man, Emil?'

'Yes,' said Emil.

'Well?'

'Bollocks.'

'How do you mean, bollocks? Yes or no?'

'Costs a lot of money.'

'Did he say yes?'

'I told him I had five hundred marks saved, that I could put down.'

'And what did he say?'

'He'd see what he could do.'

'Then it's all right.'

'No.'

'Why not?'

'Because I haven't got five hundred marks to put down.'

'How much have you saved?'

'Nothing at all.'

'Why did you say you had five hundred?'

'Because I think I can get them, Willi.'

Kufalt put on his overcoat slowly and carefully, then he inspected himself in the mirror and pulled his jacket down a bit at the back. He picked up his hat.

'Well, I'm off now, Emil.'

'I'll come a bit of the way with you, Willi.'

'Do.'

And they went, both wavering. Bruhn wanted to go on with it, but didn't quite know how; Kufalt was funny, but surely he must have got used to it in prison: 'Halves, or I'll split' was a sound principle, and a plain bit of business.

Kufalt was furious and deadly sick at heart. Had he really ever liked little Bruhn? Yes, it seemed so, he had really liked him, and never, never would he have thought . . .

'Look, Willi,' Bruhn tried to explain; 'I'll have to get out of the works, it's more than a bloke can stand, do you see?'

'Yes,' said Kufalt.

'Otherwise something will happen.'

'Yes,' said Kufalt, thoughtful once again. 'You've certainly got in wrong with the governor.'

'Can't you go and talk to him yourself, Willi?'

'No,' said Kufalt with emphasis. 'I'm through with jail and everything to do with it – understand, Bruhn?'

He stopped.

'This is where I turn down the Lütjenstrasse, Emil. My future father-in-law lives at number seventeen. I dare say you know the shop, Emil.'

But he did not move, he stood and looked at little Bruhn's round, seal-like head.

'And anyhow, I don't give a damn, Emil. Hilde's of age, and by the way, Emil,' – Kufalt bent forward and whispered mysteriously into Bruhn's face – 'I've taken care that she's fixed again, understand?'

He looked hard at Bruhn, grinned, burst into a roar of laughter and hurried, without turning, past the half-dozen houses to the Harders' door.

'Man overboard, that's all you can say,' he thought.

XXIV

After Christmas the advertisement business became very quiet, and Kufalt had again to concentrate on subscribers, so as to get some money into the till. It was a bitter comedown. One advertisement brought him eight or ten marks' commission with very little effort, and now he had to talk himself hoarse again for one mark twenty-five – four times out of five, to no avail.

By this time he had gone through all the tradesmen, who had been relatively easy victims. He now had to work his way down a street, from house to house. He never knew exactly what sort of people lived behind the doors at which he rang, nor what he ought to say to win their favour. As like as not a suspicious-looking female appeared on whom all his finest phrases would be lost; she did not even take down the chain but said, without listening, and slamming the door in his face: 'We don't want anything here.'

But it might happen – indeed it had happened – that he picked up a subscription in a quite unexpected quarter, from some Red workman's wife. Then, when he came round to the *Messenger* in the evening, the husband had already been there, making a terrible to-do and demanding his money back: they read their Socialist paper, not this filthy middle-class rag, and if he caught the windbag of a tout that had got at his wife he'd break every bone in his body. What a bastard, to talk a poor woman out of her wits!

Kraft had mildly suggested that Kufalt should be a little less excessive in his canvassing methods, and Kufalt had asked indignantly whether Herr Kraft thought that people were overjoyed at the prospect of being able to read the *Messenger*?

But then came the end of December, and the business in advertisements began to pick up again; for New Year's Day itself Kufalt had actually collected two and a half pages. But he had taken a great deal of trouble, and in addition to everything else he had roped in all the toyshops with their fireworks and the china shops with their New Year's plates. Finally, there were all the 'Good Wishes' and 'Hopes for a Continuance of Esteemed Custom during the New Year'.

There was a bittersweet smile on Kraft's face as he again handed over 215 marks to Kufalt, not without the remark: 'Easy come, easy go.'

Kufalt did not care, for, in the first place, the stocktaking sales would soon be coming along and, secondly, he now had a proper savings bank account; and in spite of all the presents he had bought there were more than a thousand marks to his credit. No, not so easily gone!

So Kufalt, scrubbed from head to foot, with clean linen and gleaming nails, went forth in holiday attire to the Harders, drank a few little glasses of mild punch, and was delighted when Frau Harder said at about half past nine: 'Well, Eugen, time for bed now, we won't wait up for the bells.'

The old man grunted acquiescence and said: 'But why don't you kids go out for a bit? It does no one any good to be stuck indoors, and by this time next year you'll be married and you may not be able to go out.'

And he surveyed his daughter's figure.

Hilde vanished, and then reappeared wearing a bright, charming dress with a pale flowery design, and a pretty twisted gold necklet . . . 'The girl looks really nice,' said Harder, astonished. The pink in her cheeks had flushed almost to red, and she cheerfully kissed her father and mother. 'All the best, sleep well into a happy New Year!'

Then the two young people went out, and the two old ones watched them from the window.

It was snowing slightly but a good many people were in the streets, and most of the shop windows were still lit up. They first strolled about for a while; Hilde admired one curtain, and he another, until they finally agreed on a third. They looked into furniture shops, and it occurred to him that there was a delightful bedroom suite in the Helmstedtstrasse that he had always wanted to show her. So they walked all the way there, only to find that Schneeweiss's, the shop in question, did not have its window lit up.

But here they were not far away from the Rendsburger Hof, and Hilde asked Willi to take her in for a few minutes; she of course wanted to show him off to some of her former girlfriends.

'That was where we first met, and I had my eye on you at once too. But you were staring at me so, I couldn't appear to have noticed you. And do you remember how you ran after Wrunka and me, almost into the lavatory? "Some lad," I remember Wrunka said. Come along, we'll only look in for a moment, even if it isn't so nice there . . .'

But he flatly refused, as people would certainly be rude and he would mind. He did not want her to be referred to in his presence as the girl with the baby, they would very likely taunt him with having been in prison, and Emil Bruhn was certain to be there. No, not on any account!

Instead, he had in mind a little cellar café on the market square, the Café Zentrum it was called; its rather musty, shabby air had always somehow appealed to him, though for some reason he had never yet set foot inside it. But no sooner did he mention it to Hilde than she declined absolutely.

'No, certainly not!'

'But why? I only wanted to have a look at it.'

'I won't go inside such a place!'

'But surely you can say why?'

'A hole like that – and what everyone says about it?'

'Have you ever been there?'

'No, and I never will. Not even with you.'

They were still standing at the corner by Schneeweiss's, the furniture shop; it was dark and bleak and they were freezing cold.

A man came by and, noticing they were having a dispute, he called out: 'Hello, Lottie, isn't he in the mood? Do you want me to help you get into his pants?'

'Come along,' said Kufalt hastily and hurried her away. The drunken New Year's reveller shouted some filth after them.

With her arm loosely slipped through his they walked briskly towards the centre of the town.

'I should like to know,' said Kufalt, emerging from profound reflection, 'why you won't go to the Café Zentrum.'

'Because a decent girl doesn't go to such a place.'

'Don't they? But such girls do go and dance at the Rendsburger Hof?'

She flung herself away from him and cried despairingly – and she really was in despair: 'Oh, Willi, Willi, why do you always torment me?'

'Torment you?' he said in amazement. 'Always torment you? Because I want to go to a café with you?'

He looked at her for a moment, her face twitched, her lips moved and she tried to speak. But she merely took his arm and said gently: 'Please take me home.'

'We're not going home yet!' he said in a bewildered tone. 'If you really won't go to the Zentrum, let's go somewhere else. How about the Café Berlin?'

She did not answer, and after a moment he noticed that she was crying quietly.

'Don't do that, Hilde,' he said, looking round him apprehensively. 'Please don't.'

'I shall be all right in a minute,' she sobbed. 'Let's look into a shop window for a moment.'

'But why are you crying? How am I tormenting you? Do tell me, Hilde darling, I don't understand.'

'Nothing, nothing,' said she, smiling again. 'I must just tidy my face a bit and blow my nose—'

'But I really want—' he persisted.

'Please not,' she said. 'We want to be cheerful this evening.'

And they were cheerful too. For in the Café Berlin there was an excellent Saxon comedian who spoke Saxon so well that he could actually be understood, and kept them laughing all the time, and a tap dancer with shaved armpits and white-powdered chest – and an older lady who sang very saucy songs . . .

The place was in uproar, everyone laughing, shouting, drinking, cheering and throwing confetti; they were soon entangled in paper snakes, and sat still so as not to tear them. Then the band played a fanfare, and it was midnight. They shook hands ceremoniously.

'A very happy New Year, Hilde, for both of us!'

'The same to you, Willi! The same to you – dearest Willi.'

They drank another small grog and Hilde's cheeks began to glow. She began to chatter about her various little friends – what so-and-so had been up to, what a bad name another had and how a third thought a great deal too much of herself . . .

'But I don't envy any of them. I've got my darling Willi. And now I've got another darling Willi – two darling Willis . . .'

She laughed loudly. And though all this chatter and laughter was drowned in the general uproar, and hardly anyone looked at the couple by the wall, Kufalt was upset. What she had said about her two darling Willis might possibly be taken in two ways, and anyway he didn't like the sound of her laugh . . .

'Come along, Hilde, let's go.'

'But you can sleep it off tomorrow.'

'We'll go somewhere we can dance.'

'Fine,' she said. She laughed. 'To the Rendsburger Hof.'

Her eyes sparkled mischievously. 'You've got another girl there you don't want me to see, eh?'

'And whom have you got at the Café Zentrum?' he asked crossly.

For an instant she was embarrassed, then she burst out laughing. 'Jealous, my poor Willi? You needn't be – I'll always be true to you and never go astray . . .'

She sang the last words to a popular tune.

The people round laughed applause. 'Good for you, young lady!'

'Come along, Hilde,' he said. And he reflected that he had led her astray, and if he had, no doubt anyone else . . .

A deep sadness came over him. 'What's the sense of it all?' he thought. 'I've nothing in common with her, I don't even like her. Then why? Just because she kept out of my way and I felt a bit of sympathy for her. Just the flesh, nothing but the flesh, it would be so much simpler with any other girl – and I don't even need the flesh . . . If a man could get out and away from it all . . . It's a bad business. If only he could start all over again.'

'What are you thinking about?' she asked.

'Nothing in particular,' he answered.

But they did not dance after all, they ended up somehow in a little wine bar and drank another bottle of sweet wine. Hilde had been depressed, peevish, saucy, jolly and talkative by turns – this last bottle simply made her tired, dead tired, and her eyelids drooped. 'Please take me home, Willi, dear.'

She stood at the street door, almost staggering from sleepiness, clinging to his arm.

'One more kiss, Willi. Oh, I'm so tired.'

'So am I,' he said.

She seemed to rouse herself a little. 'You'll go straight home, won't you – you aren't going on anywhere else?'

'Where would I be going at four o'clock in the morning? I'm off to bed at once.'

'Honest?'

'Honest to God,' he said, and tried to laugh.

'Will you give me your word of honour?'

'Of course I'll give you my word of honour. I'm going home at once.'

She was silent; she seemed somehow dissatisfied, there was something on her mind.

'Well, Hilde darling—' he said, and gave her his hand.

She flung her arms round him. 'Oh, Willi, my dearest Willi . . .' She kissed him and whispered: 'Come with me, Willi darling, the old people never go to my room . . .'

'No, no,' he said, in a shocked voice.

'But why not? I want you so much. Willi, I can't bear it! What have you against me? I can't wait till Easter.'

'Think of the boy, Hilde. It wouldn't do.'

'Oh, he never wakes up till eight o'clock; that I know. Do come. Just once, Willi.'

'No,' he said firmly. 'No, I won't. Something might happen, and they'd all talk about us.'

'They do that already. That doesn't matter.'

'No, I won't do it. Be sensible, Hilde – think, it's only a few weeks till Easter.' He took her in his arms and soothed her. And he knew that every word he said was untrue. Something would happen. But what that was, he did not yet know.

'Think how nice it will be then, all alone in our very own home, in a bright and cheerful room. By the way, I believe we can manage with the blue silk quilt instead of the eiderdown. Then we can laugh at the lot of them, and do exactly as we like; and it'll all be so much nicer than secretly like this and feeling awkward with your parents. Now I can look them in the face.'

'But you have!' she cried in agonized bewilderment. 'You have already, Willi—'

They looked at each other.

'Well, I'm going home now,' he said shortly. 'I think you've had a drop too much. Goodnight.'

He did not wait for her goodnight; he did not wait until she disappeared across the yard.

As he made off, although he did not turn, he had before his eyes an exact picture of her as she stood, staring after him with mortal terror in her face.

XXV

Of the rest of that night Kufalt had only a confused recollection, from the moment he clattered down the cellar stairs and barged into the Café Zentrum until the time when, arm in arm with his editor Freese, he stood in a deserted factory yard and stared as though spellbound into a grey, oily, sluggish stream, while Freese whispered mysteriously: 'The Trehne rises at Rutendorf, under the Galgenberg; receives in our native town the waste water from thirty-six tanneries, famed for the dissemination of the anthrax germ . . . The Trehne . . .'

A spectral night. It was improbable enough when he burst into the café – just a plain tavern parlour, without a sign of debauchery or ribaldry – and looked about him, but could see nothing through the murk of cigar smoke, and a voice shouted from a corner: 'Hey, Kufalt, you young bridegroom!'

He followed the voice and found at a corner table, in familiar converse and crouching over their grog, Freese and Dietrich: Freese flushed and red, his matted hair straying wildly over his ravaged face, and Dietrich yellow and pallid, with dull, stupid, mouse-like eyes.

'Sit down, Kufalt,' said Freese. 'That's Dietrich, I fired him on your account.'

'Delighted,' muttered Dietrich, with a slight bow.

'Drunk,' said Freese. 'Sit down, Kufalt. Drunk as a skunk. Where's your young lady?'

'Ah, young lady; I understood that,' muttered Dietrich.

'Shut your trap!' said Freese sternly. 'We want nothing of that kind from you, please – or of any kind at all . . . What'll you drink, Kufalt?'

'A beer,' said Kufalt.

'Minna, a beer, and a treble brandy for the gentleman. Minna, that fellow's going to be married, yes he is – have a good look at him.'

Kufalt looked angrily at the great fat creature with the coarse red face who set his drinks before him.

'Oh, so you're the young man that's got engaged to Harder's Hilde? I've heard about it – oh yes, you hear all sorts of things.'

'Hop it!' said Freese, and she waddled obediently behind the bar.

'A little pearl, isn't she, Minna?' asked Freese, who had not taken his eyes off Kufalt. 'Don't you like her? They all get like that, outwardly or inwardly, or outwardly and inwardly. Fat or thin, they all get like that, women do.'

'Yes – hupp,' observed Dietrich.

'Shut your trap!' roared Freese. 'I'll take you on again, I'll take you on again with five marks' advance cash down, just so I can fire you on the spot.'

And Freese felt in his pockets for money.

He found nothing.

'Give me the twenty marks you owe me, Kufalt.'

Kufalt looked at Dietrich, who blinked at him to refuse.

'Hand over, my lad, I'll stand another round.'

'Don't – you – give – it – back,' said Dietrich laboriously, as though spelling out the words. 'I – said – we're – working – together – we're working together.'

Freese burst into a roar of laughter. He laughed until he shook.

'Working together, inseparable, you two diggers, eh, what? Both digging in the same hole, hey?'

He screwed up his eyes and laughed, so that his bloated cheeks positively quivered.

Kufalt looked at him in horror, something within him trembled and he reached for his beer mug.

'So you'll take us both on?' said Dietrich suddenly in his normal voice. 'May we both work in your hole – work for the bankrupt old *Messenger*?'

There was a harsh and angry ring in Dietrich's voice.

Freese had stopped laughing, and was staring at Dietrich.

'You can perfectly well do with two canvassers,' persisted Dietrich.

Something in Kufalt's skull was turning round. 'I've drunk too much,' he thought. 'What are they really talking about? Are they talking about what they're talking about, or aren't they?'

And again he listened to the pair.

'In 1848,' observed Freese with the utmost gravity, 'Herr van der Smissen was mayor of our town. Herr van der Smissen was a real aristocrat, an honest, upright man, who wore the cleanest of clean linen . . .

'The mob gathered in front of his house and began to throw all kinds of muck and garbage through Herr van der Smissen's windows. The police succeeded that day in dispersing the mob. The mayor, who had not been present, did not return until late in the evening. Accompanied by one of the town militia, he walked in silence through the ravaged rooms . . .

'In the dining room, on one of the end walls, hung a large oil painting of his wife who had died in youth, by birth a Baroness von Puthammer. A specially filthy and odorous fragment of muck had struck the lovely lady's picture exactly on her snowy bosom . . .

'The soldier, a certain Wilms, reported that the mayor had stood motionless for about five minutes, with an utterly expressionless face, in front of the outraged portrait. Then he went to a cupboard, took out a bottle of wine and a finely cut glass and placed them both before him, Wilms, with the strict injunction that he should spend the time drinking, while he – that is Herr van der Smissen – would meanwhile get something to clean the picture. Upon which the mayor walked with a steady step out of the dining room . . . Next morning his body, covered with slime and filth, was dragged out of the Trehne, which flows at the bottom of the mayor's garden.'

Dietrich's head had long since sunk upon his chest and he was snoring. The cigar in the corner of his mouth had gone out after burning a circular hole in his shirt front.

Freese had spoken in the monotonous drone of a professional guide, and when he had finished he said in quite a different voice:

'Well, here's to you, Kufalt, we haven't got as far as that yet, have we?'

'Why did you tell me that?' said Kufalt bitterly. He cursed himself for coming to the place, he cursed himself for not being able to go away, he cursed himself for going on drinking and he cursed himself for talking to Freese at all.

'That is,' said Freese, 'a section from the history of this town, on which I have been working for the last forty years. The section will be entitled "Victims of the Trehne".'

'But I shan't be in it, you rogue!' shouted Kufalt in a sudden fury. 'You want to drive me to drown myself, don't you? But I won't, I certainly won't to please you, even if you do chuck dirt at my girl!'

He stopped in sudden shock. There was no need for Freese to point to Dietrich, and lay a warning finger on his lips.

Suddenly there rose in Kufalt's vision the lovely tall-windowed mayor's house behind the linden trees, past which he had so often trudged on his rounds. He thought he could see the broken panes, the star-shower of glass splinters tinkling onto the grass, the dark dining room lit by a single candle – and a long slender hand, with the thick blue veins and round yellow flecks of age, lifting the candlestick. From the shadowed wall came the radiant face of the lovely young woman, her slim white neck, her glorious shoulders, and now . . . and now . . .

'Do you see it?' shouted Freese. 'Do you see it?'

It was another face. 'Come with me, come just once,' said two agonized, beseeching lips.

The moment was passed, the chance was thrown away. What a fool he had been. The respite that was his had fled for ever . . .

No hand held up the candle now, it was very dark, a darkness that only gradually lifted . . .

'Had a little doze?' asked Freese. 'You shouted while you were asleep . . . He's right off.' And he pointed to Dietrich.

'I'm going,' said Kufalt, staggering with weariness.

'Wait, I'll come with you,' said Freese. 'You'll never find your way home in that state.'

He looked doubtfully at the sleeping Dietrich. 'I might tell Minna she'd better take him to bed with her,' he muttered.

Suddenly he began to grin. 'Wait a moment, Kufalt, and you'll see something.'

Kufalt tried to get away. He held on to the back of a chair, made a grab with his other hand at the nearest table, missed it, and made another attempt.

Freese soon reappeared with a piece of cardboard through which he had drawn a string. He blinked at Kufalt with malicious glee, as though he had a great joke in store for him, and approached Dietrich.

He propped him up in his chair.

'Sit up, you drunken pig,' he shouted. 'Sit straight.'

Dietrich opened his eyes, but they closed again; he gurgled once and then fell asleep. But Freese had already hung the placard round his neck. 'There, can you still read?'

Scrawled in printed letters with charcoal stood the words: 'Violator of Girls'.

Kufalt's vision first went black, then red. It seemed as though his hand was swooping down upon a beer mug which immediately went whirling in the air . . . He heard fat Minna's shriek:

'Look out, Freese . . . !' And he heard Freese's nasty chuckle . . .

Then the gurgle of running water.

Arm in arm with Freese he stood on the bank of the Trehne, the dawn had broken grey and cloudy, the sallow, oily stream rippled against the planks of the factory yard, and he heard Freese say: 'The Trehne rises at Rutendorf, under the Galgenberg, it receives the waste water from thirty-six tanneries. Famous for its dissemination of the anthrax germ . . . The Trehne . . .'

But all was a confused and spectral memory when he awoke in the afternoon.

He had dreamed it all, surely he had dreamed it all; but the New Year had started with a very bad dream.

7
Collapse

I

December, with its light clear frost, had gone, and January had come in its stead, bringing rain and bad weather. Regretfully Kufalt replaced his smart black overcoat with a shapeless yellow mackintosh.

December had been the most successful month in Kufalt's life. January set in with a series of disheartening failures. The stocktaking sales were still far off, they did not begin until 21 January, and no one wanted to take the *Messenger*.

Kufalt talked and talked – when he was allowed to talk. People listened, but they said he must know how short money was after the holiday, or they told him flatly that the *Friend* was better than the *Messenger*. The *Messenger* did not carry a quarter of the family notices that appeared in the *Friend* and that was what they mostly wanted.

On some days he had six, seven, even ten or twelve failures in succession, and with failure came discouragement. Kufalt would stand for a good ten minutes outside a tenement of twelve flats without the heart to go in; he walked up and down the street and back again, while the drizzle froze him to the bones. It would be far more sensible to go home, sit by the warm stove, and doze . . .

But here was the empty receipt book. At about four o'clock Herr Kraft expected his six new subscriptions, and he had such an offensive way of saying: 'What, only two today? Only two?'

And he rummaged among the papers on his desk.

'Besides, of your new subscribers in December thirty-seven have cancelled their order. There's really not much sense in canvassing . . .'

'Is that my fault?' asked Kufalt indignantly.

'No one mentioned the word fault,' replied Kraft with equanimity, and went on turning over papers. 'You're getting nervy, Kufalt.'

Although it was still uncertain what had really happened on New Year's Eve, Freese was friendliness itself. Indeed, he was more friendly than usual.

'Are you cold?' he would say. 'Well, there's my faithful Fridolin in the corner, go and warm yourself – I've fairly stoked him up today. Besides, I've got a job for you.'

He fumbled in the litter on his table.

'It's some write-up from the cinema. I haven't looked at the stuff. Cut out twenty lines of the worst piffle. Here's a fifty . . .'

And when Kufalt protested: 'No, no, Kufalt; only death is free of charge, and then only for the dead. You put that fifty in your pocket: a day will come . . .'

Quite unchanged – with his odd allusions, his drunkenness, the rough exterior that hid none quite knew what.

Unchanged too was Herr Harder in his admiration for Kufalt's qualities; but Hilde was changed, and very greatly changed.

No more eager kisses, hardly a yes or a no; no more poems, no more singing together.

It was half past nine. Frau Harder gave the signal for departure, goodnight was said, and the betrothed couple were alone; and now, for appearances' sake, he must stay at least half an hour longer.

He got up, lit a cigarette and began to walk up and down.

'What a stormy night,' he said, stopped, and listened towards the window.

'Yes,' she said, went on embroidering a monogram, and did not look up.

'It would be nice to stay here on a night like this,' he said, with rather an awkward laugh.

She did not answer.

He waited a moment, and then began to pace the room again. He racked his brains, and finally asked: 'Did the child eat his food better today, Hilde?'

'No,' she replied, and went on embroidering.

He paced back and forward, wondering what to say, while the

clock went ping-pang, ping-pang on the wall; at last a meagre question, and a barren yes or no.

But, as the lamp grew dim, as he looked down at her dark bowed head, at the patch of white neck that gleamed between the edge of her hair and the red collar of her jumper; as he watched her and thought of what he was doing to her and what, perhaps – perhaps – he still might do, then he felt an urge to open his mouth, and his heart, and speak.

'Hey, Hilde . . .'

She went on embroidering.

'Listen, Hilde . . .'

He came close to her.

She shifted along a little on the sofa. 'Yes?'

She went on embroidering and did not look up.

He made another try: 'Are you angry with me, Hilde?'

'Angry? How should I be?'

No, it would not come. It was not her coldness, her unresponsiveness that closed his lips – he was well aware that this came merely from wounded pride. No, there was something else.

That evening, and the white bit of cardboard with the inscription on it, haunted him.

'Why should I confess when she doesn't confide in me? Her pride is hurt, I dare say, but still I have a right . . .'

Then, a little later: 'But didn't I know it? From the very first minute she called it a child without a father. Of course she's in the right, but she could still . . .'

Feeble fool that he was, he let the moments pass and disappear. Nothing happened. He paced up and down again, puffing at a cigarette. After a long pause he said at last: 'Are the pillows hemmed yet, Hilde?'

'Not yet,' answered Hilde.

Nothing happened, except – if that could be called an event – that he called one day at No. 37 Wollenweberstrasse while on his rounds, tramped up the three flights of stairs and asked for Herr Dietrich . . .

Yes, Herr Dietrich was at home and Kufalt was promptly admitted to his room.

Dietrich was lying on a sofa fully dressed but without collar and tie, asleep with his mouth open. It was nearly noon.

'Herr Dietrich,' said Kufalt from the door.

'Hello, Kufalt,' said Dietrich, wide awake and sitting up with a jerk. 'Have a brandy?'

'I just wanted to return that twenty marks,' said Kufalt, and laid the brown note on the table by the sofa.

'There was no need to be in such a hurry! I suppose you don't want a receipt?' Dietrich had rolled up the note and put it into his waistcoat pocket. 'Well, sit you down. Good Lord, man, you look frozen. Do you go canvassing in this weather? Which part of the town are you working at present?'

'The north,' said Kufalt. 'Where the tannery workmen live.'

Dietrich whistled through his teeth. 'Pretty putrid, eh? If I were you I would stop at home and wait for stocktaking. You'll ruin more clothes than the job's worth.'

'A mackintosh keeps most of it off.'

'But your trousers!' cried Dietrich. 'And your boots! You must have a brandy at once. Or would you rather have grog? It's soon made, my landlady's got a gas ring.'

'No,' said Kufalt, with a shiver. 'I've had enough of grog. I mean I can still smell your grogs from the other night.'

And Kufalt felt he had been extremely diplomatic.

'Well, cheers,' said Dietrich. 'And may our children prosper. One more? Right! It'll do you good.'

'Did you get home all right that night?' persisted Kufalt.

'When do you mean?'

'New Year's Eve, Herr Dietrich, from the Café Zentrum.'

'Ah? You heard about that?' laughed Dietrich. 'Yes, that evening I did have one over the eight.'

'I was there too, Herr Dietrich,' said Kufalt with mild emphasis. 'We even had a talk together.'

'Were you there indeed!' said Dietrich in astonishment. 'Well, I'm blowed! Yes, I was pretty well tanked that evening.'

Kufalt reflected hurriedly. Was this assumed, or did he really not remember? He must at least have found the placard when he woke up. Or had Minna taken it off?

And, as though Kufalt had given him a sort of cue, Dietrich went on: 'Well, if you were there too, my dear Kufalt, I think it was pretty rotten of you to leave me in the lurch like that.'

'In the lurch?'

'As tight as I was. If my friend Kutzbach the butcher hadn't found me, I might actually have gone to bed with Minna!'

Dietrich was more than a match for him; and Kufalt gave up. 'Well, I must be getting on. I've got no one in my book today.'

'Have another before you go. You look awful. I wouldn't try and canvass with a face as blue as that. You will? Right, a quick one for the road.'

'By the way,' he said with sudden gravity; two fingers disappeared into his waistcoat and produced the rolled-up brown note. 'By the way – can you really spare this?'

'Certainly,' said Kufalt, confused. 'I've done rather well lately.'

'Well, if at any time . . .' said Dietrich. 'Do regard me as very much at your service. Never forget that I have always felt the deepest sympathy for your difficult – hopeless – state.'

Dietrich suddenly beamed all over his face. 'Well, this has been a very pleasant visit, Herr Kufalt. If you ever feel like looking in again, I'll always be glad to see you.'

They shook hands, and parted.

No, nothing was explained. Nothing had happened. The heavens were dark and lowering, fate might strike from any direction: Hilde, Harder, Stark, Dietrich, Freese, Bruhn, Batzke?

And then fate struck from quite a different direction.

II

On that fateful Thursday, 13 January, Kufalt slunk gloomily back to the *Messenger* office at about half past four in the afternoon. He had been out and about for seven hours, and his haul was lamentable: two subscribers. Or really only one and a half, as the Widow Maschke, who had not been able to resist his insistent talk, had only paid sixty pfennigs; he was to call for the rest on the first of next month, when her money came in.

Kufalt dreaded Kraft's rasping voice: 'Two, eh? Only two . . . Two!' He went into Lindemann's café and transmuted the widow's mite into brandy. Then he sent Pachulke the tanner's subscription the same way.

And so, shortly after five, feeling rather more jovial, he came into the despatch department, where Kraft was waiting for him.

'Only two, Herr Kraft,' he said casually, and wondered why the little shorthand typist Utnehmer eyed him with such consternation. 'It's getting worse and worse.'

'Two . . .' said Kraft, to Kufalt's surprise. 'Two are better than nothing. Go along in to Herr Freese, he wants to speak to you.'

Kufalt looked inquiringly from Kraft to Utnehmer. The girl shook her head as though to answer no.

'Why do you shake your head?' asked Kufalt in astonishment.

'I didn't shake my head,' she said untruthfully, and blushed.

'Hurry up now, Herr Freese is waiting for you,' snapped Kraft in sudden irritation.

'All right, all right,' said Kufalt, and went to the editor's room. No foreboding of disaster had yet come over him, the brandy had spread warmth and comfort through his veins; but he felt surprised at the demeanour of these two.

'Why are you so strange today, Herr Kraft?'

'I'm not strange at all. Hurry up, man.'

Freese was not alone. Near him in the armchair sat a man whom Kufalt disliked at first sight. A lean, lanky man with an absurdly protuberant belly and a dry, bird-like head, yellow all over. Behind a pair of nickel-plated spectacles glittered sharp black eyes.

Both had a glass of brandy in front of them.

'Herr Kufalt – Herr Brödchen,' said Freese, introducing them. Kufalt bowed, but Brödchen contented himself with one short, sharp nod. He looked steadily at Kufalt, and Kufalt looked at him.

'You'll be more comfortable by the stove,' said Freese genially. 'You must be frozen. How many did you beat up today?'

'Two,' replied Kufalt.

'Two,' sighed Freese. 'Two and a half marks. Can't live on that, can you?'

'Yes I can,' said Kufalt warily.

The thin man with the belly said nothing; he merely looked at Kufalt.

'Where did you go today?' asked Freese with eager interest, but Kufalt was quite aware that this interest was assumed.

'To the north,' he said shortly.

'Ah, the north,' said Freese. 'By the tanneries. Fabrikstrasse? Weberstrasse? Linsingenstrasse? Töpferstrasse? Talstrasse?'

The tall man gave a sort of deprecatory jerk, and then sat still again.

'Yes,' said Kufalt.

Disaster was in the air, so much was clear. But so much was also clear, that whatever this disaster might be, he must not submit to this strange interrogation without some protest – he must protect himself against any eventuality.

'Why are you asking all these questions, Herr Freese?' he inquired, looking at him.

Freese returned the look with reddened, fishy eyes. His tongue darted out of the corner of his mouth and licked his lips – he was certainly thinking of the Trehne – and the tongue vanished.

Freese had not answered; in his stead the thin man's quick, rasping voice suddenly rapped out: 'Light mackintosh – correct! Dark horn spectacles – correct! Sallow face – correct! Grey felt hat – that's not correct, but he's sure to have a green one at home. We'll see about that.'

'That's a cop! What a fool I was not to see it at once,' thought Kufalt, shuddering. 'But I wasn't wearing the mackintosh at the Lübeck Gate!'

With impotent fury he felt himself blush and then grow pale, his knees sagged and he had to lean heavily against the stove.

The other two stared at him fixedly. He tried to smile – but could not. He wanted to say something – but no words came. His mouth suddenly dried up.

'I am Detective Inspector Brödchen,' observed the thin man at last, when the scene had gone on long enough. 'For the sake of my friend Freese I will manage the affair quietly.'

He looked thoughtfully at his brandy glass.

'So you were canvassing in the Töpferstrasse?'

Kufalt was about to answer, but Brödchen raised his hand.

'I should warn you as a matter of form that anything you say may be used in evidence against you. You need say nothing.' He stopped, and added testily: 'But you know all about it. You're an ex-convict?'

'Yes,' said Kufalt.

'What did you get?'

'Five years' imprisonment.'

Brödchen nodded, though of course he had known this long ago.

'What for?'

'Embezzlement.'

'Where served?'

'Here in this town.'

The thin man with the belly nodded again, and said more genially: 'Well, you know all about it and I don't suppose you'll want to give us any trouble. We've caught you again, Kufalt . . .'

'What do you mean?' asked Kufalt hotly. 'I don't understand. I deny everything.'

The detective inspector nodded, and looked meaningfully at Freese, whose eyes were sparkling with excitement and glee: 'You see, he knows all about it! Denies everything in advance. Well, you were canvassing in the Töpferstrasse? You admitted that, anyway.'

'I quite admit that,' said Kufalt, utterly perplexed. (What did he mean by harping on about the stupid Töpferstrasse?)

'So you admit that. Good. And you visited a certain Frau Zwietusch?'

Kufalt reflected. The others' eyes were on him. This seemed an important question. There must be something connected with the Töpferstrasse, though what it was he could not for the life of him imagine.

'I can't say that for sure,' he replied cautiously. 'I visit thirty or forty people every day. I can't remember all their names.'

'Then you deny you visited Frau Zwietusch?'

'I didn't say that. I said I didn't know. I would have to see the house first. And the door of the flat. And perhaps the woman too.'

'No. 97,' said Brödchen.

'I've no idea, I never look at numbers.'

Silence reigned for a while.

'What's the trouble about Frau Zwietusch?' asked Kufalt. He thought he had got that out very well.

The others did not answer; the thin man asked: 'Do you possess a green felt hat?'

'No,' said Kufalt.

'What other hats do you possess?'

'A stiff black hat and a blue felt hat.'

'Blue and green are easily confused,' said Brödchen to Freese. 'In any case I had better go along with Kufalt at once to his room and look over his clothes.'

'Herr Kufalt, for the present,' protested Kufalt.

'Don't you throw your weight about, my lad,' said the detective inspector calmly. 'We'll go now, Freese. Many thanks.'

'Finish up your brandy first, Brödchen,' said Freese. 'Come along, Kufalt, you have one too. You've had a shock.'

They went, Kufalt in front, Brödchen behind. Fräulein Utnehmer assumed a surprised and sympathetic expression, but Kraft had buried himself in his ledger and did not even answer when Kufalt, rather cheerfully, said: 'Good evening.'

He was indeed feeling rather cheerful: if the officer hadn't made a bloomer this time, he'd eat his hat!

III

Outside the door of the *Messenger* office Herr Brödchen stopped and thought.

'You need not walk beside me, Herr Kufalt,' he said finally. 'Freese told me you were engaged to be married. I'll walk behind you. But if you get up to any games . . .!'

'The gun will go off!' agreed Kufalt. 'I know. I shan't be up to any games. But I wish you'd tell what's Frau Zwietusch's trouble, Herr Inspector.'

'Now for your room,' said the detective inspector crisply.

'Right,' said Kufalt, and marched off.

They met again on the staircase. Brödchen seemed rather annoyed to find that Kufalt had come there without any bother.

'You live pretty well on two marks fifty a day.'

'I've earned a great deal more than that,' explained Kufalt. 'Two hundred and forty marks a week.'

'Freese never told me anything about that,' remarked Brödchen peevishly.

'I can prove it, Herr Inspector. But you must ask Herr Kraft about that part,' replied Kufalt genially. 'It's all down in the ledgers. And the receipts are there too.'

He switched the light on in his room.

'And now all the money's gone?' said the policeman.

'What?' asked Kufalt in astonishment. 'Who on earth told you that nonsense? I've got 1,173 marks in the savings bank.'

'Oh,' said Brödchen with rising irritation. 'We'll talk about that later. Open the wardrobe, please.'

'It's open, Herr Inspector,' said Kufalt politely.

'You've got some nice stuff there,' observed Brödchen. 'All paid for out of canvassing commission?'

'My brother-in-law sent me my own things. I can prove that too.'

'Ah! Just put that hat on,' said the officer triumphantly. 'That looks decidedly green. You must admit that, Herr Kufalt.'

'Bluish-grey, I think,' said Kufalt, in front of the mirror.

'Nonsense, it's green. What's the use of denying everything? Show me your savings bank book.'

Kufalt took it out of a locked drawer.

'You've paid in nothing since the second of January? How much cash have you got in the place?'

Kufalt looked, and produced forty-six marks.

'And where are the three hundred marks?' asked the officer.

'What three hundred marks?'

'That you took out of Zwietusch's chest of drawers. Now don't go on like that, Kufalt, it's no use. I'll have your place searched this evening, and even if it's hidden somewhere else I shall find it.'

Kufalt felt very cheerful. His heart positively throbbed with joy and relief.

'So Frau Zwietusch has lost three hundred marks from her chest of drawers. Well, Inspector, the simplest thing for us to do is to go round and see her at once. And she'll tell you that it wasn't me.'

The officer looked at him attentively: 'Why are you so pleased all of a sudden?' he asked.

'Because now I know what it is, I know it's all a mistake. So let's get along.'

But Brödchen sat down. 'And why were you so frightened when you were standing by the stove?'

Kufalt was confused. 'I wasn't frightened,' he objected.

'Of course he was, terrified,' said the officer as though to himself. 'Freese will bear that out. No, Kufalt, there's something up with you, even if it wasn't you that robbed Mother Zwietusch . . . which I doubt . . .'

'I wasn't frightened,' said Kufalt, who had now recovered himself. 'But when a man's been in prison like me, he doesn't much enjoy a talk with a police inspector. You never know whether you can prove your innocence; the likes of us are always under suspicion . . .'

'It's no good, Kufalt,' said Brödchen. 'You needn't take me for a fool. I know you blokes. Somewhere around you it stinks.' Again he began to ponder. 'Well, let's go and see old Zwietusch.'

'Yes,' said Kufalt defiantly. 'It's easy enough to suspect a bloke . . . Look, Inspector, when I'm earning good money, and it's in the bank, and I'm to be married at Easter – what sort of fool would I be to mess up everything for three hundred marks?'

'There's many a fool that doesn't know it,' said the detective inspector gloomily. 'Stealing is always a fool's game.'

'Yes, and that's why I don't steal. I embezzled; and embezzling and stealing, as you know, Inspector, are entirely different things.' And he added confidentially: 'I would be much too much of a coward to steal, Inspector.'

'Indeed?' said Brödchen. 'Do you drink as much brandy as that every day?'

'I haven't drunk much brandy!'

'More than's good for you, anyway, and also more than Freese gave you. Did you drink brandy when you were canvassing in the Töpferstrasse?'

'No; I hardly ever drink brandy.'

'But you drank some today.'

'Yes . . . I was feeling depressed, because business was bad.'

'Where?'

'At Lindemann's.'

'How many?'

'Four.'

'And then what Freese stood you. That makes five. After five brandies a man's hand might well get a bit out of control.'

'I'd drunk nothing at all when I went canvassing in the Töpferstrasse.'

'We'll see about that.' The officer yawned. 'And now we'll go round and see Frau Zwietusch.'

IV

'I don't believe I've ever been inside this place,' said Kufalt, as he looked up at the tenement house at No. 97 Töpferstrasse, in the uncertain light of a street lamp.

'Belief is a religious matter,' answered Detective Inspector Brödchen. 'Why shouldn't you have been to this house when you worked your way down the whole street?'

'Good God, I don't go into every house! I can tell at once that some of them are no good, so I don't go inside.'

'Ah!' said Brödchen. 'Better be safe than sorry, but a man can be too cautious, Kufalt. Do you remember the staircase?'

'It's the staircase of any workmen's tenement,' said Kufalt surveying it. 'How could I say I recognized it? They all look exactly alike!'

And he bent down to read the nameplates at the bottom of the stairs.

'It's the second floor, ' said Brödchen impatiently, and Kufalt obediently climbed the first flight, and the second flight, with Brödchen at his heels.

'Now come along down again,' said Brödchen irritably. 'If you've been here before, I'll give you full marks. It's the ground floor, of course.'

'Inspector,' said Kufalt blithely, 'since I know what it's about, I'm not in the least afraid.'

But that was a mistake, for the policeman said with meaning: 'Since you know what it's *not* about, you mean! Knock at the door and go in first . . . I want to see . . .'

So Kufalt knocked, and a thick female voice said, 'Come in.' It was a small workman's flat that gave straight into the kitchen, and the door to the living room behind stood open. Kufalt could see two beds with white embroidered coverlets.

By the stove stood a large, flabby female clad in a shabby, dark dress, with a full white face, pendulous cheeks and dark furtive eyes.

Kufalt looked carefully at the woman; he was quite sure he had never seen her before. Then he took off his (bluish-grey) hat and politely said, 'Good evening.'

'Evening,' said the woman. 'What is it?'

Kufalt did not answer.

'Well?' he cried triumphantly to the detective inspector, who remained in shadow. 'Did she recognize me or not?'

Brödchen did not reply. He stepped out of the shadow: 'Evening, Frau Zwietusch. This is the young man . . .'

'I protest!' shouted Kufalt furiously. 'If you tell the woman I'm the man, she'll believe you. I'm not the man, Frau Zwietusch, you've never seen me before, have you?'

'Hold your tongue, Kufalt,' said Brödchen roughly. 'It's not your business to ask questions. Frau Zwietusch, this is the young man who came down the street canvassing for the *Messenger*. Did he call on you?'

'Look at me!' pleaded Kufalt. 'Please look at me carefully.'

'Hold your tongue, Kufalt!'

The woman looked helplessly from one to the other.

'I don't know,' she said. 'There's no call to look at people so close. Was he as tall as that?' she asked, appealing to the officer.

'That's what I'm asking you. Light mackintosh, dark horn-rimmed spectacles, pale face – that all fits, Mother Zwietusch, doesn't it?'

'Yes . . .' she said doubtfully.

'Was I wearing a hat like this?' asked Kufalt eagerly. 'I mean – was he wearing a hat like this? You said he had on a green hat. But my hat's not green?'

'No,' she said dubiously. 'It certainly isn't green . . .'

'But was the man wearing that sort of hat, Mother Zwietusch?' asked the officer in turn.

'I don't know,' she said. 'He took it off at once. Did I say green?'

'You certainly said green.'

'Perhaps it looked green.'

'Yes, but you must know, Frau Zwietusch,' said the officer sternly. 'And by the way, you said he kept his hat on in the room, and only put it on the table when he started to write.'

'Did I? Then that must be right. Then that's the hat right enough, sir.'

'Ah!' said Brödchen. But he was obviously very dissatisfied.

'And is that the young man?'

'At first I thought it wasn't, the other was taller and had a harsher voice. But now I almost think it is.'

'Hmm!' said Brödchen, still more dissatisfied.

'Has he still got the money, sir?' she asked ingenuously, and pointed with her thumbs at Kufalt.

The detective inspector did not answer.

There Kufalt stood. Cheerful no more, but with fear, sick fear, in his heart. For this had he struggled, for this had he suffered, to be flung back into the abyss by a stupid old woman. Brödchen needed only to take the matter rather lightly. Did she recognize him? All right, then that's the bloke, and the case is over – and he would promptly find himself in jail. Five minutes more, and she would definitely recognize him. She would believe it absolutely, and swear it in the best of faith before any investigating magistrate in the world! And he was defenceless, he had been in prison, and everyone would think him guilty; it was no use. What would happen? What in the world would happen about Hilde and Harder and Freese and Kraft? And what would happen to him!

'Frau Zwietusch,' said Kufalt in an imploring tone, 'look at me carefully. Had he got light brown hair like mine? Was it parted in the same way? Did he speak High German like me? Or Low German? Do try to think . . .'

Brödchen sat on the kitchen chair and looked appraisingly from Kufalt to the woman, and from the woman to Kufalt.

'Now, now, young man,' said the old woman tearfully. 'You're just trying to confuse me. And the officer told you to hold your tongue. You should be ashamed to steal an old woman's savings out of her cupboard, and the smug way you said, "You see to the stove so your dinner doesn't get burnt, I can wait" . . .'

Suddenly Kufalt trembled, a memory came into his mind, as though he had really sat somewhere, and really had said something of the kind . . .

But Brödchen said sternly: 'No, Frau Zwietusch, it isn't as simple as all that. And you mustn't start making up stories, please. There's a good deal to suggest that you didn't recognize the man.'

'But I tell you I did, sir,' she wailed. 'Of course I recognized him. That's the man.'

'But I've never been in the place,' cried Kufalt bitterly.

'And he was wearing a gold ring just like that on his left hand; I noticed it specially when he was holding his book to write in it.'

'You never mentioned that before, Frau Zwietusch.'

'It has only just come into my mind, sir. I'm certain he was wearing a ring like that.'

At that moment they were interrupted.

A large, stocky man in yellow bricklayer's overalls dashed into the room; in his hand was a blue enamel can, which he brandished like a weapon. His face was splashed with lime, and his long black hair was matted and dishevelled.

'Where's the bastard that stole my wife's savings?' he roared. 'Come here, you shit, I'll break all the bones in your body . . .'

And he sprang at Kufalt and clutched at his chest.

'Gently, Zwietusch . . .' said Brödchen. 'Gently,' in no great hurry to step between the two.

'Let me go, please,' shouted Kufalt. 'I've not stolen anything from you.'

And he struck the hulking creature with his fist.

All the women neighbours crowded into the open door.

It was not a powerful blow, for Kufalt was not a very powerful man. But his huge adversary at once lost his balance, staggered backwards, slipped and collapsed on the floor.

Sympathetic murmurs from the kitchen door.

The bricklayer's black, blazing eyes opened wide in blank astonishment, then he burst into a roar of laughter.

'Drunk! Drunk again!' wailed Frau Zwietusch. 'He's drunk every evening now!'

'That's the trouble about the money!' cried a shrill female voice from the door.

'They ought to be knocked on the head, the young brutes!'

'Wasting a poor man's money on their girls!'

Brödchen had observed the scene attentively. 'You'd better get up, Zwietusch. When did you start drinking again?'

'Mind your own business,' growled the man, laboriously hoisting himself to his feet with the aid of a kitchen chair. 'But if I catch that lad again . . . !'

'You'd better not be drunk again,' broke in Brödchen dryly. 'Come along, Kufalt. We might perhaps call about this again tomorrow, Frau Zwietusch, when you can see the man by daylight. Good evening.'

And he walked with the accused through an avenue of abusive women.

V

For a while they walked side by side down the street in silence.

Then Kufalt said: 'If you take me round again tomorrow, Inspector, I'm done for. She's certain to recognize me next time.'

And as Brödchen did not reply, he added: 'Now that she's been gawping at me the whole evening.'

'Ah!' observed Herr Brödchen.

Then, after a while: 'You seem to have odd ideas about our job. You think you're the only ones with their wits about them.'

'And what do you think?'

'I'm beginning to think you're a fool. And fools always make the most work.'

A pause. They walked on side by side.

'Where are we going?' asked Kufalt.

Brödchen merely growled.

'I suppose you'll let me go now? What that old woman said wasn't evidence.'

Once again Brödchen did not answer.

They made their way to the centre of the town, across the market square, into the town hall, through the police room, in which a few constables were lying on plank beds, up a dark staircase – and Brödchen pushed open the door of a small office. Here a policeman was sitting at a typewriter, a sergeant; Kufalt recognized the stripes.

'Sit down,' said Brödchen to Kufalt. 'Sit down,' he added impatiently. 'Wrede, this man is not to . . .'

'Right you are,' said Sergeant Wrede indifferently, and went on typing.

'I'm going in to see the boss for a moment,' said Brödchen, and vanished through a padded door.

For a while Kufalt sat there brooding. He would have liked to listen to the voices in the neighbouring office, but the padded door was too thick and the typewriter rattled too loud – so there was nothing to do but brood. Would they let him go? Of course they would, there was no evidence against him.

Time passed, and finally Kufalt got up and began to pace up and down.

'Get away from that door! Sit down!' shouted the man at the typewriter, and Kufalt sat down and went on brooding. 'Of course they'll let me out, then I can go straight along to Hilde.'

Again an endless wait, then the padded door opened, and with Brödchen appeared a large, imposing man in police uniform.

Kufalt jumped up, and assumed the watchful attitude he had learnt in jail.

But the police officer only glanced at him.

'Put him in the cells for the time being,' he said.

'But . . .' began Kufalt, and his voice rose to a shriek.

'Take him away,' said the officer sharply, and vanished through the padded door.

The sergeant got up from his machine and took some keys off a board.

'Herr Inspector!' shouted Kufalt. 'You know it wasn't me. Let me go, I won't run away. Look, sir,' he added confidentially; 'I have to see . . .' – lowering his voice – 'my fiancée tonight. Don't mess everything up for me.'

'Now then, what's all this, Kufalt?' said Brödchen. 'One night in the cells won't do you any harm. If you really didn't do it, you'll be out tomorrow. And it's much better to have the thing cleared up once and for all.'

He stopped and then added in a businesslike tone, 'Besides, in such a doubtful case we must have our man in our care. Take him away, Wrede!'

'Come along,' said Wrede. 'Get a move on. I've got some more work to do tonight.'

They went across a dark yard, an iron gate clashed, the officer switched on a light; a stone floor, the familiar window bars, a cell door . . .

'It's not heated,' said Wrede dubiously. 'Well, I dare say you'll be all right for one night. I'll get you another blanket. Do you want anything to eat? I can give you a slice of bread. The soup's all gone. Empty your pockets. Right. I'll come for your braces and tie in five minutes. Now get a move on.'

It was not quite dark in that icy grave of a cell. The yard lamp threw a pale reflection on the ceiling. Kufalt crouched on his bed, quivering with the cold, and stared at the grey wall.

A night in the cells won't do *you* any harm! A night in the cells won't do *you* any harm! A night in the cells won't do *you* any harm!

An indescribable fury possessed him. It was not only the cold that made him tremble.

'Just wait till I get out again, I'll show you . . . !'

And again, and yet again, 'A night in the cells won't do *you* any harm!'

Later on he heard the bells of fire engines.

That would be the thing to do, Bruhn was right; burn the place down . . . and smash their bloody heads in! A night in the cells won't do *you* any harm . . .

VI

The fire engine that Kufalt had heard was on its way to the timber works. They were on fire – on fire at last – and that kindly little seal-headed Emil Bruhn had had to suffer many things before the works were fired – on his account, but not by his hand.

He had been wrong when he said the managers had marked him down for remarking how easily timber works caught fire. That sort of thing was very often said; dogs that barked didn't bite, and the place was heavily insured.

No; they kept him on simply because he really was an uncommonly skilful workman and a grafter who knew how to keep the men at it; indeed, he liked to call himself a robot. It would be a long while before they found such a good slave-driver, and one so cheap.

The first cause for concern was when his room began to turn out bad work and the management were confronted with Bruhn's organized sabotage.

At that time Bruhn was on the verge of dismissal. But again and again he was saved by the fact that they did not want to lose him. There must be some means of bringing him into line.

It was a bookkeeper, a caustic, yellow, elderly wages clerk, who suggested that Bruhn's career should be revealed to his fellow workmen, so as to isolate him and make him dependent on the management for his protection. To the credit of the firm of Steguweit it must be said that this proposal was rejected. It was well known that the bookkeeper, who was very poorly paid, was consumed with hatred for every workman who earned good wages – especially as he had to calculate them. They laughed at him and kept him on because it was certain he would never pay anyone a pfennig more than his due. But they had no use for a proposal of that kind.

They turned instead to a Polish seasonal worker by the name of Kania, who was wasted at the planing machine. Kania, obsequious, humble, ready for any job or any unpaid overtime, loathed his fellow workers, whom he regarded as stupid, unambitious and unskilful. Always ready to denounce them and get them into any sort of trouble, he was a born foreman who thought of nothing but his factory, and thus his own advancement, until he attained his ideal of a well-furnished two-roomed flat with a wireless.

The best scheme, in the interests of the firm, was obviously to put him beside Bruhn and rouse them both to frantic rivalry.

Unfortunately both schemes were carried out, that of the wages clerk first. The number cruncher was irritated by the rejection of his admirable plan. Secretly he set the workmen against Bruhn. But Bruhn did not yield. Indeed, he even succeeded in forming a little group in his own section who took his side and did all they could to undermine the slandering majority. The foreman's actual presence was now needed to keep them busy with their nest boxes. Scarcely was his back turned than hostilities began afresh. Lockers were broken open and the contents destroyed. Transmission gear was damaged so that the enemy would be caught by the whirling belt and dragged into the machinery. Hammers flew unexpectedly through the air and the muttered insult 'murderer' was enough to unleash a fight.

There were constant petitions from the more powerful group to the management, demanding the instant dismissal of the 'murderer'. Wounds were displayed – he was responsible. Money was missing – he had stolen it. Clothes were ruined by acid – he alone possessed an acid bottle.

Then Kania appeared. Kania was no ordinary workman, employed making nest boxes; his presence implied some scheme on the part of the management, that was obvious. What it might be, was a matter of dispute; but that it concerned Bruhn they were all agreed.

Kania's arrival induced a lull which the management had so long desired. Both factions waited. Was Kania merely a spy, to report to the authorities all that was said and done? Or was he more? He was certainly a modest man. He came from the planing machine, he understood nothing about nest boxes and was unfamiliar with the art of nailing planks together. He fumbled about, squinted to the right, squinted to the left. 'He'll do about one a day,' shouted one of the men, and they all laughed. Kania laughed too. By the midday interval Kania had finished his first nest box. But the foreman rejected it; Kania smiled discreetly.

It was then agreed that there was no mystery about Kania, and by the next day he aroused no comment. Willi Blunck and Ernst Holtmann collided by the nail shelf.

'You needn't step on my toes!'

'Who's stepping on anyone's toes? You or I?'

And he stamped on the other's toes.

'You filthy murderer!'

'You filthy adulterer!' Blunck had indeed been involved in a divorce case, which he enjoyed recounting with a good deal of unsavoury detail.

'Hello, Bruhn!'

'Hello, Stachu!'

'You let Willi alone, or I'll smash your head in . . .'

'If you want your own head smashed in . . . !'

'You filthy murderer!'

A sound like the roaring of wild animals filled the room. Into the brawl, where fists had begun to fly, leapt Kania, bare-armed and bare-chested.

'Hah! Who's a murderer? You? And you? Take that! Want any more? Then take that. Get out, you dirty Pole! (This to Stachu – with the impartiality of the future foreman.) I'll take on the lot of you! Come on – you there, what's-your-name.'

In three minutes he had flung the scuffling mob apart. There were many bloody faces and swollen eyes. Stachu's cheek had been ripped open as though by a knuckle-duster; Bruhn had emerged unscathed.

Kania was shouting in a frenzy. 'Come on, the lot of you; I'm ready. Murderers, eh? I'll murder you! Hey there, you little baby, I'll crack your skull for you!'

Then, more calmly, 'Come, Bruhn, you show me how to do the job. I know my work is shit! You put me right, see?'

It never happened again. There was no more brawling. The slightest friction, the briefest exchange of words, and Kania's formidable 'Hah!' rang out and he bellowed: 'Now then, you little prick, come along here, I'll crack your skull!'; and quiet reigned once more. The word 'murderer' disappeared from the room's vocabulary; the alliance between Kania and Bruhn was plain for all to see.

Kania was quick to learn, and as long as he remained so, peace prevailed. Perhaps Kania had hoped to do better than Bruhn, once he had got to grips with the work, and so slip into the place of foreman. But in this he was mistaken. Here physical strength, in which Kania was twice or three times Bruhn's superior, was not the decisive quality; a natural aptitude, an unerring eye and a skilful hand were even more essential.

So long as Bruhn was teaching Kania, they did their work side by side; but when Kania saw he had nothing more to learn he shifted his place to the other end of the room, saying it was too cold by the window. They still called each other Josef and Emil, and chatted during the lunch interval; but the atmosphere had cooled. Bruhn was aware that Kania never took his eyes off him, that every nest box he turned out was reckoned up against him, and that Kania was working as hard as he knew how; while Bruhn tapped in his nails with smiling ease, and even helped the others, Kania's output never came near his. When Bruhn sat down to eat his meal, or went out to smoke a quick cigarette in the lavatory, Kania went on working doggedly at his bench. Bruhn came back, chatted a little, stood and watched Kania, picked up his hammer, and before half an hour had passed Kania was left behind.

The brawling and abuse had certainly ceased, but everyone in the room felt that something much worse was afoot. Bruhn sensed the hatred in the atmosphere, but took little notice of it. He relied on Kania. He had not understood that Kania had only stopped the attacks on him to convince the management of his authority and therefore his suitability for the post of foreman. For Kania the defeat of Bruhn was vital, and he quite understood the management's tactics in setting them against each other. He also realized that the time had come to change his methods and play his own game.

One day Bruhn, having gulped down his lunch, went as usual to the lavatory to smoke a cigarette. He had locked the door and was comfortably smoking, when he heard a shuffling at the door; then some crashing hammer blows; it was too late when he flung himself against the door; he was nailed in.

For two or three hours he yelled himself hoarse; when he stopped to draw breath, he could hear the whirr of the machines, the rattle of the driving belts and the rasping hiss of the great saws, but no one seemed to hear his shouts. Finally he lost patience, and flung his short, stocky person against the door until he broke it down.

When he entered the room, no one seemed to notice him, and he went straight back to his place. His tools had of course vanished, the foreman was not to be found, and when Bruhn at last ran him to earth in the boiler room and fetched him to the room, the tools were neatly laid out in their usual place. In the meantime it had been reported that a lavatory door had been broken down, and Bruhn's protestations were ignored and the damage was deducted from his weekly pay.

A few days afterwards, Bruhn had been working rather later than usual and the others had long since gone home. As he was walking along the dark corridor from the engine room to the porter's lodge a log of wood, flung with all the force of a powerful throw from a darkened upper window, struck him on the right arm; frailer bones than Bruhn's would have been broken. For three or four days he could not move the arm, and when he came back to the factory it was two weeks before he could do his usual day's work.

Those were two weeks of triumph for Kania; he began to talk to Bruhn again, and peace seemed to have returned.

Then it all started afresh. He was no longer one man's victim; there were clearly several after him, perhaps the whole section was in league against him. It was a hunt; their hunting instincts were awakened and they harried him at every turn.

Nowhere was he safe. At home, in the workshop, at the cinema or in the street, he was vulnerable to attack. His windows were broken, an unknown passer-by knocked his hat into the gutter, needles pricked him in the dark, his shirts disappeared, his hammer head was always loose, his front-door steps were covered with black ice when he came home at night. He could not enter a tavern without feeling an invisible hostility. It was now he needed Kufalt, but Kufalt he had lost. He thought about fleeing, to Hamburg, or Berlin, where no one knew anything about him and where he could plunge beneath the surface; but he must not throw away his chance with the governor, and his own pride would not let him give in.

He grew desperate, and for some time he wondered how long he could hold out. He walked like a broken man, his face was yellow and there was never a night but he woke up with a start and a shriek. The whole world was his enemy; the only time he felt he could breathe was during the few brief minutes of his interviews with the governor.

There he was disappointed.

Recently, a new ploy had started: every morning when he came to work he found his bench covered with excrement. It was thoroughly rubbed in, and amid the loud protests of the section Bruhn had to spend half an hour every morning fetching water, and washing and scrubbing, until he could start work.

However early he came, his bench was always filthy.

Bruhn complained to the management, but he was informed that the nightwatchman had found his bench clean at half past six; he had better turn up to work rather more punctually, and conduct himself so as not to be victimized by such childish pranks.

It was clear to Bruhn that this was a plot; and it was only possible to expose it if he could catch the culprit in the factory at night.

One night he got into the factory.

VII

It was easy to gain entry. The factory backed onto a narrow alley that was almost deserted at night. When the solitary gas light was extinguished, it was perfectly easy to climb over the relatively low wall and drop into the yard.

Bruhn put out the light and climbed over. The dogs, who were waiting for the nightwatchman – it was not yet nine o'clock – barked once and then came whining up to him; they fawned around his feet; they recognized him from the nights when he had regularly got into the factory to damage the goods ready for delivery.

He threw them some bread and glanced up at the four-storeyed front of the factory, towering up into the starless sky. He stopped; there was still a light in the wages clerk's office.

For a moment he stood and thought. Then he decided that someone had forgotten to turn out the light; who could be in the wages clerk's office at that time? He took out the skeleton key he had used on previous occasions, softly opened the door, chased the dogs away and immediately locked it behind him.

Again he stood for a moment and listened, took off his boots, hid them behind a pile of planks and went slowly down the corridor to the workshops. It was quite dark, and Bruhn did not dare to use a light; the nightwatchman was always on his rounds at about nine and might see the glimmer of a light at one of the windows. But he groped his way along the wall until he felt the staircase beneath his feet, and slowly and cautiously walked up it.

The stairs creaked, but that was nothing; there was so much woodwork in the factory that on winter nights, when the furnaces died down, it rasped as it contracted, so such sounds would not arouse any attention.

Bruhn was now by the door of his own workroom. He took out a second key, felt with his finger, found the keyhole, thrust in the key and turned it. The lock clicked, he grasped the door handle, it yielded, but the door did not open.

Once more he pressed the handle, but again the door did not open. For a moment he stood there thinking, then he began to run his fingers over the door; there must be something to prevent it opening.

Suddenly he stopped. Surely it must be his enemy who was holding the door on the inner side. He stood stock still and listened. Not a sound; only his heart beating with a slow and almost sluggish throb, and the rapid ticking of his watch.

The wave of fear had passed; he could lift the latch, how could the enemy be holding the door? Bruhn tried again. He couldn't make it out in the darkness, but there seemed to be something like a small hole above the latch, while the proper keyhole was under the latch – what could it be? He must flash his pocket torch on it for a moment.

He did so. It was as he had feared. The management were sick of that disgusting trick, and a safety lock had been fitted above the catch. He could now go home. Kania would be sure to know about this, and would not come; he would not catch him, and once more the reckoning must be postponed.

Intense, bitter anger surged up within him. Tomorrow there would be certainly some new abomination, devised by Kania, and applauded by all the others – and he had so longed to have it out with the bloke that night. Why hadn't they waited a day before putting on their bloody Yale lock!

He stopped. After all, had the lock been fitted that day? It could not be seen in daylight; the door always stood wide open so as to let the timber trucks through, the lock might well have been on the door for some time. And yet Kania got in; it was untrue that the nightwatchman had inspected his bench at half past six and found it clean. Kania had accomplices – perhaps the watchman gave him the key. Bruhn had waited outside Kania's lodging in the early morning; Kania was not very early at the works; he did not leave his room until quarter to seven, so it cannot be true that the bench was still clean at half past six. But all this was of no use. He could not stand and wait for Kania. The watchman would find him, Kania would catch sight of him and he could not get involved in an open fight with Kania; he must hide and catch him in the act.

For a while he stood and pondered.

It was uncertain which way Kania had got into the place. Bruhn could not hide down in the corridor, nor in the engine room gangway. There were three ways by which Kania could get in, and it would be foolish to concentrate on one; he would probably wait all night in vain. Bruhn must get into the room, and if not through the door, then . . .

He put the key into the door and turned the lock. The watchman must not find anything unusual.

The roof, of course, was a possibility, but Bruhn was no climber; his short, stocky body had stiffened during his years in prison. Besides, he should first have assessed the ascent by daylight. To break through the wall from an adjacent room, at night, and without proper implements, with the nightwatchman about, was out of the question.

Bruhn turned to go. It was no good, he always had the worst of luck. How gratifying it would have been to ambush Kania and thrash him so that he would be laid up for three weeks and yet could never prove it was Bruhn! But his luck was always out.

He walked down the stairs again.

And then stopped.

Far below he saw a glimmer of light. It might be the nightwatchman, but he could also hear a voice. The escape route was barred.

He could go through the glue room into the sawdust room and from there slip through the air shaft into the boiler room . . .

He made his way back – and suddenly heard an unmistakable voice.

He crept up to the top of the stairs and listened.

Yes, it was the voice of the enemy; he heard him shout, 'Come on down, you bastard. I know you're up there, I saw you get over the wall!'

Bruhn had nothing handy, only the two keys, but they were large and heavy; he gripped them and flung them down the stairs at the gleam of light.

He heard a cry; no, not Kania's voice, nor the watchman's voice, which was harsh and deep; it was a shrill, thin, clamorous voice, which he knew . . . There were several of them there . . . the hunt was on.

'Let me see, Herr Kesser . . . It's nothing much, just a scratch . . .'

A face came into the light of the lamp – well well, it was the pay packet man; well, serve him right, he had had enough rows with him.

'It's only a scratch,' said the watchman to Kesser, who was still whimpering. 'You'd better stay where you are, it's going to be a bit of a job to catch this brute.'

The stairs were suddenly lit up. Somebody – Kania, of course – had turned on the light, and Bruhn could just see that he was in danger; noiselessly, also in stockinged feet, Kania bounded upstairs.

Bruhn took to his heels; he ran out of the light into darkness, which made pursuit more difficult, and dashed into the glue room – it was very dark in there and the trapdoor would be difficult to lift.

He heard Kania rattling at the door of the workroom, where he had just been standing; where was the ring on the trapdoor? It must be over in the corner, and as he groped for it he glanced towards the door, which was open and, in the reflection from the staircase, stood sharply outlined against the black wall.

He had not found the ring when he saw a shadow in the doorway. The man's breath came quickly, and he listened. Bruhn crouched in his corner. He groped with his hand and grasped an iron glue-pot; he looked at the ceiling . . .

The light flashed on, and Kania roared with pleasure. 'There you are, Emil, come on out, and I'll beat your head in, blast you!' Then a crash, darkness, a scatter of glass splinters. Bruhn had smashed the bulb.

He slipped round to the opposite corner of the glue room behind the glue oven and watched his enemy, who stood cursing in the doorway.

Then all was silence . . . He looked at the dim figure; the figure stood motionless, and listened . . .

'Come on, Emil,' said Kania. 'Are you scared? You needn't be scared. I've got something that'll put you to sleep in no time.'

And he brandished a club.

Bruhn had been groping noiselessly on the glue oven, found what he wanted and with one heave of his arm he flung an iron glue-pot at the figure in the doorway.

Kania spat out a savage curse that was half a roar of pain; Bruhn had hit him. Kania had gone, he could hear him shouting on the landing, 'Bring that torch, bastards; how the hell can I get him in the dark?'

The stairs creaked.

Now was the moment. He grasped the ring of the trapdoor and raised it up; beneath him was a dark abyss into which he lowered himself, and the door slammed down above his head with a thunderous crash.

He had fallen softly, onto a heap of sawdust. Above him he heard voices shouting and talking, how far away he could not tell. He must hurry. He crawled over the sawdust – no use looking for the door, it was bound to be shut, he must find the air shaft.

He thought he remembered it was in the opposite corner, and he found it; the shaft was very narrow, but perhaps he could manage. He tore off his jacket and trousers, raised his arms above his head and got in, legs first. Then he began slowly to push himself backwards, using all his strength to squeeze himself down the narrow metal tube.

He was not far from the mouth of the shaft, not more than two or three metres, when a light appeared; the others were in the sawdust room. He heard them talking excitedly, but could not catch what they said; the air in the narrow tube was foul, his progress very laborious, there was roaring in his ears and a red mist before his eyes.

They would be searching for him in the sawdust. It would be some while before they realized he was not there, and happened on the air shaft. Doggedly he thrust himself downwards, centimetre by centimetre. Before they noticed where he was hidden he must reach the joint in the shaft, after which it dropped vertically into the boiler room on the ground floor; he could then slip down and be off before they got to the bottom of the stairs . . .

The circle of light darkened – something had blocked it – and he heard a voice: 'Give me the lamp, perhaps he's here.'

A flash of light dazzled him and a triumphant voice shouted: 'There he is! Give me the pistol and I'll shoot him in the face. Give me the pistol, watchman!'

For a moment he was paralysed by mindless terror, then he jerked himself back, so that his muscles and his bones cracked . . . and again, and yet again . . .

The opening to the shaft was clear for a moment; they were probably quarrelling over the pistol . . .

Surely they couldn't shoot him there and then, he had put up no resistance . . .

And he went on jerking himself backwards . . .

The light flashed again and dazzled him completely. Would the joint never come! Oh God, the man was going to shoot him in the face . . .

His legs swung loose; he gave a frantic push and shot downwards . . . he was choking – his lungs were bursting – he fell and fell, his mind was a blank, it was over, all over . . .

When he came to he was sitting on a heap of sawdust by the big circular saw. He looked around and listened; silence. He staggered to his feet, shivering in his thin underclothes. He listened; not a sound. Perhaps he had been unconscious merely for a second, surely they would soon be here? No, not a sound.

Then he remembered that they would for sure be looking for him in the boiler room. He had expected to drop into the boiler room, but that was of course absurd; he now realized it was not so wide a shaft; he had fallen straight into the engine room. It was dark, but he felt his way about and stumbled against the door, which was of course shut. What a fool he had been to throw away the keys – one of them might have fitted. They would be sure to come now, and they would kill him.

What should he do?

He was confused; the fall down the shaft had partly stunned him and he could barely move.

Then he thought of the windows. He was on the ground floor;

he had fallen three storeys; the windows opened onto the yard; he could climb through the ventilator over them.

He shuffled painfully towards a window. It was strange that they were not here by now. They could take him quietly, he was so exhausted. There were good beds at the police station, and the main thing was that a man could lie down on his backside.

The phrase pleased him. 'A man can't do without lying down on his backside,' he thought; but he made his way to the window, pulled the ventilator cord and looked up. It was nine feet above his head, but the windows were small wired glass panes in fixed iron frames; he would have to crawl through.

He was so weary that he had to hold on by a transmission belt; he half wished that they would come.

He grasped the belt and started to pull himself up by his hands. The pain in his arms was agonizing, there seemed no strength left in them. But his legs were worse; he tried to use them to support himself against the wall, so as to take the weight of his body off his arms, but they would not obey him. However, he slowly mounted, hand over hand, and could almost touch the edge of the ventilator when the belt began to slip round the flywheel, and he crashed to the floor.

His body struck the side of a sawing bench and he lost consciousness for a second time.

When he opened his eyes, Kania was standing in front of him. The engine room lights were on, Kania stood and looked at him with his small, black, twinkling eyes, dangled his rubber club and said nothing.

Bruhn said nothing either; he lay where he was, rigid and deadly weary. His blue lips moved, but merely set into a faintly troubled smile. His fear had gone.

'Get up, you bastard!' shouted Kania suddenly, and kicked Bruhn in the side.

Bruhn's body yielded to the blow; he rolled slowly over and closed his eyes again.

'Will you get up, you wretch!' roared Kania, and seized Bruhn by the collar.

But the moment he let him go, Bruhn collapsed once more.

'Do you expect me to carry you?' shouted Kania, and struck Bruhn savagely on the head with his rubber club. Bruhn raised his head slightly, his body stiffened as though he were going to get up; then he fell back with a faint sigh, his eyes turned to Kania with a last blue flicker of a glance . . .

'Don't sham, you pig,' shouted Kania and struck him again.

Bruhn lay still, his firm, broad, toil-worn hand had opened and the skilful fingers hung limp.

Kania looked at him, bewildered. Then a misgiving came into his mind, his lips quivered, he bent down over the lifeless form and called in a low voice, with a glance at the open door: 'Emil! Emil!'

Emil did not answer.

The murderer looked anxiously at the door; no, they would not come yet – he had time to get away. He jumped up, ran out into the passage, switched out the light and turned it on again.

He hurried into the room without a glance at the silent body on the floor, ran to the planing machines, collected a heap of shavings and scraps of wood, flung them onto a pile of planking, pulled out some matches . . . a small blue flame leapt up, he blew on it . . .

Then he dashed out. He forgot to turn out the light, he slammed the door, so that it locked, and ran down the corridor into the yard . . .

The watchman and the wages clerk came out of the engine room.

'Well, have you found him?'

'Not a sign of him,' said Kania.

'He must have got through a window. Or is he hiding behind some timber?'

'We've got to find him!'

'Damn the pig!' said Kania wearily.

He stood with his back to the engine room and watched the men's faces.

'Well, I'll search the whole factory with the dogs,' said the watchman.

'Oh, God,' cried the wages clerk suddenly; 'look!'

Behind the windows of the engine room a great tongue of flame leapt up and up – they could hear it roaring.

'He's set fire to the place,' cried Kania. 'Look, the ventilator's open!'

'He's done what he threatened to do,' said the wages clerk.

'Run to the fire alarm, you fool,' shouted the watchman. 'Telephone the police. Kania, you go to the boiler room and shut the elevator hatch or the whole place will catch fire.'

'Too late,' said Kania. 'Look!'

The third-floor windows were suddenly as light as day; they could hear roaring and crackling, and shouts from behind the yard wall . . .

'Ruined! Everything ruined,' said Kania. 'And I'll be out of a job again, damn the bastard!'

VIII

'Name?'

'Kufalt.'

'Christian name!'

'Willi Kufalt.'

'Wilhelm, you mean. Come along.'

The old, old refrain – how well he knew it.

Kufalt walked in front of the warder; a tramp was roaring in a cell, begging for schnapps: 'Just a drop! Just a little drop!'

Then the iron door clanged, they crossed the yard; the town hall was full of people who threw curious or embarrassed glances at Kufalt.

It was nearly noon the following day, but Kufalt, to whom all this was so familiar, wondered why he had been sent for so soon. Or was there to be a second confrontation?

He was now calm, but it was a dark and bitter calm. 'They can do exactly what they like with me. There is no proof against me, and they'll have to let me go. And then! And then!'

Herr Brödchen was in the room with his chief, the large and

imposing chief inspector, who had entrenched himself behind his desk and was looking over some papers. He behaved as though he was not listening to his subordinate's interrogation of Kufalt, but as Kufalt caught him looking up once or twice, he realized that this attitude was merely assumed.

'Sit down, Herr Kufalt,' said Brödchen with notable geniality.

Kufalt said, 'Good morning,' and sat down.

Brödchen cocked his head to one side and surveyed Kufalt quizzically. 'Well, have you thought things over, Herr Kufalt?' he asked.

'I have nothing to think over,' said Kufalt. 'You had no right to keep me here. The woman did not recognize me.'

'Frau Zwietusch certainly recognized you,' replied Brödchen. 'She was merely confused by the artificial light.'

'I have never been inside the place,' said Kufalt.

'Oh yes you have!'

'You'll have to prove it.'

'Frau Zwietusch will swear it.'

'She will, will she? She wondered whether she'd said the hat was green, and whether the man wasn't taller than me. You didn't believe her yourself.'

'Why do you tell such useless lies, Herr Kufalt? You have been there.'

'Never!'

'And what is this?'

Kufalt looked, and stiffened; looked again, and stiffened.

It was a receipt for a subscription to the *Messenger* made out to Frau Emma Zwietusch, Töpferstrasse 97, in the month of January: 'Received, one mark twenty-five; Kufalt.'

He looked once more, and stiffened.

A memory of that room floated to the surface of his mind, a memory of the evening before, when the fat old woman wailed: 'And you told me to go and see about the dinner, as you could wait . . .'

That, or something like it.

At that moment he had been dimly conscious of being on the right track, then the bricklayer appeared and confused him . . . So he had been there, and the recollection of it had slipped his mind among the hundreds of faces during the last few weeks . . .

His head sank to his chest and he looked at no one. 'Shot like Robert Blum,' thought he.

They gave him time.

After a long pause Brödchen said genially: 'Well, Herr Kufalt?'

Kufalt pulled himself together. Very well, he was for it. He would not get out of it as quickly as he had thought. He must resign himself to that. It was always easy for ex-convicts to get back into prison one way or another.

Should he confess, should he produce a tidy confession? If he did it now, to the police, he would perhaps get off more lightly. What would the whole thing let him in for? It was a simple theft, but he had been convicted before: a year? Eighteen months? It was a good thing he hadn't any probation to work off; that was a consolation, at any rate . . .

His brain was in such turmoil that he had almost forgotten the presence of the police officers. Then he once more felt their eyes upon him and he heard Brödchen say impatiently: 'We are still waiting, Herr Kufalt?'

(Why did he persist in saying 'Herr'?)

'All right.' Kufalt shook himself. 'Yes, I've been in the place.'

'Then why didn't you say so at once?'

'I thought I'd get away with it.'

'You thought we would let you out, and you could do a bolt, eh?'

'Yes.'

'Well?'

'I thought I'd be able to put the old woman off the scent.'

'Ah – so you took the three hundred marks?'

'Yes. Of course.'

'You took them? Stole them?!'

'Of course.'

To his astonishment Kufalt observed that Brödchen did not seem at all pleased. Brödchen gazed at him reflectively and chewed his lower lip. The other officer also stopped turning over papers and surveyed this candid criminal.

'I pinched it,' said Kufalt, feeling the need to amplify his confession. 'I needed money, I wanted to marry.'

'But you were earning a great deal of money.'

'It wasn't enough.'

Silence fell.

Chief and subordinate eyed each other. Kufalt again observed them both. Something had gone wrong, so much was clear. The chief inspector leaned towards the detective inspector and whispered something in his ear. Brödchen again looked meditatively at Kufalt and nodded slowly once or twice.

'Herr Kufalt,' he said; 'you are quite sure you stole that money?'

'Of course I am.'

'And what else have you been up to?'

The question cut through Kufalt like a knife. His heart went into spasm for a moment, and then he said with a foolish smile: 'Nothing at all, sir; that was my first attempt.'

'No it wasn't, don't tell lies! We have made inquiries. You—have . . .'

Brödchen leaned forward and glared at Kufalt.

Thoughts raced through Kufalt's brain: had they caught Batzke? Made inquiries? He had never heard a policeman use such a phrase. It was just bluff – well, he could out-glare the old bull-head: bull-head and brains, the arms of Mecklenburg . . .

He returned the policeman's glare.

And he was right; Herr Brödchen could not finish the sentence he had so craftily begun.

'If you want to find yourself in the cells for a bit, Kufalt . . .' he said instead.

'A few nights in jug won't do me any harm,' said Kufalt bitterly.

Brödchen glossed over this, obviously not understanding Kufalt's anger.

'Where did you find the money?'

'In the chest of drawers?'

'First, second or third drawer?'

'In the top drawer. No, I don't remember exactly, I was rather excited.'

'Whereabouts was it?'

'Under some linen, I think.'

'How did you find it? Did anyone tell you where the money was?'

'Oh, I just had a look round because the old woman was so long in the kitchen.'

'Ah, indeed!' Brödchen meditatively rubbed his ill-shaven cheeks. 'Indeed. And we can draw up a statement accordingly?'

'Yes.'

'And you will sign it?'

'Yes.'

'And go to prison?'

'Yes.'

'You'll get about two years.'

'So I thought, Detective Inspector,' said Kufalt cheekily, but looking at Brödchen with an air of mock humility. He had realized that they were merely bluffing, and that that statement would never be drawn up.

'Kick him out, Brödchen,' said the chief inspector suddenly. 'I'm sick of this liar.'

'Very good, sir.'

Brödchen stood up stiffly and Kufalt started to his feet at this outburst.

'And the other matter?' asked Brödchen in an undertone.

'Kick him out, I tell you! Just look at him! A bloke like that will hang himself all right, we don't need to worry. You'll soon be back again, my lad,' he shouted into Kufalt's face, shaking his fist.

'Good morning,' said Kufalt politely, as Brödchen took him out of the office.

'What on earth is the matter, Detective Inspector?' he asked when he got outside. 'Why is he in such a rage? Didn't I steal the money?'

'You clear off, young man. Get your things from the cells and hop it. I'll give them a ring on the phone.'

'But have I made a cock-up somehow? I don't understand, I wish you'd tell me . . .'

'If you get into our hands again, my lad, you'd better watch out!'

Kufalt looked into the sallow face, now quivering with anger.

'I've got them worked up all right,' he thought.

'A night in the cells won't do *me* any harm, Detective Inspector,' he said, and this time Brödchen understood.

'Listen here!' he shouted.

But Kufalt was already on the way to the cells to recover his possessions.

IX

Two hours later Kufalt was sitting in the train for Hamburg.

He felt as he had done on the day of his discharge in May: he must start all over again, and how he did not know.

It was not quite as it had been in May; he knew he would not start again in that way.

This time he would try the other route. He was sick of all this futile struggle. No more of that.

'Look,' Herr Kraft had said to him, 'we heard from Brödchen that you didn't take the money, but all the same . . .'

'Do you know who did take it?' asked Kufalt with some curiosity.

'What! Don't you know? It was old man Zwietusch himself. You're surprised!'

'And he was going to break all the bones in my body,' said Kufalt in genuine astonishment. 'What did he take it for?'

'He drinks. For eighteen months all went well, he belonged to the temperance movement, but now he's on the booze again. He's making up for lost time.'

'The old bastard!' said Kufalt with emphasis. 'And I was going to do a stretch instead of him. Did Brödchen uncover it?'

'No, he didn't. Zwietusch had deposited the money with a publican so he could go and booze when he felt like it, and the old woman wouldn't find it on him. Well, the publican reported it when he heard about your story.'

'So it's all over the town?' asked Kufalt.

'Yes,' said Kraft with emphasis. And he added hurriedly: 'And you see, Kufalt, I'm afraid we shan't be able to keep you on here. So long as it wasn't known, you understand? But now, when it's all over the place, you see. When you called at houses, we would be made responsible.'

Kufalt looked at him for a moment in silence. 'But nothing has gone missing before,' he said.

'No, no, no – I don't say it has. But all sorts of things might be said, and it would be very unpleasant for you.'

'I did my job all right.'

'You did indeed. We don't dispute that. Our best canvasser! But as things are . . . we'll gladly pay you compensation – thirty marks, no, fifty marks, eh, Herr Freese? Though you've earned good money here. But you understand . . .'

They could not get the parting over quickly enough.

'You'll have to settle up for my room here, too,' said Kufalt sullenly. 'I shan't stay here, I'll go back to Hamburg.'

'But . . .' began Kraft.

'That'll do,' said Freese. 'Give him what he wants. And, Kufalt, I wouldn't go to the Harders to say goodbye . . .'

Kufalt looked at him wide-eyed.

'Brödchen has been to the Harders.'

So that was the end of that. Very well.

'Here's a copy of our new edition,' said Freese, hurrying after him. 'Just out. There's been a big fire; and one of your . . . by the way . . .' He stopped, then added: 'Well, all the best, Kufalt.'

'It's not the Trehne this time,' said Kufalt, and tried to laugh.

'Oh, the Trehne, the Trehne,' said Freese. 'It won't flow away, you'll always find it there. Besides, in Hamburg you've got the canals . . .'

'No, sir,' said Kufalt. 'In Hamburg I'm going to make a different start. I dare say you may hear of me . . .'

He laughed, and departed; took as much money out of the savings bank as he could at short notice and packed his things, while his anxious landlady prowled about the landing muttering, 'That such people should be allowed out!' And at last he was in the train.

Farewell.

Hilde, Harder, Bruhn, prison, the *Messenger* – farewell.

Now for another chapter.

And he unfolded the latest edition of the *Messenger*.

'Filthy rag,' he murmured.

But he found something, more than a page and a half of it, in the filthy rag, which made him forget his journey.

The timber works had been burnt down.

'In spite of the most active search by the entire town and country police no trace has yet been found of the incendiary, an unskilled workman by the name of Emil Bruhn, who had lately served a sentence of eleven years' imprisonment. It is supposed that he made for Hamburg the same night. The theft of a man's bicycle, during the fire, from outside Kühn's Tavern may perhaps be ascribed to him, and he may have used it . . .'

'Well, Emil my lad, if I meet you in Hamburg, it won't be a case of "Halves, or I'll split"; I won't give you away.'

8

A Job

I

It is early February; Hamburg lies in rain and mist, damp cold and swiftly thawing snow.

When the wind whistles at night over the outer and the inner Alster people pull up their coat collars and hurry to their homes. The luxury shops on the Jungfernstieg display their glittering wares in vain, except for an occasional young couple, still warm and animated after a visit to a theatre or cinema, who stop and look into a window. 'Oh, what a lovely big aquamarine! No, that one in the old silver setting . . .'

'Yes, stunning . . . Come along, let's get home, this damp cold soaks into your shoes.'

Ten minutes later the stream of theatre- and cinema-goers has passed by, the lights in the shop windows are extinguished, iron bars rattle noisily into place, steel grilles are lowered on the inner side of the windows; the street becomes deserted, save only for the shivering girls who stand at the corners waiting for a client.

'Well, darling, what about it?'

'No time, dear, no time,' says a young man in an Ulster and bowler hat. 'Another evening.'

He hurries on. He too has his coat collar turned up, but the damp air and cutting wind seem to leave him indifferent. He whistles cheerfully to himself, and the slushy snow crackles under the firm pressure of his heels.

'My trousers'll give old Fleege a shock tomorrow,' he thinks in passing.

Outside the Alster pavilion stands a policeman. A dark and

menacing figure, sternly surveying the street, but the young man merely whistles all the louder . . .

'That's right. You're about 200 metres too far away!'

And he turns down the Grosse Bleichen.

He now slackens his step. He strolls on cheerfully still, whistling, and then stops by the window of a gentlemen's outfitter's and falls into conversation with a girl. After a while he gives her a cigarette and promises to meet her outside the same shop at eight o'clock the next evening. At the moment, unfortunately, he has an appointment.

After the Grosse Bleichen comes the Wexstrasse.

It seems as though the street lamps burn more dimly here, and there is hardly a human being in sight. The clock on St Michael's church strikes midnight.

The young man has stopped whistling and is walking quietly on. Above him tower the dim walls of the houses, without a glimmer of light; a steamer's foghorn hoots from the harbour and the sound carries so far in the moist air that the steamer might be steering round the next street corner.

When the man reaches the Grosse Neumarkt he stops for a moment and hesitates. He lights another cigarette and goes hurriedly into a restaurant, stands at the counter and orders a grog with double rum.

By the time he has downed this it is twenty past twelve. He pays and goes out into the street. He then retraces his steps and walks along the Wexstrasse again.

At the corner of the Trampgang there's a girl. But this time he doesn't wait until she speaks to him, he speaks to her at once.

And all he says is: 'Well?'

'He's at Lütt's place,' she whispers hurriedly.

'Sure?'

'Honest to God! Am I to get my five marks?'

'Two,' says the man, after brief reflection. 'Here you are. The other three when he's really there.'

'You look out, Ernst,' she says in a warning tone. 'He's a devil. He half killed Emma yesterday and knocked her bloke about until he got all his money out of him.'

'Then he's got money?'

The man seems disappointed.

'Yes, twenty marks, at least.'

'Hmmm . . . Well, see you later.'

'Honest?'

'Honest to God!' he says, imitating her phrase, laughs and moves on.

II

He doesn't turn into the Trampgang; he goes straight on, stops by the Rademachergang, peers down the dark alley, in which a dim gas lamp is burning, looks to the right, looks to the left – and dives into the Alley Quarter.

He turns right, then right again, crosses the Wexstrasse once more, disappears in the Langer Gang, walks a little way down the Düsternstrasse and disappears again in the Schulgang.

He always walks in the middle of the narrower alleys, sometimes stretching out his arms to see whether he can touch the walls on either side. Sometimes he can, but sometimes the alley is too wide.

Until then he has not met a soul. The old timbered houses stand silent and dark, as if they are long since dead; their gables tilt perilously inwards, and nothing of the sky can be seen.

Sometimes a beam of light from a tavern slants across the pavement at his feet; now and again he hears the clashing bells and cymbals of a band, or the rasp of a gramophone. The windows of the taverns are hung with red or yellow curtains.

The man is no longer in the mood for whistling; he walks slowly, he is sweating slightly, and once he feels for something in his hip pocket. All OK, but – it is going to be a tough job, even though he makes light of it in front of the girls.

Well, there's still time to go home.

He's coming into Kugelsplatz, he can already see the red glow from Lütt's Tavern.

Now for it!

Two policemen, tall young men buckled firmly into their greatcoats, the straps of their helmets under their chins and the truncheons at their belts swinging to the rhythm of their walk, march up to him.

They survey this man, out for a late stroll, with sharp, appraising eyes.

'Good evening,' says he, politely taking off his black hat.

'Nasty night,' says one of them in a surprisingly friendly voice. 'Nasty weather. Nasty neighbourhood.'

The man, who has to pass the policemen to get to Kugelsplatz, is forced to stop. The pair plant themselves in front of him and look him up and down as though he were a pretty girl.

'Can one go in there?' asks the man casually, jerking his head towards the light from Lütt's Tavern.

'Why do you want to go in there?' asks the policeman affably, in the soft Holstein dialect.

'It would interest me,' says the man. 'I've heard so much about the Alley Quarter.'

'You'd better not,' whispers the policeman, softly but with emphasis. 'They might – mess you up a bit.'

And he laughs at his own remark.

'Oh!' says the man, disappointed. 'Then where can one go at this time?'

'Home!' roars the other policeman unexpectedly. 'Straight home! We don't want any extra trouble in a place like this.'

Before he can finish the man hastily says, 'Goodnight,' raises his hat again, hurries across Kugelsplatz, runs down the Ebräergang, turns off into the Amidammachergang and emerges for the third time on the Wexstrasse. The girl isn't there any more. He goes quickly down the Wexstrasse and only four minutes later he's again at Kugelsplatz, approaching it this time from the other side.

Kugelsplatz is empty; the red glow from Lütt's window lies peacefully across the cobbled pavement.

For a moment or two the man recovers his breath, wipes the sweat from his face with a handkerchief, feels again for the steel object in his hip pocket, transfers it to his coat pocket and then resolutely presses the worn brass latch on the door of Lütt's Tavern.

III

A voice cried shrilly: 'Look out – cops!'

Silence fell upon the room.

The man closed the door behind him and blinked into the haze. All eyes were upon him.

He took off his hat and said: 'Evening.'

The portly landlord, whose fat, bluish face was distorted by an absurd, shapeless, purple nose, said thickly: 'Evening, Heideprim,' and jerked his head faintly towards a far corner of the room.

'Evening, Mister Policeman,' said a youth. 'Give us a share of the doings.'

'I'm a predator myself like you,' said the man sharply, and tried to smile.

Behind him – he was now standing at the bar – two youths had got up and were brushing against him.

'Back off!' said the man briskly.

'You leave the lad alone,' ordered the landlord. 'He's all right.'

The young men stood irresolute.

'You old crimp,' said one of them. 'We don't want a new mug. There isn't enough to go round.'

'Back off – go and sit down. If you don't sit down, I'll put you on the street. This isn't a paupers' shelter.'

The young men sat, whispering angrily.

The man at the bar had drunk a double brandy. And another.

The young men looked at him enviously. He's got what it takes!

From the far end of the room came a tall, sinister man, large-boned, with hands like battens.

He walked slowly up to the man at the bar, planted himself in front of him, and looked him up and down. It was an evil and malignant look, the low forehead under the black hair was gnarled and wrinkled, the thick-lipped mouth was half open and revealed black, rotten teeth.

'Evening, Batzke,' said the man at the bar, putting a finger to his hat.

Batzke looked at the man, his lips moved. Then he slowly raised his huge hand . . .

'No go,' said the man lightly, but his voice quavered slightly; 'got a gun.'

And the hand in his pocket lifted, so that the outline of the barrel was visible.

Batzke burst out laughing. 'A lad like you – with a gun! I'd have you down before you could shoot.'

The hand came up again.

'I've got the four hundred for you,' said the man quickly.

The other's face changed, the hand dropped. Once more Batzke looked at the man.

Then, with his hands thrust deep into his pockets, he went back to his corner without a word.

The man looked after him. Then he wiped his forehead, which was damp with sweat, and said to the landlord: 'Another brandy.'

He felt that all eyes in the place were on him, though with a different expression in them now. He swallowed some brandy and looked inquiringly at the landlord, who shook his head.

'Not now,' he whispered. 'He's got someone there.'

The man finished his brandy, paid, laid a finger to his bowler and said once more: 'Evening.'

'Bye, Heideprim,' said the landlord, and the man departed.

IV

Outside, the girl was waiting.

'Was he there?' she asked.

'Here's your three marks,' said the man. 'Wait till he comes out. Don't mention any name, tell him the four hundred's waiting for him. Understand?'

'Yes,' said the girl. 'The four hundred's waiting for you.'

'Then bring him along.'

'And what do I get?' asked the girl. 'It's cold, and my shoes are soaked through.'

'Three more marks,' said the man. 'Take it or leave it.'

'Right,' said the girl.

The man walked quickly to the Wexstrasse, looked to either side of him (he did not want to meet the policemen just then) and then hurried down it to the Fuhlentwiete.

He went a little way down the Fuhlentwiete, looked carefully about him, not a soul in sight; he opened a door, stepped into the house and carefully shut the door behind him. He made his way up an unlit staircase, opened a landing door, switched on the light and said in an undertone: 'It's all right, Frau Pastorin. Don't wake up.'

He heard the woman rustle in her bed, and then a shrill elderly voice replied: 'All right, Herr Lederer. What was the theatre like?'

'Quite good,' said the man, hanging up his overcoat and hat in a cupboard. 'A friend and his wife may be coming in – please don't disturb yourself; I can heat the water for the grog.'

'Thank you,' said the old woman. 'Sleep well. Breakfast as usual?'

'Breakfast as usual,' said the man. 'Goodnight.'

He switched off the light in the entrance hall and went into his room. There he stood for a moment in the darkness and pondered.

The wind roared round the house, whirling great flurries of snow against the windows.

'Nasty night. Nasty weather. Nasty neighbourhood,' he repeated to himself, and sighed.

He stood for a while there in the darkness, listening to the wind and the snow. 'Perhaps he won't come,' he thought.

'Yes he will. He'll come tomorrow. If he's only got twenty marks – four hundred are sure to fetch him.'

He switched on the light.

It was a neat and pleasant room, dark oak furniture, large dark armchairs, an old gun-cupboard and a stag's-horn chandelier. The bed stood behind a large green silk screen.

The man took a packet of cigarettes and a box of cigars off a bookshelf and put them on a small table. He produced a bottle of brandy, and a bottle of rum from the sideboard, and set them also on the table, together with three tumblers, three tea glasses and a sugar bowl.

He stood for a moment in thought, and listened. 'These old houses are too quiet,' he thought. Then he got out three teaspoons.

Again he pondered, and walked slowly towards the door.

Then he turned back, took his wallet out of his coat and counted out eight fifty-mark notes. He folded them together, put them on the small table and set a heavy marble ashtray on top of them. He made quite sure that the notes were not visible beneath the ashtray.

Once more he pondered. He disappeared behind the screen and emerged in slippers and a smoking jacket, carrying a pistol in his hand.

He surveyed the two armchairs, but was not quite satisfied; he pulled a wicker chair up to the table. The chair had arms, and cushions on the back and seat; he placed the pistol by the bottom cushion and covered it with a handkerchief.

Then he stepped back two paces and surveyed the scene. It looked all right; there was no sign of the pistol and the handkerchief lay as though forgotten.

He sighed softly, looked at the clock (it was quarter past one) and went into the kitchen, where he put a saucepan over a small gas jet.

Then back into the sitting room; he picked up a book and began to read.

Time passed; it was deathly quiet in the house, but the wind seemed to be rising. He sat and read; his pale, drawn face, with its weak chin and sensual mouth, was weary, but he went on reading.

Then he looked again at the clock (fifty-seven minutes past two), glanced dubiously at the array on the small table, got up and listened in the entrance hall. Not a sound. He went softly across the entrance hall, looked into the kitchen, poured some water into the now half-empty saucepan, opened the flat door and listened down the staircase.

Not a sound.

When he got back to his room he was shivering with cold; he poured himself a glass of brandy, a second, and a third . . .

He laid the book over the pistol and began to pace up and down. He walked with a light and restless step: a floorboard creaked when he trod on it, and so deeply was he immersed in his thoughts that after the third creak his foot unconsciously avoided that particular board.

There was a faint sound outside in the entrance hall, he opened the door and said in a low voice: 'Here. Don't make a noise.'

Batzke appeared, followed by the girl; he looked in better humour than before.

'Well, Kufalt, old codger . . .'

'No names, please,' said the man quickly. 'Ilse, get the water for the grog, it must have boiled long ago.'

And when she was outside he said: 'By the way, I call myself Ernst Lederer . . .'

'Do you?' said Batzke. 'Well, pour me out a glass of brandy, Lederer. Or may I take the bottle?'

V

The widowed Frau Pastorin Fleege had never had such a nice lodger as the actor Ernst Lederer, who had been with her since the end of January. Not only was he generous, and had himself said that fifty marks was much too little for such a fine room, with heating and breakfast included, and had offered seventy-five; he was also very lavish with flowers, boxes of chocolates and theatre tickets. And all that for an old woman of seventy!

But the most delightful thing of all was that he liked to sit and talk to her. She was old, her dear husband had now been dead for more than twenty years and her daughter was married to a squire up in Danish Flensburg. She seldom came to see her, and the old lady had hardly any friends left; those she did have were just as old and frail as she was and could no longer pay visits.

She had sat for so long alone in her little room and she had, too, so often been afraid of her various lodgers, male and female. They were loud and rude, paid irregularly, spoilt the furniture and were always wanting things done for them . . . But Herr Lederer, the actor!

At first she had not liked him very much. He had been loud and over-familiar when he took the room, he had laughed a great deal for no apparent reason and looked at her in a way she did not care for; then he had suddenly grown quiet and taciturn . . .

But later on she had got to know him better. Frau Pastorin Fleege had a little grey cat called 'Pussi', quite an ordinary house cat which, as a little half-starved kitten, had walked into her flat one day. She had got used to Pussi, a nice, friendly little cat; you could talk to it in the twilight and it would purr so prettily as if in answer . . .

But as it had once been a street cat, it kept its roving instincts and could not shed them. However careful Frau Fleege might be, Pussi managed to slip through an open window, or dart between her legs at the door when she was talking to the milkman – and was off.

Then followed hours, often days, of anxiety for the Frau Pastorin. So far as her old legs allowed, she would go round to all the neighbours and inquire after the cat. But so many of them were rude, laughed at her, and called her a 'silly old fool' or 'crazy-cat'. They did not understand how anxious she was; there were so many nasty big dogs round about. She knew quite well that you should not get too deeply attached to dumb animals, but her husband had been so long dead, and her daughter Hete lived so very far away.

On these occasions she cried a great deal, big, shining tears ran noiselessly down her face, for she did not sob. But life was so difficult all alone, and the good Lord might have taken pity on her long ago.

Herr Lederer had only been living with her three or four days when Pussi got out again. At first she did not mean to mention it. Pussi had always come back, but when, exhausted by her first inquiries, she was sitting by the window and a motor car screeched so shrilly outside and she started out of her chair, thinking it might be Pussi crying – then she went to him.

At first he had not understood; he had been sitting at his desk with his head in his hands, she thought he was not well . . . But then, when he lifted his head, she saw he was in trouble. She wished she had not come, but he nodded at once and said: 'Let's see what we can do . . .'

She tried to stop him, and said it wasn't serious, and she was sure Herr Lederer had to study his part for the evening . . .

She was wearing an odd little black cap, a flat object made of black glass pearls, a relic of past days, and Herr Lederer could not take his eyes off it. It had slipped askew.

So he went out to look for the cat.

He reported back to her every quarter or half an hour. He had seen Pussi in such and such a place but had not been able to catch her . . . He had bought a dried herring to attract her if he ever caught sight of her again . . . Frau Lehmann, at the greengrocer's shop, had said she had seen Pussi by the refuse bin in the yard . . .

And then Frau Pastorin Fleege had had to remind him that it was high time he went to the theatre. He was such a strange, reckless person; he had shrugged his shoulders and said: 'Oh, the theatre!', but then he pulled himself together and went.

He was back at half past eleven – never had he come home so early – and knocked at her door – she was not yet asleep – and had just said: 'I've got Pussi.'

She had come out, with a lace nightcap over her thin white hair, and wearing a bedjacket and a slip, just as her dear husband had seen her for the last time, but she had not felt embarrassed; the tears were still pouring down her cheeks.

'Now please, Frau Pastorin,' he said. 'Here's Pussi. She was just sitting by the front door. I had nothing to do with it.'

And he would not hear of any thanks, he never would. He went to the police station for her and reported his own arrival ('they're often so rude to an old lady'); he ordered the briquettes for her, and got up at eight in the morning when they were delivered, so that for the first time she got the full amount and none of them were broken; he put up the net curtains for her and carried the refuse bucket down to the yard . . .

And never a word of thanks. No, when she tried to thank him he was quite embarrassed and slipped into his room. Or he was angry, and said sometimes: 'Nothing to thank me for, Frau Pastorin, one should never thank, until the end . . .'

She often wondered whether that might mean he was going to leave her again soon.

Yes, he was an obliging, quiet, pleasant man; but best of all, in the afternoons when it grew dark he sat with her and listened to her stories about her husband and the lovely rectory in the Wilstermarsch, where her daughter Hete had been born, and where her happiest days had been spent.

He either sat silent in his chair, or paced softly up and down smoking a cigarette. (She did not usually care for cigarettes, but she thought his cigarettes smelt good.) He liked to listen, he never seemed bored, now and again he asked a sympathetic question, and they seemed to agree about everything.

In her high, clear old voice, which sometimes rose into a sort of lilt, she would talk about the rectory, with its sixty acres of land. Her dear husband had known nothing whatever about farming, but it had given him so much pleasure to till the soil himself, with a man to help him of course. He always insisted on doing his own ploughing and afterwards, utterly exhausted but tremendously happy, he would say: 'Hete' (her own as well as her daughter's name was Hete), 'Hete, now I shall preach a much better sermon at the harvest festival.'

'Was there water there?' asked Herr Lederer.

'Of course, we had everything.'

And she told him how one day in January, when little Hete was just five years old, she had fallen into the pond. And quite by herself and without crying she had got out and crept into the coach house, and there sat in the dusty old landau, taken all her clothes off and carefully hung them piece by piece up to dry: she had not meant to go home until they were all dry.

'And she was wearing her black velvet dress that wouldn't have dried for weeks. But she didn't even catch a cold. Now she has her own children; they must be quite big by now . . . That is the eldest, Ingrid – do you like the name Ingrid? They are Danish now, the children live in Copenhagen, you see, Herr Lederer.'

But now and again the Frau Pastorin remembered that she was always talking about herself; she blushed and asked pardon, and said it was time Herr Lederer told her about his own life.

But there was not much of it; he had not much to tell. He was just an actor, he went to the theatre every evening, and after that spent half the night rehearsing. No, he was not an important person, just about halfway up the programme; she had seen him on the stage . . .

Yes, she had, he often gave her tickets. She had not recognized him at first, but he explained that that was just the art of disguise. Once he had been a general and once, in a fairy story, a water spirit – so it was clear he had to look as different as possible; and, after all, it was natural she should not recognize him, as her eyes were not what they had been. His name, Ernst Lederer, had duly appeared on the programme, and she was very proud of her lodger and put every programme carefully away. But Kufalt . . .

When Kufalt arrived in Hamburg he had not gone to lodge with Frau Pastorin Fleege straight away; not until a few days later, when he had determined on a definite plan, and the unsuspecting Frau Pastorin had been a part of that plan.

He had first put up in a shabby little hotel where he had slept for a few nights. In the daytime he had tramped the streets and tried to make up his mind what to do with his life.

He reviewed the last nine months since his release: those nine months had not been good ones. He had struggled, he had abased himself, he had been cowardly, he had fawned and flattered, but he had also worked very hard – and it had all been in vain.

He realized that it was not merely the fault of all the others – Teddy, Jauch, Marcetus, Maack, Hilde, and so on – it had been his own fault too. For a while everything would seem to be going smoothly, and then something pulled him up. He could not move on steadily in a given direction; he played the fool with himself; he chickened out a dozen times and was cowardly when there was absolutely no need; then suddenly he tore into a rage and threw his weight about and upset everything, when there was equally no need. Why was he like that? Had he been like that before?

No, it was not only because he had something to hide. It was because something within him was incomplete, because he was really still in prison. And he always felt how easy it would be to return.

He had once told the governor, while still in prison, that he was like a man deprived of hands. The governor had disputed this, but it was so. For five years he had been relieved of everything, not even had he been allowed to think for himself, he had merely had to obey orders, and now he had to act alone . . . and he could not do it, deprived of hands. What was the use of work, and humiliation, and privation, when it led to nothing?

He thought of the long succession of familiar faces that he had seen return to prison during his five years' sentence. They came back, they all came back. Or else they were in other prisons, or doing what would get them back one day. Batzke was absolutely right: a man must choose his time and pull off a big thing, and then, if he had to do another stretch, he would feel it had been worth his while.

Take the case of Emil Bruhn. Kufalt now knew from the newspapers that he would never meet his old friend Emil in Hamburg or anywhere else, or ever be tempted to squeal on him. Emil had been found under the debris with his skull battered in, and an itinerant Polish workman had confessed to having murdered him and set fire to the factory.

Emil Bruhn; eleven years a slave, friendly, hard-working, with such few and trifling claims on life: the pictures, a girl and a modest job. And what had been the end of it all? An ex-convict was always an ex-convict. The most humane punishment would be to hang them all on the spot.

When had he felt so wholly at ease, when had he been so completely master of himself during those last few months and known exactly what to do and say? Where was his true home?

Superintendent Specht had complained to the investigating magistrate about him, the chief inspector had had him thrown out of the room and Detective Inspector Brödchen had fairly roared with rage at him.

When they treated him as an old lag, then he felt at home, then he could talk and act impudently – this he felt comfortable with, this was a part that he had learnt.

But if this was so, if he had really become a criminal during his imprisonment, and if he must go back again, then he needed to pull himself together for three or four weeks before the great coup was landed. He must no longer waver on the edge of respectability, he must carefully plan a coup on a large scale, while he still had money. It would not be easy, his cowardice and indecision stood in his way; he was not a natural criminal, he had become one, he had learnt to be a criminal.

So Kufalt walked about and pondered; he went into the forests and the Vierlande, he climbed the Süllberg, he looked down onto the Elbe, the ships and the villages, and all the wintry landscape; he was a man like the rest, indistinguishable from his fellows, he was no criminal type – but he was caught and fettered. And he hammered out his plan.

He became the actor Ernst Lederer, took a room with the poor little old Frau Pastorin Fleege, frequented the Jungfernstieg regularly, and sent the hooker Ilse in search of Batzke.

VI

'Send the tart away,' said Batzke.

'She's a nice girl, her name's Ilse,' replied Kufalt.

'She'll mess up our business,' said Batzke.

'I've got no business to mess up,' replied Kufalt.

A brief pause followed. Batzke looked round the room, then helped himself to another brandy.

'Nice billet,' he observed.

'Not bad,' replied Kufalt.

'When we went to see the prison at Fuhlsbüttel that day, you were pretty well cleaned out,' said Batzke pensively.

'I was,' said Kufalt.

'You couldn't have rented a room like this.'

'A room can always be rented.'

'But?'

'Yes, there's the rent to pay.'

'And the brandy? And the rum? And the cigarettes?'

'Maybe it's swag, Batzke.'

'Have you got the four hundred for me?'

'Perhaps, Batzke.'

A short pause, and then Batzke leaned forward, and said furiously: 'You fetched me here for that four hundred. Have you got it, or not?'

Their faces were now barely a metre apart. Batzke's eyes blazed with fury, Kufalt's face was pale and twitching, but his looked firmly into Batzke's.

'Look, Batzke,' he said.

With a faint jerk of the head he indicated the pistol in his right hand.

Batzke looked, stood up and shook his great carpenter's shoulders, one heavier than the other from long years of labour at the plane. He paced up and down the room and said: 'Something has come over you, Kufalt. You've changed a good bit.'

And Kufalt said: 'Look at the room here – a nice billet, says you; nifty. And the stuff. And I've got money. And the four hundred for you, perhaps, too – perhaps it's all this' – with a wave of his hand – 'that's made me different.'

Batzke began pacing up and down again.

'Well, tell me what it is you want; you didn't have that tart look for me for nothing.'

The girl came in with the hot water for the grog.

Kufalt looked at her thoughtfully, then at Batzke, then at the girl again, and said:

'Only two glasses. You can clear off, Ilse. Here's five marks.'

Batzke peered at the money, but could see no signs of anything more than the five-mark note, which had clearly been held in readiness.

And he said indignantly: 'You might at least give her a hot grog, if she's got to go out on the street again. Don't overdo it, Kufalt.'

Kufalt looked at him and grinned. 'Aha! Not in such a hurry, eh? Have a grog, Ilse, and be off with you!'

'Kufalt?' said the girl doubtfully, as she drank. 'I thought it was Lederer.'

'Did I say Kufalt?' said Batzke scornfully. 'Go and wash your ears. His name's Einfalt. And that's what he is.'

The girl looked suspiciously from one to the other with quick, darting eyes and said: 'All right, I'll go.'

'Have another, Mary, my girl,' said Batzke with a wink at Kufalt.

But the girl refused. She tossed her head and said she wouldn't be treated like this, and she wasn't going to prison for five marks and a brandy, and besides, her name wasn't Mary.

Batzke grinned.

'All right, Ilse,' said Kufalt. 'We'll meet tomorrow as usual.'

'You needn't bother,' she replied. 'You with your nasty friend and your two names.'

But she stood where she was, and surveyed the pair with a provocative eye.

'Now then, hop it,' said Kufalt impatiently.

'I shall go when I choose,' she said with rising anger. 'I won't stand for any nonsense from the likes of you. And if I went to the police now . . . I heard all you said about rent and swag . . .'

But she got no further.

In a flash Batzke was up, seized her with both his arms and said savagely: 'Now, Mary, my girl,' and crushed her so that she cried out with pain.

'Now get out,' he said. 'You know me, eh?'

He let her go. She stood there for a moment, uncertain whether she should begin to cry, and left.

'And if the job comes off,' said Kufalt, 'I'll have to get another room, just because you can't be too careful.'

'What job?' asked Batzke. 'First I've heard of it.'

The situation had strangely altered. Kufalt had been so easily the superior, it was Batzke who had made mistakes. And now Kufalt, in some mysterious way, had suddenly become the weaker party. (Was it just because Batzke had grabbed hold of the girl?)

'I've got a scheme, Batzke,' he said.

'Must be a funny sort of scheme,' said Batzke scornfully. 'You were never up to much.'

'Very well, then,' said Kufalt angrily, pushed away the ashtray and revealed the little pile of notes. 'Take your money and clear out. I'll get someone else.'

Batzke looked at the money, picked it up, counted it contentedly, put it in his pocket and said in a tone of high satisfaction: 'Now, Willi, drink your grog before it gets cold. And then tell me all about it. Old lags like us . . .'

VII

Again the wind was howling, again it was snowing, again the time was a little after eleven at night.

Batzke and Kufalt came strolling arm in arm down the Jungfernstieg, lingered now and again in front of a shop, looked contentedly at the windows and finally stopped at the jeweller's where the young couple of the previous evening had admired the aquamarine ring.

But Kufalt took no interest in aquamarines. His only interest was price.

'That's the tray I meant,' he said.

It was a large, blue velvet tray, close behind the glass in the centre of the shop window; and on it was an array of glittering, sparkling diamond rings.

Batzke whistled through his teeth. 'Yes,' he observed; 'very pretty little stones.'

'It's time,' said Kufalt. 'Come along.' He walked with Batzke to the Reesendamm; they turned and strolled for a short distance along the opposite pavement. Then they stopped and leaned against the parapet on the inner Alster, a little to one side of the shop.

'Half past eleven,' said Kufalt. 'They'll soon be here.'

He broke off and added hastily: 'Look, there's the watchman.'

A fat man in civilian clothes with a walrus moustache emerged from the Alster arcades, walked past the shop, scrutinizing the windows as he went, turned, passed the shop once more and disappeared again into the arcades.

'He's always watching the shop,' said Kufalt.

'Not a powerful man,' estimated Batzke. 'A good punch under the belt and he'd gulp for air.'

'Not on your life,' said Kufalt quickly. 'You'll soon see, there's a much better dodge than that.'

The Jungfernstieg had become lively. Crowds were coming out of the cinemas and theatres, wrapped in evening cloaks and coats, some hurrying, some strolling along for a few paces and looking into the shop windows before they disappeared into the Alster pavilion or in the direction of the Hotel Esplanade or the Four Seasons.

The weather was still bad. The passers-by hastened as they had done the night before, and in ten minutes the Jungfernstieg lay almost deserted.

'Now you'll see,' said Kufalt.

He had pulled out his watch, and said: 'Forty-two minutes past eleven. He'll be coming now.'

From among the columns appeared the fat watchman, looked up and down the street, slowly drew a bunch of keys out of his pocket, unlocked the door of the shop and disappeared inside. Then he locked the shop door from within.

Kufalt stood nearly in darkness with the watch still in his hand.

'Now he's in the shop,' he said. 'Eleven forty-four – eleven forty-five – wait, we've still time, eleven forty-six – ten seconds, twenty seconds, thirty seconds – wait – forty seconds – hell! – fifty seconds – there! Now the grilles are coming down. Come on, Batzke.'

He took Batzke by the arm and hurried him in the direction of his lodging.

'Have you got it?' he said eagerly. 'A shop with a gorgeous display like that is naturally watched day and night. But there's one thing they haven't thought about: the two and a half minutes when the watchman's in the shop letting down the grilles. For just that time he can't be on the lookout. In two and a half minutes a man can smash the window, grab the tray and run. Now what do you think about that?'

'Hmm . . . yes,' said Batzke dubiously. 'And where are the nearest cops?'

'I know all about that,' boasted Kufalt. 'One at the Alster pavilion and one at the entrance to the Bergstrasse. But he's a traffic cop.'

'Ah!' said Batzke. 'Well, we might talk the thing over.'

'Talk it over?' said Kufalt indignantly. 'What is there to talk over? There are at least a hundred and twenty thousand marks' worth of rings on that tray.'

'Better not think of that just yet,' said Batzke. 'They're in the shop window. And it's going to be a hell of a job getting them out of it.'

VIII

That night Batzke and Kufalt sat for a long time together on the Fuhlentwiete.

Batzke was once more the great man, and Kufalt had to confess himself a novice. He had imagined he had made a really great discovery. That two and a half minutes seemed to him a brilliant idea. But Batzke sat and simply laughed at him.

'Yes, that's what you think; just turn up, smash the window with a brick, grab the tray and bolt round the corner. I wish it was all so simple.'

'But where's the difficulty?' asked Kufalt angrily. 'Of course we'd have to run for it properly, but that's worth doing for a hundred and twenty thousand marks.'

'Look, Kufalt,' observed Batzke pensively; 'you're nicely fixed up here – does it all come from smashing shop windows?'

'No, certainly not,' said Kufalt.

'Just so. It will have to be a rather large hole,' said Batzke, thoughtfully, 'so as to get the tray through it quickly. And these bloody windows – I don't know, perhaps you can only make a small hole with a brick, just the size of the brick, only big enough to get your hand through and grab twenty or thirty rings. No, we'd have to try it out first.'

'How are you going to do that?' asked Kufalt. 'Are you going to smash the window just to see?'

'Fathead,' said Batzke. 'There's plenty of new buildings in the suburbs where the shops are still empty. We might go out two or three nights and practise till we can manage it right.'

'Nah, that sounds pretty risky. I don't want to be nabbed for breaking a window in an empty shop.'

'A hundred and twenty thousand marks can't be got without risk,' said Batzke. 'But there's another thing. How do we know the tray can be got out so easily? Perhaps it's fixed?'

Kufalt took refuge in sullen silence. He had thought they might bring it off the very next night. And here was Batzke making one difficulty after another.

'And another thing,' said Batzke. 'It can't be done without a car. How on earth do you suppose you can run through the streets with a tray half a square metre, at half past eleven at night, when there are still plenty of people about? If the fuzz come after you and start shooting, I suppose you'll just take the rings off the tray and put 'em in your pocket. That's how you figured it out, isn't it?'

'Oh, if you're just going to make difficulties . . .' said Kufalt with rising irritation.

'Look here, my boy,' said Batzke. 'Do you want the rings or don't you? Your idea is the way an amateur would set about it, not an old hand. Amateurs do sometimes bring a job off, but it's an off chance. No; we must have a car, and it will have to be pinched that same afternoon so that the police won't know the number. Can you drive, anyway?'

'No,' said Kufalt, viewing his cherished scheme with diminishing pride.

'And then comes the hardest thing of all,' said Batzke. 'How do you think you're going to sell the stuff?'

'Surely there are fences for that sort of thing,' said Kufalt angrily.

'There are,' agreed Batzke. 'But if you wait to fix it up until you've got the rings, he won't give you more than a thousand marks for the whole caboodle, because he's got you by the short and curlies. And he may not give you anything at all, as there'll be a reward out of at least ten thousand marks and he may not get another chance of getting on the right side of the police.'

'All right, let's drop it,' said Kufalt, furious. 'I see you don't want to come in.'

'Who says I don't?' protested Batzke in amazement. 'That two and a half minutes is a good tip, too good to let go. A job like that doesn't come along every year. No, no more brandy. I'll go for a bit of a walk and think it over. I'll come round here again tomorrow at ten.'

IX

Ten, eleven, twelve: no Batzke.

Kufalt unscrewed the stove and then screwed it up again; he poured out a brandy and tipped it back into the bottle (he must keep his head clear). Still no Batzke.

Finally he had a brandy and another, and a third; he was furious.

'He's done the dirty on me, the bastard, he's bolted with my four hundred marks and left me standing! I can't do it on my own. Or can I?'

For a moment he felt very bold. He would do it by himself. Batzke, with all his ridiculous objections, and all his talk about amateurs, would see what he, Kufalt, could do.

The rings glittered with a soft, alluring radiance; he saw himself carrying them to dim and rather vague haunts where he would have whispered talks with fences. The police were close on his heels. He leapt out of the window and dashed away into the night . . .

'Rubbish,' he thought to himself. 'I'll never do it. Perhaps I couldn't even have done it with Batzke helping. That sort of thing isn't . . . isn't in my line, but . . .'

A sudden suspicion flashed into his mind: he felt certain Batzke would nab the tip and do the job. Batzke would drop him and get away with the hundred and twenty thousand marks, and he would be left behind, penniless, done out of his scheme, without any prospects of a life that would at least be worth living – still in Frau Pastorin Fleege's flat, God knows for how long . . .

He drank more brandy and flung himself onto his bed; he was beginning to doze.

In his half-sleep it seemed to him as if Batzke came into his room. He just suddenly stood there, a dark and sinister figure in the middle of the room; he did not look round, he sat down in a chair as though the room were his own, reached for the bottle and drank, took a cigar out of the box, looked at it contemptuously, snapped it in half and lit a cigarette.

Kufalt wanted to get up and tell his visitor to behave himself. Indescribable anger and bitterness came over him, but he could not shake off his lethargy . . .

'I must be dreaming,' he said to reassure himself.

Batzke had got up. He paced up and down the room for a while. Then he drew aside the green screen, from behind which Kufalt had noticed him, and stood in silence by Kufalt's bed. He gazed down at the sleeping man.

Slowly Kufalt opened his eyes. Batzke stared steadily down at him.

'So you've come at last?' said Kufalt heavily.

'Aren't you rather drunk?' asked Batzke. 'That won't do; you can get drunk afterwards.'

'I don't think,' said Kufalt, sitting on the edge of the bed, 'that we've got quite as far as that.'

'Now listen,' said Batzke; 'I've been thinking this business over. It can be done. But I want to do it without you. You'd be no use.'

'What do you mean, without me?' said Kufalt. 'I put you up to the job and I want my share. You said yourself that a job like that didn't come along every year.'

'Who's talking about the job, fathead?' said Batzke angrily. 'We'll discuss that later on. I'm talking about bringing it off.'

'Well, and what about it?' said Kufalt.

'I don't want you with me. If I take it on, it'll be a big show. It'll be in all the papers. I'll be a big number. And I'm not going to have you messing it up.'

'Of course I won't mess it up, Batzke,' said Kufalt eagerly.

'You mess up everything,' said Batzke. 'I know you from prison days. Always nosing around, always sneaking to the governor; talking's your line. I'm not saying,' he added more mildly, 'that you're not on for a nice little bit of embezzlement, or fraud on women, like your old landlady here, where there's no guts needed nor presence of mind – you'd be quite up to that sort of thing. I'm sure you've been raising money that way . . .'

Kufalt was silent for very shame. He did not dare say that even this compliment was an exaggeration; he could not admit to the honest way in which he had earned his money.

'. . . But,' continued Batzke inexorably, 'you must keep your fingers out of this job. I admit it's a first-rate tip. I tell you what, I'll throw back your four hundred marks for it, though I'll need money badly for the job.'

'Certainly not,' said Kufalt.

'I don't want to be mean,' said Batzke, his voice becoming quite touching. 'After all, we were in jug together a pretty long time. If I bring this business off you shall have another four hundred marks.'

'You're crazy,' said Kufalt angrily. 'A hundred and twenty thousand marks, and eight hundred for me, when I put you up to the job? You can't mean it!'

'Who's crazy?' said Batzke, who had also lost his temper. 'What's all this about a hundred and twenty thousand marks? Do you suppose any fence would pay us the shop sale price?'

'No; but half of it, at least,' said Kufalt emphatically.

'You don't know what you're talking about,' said Batzke contemptuously. 'I've been making some inquiries this morning. Diamonds are very difficult to get rid of, especially a packet like that all at once. They'll have to be sent abroad; to Amsterdam or London. And the settings are worth nothing. If we get five thousand marks in all that'll be a great deal, and I'll need at least four men to help.'

'And you don't need me?'

'What for? To smash the window? To grab the tray? To go into the shop and get them to show you the whole tray full of rings, and them not smell something fishy at once? Or make a getaway at 100 kilometres an hour? What do you really propose?'

'I mean to be in it whatever happens,' said Kufalt bitterly. 'It's no good, Batzke, I know you too well, you want to do me down; and five thousand marks is rubbish, you ought to have said fifty thousand.'

'Well,' said Batzke contemptuously, 'it's hopeless talking to a fool.'

And he turned to go.

'I'll drop the job.' And he added, as he stood in the doorway, 'There's better tips, don't you forget that.'

'Right,' said Kufalt. 'But I promise you I'll stand outside the shop every evening, and if you try to bring it off, I'll squeal.'

Batzke turned quickly round. He looked at Kufalt angrily, raised his fist and walked towards him.

'All right,' shouted Kufalt wildly. 'Knock me down. But that won't help you. Not unless you kill me.'

'Very well, Willi,' said Batzke suddenly. 'We'll do it together. You go out this afternoon and get hold of a hard-baked brick. And you might get a paving stone too. And just think how to carry them so they'll be handy, but can't be seen. And we'll meet this evening about half past ten at the Lattenkamp overhead railway station. There must be some nice new suburbs round about there. You can get some good practice.'

Kufalt was not particularly pleased with this prospect. He had envisaged himself as being the one to put his hand through the hole in the window and grab the tray of rings. But he was tired now, worn out by his quarrel with Batzke, though glad he had got his way.

'Wanted to do me down,' he thought; 'the bastard. He hasn't any luck! Five thousand marks. I don't think! My share ought to be ten thousand at least. How am I to get a paving stone? You can't just pick up a paving stone off the street and take it away! And hard-baked bricks – are there soft bricks? How am I to carry the things? What a nuisance . . .'

'Well, goodbye till eleven, Kufalt,' said Batzke, who had been looking at him quizzically all this time; and a grin spread over his face.

X

At Tiedemann & Co.'s building yard, Herr Priebatsch was seated in front of a large ledger, busily making entries. From time to time he raised his head and looked at the great yard where tens of thousands of bricks, thousands of tiles, hundreds of cubic metres of sand, countless piles of timber and sheds full of cement awaited purchasers.

He noted that Gadebusch the builder's cart was still loading, and that Lange the carpenter's carter would, in a moment, stop at the sales office window; then, as was his wont, he looked towards the other end of his office and said, as was his wont, to the apprentice: 'Would you be good enough to make out the invoices, Herr Preisach, instead of dreaming?'

The door of the sales office opened; instead of Lange's carter it was a young, well-dressed, rather pallid man who entered, carrying a small case.

'I beg your pardon,' said the young man, apparently rather confused.

'Not at all,' said Herr Priebatsch. 'What can I do for you?'

'I wanted to ask whether you had any hard-baked bricks,' said the young man.

'Certainly,' said Herr Priebatsch. 'You have but to look out of the window. Fifty-four marks the thousand.'

'And you keep paving stones too?' asked the young man.

'Basalt? Granite? Composition? Ironstone? Square? Round?' replied Herr Priebatsch.

'Well, really I hardly know,' said the young man dubiously. 'Perhaps basalt, and square – no, round, I think.'

'And how many would you want? I would have to inquire about the price first,' explained Herr Priebatsch.

'Oh, not very many at present,' said the young man awkwardly, looking at Herr Priebatsch.

'Well, how many?'

'Yes,' said the young man, hesitating and looking at Herr Priebatsch with awkward deference.

'The bricks could be delivered at once,' said the manager helpfully. 'As regards the paving stones, we would need at least a week for delivery.'

'But I wanted one at once,' said the young man.

Herr Priebatsch could not believe his ears. 'One,' he said slowly, and repeated incredulously: 'One?'

It was so silent in the office that even apprentice Preisach awoke from his dreams and surveyed the customer.

Kufalt pulled himself together.

'As a sample,' he said hastily. And he added with sudden fluency, 'The thing is, my father is going to build himself a house, and he wants a sample of the bricks first.'

'The bricks?' asked Herr Priebatsch very slowly.

'And of the paving stones,' said the young man.

Herr Priebatsch had a sudden idea, and as a result he flushed very red.

'Sir,' he began in a very soft tone.

'The fact is we're going to pave a yard,' said the young man quickly.

'Sir,' said Herr Priebatsch. 'If you've come to make a fool of me in my own office . . .'

'Just samples, I assure you,' said the young man helplessly.

Herr Priebatsch began to shout.

'Get out of this office at once! Either you're a lunatic, or . . .'

But the young man had fled.

XI

Shortly before seven Kufalt again jumped up from his sofa, on which he had been lying half in sloth and half in anxious expectation, looked into the bookcase, poured out the remains of the brandy into a tumbler, gulped it down, hurried to the nearest grocer's shop and returned with a fresh bottle of brandy in his overcoat pocket.

He knew he had been drinking too much these last few days. But it was a kind of disease, or weakness. When he lay down after his hunt for bricks, the feeling had been strong within him to break free from all this, and lead a clean and decent life again. How good it had been to sit typing addresses in the Home of Peace, a clean job to which a man came freshly washed every morning. And now?

Absurd. In four hours he would be going out to smash windows, for practice. It was all nonsense. He must get out of it somehow.

Why on earth didn't he go alone to the Jungfernstieg, not for practice, and pluck up his courage at last? But tonight it was just practice – and tomorrow again just practice, perhaps, and just as often as that brute Batzke might decide. And constant bickering, and suspicion; and then what would be the result of it all?

He knew, but would not admit he knew, and so he drank some more brandy and lay down on the sofa.

Scarcely had he dropped into a doze, scarcely had he reached oblivion, than there was a knock at the door and Frau Fleege's kindly, bird-like old face looked in and she called out, 'Time for the theatre, Herr Lederer!'

He started up from sleep, and shouted: 'Leave me alone, damn the theatre!'

The head withdrew; Kufalt was ashamed for a moment, and took another drink. He tried to go to sleep again, but in vain.

So he got up and paced up and down his room, hour after hour. He heard the old woman's soft footsteps in the passage; he heard her creep to his door, to listen – he knew he had frightened that childlike, trusting heart, but was there no more to it than that?

It was not remorse, nor regret, nor resolution. It was just a process of walking up and down from one wall to the other: that he could do, that he had learnt how to do. Five paces in the cell; here it was eight. Here there were curtains; there, bars. That was the whole difference. At half past ten he would leave the house. He had been told to be at such and such a place about eleven. So he would leave the house about half past ten. Was it any different from the recreation period in prison? It was just the same.

Drink, and work up a lovely haze within him that dimmed his thoughts and senses. Drink again, until some radiant crimson sun rose in his brain and he began to believe what was not true – how it would be a good thing to go out, and he would make ten thousand marks, and this would be the last time, and he would buy himself a little shop somewhere in South Germany where he was unknown, and no one from these days would ever meet him. He would have a proper wife, and children, and never a quarrel . . .

His mind ran on and on. He had found an aim in life, the little panorama was unrolling – no need to think of this imminent ordeal. He wondered how he would invest his ten thousand marks; he considered how he would store his cigars; he calculated the possible profits of a tobacconist's shop – that was the important point.

But at half past ten he promptly slipped on his coat, took the case with its absurd contents and departed.

That evening Batzke did not keep him waiting. Kufalt threw a sidelong glance at him; Batzke was clearly in a poor way. He was walking beside Kufalt through that bitter night in a thin summer overcoat.

He did not talk; he merely said, 'Ah, there you are, let's get along.'

And he marched off.

They walked quickly, and they walked a very long way. The streets, soaking in slush and dimly lit, were nearly deserted. They did not see a single policeman all the way, and only one or two passers-by hurrying along.

Now and again they walked through fields or passed groups of allotments, and Kufalt's heart grew lighter and ceased to throb.

But when they approached a block of houses, when they could distinguish the façades, and shops, his heart beat faster, for at any moment Batzke might stop and say, 'Here we are!'

He found himself wishing they could walk on for ever, or that it were over, and they were already on their way home.

He constantly switched the case from one hand to the other. For a while he kept on, angrily reminding himself that Batzke had never once offered to carry it. Then he began to think of other things. It suddenly occurred to him that Batzke had done well to go to Fuhlsbüttel on an idle afternoon and look at the prison. Compared with this walk through the cold and wet, it had been a pleasant time. Lights out and a warm cell, and you crept under the blankets.

'I've just been thinking,' said Batzke; 'there must be a certain tension in so large a piece of glass. Mind you don't throw the stone, or it'll drop among the stuff and very likely knock our tray over. Or it may only make a small hole. You must hold the stone as short as you can and hit from above, downwards. Understand?'

'Yes,' said Kufalt obediently, but feeling far from easy in mind.

'And be careful not to put your fingers near the glass, or there'll be blood and fingerprints, and you'll have the cops onto you at once. Maybe the whole window will smash. I've never done this sort of thing. I ought to know, but I don't.'

He muttered peevishly to himself. At last he said, 'Well, we'll soon see.'

Kufalt began to feel very unwell. 'I've drunk too much,' he thought, as his stomach began to sink within him.

They walked on and on. For a time they tramped along a country road with trees on either side of it. Then houses once more, long, white blocks of houses with flat roofs. And Kufalt knew the time had come.

Hardly twenty paces farther on they reached a corner where there was a shop. Two windows on one street and one window on the other; Batzke looked up and down the street and suddenly cried, 'Go for it!'

Like a man compelled, Kufalt dropped his case on the snow, opened it, picked up the brick, holding it short, as ordered, so that he would not cut his fingers – and struck.

For a fraction of a second the window seemed to groan. Then it shivered with a crash, and the force of the blow seemed to drag the hand that held the brick out of his control . . .

He stood and stared at the window, in which there was now a gaping hole at least half a metre wide.

'Not so bad, young feller,' said Batzke, 'for starters; and for such a cowardly bloke as you are, not bad at all. But you ought to have hit a bit lower. The tray doesn't stand so high – now for the next!'

'But, Batzke,' began Kufalt in protest, for the crash still lingered in his ears . . . and wasn't that a light over there? . . . and there! . . . and there! . . . where there had been no light before.

'Hurry up!' cried Batzke. 'Take the paving stone and throw it so it falls right through into the shop.'

And Kufalt did so.

Another crash, a clatter, the dull thud of the stone falling somewhere in the darkness of the shop, a rumble and then silence.

'I thought so,' said Batzke. 'The hole's too small.'

Suddenly a female voice shrieked out over their heads. 'Help! Thieves! Help!'

'Come on, man,' said Batzke. 'Take the case. Hurry! Now then, get a move on. There's all the time God made before they get out of their beds onto the street.'

They departed side by side once more. The case was lighter now, and Kufalt too felt light. The block of houses lay behind them; Batzke was now leading. They seemed to be going farther and farther from Hamburg, out into the country.

Now they were no longer silent, they talked. Batzke was pleased. The great Batzke had admitted that he had not expected so much of Kufalt. After all, Kufalt would be quite useful. They might perhaps do the job together.

Kufalt was happy. He was gratified by Batzke's praise. But mainly because the ordeal was over. The night when he would repeat what he had just done, on the Jungfernstieg, was still far away. Until then he was free, and with a mind at ease; Batzke would make all the arrangements.

And in the exuberance of his delight he invited Batzke to a glass of grog.

XII

Next morning Frau Pastorin Fleege's lodger gave her no fresh cause for anxiety. On this occasion Herr Lederer slept soundly, as he usually did, until twelve o'clock, then appeared in a very cheerful and bright mood, asked for his breakfast and talked to her genially as he ate it, as was also his habit.

Shortly afterwards he went out. Frau Fleege then discovered the reason why she had been addressed so roughly the previous day. One brandy bottle stood empty in the corner, and a fresh one in the cupboard was already two-thirds gone.

It was clear that her lodger was in trouble. That was why he was drinking. That was why he had spoken to her so roughly. That was why, when they had been talking, he suddenly sat as though he had ceased to listen.

Frau Pastorin Fleege was perhaps the most innocent little bird in the great aviary of Hamburg, but at least she knew that this big-boned, dark friend with the evil eyes boded no good to her lodger. And she decided that she would, with great care and tact, bring the conversation round to the subject that very afternoon, and warn Herr Lederer of the bench on which bad boys are made to sit.

But unfortunately the lodger stayed out that afternoon. He did not return as usual for his afternoon sleep, and the Frau Pastorin would certainly have been horrified if she had seen him in a tawdry room on the Steindamm, sitting on Ilse's bed.

After Kufalt had slept, after all his satisfaction that the practice night was over, it had suddenly occurred to him that he still had reason to be afraid.

He had remembered that Ilse had left him in a bad temper, that she had threatened him, and that although she really knew nothing, at that moment the slightest thing might be dangerous. There was danger for him everywhere.

So he sat on her bed, and Ilse was not by any means so stupid that she did not know what had brought him there; and because she knew this, she kept on evading the matter on his mind. She had so much to talk about: the Café Steinmarder, and her want of money, and her little friends, who all earned more than she did, though they didn't deserve to, and 'By the way, Ernstel, aren't you going to give me ten marks today? I've seen such a lovely bag at Klockmann's.'

Kufalt was not going to part with ten marks without something in return.

'You could try to find out,' he said cautiously, 'where Batzke really lives.'

'Will you give me ten marks if I tell you?'

'Do you know?'

'You needn't give me the ten marks otherwise.'

'All right. Only five, though.'

'I won't get the bag for five marks.'

'Can you tell me his proper address?'

'Of course I can!'

'OK. Here you are. Where does he live?'

She leaned back and laughed. 'He doesn't live anywhere.'

'How do you mean – he doesn't live anywhere?' asked Kufalt angrily.

'Don't be such a fool,' she sneered. 'He hasn't got a place of his own. A different girl has to take him home every night. And if they ask for money, he beats them.'

'Give me back my ten marks,' said Kufalt furiously. 'You said you knew his address.'

'I said I knew where he lived. And that I've told you.'

'You give me back my money.'

There was, of course, another quarrel. Reconciliation was out of the question, and there was naturally no chance of allaying his fears. Ten marks gone, and another quarrel. He went home.

When he got home, old Frau Fleege stopped him on the landing and whispered: 'Your friend is waiting for you inside and drinking your brandy. Oh, Herr Lederer . . .'

She looked at him with imploring eyes.

'That's all right, Frau Pastorin,' said Kufalt hastily. 'I'll see you again later.'

And he went into his room. There sat Batzke, dark as night; the words stuck in Kufalt's throat, and it was all the trouble in the world to say innocently: 'Well, Batzke, any news?'

'Yes,' said Batzke, 'read that.'

And he handed him a newspaper, indicating a passage with his finger. Kufalt read:

'In the Lokstedt district last night both the large plate-glass windows in a new shop were broken by two men with a brick and a paving stone. The culprits escaped unrecognized. In connection with this case there is an interesting statement by the manager of a building yard to the effect that yesterday afternoon a young man appeared in his office and, on the pretext of wanting samples, asked for a brick and a paving stone. The police do not yet know whether there is any connection between these two events, but they are following up a definite lead.'

Long after Kufalt had read the extract, his eyes remained on the paper.

'Well?' he heard Batzke ask, and the voice sounded like the rumble of an approaching storm.

'Yes?' asked Kufalt in reply, and tried to look at Batzke. But he did not quite succeed.

'Listen,' said Batzke. 'Just you tell me where you got the stones for last night.'

'At the harbour,' said Kufalt quickly. 'Off the barges.'

'Ah,' said Batzke; 'so you're not the young man that asked for samples?'

This time Batzke's eyes were not to be evaded. The pair looked at each other for a moment, and another moment. A sudden impulse of defiance and resistance rose to the surface of Kufalt's mind, and then passed. Batzke stared unblinking; Kufalt lowered his gaze, laughed hysterically and said, 'I wouldn't be such a fool . . .'

'Oh,' said Batzke slowly, 'you wouldn't be such a fool?'

A long pause followed.

Then Batzke said quietly: 'I won't be such a fool either. It's off, Kufalt.'

He stood up and, without looking at Kufalt, took a cigarette out of the box on the table and lit it; Kufalt watched him intently. He felt that he must jump up and say something; but Batzke had walked to the door and his fingers were on the latch; then he turned.

'Shit,' he said, spat, and went.

Kufalt sat staring at the door.

XIII

'The police are following up a definite lead.'

No matter what a man might think, the words remained. He could tell himself a hundred times over that in the vast city of Hamburg it was impossible to find a young man who had stood for three minutes in a builder's office and asked a few silly questions. He could tell himself again and again that he had no intention of leaving his comfortable quarters with the widow Fleege; but he woke at night and listened to the wind outside the window, and listened towards the door and thought he could hear whispers and shuffling footsteps in the passage, and the words were still there: 'The police are following up a definite lead.'

He was still living with the widow Fleege; but he must really find some sensible occupation to drive these words out of his mind. He had too much time to brood and torment himself and drink.

For a few days he had still kept up appearances in front of his landlady, and had gone out in the evening as though he were going to the theatre. He sat in a cinema and then walked down the Jungfernstieg, stopped at the jeweller's shop and looked at the rings. They seemed to be a part of his existence. There they lay, sparkling in the strong light, as though he had acquired a claim over them in all the many nights when his thoughts had circled round and round them; and then the sight of them began to pall. And he grew weary.

It was over. Even Batzke would not take the risk now. There stood the words: 'The police are following up a definite lead.' And if one of them did risk it, the other would give him away at once. No; it was over.

He had grown weary, and one day he told the old lady in a rather hesitant manner that he had lost his engagement at the theatre and must now look for another job. But 'You needn't worry about your money yet. I still have plenty.'

'But, Herr Lederer,' the old woman had said, 'I wasn't thinking of money. I am so sorry you are out of work, and if you do get into difficulties, I have a little money saved. I would like to help such a steady young man as you are.'

And she had taken him into her room and given him some of her thin peppermint tea, and little old-fashioned aniseed cakes that tasted somehow of one's childhood; and she had told him how, when her husband was a young curate, he had lost heart because he had got stuck at three successive preaching tests. But his luck had then changed, and he had got that lovely rectory in the Wilstermarsch. She was sure that that was what would happen in his case and he would get a much better position; he must be patient.

Poor old lady, she was so pathetic and so easily upset, he must be very careful not to drink too much in the daytime so as not to shock her.

He accustomed himself to taking long walks that lasted all day. Every day he went a different way. Once he went to the Apfelstrasse and had a look at the Home of Peace. He passed it several times but saw no one in the windows. He half thought of going to Woolly Teddy and begging to be taken back into favour, to type addresses for the rest of his life.

There would be sure to be some sort of Beerboom living in the house, an even feebler wreck than himself. And he would cease to be alone in his utter, hopeless desolation.

But next day he did not go to the Home of Peace; he stood outside Herr Jauch's typing agency, and considered whether he should not march in with a superior air and engage someone to take down letters for him, at four marks an hour. He composed some wonderful business letters during the night. He would dictate all manner of orders, instructions, acknowledgements and complaints, and dazzle them all with his newly won greatness.

But he did nothing of the kind. With aching, weary feet he trudged through the slush to some little tavern, or fried-fish shop, or potato-fritter vendor, swallowed a hasty meal for sixty or eighty pfennigs and reckoned up that he could live for three or four months at least before he would need to make a move.

But these cheap meals were the merest self-delusion. And so were his calculations, for all his fear of life had passed. Life had become indifferent, grey, grim and hopeless, and all was at an end. He could of course go back to the little town and look out for Hilde Harder and tell her everything, but what would be the use?

There was nothing more to say. For him, there was nothing more to do; and a hoarse, drunken voice whispered: 'The Trehne rises at Rutendorf, under the Galgenberg . . .'

Then, for a time, things improved. Kufalt discovered a lending library; he lay in bed all night reading and drinking and slept almost the entire day. And he got up only in the evening about seven and dashed round to the library to get two or three new volumes before it closed.

But in the end, novels lost their power to stimulate him. He dozed over them. He could no longer imagine himself as the hero and he wandered aimlessly through the streets, the eternal streets and avenues, until night fell; then he gulped down tots of brandy in little drinking holes, hurriedly, as though he were really in a hurry, and ran out again. Tonight he would walk round the inner and the outer Alster to tire himself out. But he was never really tired.

And yet it was not on a walk through deserted avenues at night that he, for the first time in those disastrous weeks, did something. It was in an ordinary street, where he might any moment have met someone, or even run into a policeman.

It happened quite unexpectedly. Later on he was sure that there had been no such purpose in his mind. Perhaps he had drunk a little too much. Possibly that was it. He had been somewhere in Eilbeck or Hamm. He could never afterwards remember exactly where it had first happened.

It was late at night. A woman or a girl was walking in front of him, and the street was deserted (not that he noticed that).

Suddenly he found himself close to the girl and whispered in her ear, 'Well, Fräulein, how about it?'

She turned round angrily and said something silly, such as 'Leave me alone or I'll scream'. Something like that.

'All right, scream,' he had said, and suddenly punched his fist into her face, grabbed her handbag and bolted round the corner.

How she shrieked!

Oh, well, let her shriek. He did not much mind. He had heard people shriek quite differently in prison. And there had been nothing he could do to help them either.

We must all help ourselves. That was why he was now safely round the nearest corner. He felt warm and well at ease, and he took a bus home. At last he had done something; that night he slept soundly.

It was without doubt a shabby little bag, his first bag. But had he done it for the bag? Seven marks twenty, two keys, a crumpled handkerchief, a cracked mirror. But he still had five hundred marks at home. What were bags to him!

What mattered to him were the anguished look, the fleeing form, the agonized shrieks; the sense that he was no longer the last and lowest of humanity. He too could trample on people and make them shriek.

Yes; but you really need not go out every evening, snatch a bag and hit a girl in the face. There is no need. But when you feel like it, then do it. And if the world has been looking grey and hopeless, it brightens up again when you strike the blow; all is well once more since others too can be made to suffer pain.

You, Willi Kufalt, can now sit in the Frau Pastorin's room and talk to her about her cowshed and how, when the cow had her first calf, no one really knew what to do; and suddenly the calf was there, staggering about on spindle-shanks and making straight for the udder. But when, during the story, there's a ring at the door and the gas collector comes, and the old lady has to pay him, you watch her take a key out of her basket, a small, single, smooth key. With it she opens the cupboard and takes out a sewing basket. She lifts out the tray and underneath – take note – is the money she keeps in the house, and a savings bank book.

While she is talking to the gas man outside, you get up calmly and quietly, your pulse does not even quicken, and you look: not much money, only about a hundred marks, but there are fourteen hundred marks credited in the savings bank book; and the authorisation slip that goes with it is neatly slipped inside. Then the old lady comes back, puts away the basket and locks it up, and you talk to her again and think to yourself that sometime, next week perhaps, or in two months' time, you will take that money and the savings bank book.

And when you have got it and are gone, and she discovers that the money is missing, you will be sitting comfortably in a new room fifty streets away, with another landlady, and thinking that the world is once again a very good place.

XIV

The city is dark and grim. It is not light by day, nor is it dark by night. The moon is always slipping through the clouds, and bushes have branches like pointing arms, and you are not alone on your solitary walks, and every branch points to the trade that must be yours.

Behind your bed lies a trunk, made of some sort of imitation vulcanized fibre. And in that trunk are fourteen handbags. You often pick them up and try to recall each episode. But what is the sense of doing that? They were always the same; in the early morning, when you feel old and tired, it is so foolish to lie in bed, fingering the bags, and trying to call those faces back to mind . . . That one had a lovely painted mouth, and you dashed your fist into it, and broke the delicate little nose in senseless fury . . . In vain, in vain, this evening you must go out again. Faded memories. Again, and yet again, you seem to see the same peaked cap over the vacant youthful face, the face of a copper's nark, when you leave the house.

The face under the peaked cap dogs you, and you slink away on your dark errand. But you are well aware that you are always wearing the same overcoat and hat, and that the police have fourteen descriptions of you and soon, very soon, you must cease your forays for a while because they are on your track. Peaked cap with a nark's face beneath it . . .

You sit on your bed, your open trunk in front of you. Old Pastorin Fleege is busy in the kitchen with her little aniseed cakes. You run your fingers over the bags. Most of them are of artificial leather, but among them is a crocodile leather one, and one of white lizard skin. You like smelling those. They have brought you little, these fourteen handbags. A hundred and eighty-seven marks sixty in all. No matter; enough to buy a new overcoat and a new hat, and the peaked cap will disappear. And what will happen then?

Outside in the streets are girls and women on their way home. They come from sheltered homes, where people read in the papers about the clash of weapons in very distant worlds. And then you come and strike them in the face and snatch their bags. And the distant worlds come hurtling down on Hamburg, and they are hard and hot and merciless.

A bell rings. Why is there always a bell ringing? He hears the old widow shuffling to the door. A voice asks, a voice answers; light steps cross the passage and he puts the bags away. But not quite quick enough: one is left behind and the door opens. Who is it?

Ilse. Ilse, of course.

'Well, Ilse,' said Kufalt.

'Good morning, Willi,' said Ilse.

'Willi?' said Kufalt. 'My name's Ernst.'

'All right, Ernst then,' said Ilse dutifully, and sat down in a chair. 'Have you got any brandy?'

'No.'

A pause. A long pause.

'I suppose you've brought me my ten marks from last time?' asked Kufalt finally.

'What ten marks?' she retorted.

'Over that false address,' he said.

'I never gave you a false address,' said she.

And they both relapsed into silence.

'What do you really want?' he asked finally.

'That's a nice bag,' she said.

'Like it?' he asked.

'How kind of you, darling,' she said, and tried to kiss him.

But he evaded the kiss.

'Why have you come?' he asked again.

'I wanted to know if you were still alive.'

'You've taken your time,' said Kufalt.

'I didn't like to come,' she said. 'You were so angry when you went away last time.'

'And I'm not angry now?' he asked.

Again a long silence.

'Haven't you got any cigarettes either?' she asked at length.

'I don't think so,' he said, and lit one.

'Well,' she said, 'everyone knows his own business best.'

'What do you mean?' he said irritably.

'Everyone must look after himself,' she said at last, and flung one slim leg over the other, so that he could see a span of flesh between her stocking and the hem of her strawberry-coloured knickers.

'It's all Greek to me,' he said.

'Greece is not a bad place, when it's a case of doing a bunk.'

'Who's got to do a bunk?' he asked.

'Oh, someone,' she said.

Kufalt gazed thoughtfully at the bedspread on which the bag still lay.

'A pretty little bag,' he said invitingly.

'What's your friend doing these days?' she asked.

'Which friend?' he asked.

'The tall, dark, horrid-looking man,' she said.

'Why?' he asked.

'I just asked,' she said.

'Ah,' he said.

'Well?' she asked.

'Yes,' he said.

'Well, I'd better be off,' she said indignantly.

'Why?' he asked, with an air of great surprise. 'Have I offended you?'

'Offended?' she said. 'Takes more than that to offend me.'

'Why are you so funny, then?' he asked.

'I'm not funny,' she said. 'It's you that's funny.'

'Isn't Batzke funny?' he asked.

'Who's Batzke?' she asked.

'Oh, don't you know him?' he asked. 'Sending young narks around, is he?'

'I don't know what you're talking about,' she said.

'That doesn't matter,' he said. 'As long as I do.'

'Well, then I'm off,' she said.

But she did not go.

'Good evening,' he said.

'Good evening,' she said. 'And what about those diamond rings?' She laughed.

He felt as though he had been kicked in the stomach.

'What diamond rings?' he asked.

'There aren't so many!'

'Nothing doing,' he said. 'Gone dead,' he said. 'Your Batzke's got the wind up,' he said. 'Get lost,' he said. 'D'you suppose I'm going to pull the job off for you? Not such a fool,' he said. 'It's no go, little girl,' he said. 'Not this trip,' he said. 'Love to the boyfriend,' he said. 'Never fooled me,' he said. 'And never would,' he said. 'Goodnight, Ilse,' he said. 'Give me a kiss,' he said. 'No, the bag's much too lousy for you,' he said. 'Well, till we meet again,' he said. 'And that's it!' he said.

He was furious and drank a great deal of rough German brandy.

XV

In the year 1904 the local agricultural society at Wilster had held an exhibition, at which more than three hundred head of cattle had been shown. By some happy chance Herr Pastor Fleege, then in the prime of life, had won a first prize for his bull calf Jaromir, born of Thekla, sired by Conquistador.

This first prize took the form of a charging bull in bronze.

Frau Pastorin Fleege had an acute sense of the honour conferred by the award of this work of art. Nonetheless, in all the years that had passed, she had never got to like that bull, rampant on its hind legs and butting its clumsy horns into an invisible foe.

Among all her possessions – and they were many – she treated this bull with noticeable step-motherly neglect. Indeed, it was never dusted until the need became extreme. Softly as she whisked her feather brush over all the other objects in her household, she dealt rather briskly with the bull. Nasty rearing creature . . .

Often she did not remember until late in the evening, about nine or ten o'clock, how dusty the poor wretch must be.

That was what happened on that particular evening, as she remembered very clearly later on. Herr Lederer had received a visit from his unpleasant friend's wife and had slept unusually late. It was not until eight or half past in the evening that he had got up, when his friend's wife had long since left, and she had really hoped that Herr Lederer would come and talk to her for at least ten minutes after such a quiet day.

But he had crossed the passage and disappeared without a word. And then she had discovered that the bull with the silver plaque was thick with dust, and had set about knocking and dusting it . . .

Meantime Herr Lederer had gone out into the streets, a little tired, a little hungry, and with an unmistakable craving for alcohol.

Well, that was that. Ilse had been to see him again. She had wanted to be affectionate. She would certainly have been satisfied with five or ten marks – what was it she had asked?

'What is your friend Batzke doing?'

No, that wasn't it. She hadn't put the question quite like that. Why was she interested in Batzke, anyway?

In any case, the evening hours provided an inconspicuous background. The Alster avenues could be darker and more deserted at about eight o'clock than at midnight. Still, he must get another overcoat and hat immediately. Why he had not done so before, no one could say; not even Kufalt.

There was plenty of money in the house!

It was a motorcyclist with a sidecar, returning home from a short excursion with his wife. On the ground floor of the house in which he lived there was a tavern. The February night was rather chilly, so they both had a grog before taking the motorcycle and sidecar through the gate to Scholtheiss the taxi-driver's garage on the third yard.

But that, as it happened, they never did. When they had drunk their grog and come out onto the street again, the motorcycle and sidecar had vanished. As a result of which there was no small disturbance.

Such disturbances did not worry Frau Pastorin Fleege. Pussi was at home. The door was securely closed; Herr Lederer liked talking to his former colleagues, and seldom came home before two or three in the morning. So she got out of her tight stays and into her bedjacket, and took up the Bible. She read the passage for the day and tried, as her dear husband had done for her so many, many years ago, to meditate on it. But she found this rather hard. It was easier to spot that there was still some dust remaining on the bull's left hind leg, though she had dusted the creature only an hour and a half before.

'Understandest thou what thou readest?' she read, and wondered whether the feather brush was still in the sitting room – or had she put it back in the kitchen?

*

A man who walks for an hour can cover a long distance in a city. Many faces, and girls' faces too. Faces of pretty girls, and pretty girls unaccompanied – Kufalt had looked at them as he went on his way. What did it matter? Was he a bag snatcher? He was walking so that he could sleep when he got tired. After all, he did not depend on snatching bags: he could let them go in peace, daughters of the fat citizens of Hamburg, and then stop the last tart who had nothing in her bag but a lipstick. He was committed to nothing.

It was ten minutes past nine; are there people anywhere who watch the ticking of time and measure its passage? Time is meaningless. A great deal of time slips past, and with little profit to anyone.

The watchman at the jeweller's shop usually stood behind a pillar in the Alster arcade. He had a great deal of time. He was on duty for twelve hours. For twenty-two and a half years he had done his twelve hours' duty, and nothing had ever happened. He hardly had the sense that he was watching over such precious wares. There he stood, twelve hours out of the twenty-four, every day that God made; and, in return, he could spend the other twelve at home, raise children and quarrel with his wife. There he stood behind his pillar and watched. But he did not watch for any potential trouble; there was nothing to watch for – nothing ever happened. Everything was too well organized.

Seen another way, little Ilse was no more than a slut. She was content with the smallest offerings, and she understood nothing except the fact that she wanted some particular thing. A new bag, or three pairs of silk stockings, or a smart dress from Robinsohn's. It was on the impulse of such cravings that she went away and told Batzke all about it. And Willi knew nothing, and a rascal in a peaked cap appeared and he too said Kufalt knew nothing, and then there was a clatter outside the front door – but the problem is, how to get two men into a sidecar? How long did it take to get to the Jungfernstieg? If all the traffic lights were red, thirty-five minutes, but if they were green, twenty minutes. Eleven forty-two is the time, and they must on no account attract attention.

Time ticks on, and brings harm to all men, and to all men profit. They stand with bent heads, then they look up, and between the inner and the outer Alster runs a bridge. It is called the Lombard's

Bridge. And the trams go over it. It is really quite a lively thoroughfare, and not three minutes as the crow flies from the Jungfernstieg. On the bridge a young man says:

'Well, Fräulein, how about it?'

But before the blow falls, before fear has stricken the shrinking, lovely face, a motorcycle has long since clattered past, a window has been smashed, an old man with a walrus moustache is at his wits' end, that ancient, bird-like, fairy-tale creature, the Widow Fleege, has crept between the sheets, and a starburst of 151 diamond rings, worth 153,000 marks, has sparkled over the street – but the delicate, lovely face is disfigured, and all the lamps are dimmer . . .

Was there no one, man or woman, who sat up in their beds? Time passed, the clock on the silent, dark wall ticked on, loud and persistent.

Was there no one, man or woman? There are so many houses and such countless beds; but who thinks of those without, who cannot sleep, and must tramp the streets at night?

Another girl struck down; she will never sleep again as once she did, when she thought herself safe. And you, go home with your spoils; you too will never sleep again as once you did, when you were still at home and had a mother.

The motorcycle rattled on and on and on, throbbing like the heart of the city. It sped into the distance until, suddenly, its noise seemed to be swallowed up by the wind, blowing up from the country, where there are lakes and forests. And all is still.

The city is at rest.

9

Ripe for Arrest

I

'Now *I* am going to tell you something,' said Herr Wossidlo, looking angrily at the two police officers. 'You have spent several hours questioning me, my manager and all my employees. You have received my statements regarding the value of the stolen diamonds with barely concealed mistrust. You have suspected every employee in turn of being involved in this robbery, even my poor watchman, who has been with us for more than twenty years. Then you spent several hours investigating the robbery, both in and outside the shop. You have examined that absurd paving stone, which looks like any other paving stone, with as much care as if it had been a remarkable burglar's tool you had never seen before.

'All this is no doubt part of your professional methods. I, however, as a layman in these matters, may perhaps express the opinion that it would be rather more important to make some attempt to catch the thieves. The six or seven hours you have spent in my shop are so many hours' start for the criminals. I should like to be permitted to ask whether any of your colleagues have made any effort to catch them?'

'As to that I can give you no information,' growled one of the officers.

'And may I further ask,' said Herr Wossidlo with a nod, as though that were exactly the answer he expected, 'may I further ask whether you are following up any definite lead?'

'I cannot make any statement on that point either,' replied the same official.

'Very well,' said Herr Wossidlo. 'And what is going to be done now?'

'You will be informed in due course.'

'I will tell you something more,' said Herr Wossidlo, raising his voice. 'What you have been doing here was simply done to do something – to reassure me.

'Well, I am not reassured, gentlemen. I know nothing of police methods. But it is obvious to me that you are groping in the dark, just as I am, and waiting for something to turn up. But I have no notion of waiting until something turns up. I hereby inform you that I shall proceed independently and make an independent attempt to discover the thieves and recover my rings.'

'Detectives?' asked the second officer.

'On that point, I regret to say, I can make no statement,' observed Herr Wossidlo. 'In any case you will soon see news of me in the daily papers.'

'But what are you going to do?' said the first officer quickly and anxiously. 'We must work hand in hand.'

'All of a sudden?'

'And if you propose to offer a reward, no doubt we could offer one too.'

'I refuse to say anything,' said Herr Wossidlo emphatically.

'They may have been professional burglars,' said the second officer thoughtfully, now becoming more communicative. 'But they may be people who happened to hear about those three minutes when the shop is practically unguarded. That is why we had to question your staff as well. It must have required some pretty sharp observation to find out about those three minutes without any sort of hint from inside.'

'I don't believe a word of it,' said Herr Wossidlo. 'I read detective stories, but I don't believe that crimes are such complicated affairs. It doesn't need a professional criminal and weeks of observation to throw a stone through a shop window.'

The officers shook their heads; they plainly disagreed.

'Very well, then,' said one of them in conclusion; 'we must ask you to send us as exact a description as possible of the stolen rings, and any further information, to the town hall today. Then we will circulate it at once.'

'I will certainly do so,' said Herr Wossidlo. 'Good morning, gentlemen.'

II

'A bloody awkward business,' said one officer.

'Pompous old fool,' agreed the other.

'He'll play tricks on us before he's done,' said the first darkly.

'I'm sure he will,' agreed the second.

'Nothing to be done at the moment,' said the first.

'No,' said the second, 'we must wait till the swag turns up somewhere.'

'Yes, and by then Wossidlo will have infuriated all Hamburg with his gossip about the police.'

'I don't think it looks like one of the old hands. Besides, none of them are in Hamburg.'

'It's odd that we haven't heard a thing about it. There must have been at least four men in it. And I never heard of four crooks that could hold their tongues.'

'It must have been a bloody quick job.'

'But the tip-off!' cried the other. 'That detail of the three minutes – someone must have watched for at least a fortnight ahead.'

'The watchman saw no one, of course,' said the first man angrily.

'What are you going to say to the boss?'

'I'll propose a round-up. We can get hold of twenty or thirty of the lads and put them through it. Perhaps one of them heard something, and we can make him squeal.'

'Yes, that'll be best.'

'People seem to have funny ideas about the police,' said the first man angrily. 'As if we could find out everything at once! Of course we'll nab the blokes one day – but when?'

'Let's hope for a bit of luck,' said the second. 'That's the best chance.'

'Yes, if it wasn't for a bit of luck sometimes . . .' agreed the first.

III

The bit of luck was called Kufalt, and while the two officers were tramping the wintry streets of Hamburg in their broad, worn-out boots, Kufalt was already sitting on a bench in the town hall waiting for them.

When he saw in the paper that the robbery had taken place, that his friend Batzke had got away with his spoils, he was first afraid and then possessed by fury.

Suddenly he realized why he had been trailed by the little ruffian in the peaked cap. It was not the police who were after the bag snatcher but Batzke, who wanted to know whether Kufalt was still watching the window in the Jungfernstieg. That was why Ilse had visited him the evening before, just to check out how the land lay – for Batzke.

Fear was his first emotion. He had given the tip-off. He was in it. He had hung about the shop for weeks; perhaps his face was known there and someone would remember him. His description might even already have been forwarded to the newspapers.

But that was not all: he, the bag snatcher, whose description had appeared each time more clearly in the newspapers, could hardly move around at all.

The anger within him overcame his fear. Batzke it was who had brought him to that pass. Batzke had betrayed him again. The rendezvous under the horse's tail, the tobacconist's shop and the dud twenty-mark note, his wasted four hundred marks . . . Batzke had always betrayed him.

He paced up and down his room, brooding. Yes, he would sit down and type an anonymous letter on the spot. That would settle Batzke.

And he sat down and typed – and stopped. Five thousand marks from the fence, that would be all, Batzke had said. But rewards were always offered in the case of burglaries of this kind. Ten per cent would be the least, fifteen thousand marks, and money justly earned. Justly earned!

In a deep chamber of his brain still lurked the dream of the little tobacconist's shop, and a wife and children. Now it could be transformed into truth and reality.

He got up. He tore the typed sheet into tiny fragments, opened the door of the stove and did not shut it until he was sure the last fragment of paper was burnt to ashes.

No; he must wait until the reward was offered. In doing so, there was certainly a risk that the cops might go after him; but nothing could be achieved without some risk. They would never track him down. They would be even less likely to if he went to them.

He began to pace up and down again. He could no longer wait until the evening papers came out. The reward would certainly be advertised in the evening papers. He would go straight along to the town hall, and Batzke would be caught. Perhaps Kufalt would get the reward by the end of the week and be shot of it all.

Suddenly his fear returned. But fear of another kind. The police knew their job, and all crooks were traitors. Perhaps there were others who knew of Batzke's scheme. Perhaps they had not waited so long; perhaps they were already sitting in the town hall and would rob Kufalt of his fifteen thousand marks.

After all, what information had he to give? A single name – Batzke. He did not know who had helped him, nor who the fences were. He did not even know where Batzke lived, he only knew that one name. The name was his capital; it stood for his tobacco shop and his future. He must not let himself be robbed of that name. He must go at once.

He slipped on his coat, put on his hat and stopped doubtfully in the centre of the room.

The flush of greed faded for a moment, his desire for vengeance ebbed. 'This may go wrong,' he thought. 'It may go very wrong.'

However, he went, again hesitated in the passage, heard Frau Fleege about her business in the kitchen and suddenly felt almost touched at the thought of that old and wrinkled face.

She was the only person who had been really kind to him.

He moved in a world of enemies. He must be wary and he must be bold. But here he needed to be neither.

He opened the kitchen door.

'Frau Pastorin,' he said, 'I'm going out for a few hours. But I may be longer.'

She smiled at him kindly from under her bead cap. 'Is it about an engagement?' she asked discreetly.

'Not exactly – I may not be back again today at all. Well, my things are quite safe with you.'

'Herr Lederer,' said the old woman, and took his hand between her two old, quivering hands, 'I wish you the best of luck.'

IV

'The jewel robbery at Wossidlo's, eh?' asked one of the officers, looking appraisingly at Kufalt. 'Well, what about it?'

'I wanted to ask,' said Kufalt, 'whether there's a reward offered yet.'

'No,' said the officer curtly.

'And won't there be one?' asked Kufalt again.

'That depends,' said the officer.

Kufalt found the searching glances of the two officers very unpleasant. Any moment either of them might remember the descriptions. If only he had got himself another coat and hat before coming here. But he had not thought of anything. He had gone out blindly after the money, and perhaps there would be none.

'OK then,' he said. 'Perhaps I'll come back another time.' And he got up.

'Stop, stop,' said the officer more informally. 'Not so fast. Have a cigarette.'

He had concluded his scrutiny of Kufalt, and, having reached a pretty accurate conclusion, he thought a little further conversation might prove profitable.

'If a reward actually was offered, could you tell us anything about this robbery?'

'I don't yet know,' said Kufalt coolly. 'That depends on the reward.'

'Look,' intervened the second officer; 'I don't need to tell you, young man, that if you know anything about a crime, you have to report it. Otherwise you are liable to prosecution.'

'I know that,' said Kufalt. 'But I know no more than there has been in the papers. All the same, perhaps I could find out something because I'm in touch with certain people . . .'

'Don't you listen to him,' interceded the first officer. 'He can't help bellowing like that. Yes, the reward will be all right, the insurance company is sure to offer one. But we may have got the blokes by then. So you'd much better trust us and tell us anything you can now. We shan't let you down.'

And he looked at Kufalt with frankness.

'No,' said Kufalt decisively. 'I know nothing yet. I just meant to find out what I could, if it was worth my while.'

The officers sat thoughtfully observing Kufalt.

'Would you object,' resumed the first, 'to leaving your name and address? We might want you urgently. We'll see you don't lose out.'

'I'd rather not,' said Kufalt. 'I'll call again soon.'

'Well,' said the second officer angrily, 'if that's the case . . .'

'Don't listen to him,' said the first quickly. 'We wouldn't be mean over a big job like this. And we can also turn a blind eye when a bloke gives us a tip or two – come on, out with it.'

'That doesn't help me,' said Kufalt agitatedly. 'But I won't have the police coming to where I live.'

He added more calmly: 'Landladies are funny about some things.'

But he was thinking of the handbags in his trunk and cursed himself for not having got rid of them. He must have been demented these last few days.

'So you won't give us the address,' said the officer gloomily; 'well, we haven't got much out of you today.'

He sat and thought. Suddenly an idea flashed into his mind. He got up and said quickly: 'Wait, I'll be back in a second.'

And he departed.

'But I'm in a hurry,' Kufalt called out after him.

The first officer had already gone, and Kufalt was left sitting there with the second officer, an offensive person who never took his eyes off him.

'I want to go,' he said helplessly. He was afraid that the other officer would come back with a warrant for his arrest. He cursed himself for coming. He saw that he had made a very foolish start.

'I want to go,' he repeated.

The second officer said nothing, but kept on staring at him. Beneath the thin, reddish moustache a smile appeared . . .

'He's found me out,' thought Kufalt.

'Well, I'll go now,' he said once more, and got up.

'Where have we met before?' asked the officer.

'Nowhere. You're confusing me with someone else,' said Kufalt, much relieved. For he was quite sure that he knew no police officer in Hamburg except Herr Specht.

'My dear man,' said the officer in a very condescending tone, 'I'll soon find out. Just stay, stand as you are for a minute.'

'An hour if you like,' said Kufalt. 'But I want to go home now.'

He did not go. The other officer returned, beaming with satisfaction.

'Now listen, my lad,' he said. 'I've just been making some inquiries. There are still a few formalities to settle. But ten thousand marks will be offered for the recovery of the stuff.'

He took a chair and sat down.

'And, you know,' he said pleasantly, 'we'll have to act pretty quick, so that they don't have time to scatter the swag all over Europe. They'll be sharing it out now, and we ought to get the whole pile at a stroke. That would mean ten thousand marks for you; we police officers don't get any pickings. How about it?'

'I'll see what I can find out,' said Kufalt slowly.

'That won't do, my dear man,' said the officer briskly. 'I'm not going to let you go off like that.

'But fair's fair, and I'll make you an offer. You needn't tell me your name, nor who you are, nor where you live. And I'll give you my word of honour as an official that I won't have you followed. But . . .'

He drew a deep breath. Kufalt looked at him intently.

'. . . But you're to have a look at our photograph album. You know what I mean. And if you see the man in it who did this job, just shut the album and say, "He's in it." Nothing more. That's all we want you to do. Then I'll let you go, and you'll get two hundred marks as well, on account . . .'

'But I don't know the man yet,' protested Kufalt.

'You leave that to us,' said the officer. 'You might enjoy looking at a few of the photographs. They're very interesting.'

'But there's no sense in it,' said Kufalt helplessly.

'Sense or not,' said the officer with sudden sternness, 'if you won't, you'll stay here.'

But he was soon smiling again, and quietly placed two hundred-mark notes on the table. Kufalt looked at them hesitatingly.

'Now get on with it,' said the officer. 'Don't take all that time to think it over. Surely it's a good enough bit of business, isn't it? Which volume shall I send for?'

'I know nothing,' said Kufalt obstinately.

'You'll let the blokes get rid of the swag,' said the officer indignantly; 'and you could make such a stash of money. You're not asked to say anything. Now then – "A"? "B"?'

'Hmm – hmm.'

'Aha! But B is in several volumes. Well, you might look through them all. You don't need to say a word.'

Kufalt sat in sullen silence. He had the feeling he was caught. He was stuck in a cul-de-sac and there was no way out. He was never a match for anyone. Neither for Batzke nor for these men here.

What was the use of two hundred marks? However, he must do it, or they would not let him go.

'All right, B,' he said, and swore to himself that he would betray nothing. He would shut the volume, whether Batzke's photograph was in it or not, say, "He's there," and shut it quite at random. Then he would take the two hundred marks, so as to get something out of the transaction, and go. And he would take every sort of transport and go to all the department stores on his way home. At the China House on the Mönckebergstrasse he would go up and down in the continuous lift so that they lost all trace of him, and that would be the end of it.

He carefully chose the volume that began with 'Bi', turned over the pages and looked at the countless faces, with the strained, grimacing features and set lips of all compulsory photographs.

And as he looked at them all, commonplace faces, good and evil faces, he was overcome by curiosity to see whether Batzke really was the crook he had always made himself out to be. And he picked up the 'Ba' volume, turned over the pages and on the third he saw his friend, in profile and full-face, from the right and from the left, in the company of other 'Ba's.

'Thank you very much,' said the officer pleasantly. 'Here are your two hundred marks. All above board, you see. Well, goodbye. You're quite free to go home.'

Kufalt looked at the two policemen's faces; they were grinning with satisfaction. He wanted to say something, to bellow with rage at having been so utterly fooled. But he snatched up his notes from the table and ran out of the room, hearing the officers' idiotic laughter as he fled . . .

V

A hundred marks of his newly earned money Kufalt spent at once on an overcoat and hat. His was an ordinary black overcoat. So he bought himself a light brown loose raglan. His hat was a small blue-grey felt one, so he got a large black slouch hat. He had them packed and sent to his lodging.

As he walked on – it was now late in the afternoon – it occurred to him for the first time how thoughtless he had been. The police now knew him in his black Ulster and his felt hat. They would immediately wonder why he had bought a new coat.

It was even more stupid to have given his name and address at the shop. If he had been followed they would now know all about him. The handbags were still in his trunk.

However, he did not go home. He felt as though everything was going wrong and that no effort on his part would be of any use. Either he would emerge unscathed from this business, or he would not. He must accept both outcomes; there was little he could do.

He really ought to have eaten a meal at midday but he had not felt like eating; his appetite had gone. He would sooner drink a couple of schnapps.

He drank them. The world at once looked different. He had a lot of money on him, quite unexpected money, and he could always get fresh money when he needed it. Now at last for once he could do what he liked with his money. He had not been out with a girl for a long time, not since he had been in prison. No, not since he had been arrested nearly six years ago – he would really make an evening of it.

And he made his way in the direction of the Reeperbahn.

As he walked along it occurred to him that he had, in fact, been with girls, with Liese, Hilde and Ilse. But somehow that seemed to mean nothing, or rather to mean something different. He could not quite understand why, but when he thought of girls he couldn't help thinking of handbags as well; though there was really no connection.

There were no suitable places on the Reeperbahn. They all seemed to him like tourist traps or too refined. And then, odd as it was, the girls who prowled about the streets and whispered endearments as they passed suddenly seemed meaningless. It was as if here too his nocturnal ways had set up barriers. He was furious when they spoke to him. Yet surely it was up to him to speak first.

Finally he found himself on the first floor of a café on the Grosse Freiheit. It was just the right sort of place, with alcoves lit by shaded lamps, and little girls not too dolled up.

With them he could talk at his ease. He asked how business was. He asked after their pals and their pimps. And then they talked about the bad weather, and wondered whether they should go on anywhere else that evening, and whether they should spend the night together. And he drew up a plan, with supper and a cinema to follow.

In the meantime they drank a great many liqueurs, and the girl grew amorous and began to kiss him, which he did not like; and she cried out in a shrill, silly voice, 'Oh you're so sweet! . . . No, you're so funny!'

He chatted away to her, tried to impress her and told her jokes and laughed, but all the time he kept on thinking how stupid and boring it all was, and how much more he had enjoyed his solitary walks by night; he did not want her, nor any other girl. Once he got up, went to his overcoat and took out his cigarettes and handkerchief and keys. And the black overcoat now hung empty on its hook.

Shortly afterwards the girl wanted to go out for a moment, and he teased as to whether she would come back. He pretended he did not trust her – she just wanted to give him the slip after he had stood her ten or twelve liqueurs. And in the end she left him her bag as a pledge and said with a laugh, 'Well, that won't make you rich!'

As he came up he had noticed that the lavatories were on the half-landing. Scarcely was she out of the room than he got up (he had slipped the bag under his jacket) and said to the waiter, 'Look after my overcoat for a moment'; and went down the stairs.

But he passed the lavatories, hurried out into the street, ran the short distance to the Reichenstrasse, took a taxi and went home.

He hoped they would be pleased with the bag snatcher's coat and hat. Now they would have yet another description of him to publish in the papers. By the end of this week he would either be out of Hamburg or all would be at an end.

VI

The bag was a poor, shabby object, made of black stuff, with no money inside it. But it smelt strongly of some sort of scent; and that brought him the dreams and the desires that the girl had not been able to arouse.

He had gone to bed very early. No, he would not go out again. It was too risky. He must soon decide what he was going to do, but not that evening. Perhaps tomorrow; he had drunk too much that evening. There was a pleasant slow rotation in his head. He laid his cheek on the bag, and felt as though he were in the cabin of a ship, steaming to distant lands. The ship rolled gently, and he thought he could hear the waves gurgling faintly against the portholes and could smell the fragrance of those distant coconut islands whither he was bound.

And he fell fast asleep.

Then he thought he heard men's voices outside. He did not know exactly whether he was on board ship, or where he was – ah, of course; he was in prison, and the night guard was talking outside his door. But he could go on sleeping.

That, however, he could not do. For a voice, which woke him up fully said, quite close to his ear, 'Get up, please!'

He tried to put off opening his eyes, but the bedclothes were ruthlessly torn off him and he saw the police officer of the previous day standing by his side. The more pleasant of the two. But at the moment he did not look at all pleasant.

'Come on – wake up, lad! We've got a lot to do.'

Kufalt looked at him. 'Why are you here?' he asked. 'You gave me your word of honour . . .'

'Word of honour be damned,' said the officer. 'Read that.'

And he held a newspaper under Kufalt's nose.

Kufalt thought at first it was his latest theft of a handbag. But it was a large advertisement with the headline: 'To The Burglars'. And in it Herr Wossidlo announced his desire to get in touch direct with the burglars. He gave his word of honour he would not betray them to the police, and declared himself ready to pay them ten per cent of the value of the stolen goods. 'More than any receiver would give. With a further assurance of inviolable secrecy, for which I pledge my word as an honourable Hamburg merchant. Hermann Wossidlo.'

'Now,' said the officer, 'where does Batzke live?'

'Batzke?' asked Kufalt slowly.

'Now don't you start again with your nonsense,' said the officer angrily. 'It's a matter of minutes now. They may even meet this morning. We're having the telephones and the post and the shops watched. And we aren't going to lose sight of Wossidlo. But who knows how they may get in touch.'

'Do you really think,' said Kufalt with astonishment, 'that Batzke will accept?'

'Of course he will,' roared the officer. 'No fence will give him more than three or four thousand marks. He'll accept right enough – it's a low trick of Wossidlo's. And he'll make the police the laughing stock of Hamburg, if he can say he got his rings back in twenty-four hours. Now then, where does Batzke live?'

'I don't know,' faltered Kufalt. 'He lives with a different girl every night.'

'But you know him?'

'Yes, I know him.'

'How do you stand with him? Come on, for heaven's sake, you can get dressed while we're talking.'

'We're on bad terms,' said Kufalt, and began to put his clothes on.

'Dropped you out of the job, eh? Well, I won't ask any questions. Get after him at once, you know where he's to be found, don't you?'

'Yes,' said Kufalt in a low voice.

'Well then, in three hours at the latest we must have his address. Ring me up at once. My number is 274. Don't let him out of your sight. I'll find you all right.'

The officer was quite excited. 'Think of the fuss if it's announced in the evening papers that Wossidlo has met the burglars and got back his stuff. Do your best. You'll be well in with us. And there'll be a bit of money in it for you. You won't need to complain. What's your name, by the way?'

'Lederer,' said Kufalt. 'Ernst Lederer.'

'Oh come off it,' said the officer angrily. 'You don't suppose I'm going to swallow all that nonsense you told your Frau Pastorin about being an actor. I want to know your name.'

'Bruhn,' said Kufalt. 'Emil Bruhn.'

'And what were you in for?'

'Robbery and murder,' said Kufalt in a low voice.

'You?' said the officer. 'You!'

'It was only manslaughter, really,' said Kufalt, hesitatingly.

'Oh! Doesn't sound very likely either from the look of you. If you've told another lie—! Are you a fetishist, by the way?'

'What?' asked Kufalt.

'I asked you whether you were a fetishist! Why are you sleeping with a lady's handbag?' He pointed to the black bag on the pillow.

'No, no,' said Kufalt in confusion. 'That belongs to my fiancée. She left it behind her yesterday evening.'

'A girl in bed in the Frau Pastorin's flat?' said the officer. 'I think,

Bruhn, or whatever you call yourself, you'd better get pretty busy in the next few hours, if you don't want us prying into your affairs. And now get along. Ring me up every hour at least. Where are you going now?'

'The Alley Quarter.'

'And whereabouts?'

'Lütt's, on Kugelsplatz.'

'Right,' said the officer, rather more mildly, 'that sounds probable. Get along then. And don't you think you can give us the slip. I can pull you in any time.'

Kufalt went. And he knew that the officer, who remained behind, would not hesitate to open his trunk.

He went, so to speak, for good.

VII

Kufalt really did go straight to the Alley Quarter.

There was no sense in trying to get away at the moment for he would certainly be shadowed. There was also no sense in turning round to see who was shadowing him. That would only make them suspicious, and they would nab him all the surer.

He must lull them into confidence. He must do them a real service, and then he would get his chance. But he knew quite well that when he had got them Batzke or the swag, or both, they would pull him in over the handbags. No more question of thanks. In small things they could be generous; but as soon as it came to a matter of real importance . . .

In any case he was wearing his best suit and his new coat and hat, and had nearly seven hundred marks in his pocket. With that he could manage, provided he could get away.

Strange: while he went on his way, all the emotions that had taken hold of him during the last weeks vanished. Gone was his sense of dejection, his longing for revenge and his greed for money. Only one feeling possessed him – the desire to break away again, to shake off his pursuers and spend a few more weeks in freedom.

Even if nothing happened in those weeks, if he could only go for a walk, eat in a restaurant, drink a glass of beer, lie in a clean white bed – but, oh, please God, not prison – for a while yet!

He reached the Alley Quarter and immediately hurried to Lütt's on Kugelsplatz. It was still empty that morning. The time was not yet ten o'clock; and Lütt too was still asleep. Kufalt mobilized the landlord's wife and finally got himself taken up to the bedroom where Lütt was snoring under a checked quilt.

But Lütt was in a bad mood that morning. Of course he had no idea where Batzke might be; and he did not intend to have any idea.

'Don't pester me with all this blather. I'll have nothing to do with you. Get out. Nothing doing. Have you got a job with the cops these days?'

Kufalt climbed down the stairs in a bad mood. He went to the bar and drank two or three schnapps with the landlady, who eyed him with suspicion. She had listened through the door to his conversation with Lütt.

He was really at a loss what to do. Where in the world should he look for Batzke? The ship-owner's widow on the Harvestehude flashed into his mind. But he no longer believed in her existence.

He left the tavern, made his way to the Grosse Neumarkt, drank another schnapps and telephoned extension 274. No, nothing definite as yet. But he was following up a clue. He must get hold of a girl called Emma.

But while telephoning, he racked his brains to think how he could find out the address of this girl, with whom Batzke had hung out of late. He must ask the other tarts in the neighbourhood. But he did not know where they lived, and at that hour in the morning they would not be on the streets.

Again he dived into the Alley Quarter and wandered aimlessly up and down. Then he chatted to a young Englishman, who only seemed irritated. He was already thinking of abandoning the quest and trying to give his enemies the slip when Ilse came to mind. He ought to have thought of her first. She was in touch with Batzke. He would quite likely get something out of her.

He took a taxi, drove out to the Steindamm and rang the bell. But the landlady was sorry, Fräulein Ilse was out.

(She had a man with her, of course.)

'But you know me, Frau Maschioll. I'm Ilse's fiancé. Just call to her through the door, will you? It will mean ten marks to you.'

That ought to fetch her. But there was nothing doing, there was nothing to be done. 'You can gladly see for yourself, sir. Go along to Fräulein Ilse's room. She's really out. Look.'

And she opened the door.

Yes, she was out. Kufalt said in a despairing voice: 'But she never goes out so early in the morning. I had a date with her.'

'Oh, it was you, then, that rang her up so early.'

'Of course I did,' he said. 'She was to wait for me here.'

'No,' said Frau Maschioll. 'She told me she had to go to the town park. She had some important business there. And she was going to give me a hundred marks if it came off.'

'Ah yes, the park,' said Kufalt thoughtfully. 'Funny how things can slip out of your head.'

And he was gone.

He put off the payment of the ten marks until next time, though the landlady gave him grief all the way downstairs.

He really ought to make another telephone call and get the police to the park. But in the first place he had no time to lose, and secondly a faint new hope glimmered in his mind of scooping the spoils single-handed. He would reap all the fame himself and get free. Or, at any rate, a substantial sum of money. 'Halves, or I'll split' always goes in such cases.

He lavishly took another taxi, all the way to the park. He kept on looking out of the back window to see if he was being followed, but could see no one. Perhaps they had underestimated the amount of money he had on him and had sent a man to trail him who could not afford a taxi. Or they might have lost track of him in the Alley Quarter. Or perhaps they trusted him.

He racked his brain to think where they might be likely to meet. The park is a large place, and though Batzke was a bold man, he was not reckless. Herr Wossidlo might pledge his word of honour as a Hamburg merchant ten times over in the local newspaper: that was not going to be enough for Batzke by a long way. He would take very good care to choose a place where he could not be surprised by the police.

No; it was certainly on purpose that Batzke had acted so promptly. Even if the police had been informed, there was no longer time for them to guard the whole park. He would choose an open space where he could always get away, even if there were two or three of them watching out for him.

Kufalt got out by the casino and paid the taxi. Then he started. First through the café, which was almost deserted, then round the lake and on to the broad expanse of the festival ground. This was deserted. He kept behind the bushes at the edge of the path and peered across the broad expanse of grass, now covered with a light powdering of new snow.

Suddenly he stopped and his heart leapt. No, he was not too late. Over on the grass stood a tall man in a light overcoat, and a grin spread over Kufalt's face – Batzke had always been a tricky character!

He had brought a large camera with a stand. He was busy adjusting it while his girl (wasn't that Ilse? Of course it was Ilse!) stood by a snow-laden tree in a pretty photographic pose.

'First rate,' thought Kufalt; 'about as innocent as a bloke could look.'

And he thrilled with a sort of pride at his colleague's astuteness. 'The cops haven't got him yet by a long way, even if there's one behind every bush.'

From the opposite direction a tall man was walking across the grass towards the pair, carrying a briefcase. He had horn-rimmed spectacles and a grizzled pointed beard. He strolled innocently through the soft, fresh snow towards them, stopped a few paces away, so as not to invade the picture, and seemed to be asking a question.

What it was, Kufalt could not hear, he was too far away. He kept behind his bush. But the little group appeared to be quite unconcerned. They did not once look round.

Ilse stayed quietly beside her tree. Batzke had taken every precaution. Kufalt noticed her slip one hand into her pocket, and there hold it rather tense, with elbow crooked. He knew that movement. Batzke had armed his girl with a gun for this encounter.

Meanwhile the two men had fallen into conversation. They still stood a polite three paces apart. Each seemed to regard the other with a certain respect. Batzke had ceased to attend to his apparatus. He had bent down over the snow and was engaged in unpacking a round parcel. Not a very distinguished receptacle for rings worth a hundred and fifty thousand marks, Kufalt thought. It appeared to be an old preserved-food tin wrapped in newspaper, as far as he could see.

Batzke seemed extremely indifferent. Kufalt would have thought that the exchange of rings and money might have presented certain difficulties. But Batzke calmly handed his tin to the man with the pointed beard. Then he too slipped a hand into his coat pocket.

The man said something with a smile, and Batzke took his hand out of his pocket again and looked on pleasantly while the other picked ring after ring out of the tin, examined it and dropped it into his briefcase.

Indeed, a minute later the two businessmen had got to the stage where burglar Batzke was holding merchant Wossidlo's briefcase. It was more convenient, and quick.

Then Wossidlo threw the tin into the snow, felt in his coat pocket, produced a bundle of paper and gave it to Batzke. Batzke gripped the briefcase under his arm and began to count. Wossidlo, the great merchant, seemed to be a considerate person. He had actually remembered not to bring thousand-mark notes, which crooks always find so difficult to change, but smaller ones, which Batzke took some while to count.

Then the briefcase finally changed hands. Ilse left her tree and went up to the pair. Herr Wossidlo gravely lifted his hat, and the parties took their leave. Herr Wossidlo turned back towards the opposite side of the public ground; but Batzke, arm in arm with the girl, made his way towards Kufalt's border of bushes.

Lonely and abandoned, a black speck on the expanse of snow, the photographic apparatus remained standing on the grass, a sole indication that Herr Batzke was perhaps in rather a hurry.

The scheme of waylaying Herr Wossidlo, and by a bold stroke relieving him of the diamond rings and the briefcase, Kufalt rejected at once. The disposal of such things seemed more difficult than he had believed. And cash is always king. Especially when a man cannot go back home.

Batzke, then. Batzke was certainly not an easy customer, but Kufalt had tried something of the kind on him before and was convinced that he would bring it off again. He was not going to make any excessive claims. He would only ask for three or four thousand out of the fifteen – a sum to which Batzke would certainly agree.

The pair approached, walking in the direction of the casino, along Kufalt's path. Kufalt had to move quickly to catch up. They were both quite at ease, feeling perfectly secure; they did not even glance round the bend in the path that hid Kufalt from their view. So he was able to appear quite suddenly at their side and say:

'Morning, Batzke. Morning, Ilse. Fine morning.'

Batzke was not in the least taken aback, but Ilse gave a faint shriek.

'Hello,' said Batzke, in the best of humour, 'is that you, Willi? How much? I'm in a hurry.'

'I'm sure you are,' agreed Kufalt; 'ditto.' And as he saw Batzke in such a sunny mood, he said casually: 'Five thousand.'

'Eight hundred as agreed,' said Batzke.

'Eight hundred were agreed on five thousand,' said Kufalt; 'it's rather a different situation now.'

'Then two,' said Batzke, 'to leave me in peace.'

'Four,' said Kufalt obstinately.

'Three,' said Kufalt finally.

'You aren't going to be so stupid,' protested Ilse angrily.

'Shut your trap,' said Batzke; he took the thick packet of money out of his pocket, looked round, said quickly, 'The coast's clear,' and as he uttered the words crashed his fist onto Kufalt's chin, who flung up his hands and staggered backwards . . .

Then his head was pummelled with blows as if from a hammer, everything before his eyes went red, then black, and he collapsed.

VIII

It was an effort for Kufalt to wake, remember what had happened and where he lay.

Even before he opened his eyes, while consciousness gradually returned, he had a feeling of chill and dampness around him. He drew up his knees, his hands groped about, as though in search of a blanket. Then everything again vanished for a while, but the cold returned, and the hands clutched for a blanket in vain.

This time he opened his eyes a little and shut them at once. The air about him was dim and grey, and full of falling flakes of snow. He could not understand.

But the cold grew more intense; he sat up slowly, his head felt strangely heavy and confused. He looked about him in bewilderment. In the thick, clammy greyness of the late twilight he could make out bushes, the stump of a tree, half enveloped in snow. He closed his eyes again. He must be dreaming.

The cold grew more menacing and insistent and as he opened his eyes for the second time, and again saw the same bleak bushes and the same snow-covered tree stump, he tried to remember how he had got there.

His head was agonizing, and seemed as though it must burst. He put his hands to it, felt several bumps and bruises – and slowly his memory returned to Batzke . . . and the blows . . .

He staggered to his feet and looked around him. He was not lying on the path, where he had had his argument with Batzke, but in some bushes where he must have been dragged.

He noticed something black in the snow and picked it up. It was his hat. He held it in his hand and walked slowly away. He had not far to go. Only six or eight paces. There he stood on the path where he had been attacked by Batzke. Batzke had not taken much trouble over him; nonetheless he had lain undiscovered, not merely for minutes but for hours. It was already nearly dark.

Just to have him out of sight for the first couple of minutes.

He found it very difficult to walk; every few steps he was suddenly overcome by dizziness and had to fling himself against a tree so as not to fall down. That he must not do. He felt as if he would never get up again.

As he tottered painfully over the short distance he could have walked so easily a few hours before, he thought all the time of his pleasant room in the widow's flat, of his bed, of the open bottle of brandy that still stood in his cupboard – how he longed for it now. Of Batzke, of the rings, of the money, he no longer thought at all. He was no more than a wounded beast whose sole impulse was to creep back into its lair.

But by degrees, as he made his way along, the attacks of dizziness diminished, his step became firmer and his memory stronger. At first he was like a man who wanted to say something and then, the moment he opened his mouth, forgot what it was. There was something he had to bear in mind, something that was not as it should be. Surely it was something connected with his room?

Then it came: he was sitting on the edge of the bed and someone was talking to him. He got up and began to dress: 'Are you a fetishist?' asked the other.

Kufalt saw him, oh he saw him as though he were then standing at his side in that wintry and deserted park – the policeman who made it impossible for him to go back home.

His head began to swim once more. He steadied himself against a tree. Suddenly the cold got to him and he shivered violently; his teeth chattered and he had to vomit.

'I'm shit scared,' he thought.

Then the attack passed, but he stood for a long time motionless, against his tree. The evening drew on. It seemed to him that the driving snow grew colder and more cruel and the wind howled more wildly.

There were noises all around him, the rustling of the pines, the creaking branches – a dim memory came over him of another night like this. A girl had then been with him, what was her name? And that night too had come to a bad end.

Past, and gone.

At last he went on. He only went on because he could not go on standing where he was. But he walked slowly on. The lights of the park café came into view. Good. He could no longer turn to men for help. But he could drink a schnapps or two. That would cheer him up.

For a moment he thought of what he must look like. Whether he could go into the café without attracting attention. He knocked the snow off his coat as well as he could, set his hat straight and waited until he reached a lamp to look at himself in a pocket mirror.

It was a pallid, spectral face that looked at him out of the fragment. But that might be the effect of the light. Still, it was not too bad. On his chin was a large red bruise. Batzke had struck as hard as he knew how. In the centre of the bruise the skin was split and blood had trickled out. He felt in his breast pocket for his handkerchief and wiped the blood away. Now he could go into the café.

No, he could not. As he took the pocket mirror out of his waistcoat pocket, and then as he took his handkerchief out of his breast pocket, he had a definite sense that there was something wrong. He felt in his breast pocket, on the opposite side, and it was so; sure enough, his wallet with his papers and his seven hundred marks had gone.

For a moment he thought of going back to the place where he had been lying, in case it might have slipped out. But that would be no use. The wallet was too large and had always been inclined to stick in his pocket – it could not have slipped out of its own accord. His friend Batzke had done this. He had cheated him of his share, knocked him senseless and then relieved him of his last money. All was as it should be. It was all of a piece with his life of the last few weeks, in which he had gone more and more steeply downhill towards an end, which – close your eyes as you will – was nonetheless coming inexorably closer.

No. Now, when there was every reason for it, he felt no hint of fury or despair. On the contrary. It was just as though, at this last and bitterest blow, his almost exhausted powers of resistance had been rekindled. As he painfully made his way along, with his head again and again refusing to work, he had first to abandon the thought of any help from men – he was alone. Then the thought of his home with the kindly old Pastorin – he no longer had a home. Then the thought of money. His little treasure, so laboriously saved, or stolen at such peril – of that too he had been deprived.

There was no more help in alcohol. What help there was must come from himself. Some weeks ago, when things were going relatively well, he had often toyed with the idea of giving himself up at a police station, or doing something that would get him arrested, just to land himself back home, in jail – but not now.

He stood under his tree, half frozen and half dead, and mulled over a plan by which he could again lay hold of money and win freedom for himself – even though he did not know what to do with it.

IX

Frau Lehmann's greengrocery shop was not on the Fuhlentwiete itself, but round the corner in the Neustädter Strasse. Kufalt was there known as Herr Lederer. He had inquired there for Frau Pastor Fleege's cat, Pussi. And he had now and then bought things from Frau Lehmann for his landlady.

So he met with a friendly welcome when he appeared a few minutes after seven and bought ten eggs and two bottles of beer. But while they were being packed up, and before he could pay for them, poor Herr Lederer felt faint. Frau Lehmann hurriedly fetched him a chair and sent the one assistant still remaining to the tavern at the corner to get an eighth-litre of brandy for the poor gentleman.

What a state he was in! He explained in the meantime that he had fallen down on the street. His chin had hit a kerbstone and his head was still dizzy, he said.

When the girl appeared with the brandy, Frau Lehmann wanted to send her round for Frau Fleege, but Herr Lederer would not hear of it. She was an old lady, and the shock might be the end of her. And he would soon be all right. Might he sit for five minutes in the warm room behind the shop?

Of course he might. He took the brandy with him and then, while Frau Lehmann was clearing up the shop, he asked her, this time in a more cheerful tone, for twenty cigarettes. He took them, disappeared into the back room and shut the door.

He then gulped down the brandy, lit a cigarette, opened the window and jumped out into the yard.

He knew that yard well. In it stood the refuse bins in which Pussi loved to rummage for her scraps of herring. He climbed onto one of the bins and pulled himself up the wall. He was then in a garden, at that time of year quite deserted. He hurried across it, pulled himself up the farther wall and stood in the yard of the Fleege house.

The hardest part was now to come. He had to go from the yard into the lit stairway; possibly the policeman whom he had noticed in the Fuhlentwiete would be just outside the front door. Or he might arrive at the door that very moment and discover him on the staircase as he ran, with no concealment possible, up to Frau Fleege's flat.

However, he must take the risk, and hesitation was folly. So he hurried into the stairway, ran up the stairs and opened the door. Not until he had opened it did he dare to look down. The coast was clear. Now all depended on a successful return journey.

He opened the door quite softly and tiptoed into the hall. Then he pulled the door noiselessly to, and stood listening. In the kitchen nearby there was a light and the clatter of saucepans. The old lady was cooking her supper. Just as well. He would be sorry to do her any harm.

He did not go into his room at all. He went straight into her living room and closed the door softly behind him. It was dark, but not that dark. The street lamps threw a reflection on the ceiling and he could make out the little sewing table by the window. It needed only an instant for his fingers to close on the bunch of keys. But that he did not want. His fingers felt again, and under a handkerchief they came upon the smooth and very serrated single key.

He tiptoed quickly to the cupboard, felt for the keyhole with his other hand, inserted the key, opened the door, which creaked a little, and stood for a moment listening; not a sound. His fingers felt in the upper drawer, grasped the smooth, deep sewing basket and lifted it out. He carried it to the sofa table, opened it, took out the tray, laid it beside the box – and in that moment the door clicked, the light came on and old Frau Pastorin Fleege stood in the doorway.

He stood as if numb. She looked at him helplessly. He saw the horror in her face, her lower jaw began to quiver and tears ran down the old wrinkled face . . .

He did not know what to do. There she stood and wept. He looked confusedly into the basket, opened the inner compartment, saw the money, the savings bank book and reached out for them . . .

'Oh, Herr Lederer! . . .' she whispered.

Suddenly he heard himself speak. While he snatched up the money and the book, he heard himself whisper: 'Sit down at once, don't make a sound. I won't hurt you.'

She whispered again in even deeper horror and bewilderment, 'Herr Lederer! . . .'

Then she made as though to go out into the passage.

Three leaps, and he was beside her. He gripped the little, fragile, helpless, quivering form, laid his hand over the sobbing mouth, dragged her through the sitting room into the bedroom, laid her on the bed and whispered once more, 'Lie quiet for three minutes. Then you can scream.'

He ran out of the bedroom into the sitting room and looked wildly round him for a moment; where had he put his hat? Fool! It was on his head. She would scream in a moment.

He ran down the passage to the door and stood for an instant listening.

Not a sound, all was deathly still. He grasped the handle of the door, turned it very carefully, noiselessly and inch by inch he opened the door, peered out onto the landing, saw nothing, hurried out – and stepped into the arms of his policeman.

'Ah, Kufalt, didn't I tell you I'd find you again?' And to one of his men who stood behind him, 'Have a look round at once, in case he's been up to any games.' And again to Kufalt, 'Well, how's life? Not so good, eh?'

10

North, South, East, West – Home's Best

I

The house stood at the top of a precipitous little road immediately under the castle rock. The schoolboy's room lay up four flights of stairs, each one narrower and steeper than the last, at the peak of the gable.

If the boy went to his window and the day was clear, he could see over the roofs of the little town, over the broadish river valley, over the gentle wooded hills that edged the other side of it as far as the rugged basalt ridges clad in dark firs and pines, known as the Great Owl.

He often gazed at them, for under the Great Owl, a bare hour's walk away, lay his home, the estate of Triebkendorf.

The boy stood at the window and in his imagination he climbed down the steep path to the Great Owl. Torrents of rain had swept the soil from the path and he clambered cautiously from rock to rock. Many of them were gripped and held steady by tenacious strands of roots washed bare; others shook as he slipped on them and threatened to roll downwards if he lingered.

Gradually the path grew gentler, the trees closed in and he seemed to be walking through a cool, green hall. Then it grew lighter, and he stepped out of the forest; the mountain path had climbed the ridge and come out onto a fertile plateau.

A few more steps, the path turned the corner of a hedge, and there was the village. It was more of an estate than a village, with the long, bare cottages of the labourers always enveloped in a damp reek of rotting potatoes.

At the end of the path rose the tall, grey stone gateway leading into the estate. And immediately opposite, on the farther side of the yard, flanked by barns and stables and sheds, stood the great house. But that was not important. More important was the small red-brick house on the right of the yard near the gate, with its six windows beneath the low roof, which was the boy's home. It was quite insignificant; a little red box of a place, a steward's house, such as are to be found on thousands of estates, with whitewashed walls, worn planking and smoke-stained kitchen – but there he was at home.

Two lime trees stood outside the door, tall strong trees, towering above the roof and the chimney. They had always been there, since he was quite small, proud guardians of that little house. When the weather was at all clement, his mother wheeled his perambulator out into the yard. How often had he looked up at that marvellous golden wilderness of leaves trembling faintly in the breeze and reached up at them with tiny hands.

He learnt to know the trees; the transparent network of their winter garb, when the sky peered down through the gnarled black serpentine branches. Then, later on, when they came to fullness, and nothing could be seen but a great canopy of green. Soon they blossomed, and the trees rang like great bells with the incessant humming of the bees. At last the leaves shrivelled and grew yellow, and dropped, one by one at first and then in fluttering clouds. Every gust of wind drove them across the yard, where they lay heaped in the horses' drinking troughs, against the rubble walls of the stables, and the whole place was filled with their acrid, mouldering smell.

When the boy grew older and moved from his parents' bedroom into the gable attic, and learnt to sleep alone, it was the lime trees that brought him comfort when he felt frightened in the solitary void of night – he knew every sound they made, indeed he had grown up at their side.

The boy stands at the window of the pastor's house at the top of the steep street and stares at the Great Owl. He imagines he can see his mother's smooth head bowed over her sewing at the window. His father comes out of the stables with his riding whip in his hand. He stops by the wooden frame in the centre of the yard from which hangs an old ploughshare.

His father pulls out his watch, waits a moment and then says to the foreman: 'One o'clock!' The foreman strikes the ploughshare with a hammer and the sharp metallic clang echoes all over the yard.

From the stable door comes the first team of horses. The workers range themselves in rows outside the steward's house. The casual workers in front, first the lads, then the girls. Behind them the estate labourers, first the women, then the men . . .

He sees it all, as he has seen it a hundred times before. And that is why he sees it now, from the window in the pastor's house, across seven lines of hills and seven valleys.

The bells in the valley begin to peal; it is Saturday afternoon, a holiday. The schoolboy sighs. He no longer looks at the Great Owl, he looks across the little town; over by the river stands the high school, which explains his presence in that place. Then he looks down into the street, at a house on the other side, a little below the pastor's, where there is a dressmaker's shop. There too they were packing up, as it was Saturday afternoon. A bevy of girls bustling about and putting their belongings away: daughters of the more substantial townsmen who had been taking a sewing lesson.

He has often noticed one of them, a slim and cheerful fair-haired girl, and when she looks across at him he nods.

She nods back; and for a few moments they stand at their respective windows. The fifteen-year-old schoolboy and the little blonde girl. They nod again, and laugh.

Suddenly he has an inspiration. He makes a sign to her, runs back into the room, picks up the empty envelope of a letter from his mother which had come that morning, and dashes back to the window.

She looks at him, he waves the envelope and nods meaningfully. She looks doubtfully back at him, and then nods slowly in reply . . .

He dashes away from the window and down the stairs.

On the first landing he stops; she has also run down a flight, and she has also stopped. He waves the letter again, and they both nod.

Next flight, another nod.

Last flight, last nod.

He flings open the heavy, creaking oak door and runs out onto the rough, cobbled street.

In the middle of the street, between the two houses, they meet.

'Good day,' he says awkwardly.

'Good day,' she answers shyly.

And that is all for a few moments.

She looks doubtfully at the letter in his hands. An odd-looking envelope, torn open, with a stamp and a postmark.

He too looks at the envelope.

'Please give me the letter,' she says quickly.

'I haven't got one,' he says. 'I only wanted to get you to come down.'

Pause.

'I must go back,' she says.

'Eight o'clock this evening by the town wall,' he urges.

'I can't,' she says. 'My mama . . .'

'Please!' says he.

She purses her lips and looks at him. 'I'll try,' says she.

'Please!' he says. 'Eight by the town wall.'

'Right,' she says.

They look at each other. Suddenly they both burst out laughing.

'Aren't you funny with your letter,' she laughs.

'You bet!' he says proudly. 'I caught you at last.'

'At eight, then.'

'Punctually.'

'Till then.'

'Bye-bye.'

Back indoors again; and upstairs. Only a couple of hours till eight, only a couple of hours till eight – it sounds like a song to him.

But he doesn't sing that song for long.

The moment he sees the fat dressmaker, Gubalke, with her white, short hair, cross the street, ring the doorbell and go in – the song fades on his lips. The boy forces himself to continue, but it is a faltering effort and often comes to a stop when he leans out of the window to see whether the dressmaker has come out again.

No, she has not, and the empty workroom opposite wears a bleak and ugly grin. A couple of hours till eight? An eternity till eight.

Then she comes. She crosses the street to her house, but as she stands in the doorway she turns, catches sight of the boy at the window, glares and shakes her fist at him. Then the door slams behind her.

'Nothing much can happen. I really haven't done anything I shouldn't,' he tries to reassure himself.

Then comes a knock at the door and Minna the maid, a bitter old nag, says: 'The Herr Pastor wants to see you; at once!'

'All right,' says the boy, and starts to comb his hair in front of the mirror.

'At once. This very minute.'

'I'm coming!'

'You're in for it!'

'You sour old lemon!' says the boy, and runs down the two flights of stairs to the pastor's study.

He knocks; a voice – a smooth and oily voice – says, 'Come in,' and he stands before his pastor.

The voice is ominously smooth. The homily begins: shocked and disappointed – wanton flirtation – desecration of a godly household – clandestine correspondence – a mere boy, too . . .

'What is to become of you later on if you begin like this?'

'I never wrote a letter.'

'Your denial completes the picture. Minna saw it, as well as Frau Gubalke. The whole street must have seen it. Tomorrow the whole town will know what kind of person is living in my house . . .'

'But really I didn't . . .'

'I have no intention of discussing the matter. Go up and pack your things. I have already telephoned your father. I will not have you another night under my roof.'

The boy's mouth begins to quiver . . .

'Please, Herr Pastor, please . . .'

'That will do. Going with girls at fifteen. Disgusting. Simply disgusting.'

The clerical forefinger rises in menace. Then it points to the door and the boy can do nothing but go out.

In his room he is alone; but he cannot pack for crying. Minna brings his clean linen. 'Yes, howl away, you nasty little boy!'

'Get out, you old lemon!' he roars, and finds he can howl no more.

And while the day, with all the lively, cheerful noise of Saturday afternoon, passes over into evening, he sits there on his oilcloth sofa, with his trunk, half full, on a chair; he cannot bring himself to pack it because he cannot believe that all is really at an end . . .

Shortly after seven he hears his father's bicycle bell. He dashes to the window and shouts: 'Father, come up to me first!'

But though his father nods, he does not come. The pastor has intercepted him, of course; for Father is a man of his word.

Another five minutes to wait, then the stairs creak under Father's heavy riding boots and he comes into the room.

'Well, my boy? By the waters of Babylon they sat and wept, eh? Too late. Too late. Tell me all about it.'

Father is always splendid. The way the great, strong man sits there at the table on a little chair, in his leather-strapped riding breeches, his green shooting jacket, with his ruddy tanned face and the snow-white brow above it – the white skin sharp-edged against the tan at the line of his cap – and the way he says 'Tell me all about it' – makes everything seem easier at once.

He listens. 'Right,' he says at last. 'And that is all? Right. And now I'll go down and see your pastor.'

But he soon reappears and his face is rather flushed.

'Nothing doing, my son, it seems you're a very bad lad indeed. Well, you'd better come along home with me. Mother will be very pleased to see you.

'We'll leave your trunk here. Eli can fetch it tomorrow. He's got to come into town anyhow. You can stand on my back wheel so long as the road's flat. When we get up into the hills we'll both push. We'll be home by eleven.'

'But what about school?'

'I'm afraid it's all up with the high school, my boy. He's sure to shop you to the head. We'll see tomorrow, I'll ride over.'

And so they depart. Father on the left of the bicycle, son on the right. Minna laughs at them out of the kitchen window.

'You old cow,' shouts the father, flushing angrily.

'I always call her a lemon,' says the son.

'Lemon's much better,' agrees the father.

'Um, Father,' begins the son cautiously.

'Well?'

'It's just on eight . . .'

'Yes, the town hall clock will be striking in a minute.'

'And we're passing the town wall . . .'

The father whistles slowly. 'Oh, that's how the wind's blowing, is it?'

'It's only because I fixed it up with her. I can't just leave her there. And I'd like to say goodbye.'

'I really don't know whether I ought . . .'

'Oh, do, Father, please!'

'All right. I don't think I ought; but I will. And not longer than five minutes.'

'Of course not.'

'I don't want to be in this,' says the father thoughtfully. 'I'll stay here with the bicycle. When the five minutes are up I'll whistle my usual whistle. And you must come at once.'

'Very well, Father.'

She was already waiting.

'Good evening. How punctual you are!'

'So one ought to be. Good evening.'

'It's just striking eight.'

'Yes, I can hear it.'

The conversation, which has begun so cheerfully, suddenly halts.

At last he says: 'Did you get away all right?'

'I told a bit of a fib. And you?'

'Oh yes, I managed it.'

'Is anything the matter?' she asks suddenly.

'No, nothing. What should there be? It's nice this evening, isn't it?'

'Yes. Rather close, though.'

'Perhaps it is. I'll have to be going soon . . .'

'Oh . . .'

'There's my father waiting over there . . .'

'Where?'

'There. The man with the bicycle. Just put your head round the bush . . .'

'And he knows—? And he let you?'

'Yes, my father's like that.'

She looks at him a moment.

'But I'm not like that, I don't think it's nice of you.'

He blushes slowly.

'I wouldn't have thought it of you.'

'I . . .' he began.

'No,' she says; 'I shall go home at once.'

'Fräulein,' he says. 'Fräulein, I have to leave. The pastor has turned me out, because . . . You understand . . . Frau Gubalke complained.'

'Oh dear, oh dear!' she cries. 'And my mama . . .'

'Probably they will expel me from the high school.'

'If my father hears of it . . . !'

'Mine wasn't angry.'

'And what about my school? . . .'

'You must put all the blame onto me.'

'Oh, you – and there wasn't even anything at all in that envelope.'

'But I'd like to write to you,' he says.

His father whistles the tune: *Don't – you – love – me – any – more?*

'Oh God, the five minutes are up. I must . . .'

'Go away then, do. You've got me into a pretty mess.'

Don't – you – love – me – any – more?

'And I don't even know your name, Fräulein?'

Don't – you – love – me – any – more?

'Yes, and get me into more trouble!'

'But, Fräulein, it really isn't my fault!'

'And what am I to say at home?'

Don't – you – love – me – any – more?

'Fräulein, I must . . .'

'Yes, you go along home to your father, who isn't angry. But I . . . ?'

'Please shake hands with me, at least.'

'Well, really!'

'But we may never meet again.'

'Much better not. And I thought it would be so nice. Oh God, here comes your father.'

'Well, my boy, I thought you promised. Good evening, little fairy. Have you two had a quarrel?'

'I . . .'

'We . . .'

'Shake hands, goodbye!'

'Goodbye!'

'Goodbye!'

'And now we must be off!'

Again they look at each other.

'It's all my fault,' says the boy ruefully, and his lips quiver.

'Yes,' she says. 'Never mind, though. I was just a bit upset at first. But I'll wriggle out of it somehow.'

'Now then, you two – time's up. You're much too young; and much too green.'

'Well, all the best!'

'Yes; thank you. Same to you.'

'*Auf Wiedersehen!*'

'Perhaps we really shall meet again.'

'Goodnight, little lady. Come, Willi.'

Beyond the bridge, the road began to ascend. 'Jump down, my boy,' said his father.

And as they walked beside the bicycle, he went on: 'There's no hurry. We shall get home in plenty of time.'

'When do you get up nowadays, Father?'

'At my usual time in summer. At four. I have to look after the feeding and milking myself. The student hands can't be trusted.'

And after a pause he asked casually: 'You don't care for farming, do you?'

'I don't think so, Father.'

'Any other ideas?'

'Yes . . .'

'Yes? What do you mean by yes?'

'I'd like to keep on at the high school.'

'I don't see how that's going to be managed. The pastor and the head are too good friends.'

'But couldn't you send me to another school—?'

They walked for a while in silence.

'Look, Willi. It has already been hard for me. I don't earn much, as you know. And there's your sister. I'd have carried on, as things were, but now it's finished. As a matter of fact it's just as well for me that this has happened. I wouldn't have said anything. But as you've brought it on yourself, I think we'll leave it so.'

'But I haven't done anything!'

'You've at least done a very foolish thing. You were thoughtless anyway, Willi. You must learn that you can do as much damage by doing what's foolish as by doing what's wrong. And it's not always possible to put things right again. After all, you're out of this pretty well, you're going home with your father, and the storm's over. Later, perhaps you won't be able to go home afterwards.'

The father sighed gently, and pushed his bicycle more slowly uphill. The son walked in silence at his side. Dimly it went through his mind: his father was surely being unfair; he had done nothing wrong; and yet his father seized the excuse to save money and take him away from school. If it had been possible for so long, surely it could go on further. Merely because he had run out onto the street with an empty envelope and talked to a girl for two minutes, his father wanted to save his school and college fees. It didn't seem right.

The road mounted the hillside between high forest walls; and above them, edged by the marching lines of trees, hung a long, glowing strip of deep blue sky.

'How about business?' asked the father at last.

'Oh no!' cried the boy in a tone of disappointment.

'Not a shop,' said the father reassuringly. 'I had thought of a bank.'

'Ah,' said the boy.

'Well?' said the father encouragingly.

'I really don't know,' said the son, doubtfully.

'When you've had a crack on the head,' said the father, 'it's no use making a song and dance about it, you must just think over what went wrong and try to put it right. Well, you can stay at home quietly for two or three weeks. You might help me with the wages accounts. I never have time for them during the harvest. Right . . . hop up again, I can ride for a bit now.'

The boy stood on the back hub, with his hands on his father's shoulders. The bicycle purred downhill, and a cool refreshing breeze blew into his face.

'I don't even know her name,' he said suddenly.

'What?' shouted the father, who had not heard, in the rush of the descent.

'I don't even know her name.'

'Whose name?'

'The girl's.'

The father stepped so hard on the brake that the son was jerked onto his shoulders. The bicycle almost stopped.

'I really ought to tell you,' said the father, pedalling slowly on, 'to get down and walk home; so as to give you time to think. Are you still set on what's past and over? Do you mean to carry on with a piece of foolishness that only got you into trouble? Oh, Willi, Willi, I'm afraid I'm making life too easy for you again. I hope it won't be too much for you one day.'

The bicycle sped on and the son did not answer.

Then they rode over a bridge; they could hear the gurgle of water as they passed; the road curved, the reflection from the bicycle lamp flashed onto a wall of trees, then something black and tall and massive rose up in the darkness.

The father rang his bell.

'Mother's sure to hear that.'

They rode through the gateway in the massive wall; the windows of the steward's house were brightly lit. As they approached the door opened, a glow of light came forth and in it stood the mother . . .

The bicycle stopped with a rasp of brakes.

'There you are, Willi,' said Mother. 'Come in quickly. You must be terribly hungry. I've kept some pea soup for you from dinner.'

II

One lovely morning in early spring, Herr Gröschke, of the Public Prosecutor's Department, said to his assistant, Söhnlein: 'I have the Kufalt case on Friday. Go through the papers and draw up a summary for me. Take each offence separately; and make a note of the penalty provided in each instance. I want to have the details clearly in my mind before I ask for sentence.'

'Certainly,' said Herr Söhnlein, and plunged into the papers.

Söhnlein had two passions: the cultivation of cacti and criminal law. But the second passion was the stronger. He was in some senses a legal arithmetician; persons disappeared under his hands, clauses and sections remained. Then they too dissolved into figures. Things had happened, passions had been let loose, desires and schemes and conflicts – they passed, and nothing was left of them but figures. And on Friday Herr Gröschke, of the Public Prosecutor's Department, would use these figures.

Here was the case of Wilhelm (not Willi) Kufalt.

Sentenced in 1924 to five years' imprisonment for:

> 1. Embezzlement, under § 246 of the Code.
> 2. Major forgery of documents on several occasions, under § 268 of the Code.

'Good; and now let us see what is up against him this time.'

And he wrote:

> 1. 14–15 'independent' thefts of handbags, as the prisoner planned each one separately . . .

'The appropriate paragraphs of the Code are certainly—'

> § 249 (Robbery), and also § 223 (Violence), in conjunction with § 223. a., as the violence was the result of a premeditated attack. In accordance with § 73 of the Code the penalty to be applied falls under the terms of § 249 of the Code. Robbery and violence are to be dealt with and punished as a single crime:
>
> 1–15 years' maximum security; under extenuating circumstances, from 6 months' to 5 years' imprisonment.

'But the robbery was committed on the public highway.'

And he wrote:

> So the case does not come under § 249 of the Code, but under § 250, Subsection 3:
>
> 5–15 years' maximum security; extenuating circumstances, 1–5 years' imprisonment.

'Now for number 2.'

And he wrote:

> 2. 'Theft' of the savings bank book and of 37, 56 marks in cash is a theft 'approximating to a robbery', and is to be dealt with under the latter category in accordance with § 252 of the Code. (See also § 249 of the Code.)
>
> 3. Prisoner planned the shop window burglary and was accessory before the event: § 243, Section 1, Subsection 2, 49 of the Code:
>
> From 4 months 15 days, to 1 year, 4 months, 15 days' imprisonment. Alternatively – from 1 year, to 9 years, 11 months' imprisonment; extenuating circumstances – from 22 days' imprisonment, to 4 years, 11 months, 29/30 days' imprisonment.
>
> Even when the offence was committed against the will of the accessory, he is still liable. The accessory made no with-

drawal that would relieve him of liability, and his efforts materially assisted the success of the crime.

4. Attempted blackmail of the leader of the gang, § 253, Section 43, ff, of the Code:

From 7 days, to 4 years, 11 months, 29/30 days' imprisonment.

'There,' said Herr Söhnlein to himself, with much satisfaction. 'A very neat bit of work. Now I had better add up the total term of imprisonment incurred. There is no question, I think, of extenuating circumstances.'

And he plunged into earnest calculation:

1. Robbery accompanied	1 year	2 months' imprisonment
by violence, 15 separate		8 ” ”
occasions; extenuating		9 ” ”
circumstances:		10 ” ”
	1 year	3 ” ”
	2 years	—
		7 ” ”
		8 ” ”
		11 ” ”
	1 year	2 ” ”
		9 ” ”
		10 ” ”
	1 year	—
	1 year	4 ” ”
		9 ” ”
2. Theft:	2 years	—
3. Accessory in burglary:		3 ” ”
4. Attempted blackmail:	1 year	2 ” ”
Total	18 years	1 month imprisonment.

Suggested sentence: 10 years' imprisonment.

'There,' said Herr Söhnlein, surveying his achievement with a loving eye. 'That's just about right. I've put it rather high, perhaps, but something is always knocked off.'

III

The large, green, closed car gave one raucous hoot outside the gateway, a warder's face appeared at the window of the porter's lodge, nodded to the police driver, and in a moment or two the great double gates swung slowly open.

The van drove under the archway, across a yard and stopped in front of the Administration Building.

The driver clambered down from his seat, two policemen emerged from the back of the van and almost at the same moment four officers appeared from a door, one in plain clothes.

'Delivery,' said one of the policemen.

'How many?' asked the man in plain clothes.

'Five,' said the policeman.

'Right,' said the other. 'Anything special?'

'I don't know. I didn't particularly notice. We had to handcuff one, he's got form.'

'What's his name?'

'Wait a minute. Here it is – Kufalt. Seven years. Robbery, burglary and I don't know what else.'

'Did he try to bolt?'

'Dare say. No idea. He was quite quiet in the van.'

'Fetch 'em out, then.'

The two policemen went into the van and opened the cell doors. Out came a cloud of reeking tobacco smoke.

'Pigs,' said the policeman. 'I particularly forbade you to smoke.'

Then the prisoners came out.

First, a little old man with a white death's head, who looked nervously about him. Then a young man with black, curly hair, in a smart suit and faultlessly creased trousers, who surveyed the officers with a condescending air, whistled softly, and put his hands into his pockets.

'Take your hands out of your pockets at once!'

The man did so, very deliberately.

'A bit fresh this morning, Inspector,' said he. 'I think old papa has shat his trousers for fear.'

'What?'

'He stinks like a toilet anyway.'

'Look,' said an officer savagely to the old man, 'is that true?'

'Ohgod, ohgod,' wailed the old creature. 'Don't be hard on me, sir . . . I couldn't help it . . .'

'Stand right over there. The storeman will have a few things to say to you, I shouldn't wonder . . .'

Meantime, numbers three and four had clambered out of the van. There was a tall, lanky man in a very shabby suit. 'Morrrning, Panje Inspector,' he said.

'Hold your tongue. Polish, aren't you? We don't want any good mornings from the likes of you.'

But the fourth was a comfortable and corpulent personage who looked like a respectable taxpayer. 'Good day, Deputy Governor Fröschlein. Good day, Herr Fritze. Good day, Herr Haubold. Good day, Herr Wenk. You've become a senior warder, have you? Fine, I congratulate you.'

And he added with an apologetic smile: 'Here I am again, but it's only a small matter this time. Nine months. An unfortunate little accident in my profession.'

The officers grinned delightedly.

'Well, Häberlein, what was it this time?'

'Oh, not worth talking about. People are so silly; they've got no sense of humour.' And he continued, with a sudden air of anxiety: 'Will I get my old job in the kitchen? No one cooks as well as I do, you know, Deputy Governor.'

'And no one eats as much as you do, Häberlein. Well, I'll have a talk to the work inspector. Now then, last man. Oh Lord, what an object!'

'You may well say that,' grumbled the warder.

Kufalt clambered painfully out of the van. His suit hung in rags, half his head was wrapped in a blood-soaked bandage and one arm was in a sling.

'What on earth have you been up to, my lad?'

'I had a fight with a bloke,' said Kufalt.

'Looks as if the bloke won,' observed the officer. 'Warder, take off his handcuffs, he won't try to bolt now.'

'I certainly shan't,' said Kufalt. 'I'm very glad to be here.'

'Squealed on somebody, eh?' said the officer. 'Isn't your friend coming here too?'

'I don't think so. He got hard labour.'

'You ought to be glad; he's a hard hitter, he is. Off you go!'

IV

'What am I to do with you?' said the storeman pensively. 'It's a regulation that a prisoner's to take a bath on admission. But I don't know how you're going to manage it with all those bandages.'

'Oh, that'll be all right, Chief Warder,' said Kufalt ingratiatingly. 'It looks worse than it is. I'd like a bath very much. A bloke gets so dirty when he's on remand.'

'Just as you like. Peter, look after him. But don't put him under the shower. This time we can use the bath.'

'Right,' said the storeman's orderly, an elderly bald-head. 'Come on, you fresher.'

'Is there a warder present in the bathroom?' whispered Kufalt.

'He just has a look in at the most. Got anything?'

'Perhaps. Are you safe?'

'I'm all right,' said bald-head proudly. 'I've never done anyone down. You can trust me with what you like, and I don't pinch any of it either. Done a stretch before?'

'Yes,' said Kufalt. 'Five years.'

'And now?'

'Seven.'

'Some stretch!'

'Pah. Seven years is nothing, I can do 'em on my head.'

'You've got a nerve.'

'What are you on about! What's the work inspector like? Is it easy to get a cushy job?'

'Depends,' said the orderly, turning on the tap. Water gushed into the bath. 'Like it hot?'

'Middling. Now let's see. Help me to undress. I can't use my arm much yet.'

'Who knocked you about like that?'

'My pal. He tried to throw me out of a third-floor cell window.'

'Ouch!'

'But I bit him in the hand, and he didn't half yell, I can tell you! What's the old man like?'

'Not so bad. He doesn't have much to say. Did you pull off anything worthwhile?'

'A hundred and fifty thousand,' said Kufalt solemnly.

'What!! Go on!'

'Didn't you read in the paper about the jewel robbery at Wossidlo's in Hamburg?'

'Sure. What about it?'

'That was my job.'

'You don't say!' The orderly stared at him in admiration. 'Did you manage to put any aside?'

Kufalt smiled significantly. 'Ah, that's what we don't talk about. Perhaps I'll give you a surprise one day. Now then, just see if there's anyone around, will you?'

'All clear,' reported the orderly obediently.

'Right. Then unwind the bandage from my arm. So. Slowly, so it doesn't drop into the water. There's the first packet of tobacco. Right. Shove it under the bath. There's some plug in the tin box. Here's another packet. And here's the third. And there's cigarette papers too, and matches. Thank the Lord I can shift my arm again; it had gone dead.'

And he swung his arm energetically.

The orderly was dumbfounded. 'Well, I'm damned! Isn't there anything wrong with your arm, then?'

'Course there isn't. The infirmary orderly fixed that up, for a packet of tobacco. Listen here, mate. If you keep your mouth shut and don't split, there's half a packet for you.'

'A whole packet,' demanded the orderly firmly.

'Nothing doing,' said Kufalt as he hopped into the bath. 'I've only got three.'

'Well, there's more where they came from.'

'I don't know, I'll have to look around a bit first and see who'll do my bits of business for me. When does the doctor come?'

'The doctor? Tomorrow.'

'Damn. I'll have to take my bandage off. Are the cells here searched much?'

'No. You'd better stick your baccy in your mattress, they never look there. You can smoke after lock-up. The nightwatch won't split.'

'That's good. All right, I'll give you a packet. I can always get more. But you'll have to give me a nice new outfit at the store.'

'I will. We'll fix that up right away.'

With a sigh of satisfaction Kufalt stretched himself in the bath. 'It really is good to be inside again, you can lead a regular life again.'

'That's so,' said the orderly. 'But seven years – well, don't forget me.'

'When you've done five years, seven don't seem much more. And perhaps there'll be an amnesty. The main thing is not to run out of tobacco, and to get a soft job. But I'm not worrying, I'll look after myself all right.'

V

The first exciting day, with all its comings and its goings, interviews and distribution of clothes and outfits, was over; it was after lock-up, and Kufalt was sitting alone on his bed in cell 207.

The prison was filled with the old familiar evening noises: a bed swung down onto the floor, a prisoner fell to whistling absentmindedly in his cell and his neighbour burst into shouts of protest, two prisoners on the storey below were talking out of their windows, a bucket lid clattered, a watchdog howled in the yard.

Kufalt was at ease; Kufalt was at peace. He had got an excellent cell and his outfit was first-rate, the brushes almost as good as new. Behind the bucket he had found some tinder, flint and striker, so he would not need his matches, and he already had something to swap. He had got a clean suit of clothes and good shoes, and his underclothes were also good; the coarse shirt did scratch him a little, but he would soon get used to that.

He had had a talk with the work inspector, who seemed to be a decent sort; as soon as Kufalt was reported well, he was to be put into the aluminium workshop and set to file down castings, a job he knew nothing about, but he quite looked forward to it. It would be a change, at any rate; there was no net-making in this prison.

Darkness fell quickly; he sat quietly on his bed, his tobacco tucked away in his mattress. He was waiting until the nightwatchmen had padded past in their list slippers. When they had gone he could enjoy a cigarette in peace. A man had to mind his eye to begin with until he knew what risks he could take.

Tomorrow he would polish his bucket lid, which was not at all as it should be. He could certainly get some polish in exchange for a couple of matches, and a spotless cell would earn him favour with the chief warder. Next, he would clean his windows, but there was no hurry; there was all the time in the world before him.

He must get himself reported fit for work as soon as possible, as life in his cell would otherwise be very dull. Library books would not be given out for two days; in the meantime he must manage with the Bible and hymn book. He must make up to the book orderly so as to be sure of getting good, thick volumes. For the present he would only be given one book, which would have to last him the entire week; but he was counting on being put into category two after six months, when two books a week are allowed.

As an old convict he had resolved to get on good terms with everybody; it was not difficult, and he had learnt his lesson. He had even asked to be taken to see the chaplain; this time he would not be such a fool, he would take care to keep in the chaplain's good graces. His quarrels had never done him any good, and a man must know how to learn from his own follies.

He wished he could hear the watchmen shuffling past his door – he longed for a cigarette.

But he was better off in here than outside. Outside, he had just smoked away without thinking, but here – since he had climbed out of the Black Maria a good eight hours ago, he had not smoked at all. That had never happened outside. And there never seemed time outside to read a book in peace and quiet. He would take care to get a book of travels. Hedin's books were always nice, fat volumes and sometimes there was an illustration with a woman's bare breast or legs. Oh yes, it would be fine.

'Click,' and his cell was suddenly lit up.

He jumped to his feet and stood to attention. The slide over the peephole had dropped, but the little gaping aperture confused his vision and he could not see the eye outside.

'You lie down, my lad – want a nurse to tuck you up?'

'And wouldn't that be nice, Chief Warder.' Kufalt grinned at the iron door, and pretended to undress at once.

'Well, goodnight.'

'Goodnight, Chief Warder. And thanks very much.'

'Click,' and the cell was again in darkness.

Kufalt leaned against the door and listened.

He heard the steps depart, then he heard them on the other side; the staircase creaked, and all was clear.

He picked up the cigarette he had already rolled, and a match – he would use a match this time, it was easier – pushed the table under the window, put the stool on top of it, and clambered up cautiously in the darkness.

Then he hooked one arm round the ventilator, lit the cigarette and puffed out of the window.

How good it tasted – he flooded his lungs with smoke; a cigarette in prison was glorious, it was the best cigarette in the world.

'Hello, new boy,' whispered a voice.

'Yes?' he answered.

'Are you smoking?'

'Can't you smell it?'

'Bring me a bit of baccy tomorrow at recreation. I'm your neighbour on the left.'

'I'll see about it.'

'No, you've got to. I'll tell you a bit about the cops on our landing. Then you can get a cushy job quick.'

'Why haven't you got one?'

'Oh, I'm going out in five days.'

'Good for you. How long have you been in?'

'A pretty good stretch – a year and a half.'

'Call that a stretch! I'm doing seven.'

'Well, I never . . . What are you in for?'

'I did the jewel robbery at Wossidlo's on the Jungfernstieg. You must have heard of it.'

'You bet I have! Seven years is cheap for that. Have you got any doings left?'

'Quite a nice little packet.'

'Look here, mate . . .' began the other man.

'Well?'

'If I got a letter out for you, and you wanted any money slipped into the prison, you can trust me. I won't split. I won't tell the cops where the goods are . . .'

'I'll think it over.'

'I've only got five days left.'

'I'll let you know. What are you in for?'

'Embezzlement . . .'

'Well, I'm not likely to let you get your hands on my money . . .'

'I wouldn't steal from a pal; what do you take me for? I'd skin a greasy old grafter any time. But a pal – and in for seven years! Now you give me a letter, eh? Has your girl got the stuff?'

'Perhaps . . .'

'Listen, mate,' said the other man eagerly; 'I can buy you anything you want. I can slip it into prison all right, don't you worry. And you needn't bring me any baccy tomorrow, I've got plenty.

I only said that because I thought you were green. I can give you lots of baccy, and cigarette papers too. And I've got a nice bit of toilet soap that you might as well have . . .'

'Well, goodnight,' said Kufalt. 'I'm going to turn in. I'll think about that letter.'

'You do as I say, and mind you don't get mixed up with any of the orderlies, they'll double-cross you. Psst, are you still there?'

'Yes, but I'm going now.'

'How much was it?'

'Oh, about fifteen thousand. But I've spent two or three . . .'

'You don't say! And has your girl got all that! I'd do ten years for that. Twelve years . . .'

'G'night.'

'G'night. I won't forget your baccy.'

Kufalt slid softly down from his throne, cleared everything away and got into bed.

The man was a fool, but he might be useful, the sort of fool who let himself be stung. What a shock he would get if Kufalt gave him a letter and told him to go to that uppity little typist at Jauch's typing agency and ask her for a thousand marks, or better still, to Liese. She would put him through it properly.

Kufalt had drawn the blanket well up over his shoulders, it was pleasantly quiet in prison, and he was going to have a sound night's sleep.

How good it was to be back home again. No more worries. Almost like home in the old days, with his father and his mother.

Almost?

It was better. Here a man could live in peace. The voices of the world were stilled. No making up your mind, no need for effort.

Life proceeded duly and in order. He was utterly at home.

And Willi Kufalt fell quietly asleep, with a peaceful smile on his lips.

Afterword

Hans Fallada, the son of a senior member of the German judiciary, was no stranger to a prison cell. When *Once a Jailbird* was first published, in March 1934, he had already spent a total of almost three years behind bars, for he had been sent to prison twice in the 1920s for embezzlement, as a result of his alcohol and drug addiction, and in 1933, shortly after the Nazi regime came to power, he had been arrested again, this time on the much more serious charge of plotting to assassinate Hitler. Fallada was therefore familiar with the criminal justice system and his experience of prison life made him a passionate advocate of prison reform.

After completing his first prison sentence, in 1924, Fallada published an essay entitled 'A Voice from the Prisons', in which he criticized a number of aspects of prison policy. For example, he considered it unacceptable that prisoners on remand were held in worse conditions than prisoners who had already been sentenced. He took the view that a prison sentence should entail the loss of liberty and forced labour, but should otherwise not be excessively harsh. Furthermore, he saw no reason why the prison library should be so poorly stocked or have such restricted opening hours or why prison windows should have opaque glass that prevented prisoners from seeing the world outside. And he was particularly critical of the complete absence of a coherent rehabilitation strategy. Having suffered from a lack of information about entitlement to remission himself, he demanded a more transparent remission system that would provide clarity about both the process and the expected outcomes.

Fallada developed his ideas on prison reform, particularly on the care and resettlement of offenders, further during his second term in prison, from September 1925 to May 1928. Shortly before his release he wrote an (unpublished) essay in which he described the disorientation, vulnerability and helplessness of men who had been locked up for years and he urged the prison authorities to make transitional arrangements for prisoners coming to the end of their sentences. The absence of such arrangements forms a major theme in *Once a Jailbird*, where not one of the former prisoners succeeds in coping with life on the outside. Shortly after his release, Willi Kufalt begins to long for the peace and quiet of his prison cell and the ordered existence provided by the prison regime. He even thinks of prison as 'Heimat', which means not just 'home' but a place where his material, emotional and psychological needs are met and where he feels a strong sense of belonging. In attributing such feelings to his protagonist, Fallada is delivering a trenchant critique of a prison regime that he regards as failing utterly in one of its primary functions: the task of rehabilitation. The aim of the novel, according to the outline that Fallada sent to his publisher, Ernst Rowohlt, in April 1932, was 'to show how the current criminal justice system and modern society as a whole force anyone who has broken the law only once into a life of crime'.

For Fallada, writing was an important survival strategy in prison. While serving his first sentence, he kept a prison diary, which began with an account of his journey to the prison and went on to describe his day-to-day experience of life in a prison cell. The entry for 24 June 1924, four days into his sentence, records: 'It would be hard if I didn't have this joy in the evenings of being able to write. It is almost as if I lived only for this.' Gradually he engaged in exercises in creative writing and, by the end of July, he was noting ideas for novels, including one about the rehabilitation of a former prisoner, thanks to the support of a 'simple young woman'.

By the summer of 1925 he had started writing a novel about prison life, the work which was to become *Once a Jailbird*. The provisional title, 'Robinson in Prison', contains echoes of one of Fallada's favourite books as a child: Daniel Defoe's *Robinson Crusoe*. He establishes the connection in the first sentence: 'A man who arrives in prison is like Robinson Crusoe, washed up by a storm on a desert island. All the skills that he has learned on the outside are of no use to him. In fact, they are more likely to be a hindrance. He has to start again from scratch.'

Work on the prison novel came to an abrupt end in September 1925, when he was arrested a second time for embezzlement and sentenced to two and a half years in prison. On his release, he, like his protagonist Willi Kufalt, made his way to Hamburg, and it was here that he met Anna Issel, 'a simple young woman', who became his wife in 1929 and who played a pivotal role in his rehabilitation. He thus realized in his own life the idea that he had noted as a possible plot for a novel back in 1924.

Although Fallada began work on another novel, *A Small Circus*, in 1929, he did not abandon his prison story completely, for he sent an extract to his publisher, Rowohlt, in November of that year. Following the completion of *A Small Circus*, he returned to it briefly in the spring and summer of 1931, but abandoned it again as 'too dark for these summer days', in favour of a more light-hearted project. This turned out to be *Little Man, What Now?*, the tale of the trials and tribulations of the 'little man' Johannes Pinneberg and his wife Emma, which quickly reached the top of the bestseller list in 1932 and brought Fallada fame and fortune, not just in Germany but also internationally.

As a result of this literary success, he was able to move to a villa in an idyllic setting in Berkenbrück, on the banks of the River Spree, east of Berlin. He initially rented, and then agreed to buy, the property from an impoverished elderly couple, whose business had fallen victim to the economic crisis. In January 1933, now settled with his wife and son in a new home, Fallada could devote himself again to his prison novel. He decided to adopt the point of view of a released prisoner, because he wanted to arouse sympathy for 'these unfortunate human beings, ninety per cent of whom revert to crime' and thereby make a contribution to improving their situation.

Because of his own background and experience, Fallada was well equipped to narrate the novel from Kufalt's perspective. In particular, he understood the anxieties of a prisoner facing release and the difficulties of making a fresh start. He was also familiar with the fringes of the criminal underworld. The description of Kufalt's release in *Once a Jailbird* is modelled closely on Fallada's own experiences after leaving Neumünster prison in Schleswig Holstein, in the spring of 1928, and moving to work in a typing agency in Hamburg. As in his previous two novels, his keen ear for the linguistic characteristics of a wide range of social groups finds expression in lively and credible dialogue.

In Berkenbrück, Fallada had a study of his own for the first time, and the family congratulated themselves on the tranquillity of their new home, which was within reach of Berlin but removed from the unrest and upheaval that accompanied the Nazi Party's rise to power in the first three months of 1933. This tranquillity came to an abrupt end on 12 April, the Wednesday before Easter, with the arrival of Nazi stormtroopers, who had received a tip-off that Fallada was involved in a conspiracy to assassinate Hitler. The tip-off had come from the former owners of the villa, who denounced Fallada to the authorities in the hope of reclaiming their property free of charge. After conducting a thorough search of the premises – and finding no incriminating material – the stormtroopers took Fallada to a nearby town, where he was placed in 'protective custody'. This was a type of internment without trial, instituted by the Nazis in February 1933, with the aim of locking up their opponents for an indefinite period of time.

Finding himself once again in a prison cell, Fallada turned to writing as a coping strategy and continued to work on *Once a Jailbird*. In the ten days it took his wife and his publisher to secure his release, he completed seventeen pages of the novel.

Following his release, Fallada sought redress for wrongful imprisonment – only to discover that the people who had denounced him were Party members, and therefore above the law. This plunged him into a nervous breakdown from which he did not fully recover until the autumn, by which time he and his family had moved to a smallholding in a remote corner of Mecklenburg. It was here that he was finally able to complete *Once a Jailbird* in November 1933.

In the years that Fallada had spent writing this novel, his fortunes had changed dramatically. In the summer of 1924 he had been a social outcast, a prisoner battling to overcome alcoholism and drug addiction. By the end of 1933 he was a happily married family man, who had fulfilled two lifetime ambitions: to become a successful writer and to own a small farm.

The fortunes of Germany had changed drastically, too. The Germany in which *Once a Jailbird* was published, in the spring of 1934, was very different from the Germany where the idea had first been conceived, almost a decade previously. The Wall Street crash of 1929 and the ensuing economic turmoil had paved the way for the rise of fascism. In the year since the Nazi regime had come to power, the democratic institutions of the Weimar Republic had been replaced by a one-party state, the campaign against any individuals or groups regarded as 'un-German' had been given a legal basis, and the books of the German humanist tradition had been publicly burnt.

Fallada was aware that *Once a Jailbird*, with its sympathetic portrayal of a petty thief and alcoholic, who 'was not a natural criminal, he had become one, he had learnt to be a criminal', was not likely to meet with the approval of the new literary authorities. He therefore insisted in January 1934 – against the advice of his publisher – on adding a foreword, in which he hoped to placate the Nazi literary establishment by claiming that recent changes to German society had solved the problems depicted in the novel. The foreword to the first edition reads as follows:

> The author of this novel is preaching to the converted. The so-called humane treatment of prisoners, whose ludicrous, grotesque and regrettable consequences are told in its pages, is no more. As the author was writing, this piece of German reality was also changing.
>
> If Willi Kufalt, this brother-in-the-shadows of the 'little man' Pinneberg, now appears on the scene, it is because his creator has high hopes of him. Let's put an end to empty humane talk about those imprisoned, but, instead, find work for released prisoners. No empty career counselling, but understanding. No forgiveness, but 'forget the past. Now show us what you can do.'
>
> As with *A Small Circus* and *Little Man*, the author could only depict what he saw, not what might be. This and this alone he considered his task.

The advice of his publisher proved to be correct, however. On the one hand, the foreword alienated Fallada's established readership, such as his fellow author, Thomas Mann, already in exile in

Switzerland, who noted in his diary on 14 March 1934 that 'in order to be published in Germany, a book has to disown and deny its humane philosophy in an introduction'. On the other hand, it also failed to convince the Nazi reviewers, one of whom described Willi Kufalt as an example 'of those degenerate human beings for whom we have established protective custody nowadays'. In this, his first brush with the Nazi literary authorities, Fallada's assumption that an ingratiating foreword would make his realist, socio-critical novel acceptable to the regime, showed great political naivety. In the course of 1934, he came to realize further the futility of such a strategy, after his next novel, *Once We Had a Child*, received devastating reviews and the Propaganda Ministry recommended the removal of *Little Man, What Now?* from all public libraries. By the end of the year, it had become clear that the socio-critical, humanist novels that Fallada wanted to write would no longer be tolerated in his native land.

It was not until 1946 that a second edition of *Once a Jailbird* could be published. It was, in fact, the first Fallada novel to be published by the newly founded Aufbau publishing house in the Soviet sector of Berlin. In the intervening years, Fallada had lived through fascism and a world war. His first marriage had ended in divorce in the summer of 1944 and, shortly afterwards, he found himself behind bars again, this time in a Nazi psychiatric prison. Here, once more, he took up his pen, this time to confront the many problems that beset him. The short story 'The Man Who Was Mad About Children' was part of his strategy to effect a reconciliation with his wife. His battle with alcoholism found expression in *The Drinker*, one of the best novels on the subject in any language. In his *Prison Memoir 1944*, he gave an account of his experiences under the Nazi regime and dealt with the consequences of his decision not to emigrate. Alcoholism and his contempt for the Nazi authorities were dangerous topics, and would have cost him his life, had he not written an almost indecipherable manuscript and managed to smuggle it out of the prison.

When the war ended, Fallada was willing to play his part in reconstruction. In May 1945, he was appointed mayor of Feldberg, the town in Mecklenburg where he was living at the time, and at a public meeting in December 1945 he underscored his belief in a new, democratic Germany, a Germany that would guarantee intellectual freedom. This is the context in which he wrote the foreword to the second edition:

> One of the first acts of the Nazis was to put this jailbird book on the black list. And one of the first acts of the new democratic Germany is to publish it again. To me this is almost symbolic. Every line of this novel contradicts the view and the treatment the National Socialists held about and meted out to criminals. Now is the time for humanity again, albeit a humanity free of all sentimentality [. . .].
>
> In this new reprint I have changed nothing from the first edition. I may now think differently, in some respects, from eleven years ago when I wrote this book. All the more reason not to change anything! We can't change our books according to each different phase of our life. And by and large what I wrote then is compatible with what I feel now.
>
> So, out you go in the world, book. I hope you can do your bit to humanize the world a little, after twelve years of brutalization.

At the same public meeting, Fallada expressed the view that, despite the horrors of the previous twelve years, 'a seed of decency has survived. It is our duty to preserve this seed of decency, to pass it on, to sow a whole field from this one seed.' The theme of decency ('Anständigkeit'), which was introduced in *A Small Circus*, was the cornerstone of Fallada's philosophy of life. In *Once a Jailbird* Fallada places decency at the heart of a universal issue: the care and resettlement of offenders. Yet decency is a quality that is ascribed to only two characters in the novel: the prison governor and a prison tutor. Outside the prison walls there is little sympathy for a former inmate.

Once a Jailbird deals with an issue that is as relevant today as it was when the novel first appeared. For, as Fallada wrote in a letter to his publisher in January 1934: 'It doesn't really matter what Kufalt does; whatever happens, he's caught fast in a trap and he cannot struggle free.'

Jenny Williams, 2012

PENGUIN MODERN CLASSICS

ALONE IN BERLIN
HANS FALLADA

'A truly great book .. an utterly gripping thriller' Justin Cartwright, *Sunday Telegraph*

Berlin, 1940, and the city is filled with fear. At the house on 55 Jablonski Strasse, its various occupants try to live under Nazi rule in their different ways: the bullying Hitler loyalists the Persickes, the retired judge Fromm and the unassuming couple Otto and Anna Quangel. Then the Quangels receive the news that their beloved son has been killed fighting in France. Shocked out of their quiet existence, they begin a silent campaign of defiance, and a deadly game of cat and mouse develops between the Quangels and the ambitious Gestapo inspector Escherich. When petty criminals Kluge and Borkhausen also become involved, deception, betrayal and murder ensue, tightening the noose around the Quangels' necks ...

'Fallada's great novel, beautifully translated by the poet Michael Hofmann, evokes the daily horror of life under the Third Reich, where the venom of Nazism seeped into the very pores of society, poisoning every aspect of existence. It is a story of resistence, sly humour and hope' Ben Macintyre, *The Times*

'[*Alone in Berlin*] has something of the horror of Conrad, the madness of Dostoyevsky and the chilling menace of Capote's *In Cold Blood*' Roger Cohen, *New York Times*

Contemporary ... Provocative ... Outrageous ...
Prophetic ... Groundbreaking ... Funny ... Disturbing ...
Different ... Moving ... Revolutionary ... Inspiring ...
Subversive ... Life-changing ...

What makes a modern classic?

At Penguin Classics our mission has always been to make the best books ever written available to everyone. And that also means constantly redefining and refreshing exactly what makes a 'classic'. That's where Modern Classics come in. Since 1961 they have been an organic, ever-growing and ever-evolving list of books from the last hundred (or so) years that we believe will continue to be read over and over again.

They could be books that have inspired political dissent, such as *Animal Farm*. Some, like *Lolita* or *A Clockwork Orange*, may have caused shock and outrage. Many have led to great films, from *In Cold Blood* to *One Flew Over the Cuckoo's Nest*. They have broken down barriers – whether social, sexual, or, in the case of *Ulysses*, the boundaries of language itself. And they might – like *Goldfinger* or *Scoop* – just be pure classic escapism. Whatever the reason, Penguin Modern Classics continue to inspire, entertain and enlighten millions of readers everywhere.

'No publisher has had more influence on reading habits than Penguin'
Independent

'Penguins provided a crash course in world literature'
Guardian